EDGE OF THE

VOID

A NOVEL BY
MICHAEL D. KURZ

Morgan Marie Productions, Inc.
Box 1948, Vail, Colorado, 81658, USA

This novel is dedicated to the people who encouraged me; my father Jack, my mother Betty, my wife Kelli and my long lost friend Jim, who told me that, "To be a writer, you need to do it every day." Also, a special thanks to Germ Boy who helped me get it right and my Aussie mate, Mark who cajoled me to get the story out of the computer and onto the printed page.

I'm standing on the edge of something much too deep.

—SARA MCLAUGHLIN

Part One

"Intrigues of the Few"

The Fensfjord, Norway

Chapter 1

"The Builder"

Making one hundred forty-five knots through a blizzard was a visually and viscerally terrifying experience. Even the robust drone of the helo's turbines didn't dispel the crew's fear. When the gale lulled the ship lurched forward and the battle-hardened but very human aviators in the front seat looked at each other wide-eyed. The snow was getting heavier and in the weird perma-twilight of the Norwegian fall it seemed like the helo was suspended in a bowl of milk.

Blending subtle manipulations and forceful yanks on the flight controls, Navy Lieutenant Joe "Guido" Gallinari imposed his will on the bitter air. Flying through a monumental crevasse with five hundred meter high granite walls left no room for error.

This was one weird mission. Get there (which seemed as every second went by, the hardest part). Load a hefty package. Haul it back to the carrier and debrief. Seemed simple, but when the Air Boss asked for volunteers they knew there was more to it. Gallinari and his men knew little more and they would remain ignorant of the details. They didn't need to know. This mission wasn't directed by the Navy, the Department of Defense or the U.S. Government but by The Ten, a shadowy organization of global guardians whose very existence was known to only a handful.

And, what if they didn't have the whole picture? This crew had been to Hades and back with Guido at the stick and aside from the usual concerns about flying in inclement weather, they were confident to a man that the mission would be accomplished. So, Gallinari wrestled with the controls, the helo's computer dispassionately proclaimed altitude and air speed alerts that would make most men scream for their mommies, and they flew dutifully onward.

In her laboratory, Dr. Eva Luknar zoomed a long screw into a wooden crate. Liver spots on the hand that gripped the power driver revealed the builder's advancing age and a rash of half-healed cuts and fresh scratches testified to the difficulty of her task. The doctor gave a little grunt as she torqued each fastener home. They were placed chock-a-block like rivets and left no doubt of the scientist's obsession with sealing in the contents.

The crate occupied the center of a brightly lit and well-organized room - the largest in her laboratory. The facility was without frills and like the woman herself, made of stern stuff. Corrugated steel walls arched upward, Quonset-like. Harsh lamps nestled in polished reflectors hung from the ceiling; their ranks intermittently broken by the glow of plasma heaters (one of her useful inventions) that emitted a pleasant, low-end thrum.

The walls were lined with racks and stacks of electronic components, all upright, clean and labeled. Some of the gear was operating and a motley bank of light-emitting diodes blinked at her like an out-of-synch theater marquee. In the middle of one wall, highlighted by a single spotlight as if it were a treasured gallery work, was one schematic that plainly served no scientific purpose. It was a beefcake poster of a young, well endowed, nude male, looking to camera with a naïve attempt at a sultry smile. The image was peppered with greasy little fingerprints in the predictable places.

At one end of the structure was a huge titanium-clad door. Its brushed finish suggested a bank vault. Though the portal was in itself redoubtable, the scientist had installed an added security measure. Powerful laser beams overlaid the door like neon ladder rungs, six inches apart, floor to ceiling. They'd sear right through an erstwhile intruder. A narrow gauge track imbedded in the floor led beneath the door to the outside, the rails gleaming in the intense ruby hue of the lasers.

Eva didn't get uninvited guests but in the last year she had retained a small cadre of local workmen for odd jobs here and there and it worried her that nosey observations and subsequently embellished tales of her activities may spark curiosity among the locals. Anyway, adequate security or not, she couldn't keep her work under wraps forever. It was time to get her machine to America.

As Eva labored, a drop of condensation from the ceiling fell into the laser grid. A brilliant spark snapped as the beam fried the water into steam and the scientist's hair tossed as she whirled to confront the noise. Realizing what had happened; she straightened her sweater, smoothed her hair back into place and yipped a curse in Norwegian.

At sixty-one years of age Eva Luknar was an attractive woman. Her features were somewhat angular but symmetrical and strong, hinting at the masculine. Her bright, blue-gray eyes were set off by a weathered, permanently tan complexion, though the skin on the rest of her body had rarely been exposed to the sun. For most Norwegians, it was so.

Eva took a deep breath to shake off the distraction and put the power driver on the cart at her side. She stood, stretched her lithe frame and exhaled. There was something very sensual about her. She wore boots and black tights that emphasized her well-toned legs and shapely glutes and even in her loose sweater her ample breasts commanded attention. From tip to tail, she was a formidable physical specimen - astonishingly youthful in form, but no longer the carefree ingénue with a trail of broken boy-hearts at her feet. Still, she had the ability to unleash a devastating come-hither smile when she was moved to do so. During these last days though, her movie star straight, snow white teeth were masked behind the dense barricade of a permanently serious expression. Her *joie de vivre* had been murdered by her latest and last creation.

Refocused, Eva ambled to a control knob on the wall. She turned it and a round window port vacuumed open before her, providing a good look at the bad weather.

"The Americans will need good fortune this night," she thought as she hugged her sweater tight around her and closed the port.

Turning, she regarded the entirety of her project. The crate, taller than she and nearly eighteen feet in length, rested on an electrically-powered undercarriage, itself mounted on small, railroad-type wheels set onto the recessed tracks. The simple box atop the sturdy rig belied the complexity and horror of the danger within.

Kneading the knots from the muscles in her forearms, the doctor picked up the power driver, exchanged the exhausted battery pack for a fresh one and poured the last handful of screws. The Americans, she hoped, would soon land.

CHAPTER 2

"CONTACT"

It was normal for the atmosphere in a Navy helo to be a jumble of nervous chatter and ballsy bravado but tonight in the Blue Betty (the pilot's affectionate nickname for this particular helo) things were happening at hyper speed. As Gallinari plunged the helo into the amorphous snow tunnel his armpits moistened. Secretly he wished for a bungee cord to strap his feet to the pedals. Every few seconds there was air between his butt and the seat as Betty was spanked by another downdraft. When next she caught the air and bucked upward he was pounded back into the inadequately padded chair. So it went. It was more bronco riding than flying.

"Yep," he thought, "this is a regular helo rodeo and I'm riding the baddest bull in the ring."

"Talk to me Chef," Gallinari barked into his helmet mic.

Gallinari had handpicked his communications officer/radar intercept officer, Ensign Tyrone "Chef" Cooksey, and his co-pilot, LJG Tony "Magoo" McLachlan. They had last served together aboard an attack ship back in 2028 supporting SEAL team assaults against the "Shadow Lotus" Japanese terrorists in the coup attempt on Okinawa and they knew each others' fine points and foibles well.

For this trip, The Ten ordered the Navy to manifest a crew of three. That meant everyone had plenty to do. The finesse in this mission would come not just from each man's individual talents and skills, but in knowing how to apply them in harmony. It was all about intuition and trust. Anything less than perfection; bad decisions or maverick moves, could cost lives. Theirs.

As the helo bore down on the objective, Gallinari knew his guys had it together. He was only worried about one thing - the one thing he couldn't control. Would their luck hold? Naval aviation was risky business over the long term but in his mind he was the best and so far he had been successful at maintaining the delicate balance between the physics of flight and the persistence of gravity.

Despite Gallinari's hubris his doubt and the storm were thickening. It was getting dangerous to fly and the pilot had to fight back his mounting anger. The way he saw it he was playing delivery boy for some mysterious cargo, making a pickup from a person or persons unknown at an obscure LZ and bringing it back to the carrier for an unknown purpose. It was not, for him, enough information to justify the risks he and his crew were taking. But then, it wasn't his place to question orders. He wouldn't get straight answers had he asked. Why in hell did he volunteer for this one? Oh yeah, the extra pay.

Qualified in four rotary-wing and five fixed-wing aircraft types, Gallinari had achieved every aviation goal he had set for himself. None of those accomplishments were of any comfort at the moment. He was feeling strangely pessimistic and his stomach was queasy. He'd never felt anything like it. His innards weren't just unsettled by the turbulence, they were reacting to strong signals from his subconscious. He was trying to shake it off when Cooksey's voice crackled in his headset.

"Skipper, I've got one bodacious transponder squawk at zero one two degrees, ten kilometers out."

"Thanks, Chef," the pilot checked back. "Magoo, lay that course."

"Aye, Skipper. Mark is zero one two degrees. The way we're crabbing in this wind we're going to have to put Betty's nose at three four five to get there."

"Tyrone, what's the transponder ID?" Gallinari asked.

"No ID protocol," the communications officer replied. "Just three letters - E-V-A."

"EVA," Gallinari echoed, not knowing what to think about the unusual squawk. "Let's lock it in and go for voice contact. We've got to get Betty on the ground. She's gettin' jumpy again and my six is black n' blue," he said, referring to the clock face position of his posterior.

"Aye, Sir." Tyrone spoke in the clipped tone of a man responding to command authority. He switched the radio to the designated frequency and spoke.

"Echo niner niner to E-V-A do you read me, over?"

There was only static. He strained to hear a reply, ratcheting up the gain control in his headset.

Back in Eva's workshop the nearly exhausted scientist stood back and gazed at the machine one last time.

Made of sophisticated alloys covered in coat upon coat of hospital white enamel, it resembled a streamlined, overbuilt pram without wheels. The treatment table was fabricated of stainless steel and the red leather patient bed was overstuffed and inviting. The hood that held the beam generator formed a cove where the infirm were to have rested. There was a television monitor recessed into the hood, so patients could view relaxing images during the short but intense treatment that would dissolve their otherwise inoperable tumors and make them well again. But then, no one got well. Her dream of a cure had vanished in the abject terror of an uncontrolled chain reaction that not only had destroyed the targeted tumor, but the afflicted organism as well.

After fourteen years of work the device she had once affectionately called "Victoria," to celebrate her triumph over cancer, had become a monster. She now called it, "Medusa."

The physics of the device were fairly simple and demonstrated exquisite science. It focused an intense, modulated particle beam precisely guided through a micro-incision to the core of the lesion or carcinoma. There, *in situ*, it unleashed its power, the harmonic energy of the ray dissolving the bonds between the carbon atoms that comprised the morphology of the invading cells, turning the mass into a harmless residue the body would metabolize in its own time.

During the tests on small mammalian tumors it had worked even better than anticipated. A short burst of energy, an intensely bright flash of blue light, and the tumor was neutralized - cooked to nothing more unpleasant than smelly, yellow-green steam. Even intricately involved tissue could be cleansed. If just a small part of the invader could be exposed, the beam frequency could be calibrated for its particular molecular characteristics and it would be destroyed.

After the first few tests Eva was giddy. At last the dark foe that had viciously ended her mother's life, and brought so much suffering to so many over the centuries, would be vanquished.

Then her joy evaporated like ether with the truth of her failure. The daunting irony of good gone bad had brought her to the brink of dementia and ultimately to the events of today. The journey had cost her everything and now Eva was a shell - desperate, empty, broken and as hideous in her mind as the snake-haired Gorgon herself. A quotation from the *Bhagavad-Gita*, the ancient gospel of Hinduism, permeated her dreams and taunted her as this day approached. "*I am become death, the destroyer of worlds.*" She must be done with it.

Although she had taken every imaginable security precaution and had chosen a research site that guaranteed isolation, she was realistically cognizant that word of her "accidents" had gotten out. There was no way to assure that her contract technicians and repairmen had not drawn their own conclusions about the purpose of the beam she invented.

Someone must know that her machine was capable of killing. There would be people who would be interested in that. They would find a way to take it from her and make it more terrible and that could not be allowed. She had to get the machine into more competent hands. The time for her to make it safe had run out.

Clearing her head of the melancholy, Eva closed and fastened the crate's sidewall, saying a last goodbye to the device that at one time had given her so much joy. She drove the last screw and slumped to the floor, her back against the big box. Then, she heard Tyrone Cooksey's voice scratch over the digicom.

Resigned to the coming events, she dropped her face into her swollen hands.

"The end begins," she thought.

She rose slowly and turning toward the crate, brushed her hand against the titanium cassette she had fastened to its front. Through the mist clouding her eyes she read the engraved cover plate.

> ACCESS ONLY: Dr. Lawrence G. B.
> Craigh, Chairman, Department of Nuclear
> Medicine, University of Illinois Medical
> Center, Chicago, Illinois, U.S.A. Anti-
> tamper device armed, fail safe encrypted.

A corner of the cassette flicked open at her touch. Behind it, a retina-reader confirmed her identity. Eva blinked twice and three short beeps accompanied by the glow of an indicator lamp on the panel confirmed that the anti-tamper device was armed. She blinked twice more and the cover closed.

"Beep, beep, beep, beep."

Inside the crate a detonator, five pounds of Semtex high explosive and a cache of microswitches and sensors would assure that, unless Dr. Craigh's retinal ID was confirmed within seconds of beginning the disarming process, the machine and everything within a ten meter radius would be obliterated.

With a vacant stare in her eyes and Tyrone's redundant attempts to hail her in her ears, Eva turned her face skyward and prayed to a God she had never before addressed.

"Help us all."

Chapter 3

"Well rid of it"

Eva shuffled to her digicom, took a deep breath and keyed the mic.

"Echo nine nine, this is Dr. Eva Luknar, I hear you."

"Contact, Skipper," the Chef shouted, "E-V-A is a name. Eva.

"Dr. Luknar, this is echo niner niner, U.S. Navy helo, I read you too. Five by five. ETA your position is fourteen minutes, that's one four minutes, do you copy?"

"Yes, but call me Eva, please. How are you called?"

"Echo, niner, ni…" He replied, but was cut short.

"No, my boy. I'm not of your Navy. I just want to know your name," the scientist chided.

"Tyrone, ma'am. My given name is Tyrone. Can you give us landing instructions and weather conditions at the LZ? We're having a rough time of it up here," he understated as Betty bucked again and bashed his helmet into the transmitter console.

"We've got your transponder signal, but we can't see you."

"I'm sure you'll do just fine. I've seen movies about you American heroes. I can't give you a heading because I don't have radar. I can't see you either"

She read the indicators at on the weather station next to her digicom and flipped a pair of toggle switches on the wall.

"I've just turned on my helipad lights. You should see them soon. I have forty-three kilometers per hour of wind steady from the north-northwest and heavy snow. I can't see much out my window. I'm guessing visibility is four hundred meters. Helipad elevation is zero two eight four meters. My loading dock faces east. Please position the center of your cargo door on the red arrow marker. Your cargo will be loaded mechanically. You will have just a few minutes on the ground. Please confirm that you have these orders. We will not be making, how do you say it, 'small talk' and you are not to attempt to enter this facility. Is that clear, Tyrone? Any attempt to compromise the security of this facility will be met with maximum deadly force. Are you a crew of three as I specified?"

"Yes, ma'am."

"Good. You sound like a nice boy and I don't want to have to send you and your friends to the halls of Valhalla at such a young age. Clear?"

"Ah, Norwegian hospitality, Skipper," the Chef said, off-mic. "Copy Eva. I guess we won't be able to use your bathroom, huh?" He chuckled to no reply.

Feeling chastised, in a more serious tone, he keyed his mic.

"ETA is now twelve minutes. Echo niner niner, out."

It bothered the Chef that this Norwegian civilian with a voice like honey and a motherly manner, used the term "maximum deadly force." This was someone on edge. Banter was ill advised.

"Yes, out," The scientist replied.

Suddenly and simultaneously Guido and Magoo caught a fleeting visual of helipad lights and the intercom hummed with the mantra of Blue Betty's landing procedures. Changes in distance, heading, speed, fuel status and altitude were called out rapid fire.

The helipad was a gaudy sight in an otherwise monochromatic vignette. Violet high intensity lamps set in concentric circles strobed inward from the pad's perimeter. A red chevron of animated arrowhead markers pointed away from the side of an arch-roofed building toward the pad's center.

As they approached the snow-shrouded hump of a building they could just make out a series of skylights broadcasting bright shafts of light into the blackness. Just to the north and attached to the lab by a like-constructed half tube, the men in the front seats intermittently caught glimpses of a three story stone structure - perhaps living quarters. The light coming from the few illuminated windows in the fortress-like residence was a warm, incandescent yellow in contrast to the garish helipad strobes and the harsh fluorescent escaping the Quonset. Smoke rose from the largest of several chimneys and was immediately buffeted away.

The helo was on final approach now and Eva could hear the craft's engines above the howl of the wind.

"Prepare for landing," Gallinari commanded.

"Aye, Sir," the crew responded in tandem.

Gallinari needed all his pilot stuff to put Betty down. The cross winds above the pad were brutal. Fortunately, as he began his descent, he could see the pad was encircled with high walls that blunted the maelstrom and held the drifting snow at bay. It was problematic that the closed revetment would deliver one hell of an updraft as he tried to kiss the craft to the surface.

Fog from the snow melted by the pad's deck heaters added to the out-worldliness of the scene. It clung tenaciously to the surface, dense as soup, before it was dispersed by the powerful wash from helo's main rotor. With the deftness of a diamond cutter, Gallinari flared the huge Sikorsky and set it down with a reassuring thud.

"Let's get busy," the pilot ordered.

"Right, Skipper," Tyrone answered.

"Eva, this is echo niner niner. We are down and standing by. How would you like us to proceed? Please acknowledge."

The scientist replied curtly.

"Open your cargo door when you have dressed for the elements. The air temperature is twenty-eight degrees below zero, Fahrenheit. Please young man; do not leave your aircraft. Any attempt to do so will be met with hostile action. Do you understand?"

"Yes, Ma'am," he said, growing irritated with her brusqueness.

Then Magoo saw another sign that this woman was all business.

"Check it out, Skipper," he said in a serious tone, nodding to direct the pilot's attention.

Directly in front of the aircraft was a tube about the diameter of an oil drum mounted on the inside wall of the landing pad. As the pair watched with mounting dread, the hatch cover cantilevered up and back, revealing the unmistakable sighting wand of a pulse laser cannon. They looked at each other to confirm it was actually there. Looking back to the weapon, they saw the ominous red beam of the sight bloom on Blue Betty's windscreen and bathe the cockpit in an eerie glow. One shot at this range would drill the helo from nose to tail in a sizzling instant.

"Tyrone!" Gallinari said, noticeably tense.

"Acknowledge her instructions and stow the chatter. There's a god-damn laser cannon looking up my nose at point-blank range."

"Aye, Sir," the young officer shot back. "I've got it on my console. It's for real and it's locked on."

Switching his mic from intercom to broadcast, he spoke carefully.

"We'll comply precisely with your instructions, Ma'am. Rotors are at idle. We're opening the cargo hatch and remaining at our stations awaiting your orders."

"Prepare to receive your cargo, Tyrone", the scientist said, assured that the Americans knew she was firmly in control.

She began to think that she could trust these men and that the device would safely get to the only human on earth who may be able to tame it and if he failed, to have the good sense to destroy it.

Eva walked to the glass-walled booth that contained the controls for the laboratory bay door and the cargo loading machinery. Inside her bulletproof niche she would be secure against surprise attack and could activate any of the self-defense munitions she had installed in anticipation of such an event. She thought it unlikely that the Americans would attempt to harm her. However, if the secrecy of their mission had been compromised, she was prepared for interlopers. As a final precaution, Eva touched a few numbers on the keypad before her. The "Facility Destruct" sequence was now activated. As the computer acknowledged the command with a feminine but monotoned, "Facility destruct sequence engaged. Standing by," the doctor began the onload procedure.

On her video monitor, she saw the helo's cargo hatch slide open and switched on the motors that raised the outer door. She stroked the key sequence that controlled the door lasers and eased forward the toggle switch that moved the dolly bearing the crate. As the ungainly rig crawled toward the helo door, she was already feeling relieved.

In the last few months, she'd been having wretched dreams. She kept seeing the damned machine like it was alive, with the once benevolent-looking beam cove morphing into a macabre mouth that shrink-wrapped itself around the terrified patient's head; the helpless being inside frantically flailing its arms and legs in a vain attempt to escape. Her ears rang from the dream patient's screams as the device turned the human form into a pool of putrefied sludge. How had the magnificent medical miracle in her mind become the instrument of such a horrible death?

Realizing that what she had imagined was not the worst that could happen she began to hurry at the controls to play out this last act of her defeat. After what seemed like half an hour (in real time it was only a few minutes) the helo devoured the crate and it clinked to a stop against a détente on the helo's deck. Two heavy mechanical clamps locked the container in place. The transfer was complete.

From his position behind the payload, Tyrone leaned forward to see if he might glimpse the ubiquitous lady scientist, but the lab's door was already closing. Even so, he gingerly extended his hand and waved farewell. Eva saw the gesture and she said to herself, "God speed Tyrone. God speed you Americans."

The door to the lab shut with an authoritative tremor. Tyrone closed the helo's cargo door.

"Damn nice place, Norway," he thought as the last snowflakes melted onto the deck. "If you're a Popsicle."

Working quickly he made the crate fast with heavy retaining straps. After locking the ends in place with firm tugs, he returned to his station, shedding his gloves along the way.

"Let's get out of here, Skipper," the radioman said, his teeth chattering from his brief encounter with the cold.

"That's a wrap boys, let's head for the crib," Gallinari said, half giving and order and half expressing his joy that this bizarre bullshit was about to end.

As he brought the Blue Betty's turbines to take-off power, the drivers saw the missile launch tube closing before them. The red light stopped blinking and to the crew's relief, Tyrone's threat console reported the weapon's "safe" status.

"The cannon's off line, Skipper."

"I heard that, Mr. Cooksey. Prepare for takeoff," Gallinari said, raising his eyebrows at his co-driver.

McLachlan exhaled, flapping his lips.

"Let's go home."

Gallinari throttled up and twisted the collective control to maximum, simultaneously applying left anti-torque to counteract the clockwise force of the main rotor. As he added forward pressure on the cyclic the helo rose and Blue Betty and the already emotionally decompressing crew made a hasty exit. They hadn't climbed to ten meters when the doctor switched off the helipad lights. No lingering good-byes here.

McLachlan was really looking forward to getting back aboard the carrier and returning to his normal duties. But, even as the most difficult part of his mission was about to end, the hairs on his arms were standing on end.

"Knock it off," he said to himself. "The creepy part is over."

Back in the lab, Eva shut down the controls in the booth and commanded the computer to, "Maintain destruct sequence standby status." As she walked away she could hear the computer voice fading in reply, "Acknowledged. Maintaining destruct sequence standby."

Nearly exhausted after the ordeal of packing and dispatching the crate, Eva slumped down at the keyboard on her communications console and keyed in a final coded InterVid message to the man to whom she had passed her crown of thorns.

> Http://uicmedcen/privcom/lgbc
> As of 2130GMT this date, device is yours.
> Wish you well.
> Continued covert control is imperative.
> I suspect compromise. End. Eva.

Chapter 4

"Last dance with the demon"

The machine was barely gone and Eva was in denial. She had to make one last attempt to uncover the secret of controlling the chain reaction. If she could just find a thread, a clue, a subatomic particle of hope. There were a few hours until for good or bad, things would be completely out of her hands. She threw off the heavy sweater she wore in the lab. Going against the grain of her habit, she didn't return the garment to its proper hook on the wall but let it fall to the floor.

She slapped her cheeks vigorously a few times to force some measure of alertness, walked to an arched doorway adjoining the passage that led to her residence and voiced a command to the sensor on the wall. The door to her computer room slid open with a whoosh.

Unlike the winter-rage without, the doctor's computer room was a cocoon of serenity. In her nexus of knowledge, with the hum of cooling fans providing a background of white noise, Eva melded her brain with sophisticated mathematical software, the teachings of the best scientists of today and yesterday, and three dimensional holographic models of every component of energy and matter in the known physical universe.

When she began her work sessions Eva entered a zone that turned time to molasses. She moved with it, a helpless fingerling in a phlegmatic river of chronometric ooze. Often her physical surroundings faded to a fog around her. During these times she was apprehensive. Awash in a tsunami of alpha waves, she was in a state of such overwhelming disassociation that the sun's rays from the skylight above seemed to pass through her and shadows from the hardware danced about the room in a frenzy.

The trances often led to queer incidents. She divided her recollection of the experiences into those that were funny and those that were scary. A few times she blacked out from hypoglycemia and bonked her head on the glass of the computer monitor or keyboard. Food didn't matter at such times. Twice, she urinated in her chair because she failed to attenuate to the pressure building in her bladder. It took the demanding sensation of warm and pungent rivulets running down her thighs and ankles to bring her back to reality. Other events were decidedly nightmare-like – as in the time she forgot to close the access door and was stung by an aggressive wasp that had nested in the lab's rippled roof. She didn't notice it until her bath that night.

It was only in this twilight of consciousness that Eva was able to focus on the mathematical minutia that would bring her answers. And, she wanted this answer to the depths of her being. To the exclusion of nearly every other activity and pleasure in her life, she had labored to uncover the secret of focused, instantaneous disintegration of foreign tissue - the ultimate weapon against the cancers that had plagued multicellular animal life since it crawled forth from the primordial soup.

As much as Eva wanted to become humanity's benefactor though, it was, selfishly, hope for her own salvation that drove her. The world was turning away from her time. It was a mean, stupid, graceless place now and she had inadvertently contributed to the decadence. If her efforts over the next two hours failed, her beautiful healer might become the doom of mankind. She couldn't live with that. Eva trembled a little, took a deep breath, exhaled forcefully and voiced the program launch commands to the computer.

Chapter 5

"Defeat"

There was one narrow intellectual alleyway Eva had left to explore. It had to do with the machine's power supply. As fast as she could and still be understood by the computer's voice rec software, she blurted out commands. Schematics leapt onto the holographic image platen at a pace that would make a bystander woozy. As she fell into a rhythmic patter with the CPU her spirits buoyed. She had a hunch. Though it went down a path she'd tread thoroughly during development, she didn't remember looking under this specific empirical rock when she was troubleshooting. A quick review of her notes confirmed that she had not.

Until this moment, Eva thought the problem with the machine was that the chain reaction created by the beam was inevitably self-sustaining. As the TVap, or tumor evaporator beam, impacted the patient's tissue, it immediately began to disrupt the valence bonds between the carbon atoms. That effect at the tumor site was intended. It was how the cure was affected. The problem was that it wasn't only the tumor that was comprised of carbon-based molecules. So was the healthy tissue that surrounded it and all organic animal tissue and every plant, fungus and microbe on Earth. If the disintegrating effect of the beam could not be confined to the tumor or the epithelium surrounding it, the entire organism would be vaporized.

Initial tests worked simply because the prototype machine had been used on small animals. The power needed to vaporize such small lesions was insufficient to initiate the chain reaction and the machine reliably eliminated the tiny clusters of diseased cells at first contact with the beam.

However, when the device was used on larger tumors in higher animals and the beam's delivery power was increased, the results were catastrophic. Surrounding tissue, complete organs and in one macabre case, most of the organism being treated had been mercilessly disintegrated. Eva never forgot the gruesome sight of a Chimpanzee as it dissolved from the liver outward on her table. The creature just came apart. Its bones exploded when the heat created by the chemical reaction of the unraveling marrow molecules had no place to expand and ragged shards whizzed through the air around her. Blood and bile turned to goo and the terrified animal's bifurcated upper and lower halves wriggled in the restraints until all but a few random slabs of hide and muscle were turned to a puddle of pungent yellow paste. The noise of the process - the wailing of the animal and the wretched "fizzing" of the soft tissue as it decomposed had been digitally recorded or she never would have believed it. It took less than ten seconds for an ape weighing sixty kilos to be turned to three kilos of viscous slime.

That was all frightening enough but when the reaction started to consume the machine's casing and a part of the laboratory floor, the doctor saw the lid on Pandora's Box had burst wide open.

Theoretically that should not have happened. Theoretically an increase in the energy delivered to the containment beam, set to correspond in a perfect one-to-one ratio with that used in generating the TVap beam, should have safely restricted the beam's effect to the tumor site. It should have worked. She had spent exhausting hours working on complex formulae that govern plasma/matter interaction and force field dynamics. By everything she knew and everything the computer calculations could tell her, the containment field should have worked. Should have worked.

Now, as she propelled her thought processes into overdrive and the computer strained to deliver the data, she thought she was closing in on the real problem. It wasn't in applying too much power to the beam generator; it was getting more power to the containment beam!

The solution hit her like an uppercut. It was so obvious. Why hadn't she seen it? Of course. The application ratio was wrong.

Because the chain reaction grew, not mathematically in its effect but geometrically by a power of four, the number of covalent bonds in the carbon atom, wouldn't increasing the containment beam's energy by the power of four control the spread of the effect? Could it be that simple?

"Yes," she said under her breath, a reluctant anticipation building as she posed the problem to the mainframe.

"Yes!" She screamed with hysterical joy as the computer worked on the problem and her anticipation rose.

Then, a despondent "No!"

Her eyes bulged until her lids seemed to disappear and anguished tears scoured her once-lovely face. Her gut convulsed with the tragedy of her failure and she cried out until she was nearly hoarse.

Spent, she collapsed face down on the hologram platen, her arms over her head. After a few whimpers she sat up, wiped away her tears with the sleeve of her shirt and was still. The ghostly-green holo image of a complex, still-calculating formula, swirled menacingly across her face and mocked the broken woman. Her expression was blank and she stared like a zombie. There would be no reprieve. No epiphany at the eleventh hour. No redemption. Just a guaranteed death sentence for any patient subjected to the treatment.

Once the TVap beam was generated using anything more than a miniscule power level it couldn't ever be contained. If the primary beam were being delivered with 800 volts of power behind it (the minimum input needed to dissolve even a modest sized tumor in an adult human), the containment beam would only be effective for a millisecond. As the chain reaction that killed the tumor spread, containment must instantaneously increase to 800^4 volts. A fraction of a second later, it would have to increase again to 800^{16} volts, then to 800^{64}, 800^{256}, and so on. The technology to make that happen without instantly frying the machinery, the patient and the room they were in, didn't now and may never exist. Worse, at higher TVap beam delivery voltages and amperage, and without containment, she was sure the beam's effect would be transmitted through the organic molecules in the air, making it possible to generate a wide area chain reaction.

The tears welled in her eyes again as Eva imagined the effect continuing unabated through the sky and into the ground and over the surface of the Earth until the planet was turned to wasteland.

It was over for her and her pathetic creation.

Eva sat up and spitefully cut the power to the computer. Flashing and announcing the consequences of incorrect shut down procedures, it seemed to sigh with her as the energy drained from them both. Running on emotional fumes, she walked out of the cocoon to the communications console and keyed in her last message to the outside world. Unfortunately, in the fog of her depression, she selected the wrong one of two address options and sent a text message in the clear; unencrypted, over the commercial e-mail side of the InterVid network.

http://www.uicmedcen.edu/lgbcraigh/mail.
html
Cannot generate sufficient power to contain
TVap effect. Exponential increase required
to stop chain reaction. Device useless as
treatment modality. Imperative you destroy
prototype and plans if you fail to remedy my
errors. Files here gone tonight. Sorry.

Eva sent the message and without a backward glance entered the decontamination chamber that separated the lab from her living quarters. There she stripped and stepped into the shower. This time she didn't perform the routine scrub down with the pumice stone, scratchy brush and harsh soap. She just rinsed languidly in the steaming water. She wanted to be clean when she crossed over but contamination wasn't an issue. Still, the water hissing at her from spray jets in the ceiling, floor and walls could not scour away the filth she felt inside. She turned off the water and for a brief moment stood there, frozen in place by the realization that her life had been a waste. The vapid look in her eyes announced the departure of her soul.

She opened the far doorway and passed through, not bothering to close it behind her. She dressed in the fuzzy terry-cloth robe and mules she kept in the dressing room and opened the outer door to her quarters. Oddly, she was hungry. As usual her Elk Hound, Knute, was sitting on the venerable braided rug just inside. Seeing him cheered her and she reveled in the dog's attentions.

"Nuti, Nuti," she squealed as they wrestled. She buried her head in her companion's luxuriant fur and for a fleeting moment, she thought about staying around for a while. Then the giggles and the snuffling stopped and she knew she would go ahead with her plans. The dog was hungry too. He padded to his bowl anticipating his meal and cast his bright eyes up at her, his tail wagging furiously.

"Ja, Nuti, we eat soon," she said sympathetically. "But I must dress first. Then we have our last supper."

She ruffed him behind the ears and walked through the darkened great room adjacent to the entry. It opened on a huge parlor with a magnificent log fireplace on one end. Overstuffed chairs and long, low divans bordered an ancient rug woven with Norwegian folk designs and runic symbols. She had the home built to resemble her childhood home in Seljord, Telemark filke. She so loved the ornate and colorful wood furniture her mother had used to decorate her room. The stuff was everywhere. It served well to counter the dark shadows cast by the high and deeply carved beams that formed the structure's caliginous interior.

Turning to her right, Eva climbed the thick plank stairs to the second story. The dry wood creaked as she ascended past the gallery of dusky portraits of her ancient clan. Since the 1650s, as far back as family records were kept, the Luknars had been scientists of one kind or another. Physicians mostly. There had always been a hint of inscrutability about them, though that was not unusual during the nascent days of the healing arts. There were no x-rays then. If you wanted to know how something worked, or what a chemical compound would do to someone or something, you had to investigate and experiment. Sometimes that meant working opportunistically with a cadaver or an animal claimed by old age, accident or infirmity. Sometimes however, the test subjects were more viable and less amenable.

Most of this exploration was above board and honorable but in the best interest of science, or in the worst interest of curiosity, liberties were taken. That's what the townspeople held in their collective memory of the Luknars. So, after matriculating at the Norwegian University of Science and Technology in Trondheim, and graduating Summa Cum Laude from M.I.T., Eva took extra care to isolate herself from prying professional eyes and inquisitive neighbors by building her little castle on the Fensfjord, forty kilometers east of Solheim.

Unwilling to settle merely for geographic isolation, she specified further that the place be built in a great rill - a high-walled, narrow valley that cloaked it from all but those who knew its precise location. The only access was by helicopter and her visitors were few and by invitation only. Although she did have a mildly deranged, and very attractive young sled-driver visit once in a blue moon. She hadn't seen Markus for quite a while. It had been months, she thought. She hoped that, afterward, he at least would think and speak well of her.

Chapter 6

"Out with a bang"

Eva was nearing exhaustion. The strain of losing her precious invention to a technological conundrum and then casting its fate to the wind had shredded her spirit. There was nothing left to do but eat a good meal and vanish into the great beyond where she would meet her final judgment.

Eva didn't fear death. Common sense told her it was inevitable. She was comfortable with her interpretation of "the great purpose" as she called it. She was not superstitious, didn't believe in the supernatural and was intolerant of those who attempted to recruit her into organized religion. She didn't need anyone to shout her flaws from a pulpit. And, she knew many would say after today's events that she had run away like a coward. No matter. She wasn't about to cower in her solitude until someone did something bad with her machine and they came for her.

She swiped at the condensation clinging to the inside of the curved windows of her bedroom turret and through the wavy distortion saw the storm hadn't abated. That was good. The cloying wetness would minimize the fallout and downrange effects of the small thermonuclear blast she would soon unleash.

A zero point one five-megaton detonation was not an insignificant event but according to her calculations, the most devastating effects would be limited to a quarter mile radius. There should be no civilians or civilian aircraft in the area and the helo carrying her machine would be long gone; probably on its way to refueling in Bergen or even Stavanger. Soon it would be en route to a rendezvous with an American aircraft carrier, she guessed somewhere in the North Sea.

Dropping her robe and kicking off her mules, Eva walked to the full-length mirror on the closet door. Avoiding eye contact with her reflection, she considered the form of the woman before her. Her eyes, her most striking feature, were large, intelligent, angled playfully upward at the corners and set not too deeply atop firm, elevated cheekbones. Using her fingers as combs, she pulled her hair upward and away from her face. Deciding to wear it loose, she let her hair fall and, twisting her legs to hide her mons, let her hands stroke down over her breasts and the flatness of her stomach to settle lightly on the trimmed tuft between her legs. She blushed into the mirror.

"You're a naughty girl, Eva," she said.

She thought about making love to herself right there, but hesitated. The events of the day had rendered her incapable of arousal. She turned and pulled the handle to open the closet door. A fluorescent fixture tinkled on overhead. Stepping inside the spacious wardrobe Eva pulled a knit tunic from one of the tall columns of bins on the wall and tugged it over her head. Then a pair of snug, well-worn Wranglers. Another reason she liked Americans. She stepped into the jeans, zipped the fly and stepped back to consider her footwear. She chose the wooden shoes she bought on her last trip to Amsterdam. They were traditionally Dutch and the vamps were stained in Delft blue with a delicate tulip and leaf design that amused her. These were not the flashy colored and thickly glazed souvenirs the tourists bought for their mantelpieces. They were her house shoes and she treasured them.

Finished, she thumped over the plush carpet into the bathroom and drew a brush through her damp, thick mane. Habitually, she scorned makeup but this evening she decided to add just a touch of lipstick. She painted on the glossy gunk, pouted at herself, blotted and, discarding the used tissue onto the floor, turned to head down to the kitchen. Her stomach growled vigorously to remind her that she hadn't eaten in a day. Or, was it two? She left the bedroom lights on and the closet door ajar as she and the dog dismounted the back stairway.

Cleverly, Eva had used a modest quantity of the radioactive materials she used in her work to power a small and efficient reactor. This generated the steam and electricity she needed to survive in the hostile environment of the Fensfjord and provided her with the independent energy supply she needed to carry out her experiments without the bother or potential hazards of commercial power interruptions. She often heard the hum of the retrofitted machine and the clank of the plumbing through the walls, as she did now beneath the stairwell as it warmed the big stone house.

Tonight, with the push of a button, the friendly genie in the reactor core would overload and become her angel of death.

But first, to the kitchen for a few glasses of Macon Villages, a plate of her country's best gravlox with capers and thin strips of fresh fennel, a succulent venison steak (a thoughtful gift from Markus's last visit), sautéed onions and dried mushrooms, warm rolled lefse spread with lingonberry jam, a glass or two of Chateauneuf-du-Pape, a flute of her treasured Lillie Aquavit with its faded gold color and hint of caraway, a last Cappuccino and some time with Knute - the only male in her life that had never disappointed her. Then, the sauna.

"What could be better to send us on our way, eh, Nuti," she said to the dog.

His tail whipped as he waited for her to descend to the landing. Eva tickled the fur on the hound's plush, black-masked face, gently tugged his raggedy bandana (She had seen such an accoutrement on a Steamboat Springs ski poster once and thought it *avant-garde*.) and chirped, "Let's eat," to her now very enthusiastic pet.

She wasn't sure when she had fed him last, either.

Wooden clacks and toenail clicks on slate tiles announced their arrival in the warm and spacious kitchen. Although she never entertained and rarely prepared more than quick snacks to maintain her energy, the place was professionally designed and equipped. A stiff rank of Danish designed guest stools stood on one side of the island counter. She had a slab of mica-flecked granite from the Dolomites custom-cut to accommodate a three-tub sink and waterfall faucets. Stainless steel appliances echoed the glow from the firewood and a thorny hedge of somewhat dusty pots, pans and utensils dangled from a chain-mounted, ovaline rack above her.

Though it happened infrequently, she relished the time she spent tinkering here. The kitchen didn't stink of the failure that permeated the lab and errors made here left only a momentary bad taste.

She selected a fine, cut crystal stem from the sideboard, opened the white Burgundy and poured a lavish serving right to the brim. Sipping the wine she toddled to the refrigerator, retrieved the thawed venison loin and sliced off a thick strip. As she held it for the Elk Hound to see, she smiled at him and said, "Tonight, my Nuti, we have no rules."

The dog watched and Eva cooked. She made an admirable mess and did a credible job preparing the food, though the presentation was unadorned. As the storm raged at the windows Eva lingered over her meal. Knute had made somewhat shorter work of his very rare deer steak - unencumbered by etiquette and utensils as he was. Now he lounged near the soporific warmth of the coaling embers on the hearth, the languid sweeps of his tail rhythmically dusting the floor. Under the influence of the wine, Eva thought the appendage kept time with the music like a furry metronome.

She had selected disks for her old audio player with just the right tone to match her mood, her peculiarly heightened senses, and to embolden her to bring about the dreadful but foregone conclusion to the evening. She started with Liszt's *Les Preludes* with its solemn initial theme and triumphant, spiritual climax. Wagner's *Ride of the Valkyries* followed; an unavoidable cliché in her current state of mind. Then Beethoven's *Fifth*. Finally she allowed herself the solace of a closing double-play of Beethoven's *Moonlight Sonata*.

It was during the reprise of that melodic poem that Eva savored the last, heady swallow of the aquavit and threw her arms around her Elkhound for a final farewell.

She knew she would get maudlin when this time came but she didn't anticipate the sharp pangs as she told her intimate;

"Knute, my friend and my protector, I shall miss you. We have been closer in our time together as woman and beast than most people who are blood relatives. You are a noble spirit, my dog of the Vikings, and you have served me well. I hope I have done the same. I regret that I must cut short our time together, but I trust you will forgive me and that if there is any mercy in the cosmic scheme of things we will meet in a brief time in Valhalla, where mead will flow and there will be always games to play and rubber balls to chase and sweet young girls to brush you and run the meadows at your side."

She grabbed hands full of his fur, kissed his forehead and hugging him tight to her breast, whispered, "Goodbye, Nuti, my dear."

She released him. The Elkhound shook free his fur and wagged his great ears, springing to all fours to look at her. He understood. As if in forgiveness, and to grant Eva the relief of his approval, he barked a voluminous single "woof," lowered his head and swayed side-to-side, his tail wagging wildly, as if to say, "I'm ready!"

Dabbing her tears with her sleeve she took the self-destruct remote control from the cooking island and began the short walk down the narrow hallway to her sauna. Along the way Eva shed her shoes and clothes. The dog sensed his mistress was at peace. In turn, he took the doctor's jeans and then the tunic in his mouth and playfully shook each with a growl before casting it aside. He knew better than to chew her beloved shoes. Eva put the remote in one of the cubbies atop the clothes pegs in the hallway, spun the timer full on to the stop and stepped into the familiarity and comfort of the little redwood room. Though it took fifteen minutes to warm, Eva didn't attenuate to the clammy air as she waited. Her mind was busy replaying a lifetime of memories at fast forward. She feared that as the moment of her death approached, she would not be able to squelch her recollections of the bad times; her father's death in a spring avalanche in France, her mother's surgical mutilations and lingering death, her inability to attract a mate, the torment of her failure with the machine. Surprisingly, she was able to keep her thoughts pleasant.

She recalled skating with her father, her tiny hand in his, on the frozen pond behind her childhood home. She smiled as she thought back to her mother making lefse on the tiny wood-fired stove that warmed their cabin in the quaint ski village of Voss. And, she remembered the passionate, raucous love-making with Markus and his gifts of contraband (cannabis and absinthe) that made his visits so thrilling. It was as she conjured the image of him and their sometimes-weeklong dalliances that she felt the air around her warm and the beginning of a tingle between her legs.

The memories began to overwhelm her and she caressed her temples, allowing her fingertips to brush over the strong line of her jaw and over the fullness of her lips. Her fingers continued their sensuous exploration as she crossed her arms, cupped the roundness of her shoulders and let her forearms cradle her breasts, nipples perking. Her breathing deepened and went husky. As she gently pressed her fingernails into the pink areolas, a quivering moan escaped her lips. Her hands glided halt-ingly downward, her arms uncrossed and she spread her legs, allowing the palm of one hand to briefly visit the sensitive, pulsing outer lips of her moistening vagina. She began to writhe on the slatted wood bench, deeply stroking the taut muscles of her thighs; massaging first the front then the backs of her legs. The pleasure and the heat made her glow. She drew her legs up until her knees pressed deliciously against her breasts. She put her heels beneath her buttocks, exposing the full wetness of her inner labia and the opening to the hot pink and pale purple tunnel her lovers and she had so enjoyed during her all-too-infrequent surrenders to corporal pleasure.

She gasped as she wound her fingers into the delicate, soaking folds of flesh around her clitoris. Her orgasm began as she pressed the erect pink button hiding there. Her stroking became fevered and her feet left the bench as she used both hands to deliver a shuddering climax. Arch-ing, she threw her shoulders back, tossed her head left then right, rasped a short breath and screamed out the unbridled thrill of her ecstasy.

Satiated, Eva stretched out lengthwise on the bench, her arms at her side, and began to regain her composure. She lay that way for a long while, ignoring Knute's plaintive whines and the scratching at the door.

As she quieted and her heart found its normal rhythm, the heat of the sauna became oppressive and she knew it was time. She sat upright, stretched, rose to her feet and opened the door. Knute lay just outside the door on a hemp mat. When the hot air of the sauna met the cold air of the hallway, Eva was nearly obscured by a cloud of diaphanous vapor. When it dissipated she saw the Elkhound had come to an atten-tive sit. He cocked his head and looked at her. His tail stopped wagging and he stared, as if accusing her of indiscreet misconduct. She laughed at his expression, smiled sheepishly and, disregarding the chastisement implicit in the canine's gaze, said, "Go for walk?"

She turned nonchalantly to the cubbyhole and took the remote, thumbing the selector switch from *Standby* to *Detonate*. The device beeped in acknowledgment and she placed it back on the shelf. A green LED stopped pulsing and a red one took over. The numerical display counted down - 00:00:**20**, 00:00:**19**, 00:00:**18**...

In the lab and the house, warning lights strobed and the computer's "voice" blared over the loudspeakers.

"Warning. Warning. Destruction imminent. Destruction imminent. Warning. Warning."

She and Knute turned down the hallway and Eva opened the door that led to the small yard behind the house. She was surprised, not so much by the snap of frigid air on her body as by the calmness of the night. The storm had subsided.

A full moon lit the landscape, a harsh spotlight on a frosted stage. The naked leading lady and her faithful hound were the only players before the crowd of spirits gathered there. Under the brilliant moon the fuzzy aura of the newly fallen snow and the high walls of the fjord made Eva felt as if she had already transcended her wicked existence, but it would be a moment yet before the explosive trigger lit the mini-bomb.

Head held high, Eva pranced elatedly through the snow toward the moon above the rocky horizon in the distance. She was reaching out to touch the silver-white orb when the bomb detonated with the flash and thunder of Thor's hammer. Neither she nor Knute felt the blast. They didn't see the hellish blue-white hemisphere of self-rending atoms engulf them. They were oblivious to the cloud of fire, smoke and steam rising out of the crater that had once been her home. They were only nano-bits of energy now; obliterated as the fury of the blast ripped outward.

The shock wave shrieked its pain over the landscape and the night grew darker. Avalanches born of the blast were launched from every slope and precipice in the tiny valley and beyond. The earth groaned and spoke her miserable eulogy.

Chapter 7

"In the wrong hands"

Minutes after the Naval aviators left the scientist's landing zone, the Blue Betty began to balk at the ice she was ingesting into her turbofans. Power was falling off and visibility was down to zero. It was time to put her down again. Aware he was pushing the helo past the point of safety and himself past his ability to get them all home, Gallinari laid it out for the crew.

"Well ladies, we've got two options," he said with sand in his mouth. "We can set down and wait this out, or we keep flying and take our chances. Frankly boys, I don't think Betty can handle it."

Neither pilot had ever attempted a landing in deep snow and both were apprehensive about learning to do it here. But, before anyone could voice an opinion about what to do, the pilot made the decision.

"Make yourselves fast for landing."

"Please be gentle man," Cooksey said to himself, relying on his sense of humor to calm the butterflies. It's my first time and I don't want it to hurt."

Tyrone always turned to humor when things were going badly. It was a habit since he was a kid and his father told him the only way to banish the monsters from under his bed was to tell them jokes. He said monsters hated jokes, especially the stupid jokes little kids made. Tonight Tyrone was hoping his father was right.

With Gallinari and McLachlan driving, Tyrone believed down to his toes that if there was a chance to get through this, they would. He pulled his seat harness tight, snapped his helmet visor down, and started reciting every dumb "Knock, knock" joke he knew.

"Knock, knock."

"Who's there?" He answered himself.

"Who." He said.

"Who, who?"

"What are you, an owl?" He chuckled at his poorly timed delivery.

"Stand by gentlemen," Gallinari spoke softly, bringing Tyrone back to the reality of their plight, "Let's see if we can find the bottom of this."

The snow cast into the air by the rotors made *terra firma* a moving target and it seemed as if Betty was stretching her landing gear to tiptoes to touch solid ground.

Without visual cues to aid him and with no chance of returning to the LZ, Gallinari would have to put the chopper down just three nautical miles from the doctor's compound in something he was sure would be like quicksand. He was also dreadfully unsure about their ability to take off again. Even if they were able to find solid ground, he was thinking they'd be quickly frozen fast or less quickly, but as disastrously, entombed by the drifting snow. Though he was controlling his temper to keep his head clear, he was still pissed off at the mission, the doctor's lack of hospitality, the weather, and the threat of smashing Blue Betty into pieces with his ass strapped to her, a few thousand pounds of fuel, and "God knows what" in the cargo bay. As Gallinari began his descent, he voiced his most fervent and heretofore effective landing prayer.

"Please Lord, get my ass on the deck in one piece."

Feeling his way very, very gently, Gallinari lowered the craft toward the place he thought he would encounter the ground. Foot-by-foot, then inch-by-inch the massive helo, now with the main rotor producing its own ground blizzard, floated toward the surface.

"Grab a bulkhead boys, we're goin' in," he urged his crew-friends.

Just as he thought he and the instruments were both going to let them down and a brutal smack would be the next sensation he felt, Blue Betty floated into the pillow of powder snow and settled.

"Power off, Skipper." McLachlan exhaled. "You did it."

"Yeah, Baby!" Tyrone yelled, not complimenting his driver as much as he was praising the Big Pilot in the sky.

As the engine revs dropped and Gallinari moved the flight controls to neutral, he sat for a brief moment and thought once again he had cheated death. Now, it would be a waiting game to see if the storm would subside or if they would be sending transponder signals to the air-sea rescue satellite.

They had enough battery power for a few hours but the unplanned landing, downtime and additional take off dictated a refueling stop in Bergen before they would be safely able to fight the North Atlantic winds and touchdown on CVN78, the U.S.S Ken Nighthawk Kendall.

Named for America's first Native American president, the Kendall was a Nimitz Class flat top; the largest, best equipped and most powerful nuclear powered aircraft carriers of the modern era. Aside from the ship's awesome ability to make war, her state of the art uplinks to all manner of satellite-borne tracking sensors made her very efficient at saving lives as well. Still, even in this decade, the success of surface and deep-sea rescues depended on the vagaries of the weather. With the severity of the storm sitting on the Blue Betty, even the hyper-sharp eyes of the radar imaging satellites would find their precise location elusive.

Markus Haukken put his sled dogs to bed about twenty-one thirty hours the night of the storm. He saw the barometer drop on his weatherlink unit and knew he must make what shelter he could immediately and ride it out. After sipping the last of the liquid water from his flask, he decided that at dawn, if the snow had abated, he would drop in on his old friend Dr. Eva. She wasn't so young anymore but she still knew how to make wonderful love to him and she paid him well for the black market supplies he brought her - the marijuana, American cigarettes and lingonberry jelly for her lefse. But, first things first. This storm was fierce and Haukken, who had survived a lifetime of Norway's terrifying storms, knew that he would be challenged to make it through the night.

Haukken was a magnificent Nordic specimen. He was broad-shouldered and muscular, nearly two meters in height with a leathery complexion and dark blonde hair that he wore long against the elements. He had ham-huge hands with hard-callused skin padding his palms and the wear points of his stubby fingers.

"Not pretty, but pretty good for my job," he used to say, amusing only himself.

Others who saw his hands thought they looked more like a Husky's than a sled-driver's and they said so whenever they wanted to poke some good-natured fun at the big musher.

Their jokes didn't matter much to Markus. He was as quiet and contemplative as he was large. To Markus's way of thinking, people said very few things worth listening to. He preferred listening to the natural sounds of newly sharpened runners slicing the snow crust, the barking of his beloved team in the crisp morning air, and the screech of the sea-birds that colonized the fjords' nooks and crannies.

Markus's lead dog, Tracker, out of old age or just a fatal inability to distinguish between dreams and reality any more scorned the communal warmth of the pack as they settled in this night and trudged to the end of his lead to be at the vanguard of the team. The loyal and immensely strong Husky-Malamute mix froze to death in an hour. Two others in the pack succumbed just after midnight, bitten through by the desiccating teeth of the wind.

"This is very bad," Markus fought back tears on finding the corpses.

His biggest worry was that he and the dogs that hadn't yet been claimed by the cold would become dehydrated. Throughout the harsh day he and the dogs had been working at maximum effort and without the means to melt large quantities of snow; they wouldn't be able to hydrate fast enough to keep pace with sweat they were evaporating. It was only a matter of time before exhaustion and hypothermia would set in. Leaning into the wind, he staggered to where the remaining dogs lay and tucked the four smallest of them into thick woolen blankets from the sled. When he was finished he took a knee, bowed reverently and spoke his piece to the deities who would measure out the remaining thread of his life. Then, he pulled himself into a ball in the lee of the sled to await his fate.

He didn't know how long he slept but as his wits returned, he sensed something was different. The wind had stopped. There was no howling in his ears. The dogs stirred, too. Markus lifted his stiff and sore body from the drift surrounding him and pulled his parka hood back to see... stars! Millions of bright, beautiful, wonderful stars!

The storm had passed. The dogs bolted their blankets and began to bark, straining at their tethers. Markus knew that even though he had been spared for the moment, he and the team were still in peril. He must work quickly to reduce the weight of the sled and hope that the remaining dogs could find a little refreshment from the snow packed around their muzzles. Now, his visit with Dr. Eva would not be an impromptu social call, but a life-saving necessity. He reckoned it was eight kilometers to her compound.

Putting his fear and regret for the death of his precious dogs aside, he made ready to press forward. His eyes were swollen and burning from the hours in the ripping wind and tears flowed freely down to augment the hoary mask of icicles cementing together his mustache, beard and collar. Attempts to move any of these parts independently of the others were not just annoyingly difficult; they were painful and yanked his whiskers. With more effort than he planned to expend, he pulled at his parka and broke the grip of the ice binding the pocket where he kept his GPS unit. With a little luck, his body heat would have kept the batteries warm enough to keep the thing functioning and it would show him the direction and distance to Eva's front door.

Then, he heard it - a sound like whining engines. This couldn't be. But, unless he had finally been driven mad by the cold, he heard an aircraft taking off. It was close by. The dogs were barking excitedly, both at the noise and the smell of Markus' puzzlement. With a single, powerful stroke the musher pulled his survival knife, moved to his rig and cut away the dead animals' harness traces.

"Goodbye Tracker. Farewell, Rolf and Naomi," he choked through the emotion.

No matter how many dogs he'd lost to old age, disease or mishap, the loss of a co-worker was always difficult. But, there was no time to grieve. The wind wouldn't stay down for long and it was time to investigate the source of the strange noise. Maybe someone needed help more than he did.

Markus righted the sled while the dogs tried to shake off the snow, their noses pointing toward the sound. Markus moved two of the dogs to new positions to balance the loss of the dead ones and, for the first time without Tracker at the lead, the team, reluctant and somewhat confused, lurched forward.

"Go, go, go!" Markus yelled releasing the brake and shoving mightily to give the dogs his best assist.

Within a few meters the sled trimmed up and rode atop the snow as the decimated team strove to gain speed. As they labored and gained momentum, Markus pulled the heaviest objects he could find from under the tarp that covered his cargo. He was well aware that whatever was making the loud noise, it may not be there when he arrived. Casting off bundles, boxes and gear on the fly, he screamed to his team.

"Pull, doggies. Get on. Get on you dogs. Go, go, go!"

The sled was now gliding smoothly, although at an agonizingly slow speed. Digging in to give their all, the dogs began climbing the long slope to the top of the snow dune Markus thought concealed the noise-maker. As they neared the top of the ridge, he could see colored lights flashing, the sound grew in volume and pitch and the dog's barking became frenzied. Suddenly, the dogs sank into the backside of a mogul, tripped, yelped and smashed helplessly into the tip of a snow-covered boulder. The sled continued and struck the mess, dogs first, then rock. The collision launched the sled into the air like a snowmobile at full throttle and it began to flip stern over prow. Markus, still clinging to the sled's drive bow, felt the nose-down pitch but he was helpless to stop the debacle in progress. In what seemed to the driver to be slow motion, the back end of the vehicle tore loose from his grip and he flew as if flung from a catapult. He landed face first, his full weight crashing cruelly into the hindquarters of the two lead dogs.

Suki, the smallish but tough Samoyed bitch yelped but Erik, the young Malamute, gave a prolonged howl as the musher's shoulder drove into the dog's backside. Markus felt his collarbone snap. The sickening sound of the bone-crushing collision and the sublime pain of his injury mingled with the disorientation of his flight. In the swirl of sensory overload he lost consciousness and thumped to the snow in a heap.

He couldn't have been out for more than a few seconds when his consciousness rushed back. Markus stood, wobbling. He was groggy, but still he heard the engine noise.

There was no time to right the sled or tend to his team. He had to find out what that blasted noise was all about. Listing under the pain of his injury, Markus clawed at the wreckage and miraculously found his snowshoes. These were not the heavy old wood and leather "tennis racquet" models mounted on the wall of his grandfather's tavern, these were aluminum and graphite composites with fast-on, hinged bindings that would let him run on top of the snow. If he could just get them on over the cursed ice clinging to his boots. Finally, he secured them and stumbled past the wounded and confused dogs toward the sound.

He was just a few meters from the crest of the hill when the noise came to a crescendo and the craft ascended. It was a military helicopter. American, Markus thought, though it didn't matter who they were. In desperation, he began to jump and wave his arms, one up higher and less painful than the other, when the craft yawed and turned to face him.

"Yes, yes," he screamed joyously, anticipating his rescue.

"Skipper, do you see that?" McLachlan asked.

"Holy shit," Gallinari replied. "Is that a man down there?"

"What?" Tyrone asked. "Where?"

Gallinari rotated the helo to center the unidentified snow creature in the windscreen and hovered to get a better view. The ice crystals kicked up by the main rotor were too much for Markus. He turned away, lost his balance and tumbled back down the steep drift. The fall saved his life.

As Markus tried to regain his feet and the men at the controls of the helo strained to identify the snowman in the moonlight, Eva Luknar's bomb went off.

The light energy from the blast hit the helo first, screaming through the wide-open irises of the aviators in the front seat, searing their retinas. The shock wave was the next to arrive and the superheated air engulfed the aircraft. The vacuum it caused as it sped past the fuselage imploded the helo. Crushed to half its original size, the craft hung in the air for a split second before the compressed and superheated aviation fuel in Blue Betty's tanks exploded. Overwhelmed by the shriek of the atomic blast, the craft's destruction was noiseless.

The helo, the valiant crew and Dr. Eva's machine were now just chunks of flaming matter departing the scene. Ground zero was just far enough away that the shock wave left most of the helo's heavier metal components intact but the invisible force of the wave's impact sent it sidelong through the air. Dropping onto the snow with the trajectory of a molten curveball, Blue Betty's fiery carcass flew just a few meters over Markus's head. Astonishingly, the lip of the snow dune that had obscured the snowbound helo from Markus's view had provided a life-saving burm that shielded him from the worst of the blast, though it didn't save him from being covered in hot slush.

"Hell," he thought as he was mashed into the surface. Everything seemed to be in motion around him. As he fought to stay coherent, he heard a deep bass thunder in the distance and the earth churned beneath him.

His next memory was being vaguely aware of his own breathing. Then a surge of pain rudely announced the full return of his senses. After three or four nauseating attempts at focusing, he was successful. The sight before him made him scream. He thought he was in hell. But it was no demon's face that confronted him. It was Marit, his prized breeding Husky. Her empty, steaming eye sockets, seared snout and singed fur were just inches from his nose. Her canine teeth formed a ghastly grin that mocked his survival.

He shrieked into the foul night, "Death take me! Lord my God, please, please-"

Then a horrifying howl scaled the stone walls of the fjord. Markus thought he had imagined it. Or was it he who had screamed, again? He was on the brink of going into shock and could not trust his perceptions. Now, a faint groan crawled into his ear.

In English it said, "Help...me."

Markus crawled apprehensively in the direction of the sound, his snapped clavicle allowing only an awkward, lurching,S crabbing approach. He heard it again and, through the haze, he was able to discern the source a few meters ahead. The plaint issued from a steaming, quivering bundle of cloth. When he got to the thing, Markus beheld the image that would disturb his sleep for the rest of his life. It was a soldier in a charred parka and half-melted helmet. It was Tyrone Cooksey, or what was left of him.

He was on his back, arms akimbo, like a child in a snowsuit ready to make an angel. He was barely distinguishable from the bed of ashen slush on which he lay. Markus tried to assess the man's injuries. At first, they didn't seem serious. It looked as if his limbs were buried in the snow and there were some burns on his neck where his flight suit had left the skin exposed. He must have been thrown clear of the helo when it exploded. Maybe he wasn't too bad off. But, when Markus looked closer at the fallen warrior he saw the man's limbs weren't in the snow. They were, they were…lopped off. Below the elbows and below the knees there were only black pools of congealing blood.

The musher yelped, reflexively standing and staggering backward. His head began to spin, his ears began to ring and, as the sky twirled above him, he fainted again.

This time, consciousness returned with the deep-throated whistle of a steam locomotive. As he pushed himself to a sit, the pain in Markus's shoulder bloomed and he bellowed an angry cry. It seemed as if, in this nightmare, rage was all he could do.

Tyrone groaned again.

Casting aside his revulsion Markus leaned over the man to render what aid he could to the stricken…*sailor*, he saw as he read the toasted leather patch on the man's flight suit.

"You are Ensign Jerome Cooksey, U.S.N, yes Mister?"

Tyrone opened his eyes, but through the scorched and distorted visor, he could only make out the Samaritan's outline.

"Who..?"

Markus lifted the Ensign's head in one of his huge palms and pulled off the helmet. Tossing it aside, he shook his head at the sight of the callow young face and spoke, happy to have someone to talk to.

"I don't know what has happened, Mister Sailor," the musher said apologetically.

"An explosion knocked you out of the sky."

"B-B-Betty?" Tyrone stammered, shivering.

"I don't know anything about her, but your helicopter is gone, Mister," Markus said, in the most comforting tone he could muster.

"My mates?"

"Gone to heaven, I hope. Let me try to stop your bleeding," he said.

"Too late for me," Tyrone said, fighting death with all his might. "Please, listen." "Please...listen," he said, weakening.

The sled driver bent low, his ear to the dying man's lips.

"Eva Luknar?" Markus bolted upright in disbelief. This man was talking about his Dr. Eva. What under the midnight sun would the American Navy have to do with Dr. Eva? Was the explosion from her compound? Did they bomb his friend and lover into dust? No, the Americans were too noble for that and they certainly weren't so stupid as to kill themselves in such an attack.

He bent low again to hear the rest, as incredible as it was. Markus learned about the machine. Tyrone knew it had been blown to smithereens in the blast but he also impressed the sled driver with the importance of finding any shred of documentation that may have been packed in the crate.

"Find the plans, please," he begged. "You must find the plans...look for...computer...disks," he gasped between deep, wheezing breaths. "Dangerous," he sighed. "Don't touch anything without gloves...radiation in the crate...I think."

"Radiation in the crate?" Markus repeated, almost losing his dour mood to a laugh. "If that bomb was what I think it was Mister, the crate is not the only thing that has radiation."

Tyrone didn't hear Markus's speculation. He was gone. His eyes stared emptily into the sky.

Markus winced at the young warrior's passing; gently pressed Tyrone's eyelids closed with the palm of his hand and prayed.

"God, take this man's soul to heaven, and God...help me."

Looking at the burning remnants of aircraft pieces through the steam and smoke, Markus thought seriously about evacuating the area on a dead run. The idea of dying here was unappealing. The thing was, even if he did risk additional contamination to search the wreckage, he didn't know what he was looking for.

He had no transportation. His dogs were dead. In the bitter cold and the infected aftermath of the bomb surrounding him, he was fast losing confidence that the survival skills that had saved him so many times before would be of any avail. Maybe someone else was alive, maybe this Betty, and there was yet some good he could do before he lost his life.

The heat of the blast was dissipating rapidly into the cloudless sky. The slush was already re-freezing and the steam was evaporating as he watched. He felt the cold closing in. Chilled, in wet clothes and without shelter, he would only last a little while. Maybe, if Tyrone was right and not just deluded by the trauma of his injuries, there was something of significance in the wreck and there would be other people on the way. Surely the Americans would be searching for the downed helicopter. If he could just hold out until they arrived.

A shiver wracked Markus's body. He decided to warm himself by conducting his search at a quick march. But where were his snowshoes?

"Thank God," he thought as he looked down and saw the safety straps still attached to his ankles.

Without the shoes, walking on the re glazing ice would be impossible. He knelt down, remounted them, ripping his fingernails on the frost-encrusted buckles, and stood defiantly.

Since saving his own hide was now improbable, he steeled himself to the task of trying his best to fill the request of the young man who had just died in his arms.

"Odin, guide my eyes," he prayed.

The Christian God was good, but in times of dire need like his current predicament, he thought the ancient Norse gods more accessible.

"Put Loki back in his chains and help me find these plans," he cried, beseeching the Scandinavian god of wisdom to reign in the fire demon and god of strife.

All he could see in the murk was bits of debris, each it seemed licked by multicolored flames and producing its own acrid smoke, like a vast field of volcanic fumaroles. Undeterred by the apparent hopelessness of his endeavor, the big man started to circumnavigate what he thought would be an adequate perimeter for his quest and began an inward spiral toward the larger pieces of the helo's fuselage. The smaller junk was so misshapen and covered in soot that as close as he looked, he just couldn't determine their form or function. He didn't know what he was looking at or for and he was getting nervous that as he approached the center of the debris field, he would encounter whatever it was that had prompted the dead American to warn him about the radiation.

As he neared the main body of the wreckage dense smoke overwhelmed him and he turned away to catch his breath and clear the sting from his eyes. Just then, the last of the steam vanished overhead and dazzling moonlight washed the scene. Through his tears, Markus caught a silvery flicker reflecting off a shiny object partially buried in the crust. It was just a couple of meters away.

Markus reached into his belt, drew his knife from its sheath and began to hack at the ice binding the object. In a few strokes it was free. Heeding Tyrone's warning, he pulled his arms into his parka; picked up the object using his sleeves as mittens, and brushed the frost from its surface.

"Nothing" he thought, noting the object's resemblance to the old laser disks he played with as a child.

"Old music or a movie," he thought.

Inspecting the case closer, he wondered if his initial assessment was correct. It surely looked like a compact disk. Dr. Eva had lots of them.

"Too bad," he said aloud and thought, "It is probably ruined by the fire and so is Dr. Eva."

Markus cried. He was fatigued, confused and gamely fighting off shock and hysteria. He'd lost everything, witnessed Tyrone's death, and now it seemed he wouldn't find the thing the Americans wanted. Whatever it was, Markus thought it must be of tremendous import to have caused so much death and destruction. The thing he held was worthy of closer inspection.

The sled driver turned the small case over and read the single word etched into the obverse side. "Medusa," it said.

"I don't know this band," the driver said aloud, "It sounds ugly."

It was as he was trying to open the case with the point of his knife blade, that he heard it…a throaty thumping, off in the distance. It was coming from the general direction of Dr. Eva's compound. It was another helicopter and it was approaching fast.

"Thank you Odin. Thank you, Jesus. Thank you Buddha," Markus stood, and shouted hoarsely into the sky, his good arm raised to hail the craft. Then, with all the energy left in him he yelled, "I live!"

Surely this must be the Americans looking for their lost comrades. Fearful that the men in the approaching aircraft wouldn't see him, Markus took the metal case in his bare hands, adjusted his stance to catch the moonlight and tried to signal the new helicopter. After a few misses, it worked and he saw a ray of light reflect back to him off the aircraft's windscreen. The helicopter banked sharply and bore down on him. Markus's relief was immediate and joyous. He began to whoop and jump like a footballer who just scored the winning goal at World Cup.

In the helicopter, the dark figure in the co-pilot's seat commanded, "Hit him with the light."

As the craft hovered over him, Markus covered his eyes against the harsh searchlight. He didn't understand why the craft stayed aloft.

"Come down you men and take me home, I have a present for you," he shouted waving the disk case at them.

"Shoot him," the pilot instructed to the gunman in the rear. The helo yawed and presented its flank. Markus saw a muzzle flash and felt something hit his chest. The impact knocked him to the ground with a thud and he slid two meters across the ice on his back. He struggled to see what hit him. He couldn't raise his head enough to inspect himself and he couldn't feel his legs but he felt something warm trickling down his left side and his ribs hurt. It was as if he was frozen in place. As the helicopter set down, he knew this wasn't a rescue and began to panic. His breathing was labored and though he tried with all the strength left in his body, he couldn't speak.

He heard the engine wind down and the crunch of footsteps. They were coming at him out of the searchlight's glare. Suddenly, the light changed as if a large object, no…two large objects put him in shadow.

He heard one of them say, "What have we got here?" in a thick, Slavic accent.

"Were you aboard this ruined helicopter? Are you CIA? Maybe an American soldier?" One dark figure said.

"Look in his hand, Klax," the other figure exclaimed. "He's got something there."

The nearest shade reached down and snatched the case, turning it over to read the label. Thinking Markus knew what he had, the man said, "Thank you my hopeless friend, for this gift. It's too bad. You lose.

"Is that what we seek, Mr. Klax?" His henchman asked.

"No, fool, we seek the machine. But, we failed. It's probably shredded and melted into this blasted ice. Never mind what this is. Prepare for take off," Klax said, sternly.

The pilot looked again at the prostrate sled driver, the blood from the hole in his chest seeping into the ice beneath him.

"Should I shoot him again?" The gunner drew his sidearm a demonic grin on his face.

"Leave him," Klax said. He will freeze soon enough.

Disappointed, the man holstered his gun and turned toward the helicopter, muttering.

Markus heard the helicopter's engine rev for takeoff. Ice crystals kicked up by the rotor battered his face and he watched helplessly as the aircraft rose, doused its baleful eye and diminished in the distance.

Chapter 8

"The wrong side of the bed"

The alarm pierced the silence like a klaxon in a confessional. In the rumpled bed, the man's eyes snapped opened and focused. The red digits on his vidcenter declared zero six fifteen, Sunday. It went off two hours earlier when he was on duty. He fumbled for the remote on the nightstand and switched on the Armed Forces News Channel. An atypically attractive female officer in studio makeup and a crisp uni was detailing overnight events around the world; or at least the Defense Department's approved version of what happened.

Luke Forster, CAPT, U.S. Army, BNFL (but not for long) awoke with the hangover of vivid nightmares that would darken his mood all day. Even the thrill of his impending separation from the service after nine long, nasty years brought him no joy this morning. He cursed unintelligibly, extricated himself from the tangled bedding and stumbled toward the bathroom. A night-light glowed meekly through the bathroom doorway, adding a theatrical wash of light to his naked form. He was tall, dark-haired, early thirties and Ranger fit.

Stretching his brawny arms to the ceiling he arched his back, yawned and approached the commode. Taking matters into his own hand, he relieved the pressure on his bladder as he confronted himself in the mirror. Sable eyes surmounted by a thicket of black brows looked back at him. Here and there the whites of his eyes were shot with clusters of red but in total, in their wide-set sockets, they presented an image of attentive intellect. Between them sat what he thought to be a serviceable, if somewhat dog-like nose. Underneath full, wide lips was a strong chin made friendly by the vertical bisection of a small cleft. He had small ears for a man his size and they were pinned back a little - out of the way. He finished his toilet, flushed, left the lid and seat up where they belonged, and scrubbed his scalp with his fingers to force some circulation to his brain.

As he smacked his lips to fight back the desert in his mouth, he experienced the unpleasant remnants of the carnitas he had wolfed down at the Riviera supper club just a few hours ago. Since Tricia's death, the bar had become a second home. Another pass with his tongue and the latent taste of tequila returned. So did the knot in his neck; most likely the penalty for the two freebies he and the bartender gulped at last call. Leon had a limp wrist when it came to pouring the magic juice from the blue agave and he never used a shot glass to measure portions for his amigos. Half a tumbler was so much more, *simpatico*.

Reaching into the morass of the hell drawer beneath the sink, Luke managed to locate a crumpled foil packet; a few strands of hair and a ball of towel lint decoratively attached. He plucked it from the hairbrush on which it was impaled. The autofaucet filled his glass. He ripped open the packet and dropped in the twin white tablets. Nothing happened. No fizz. Nothing. They just sank to the bottom of the glass, inert - like little albino hockey pucks.

Mumbling, "fuckin'" something, he slammed the drawer closed, grabbed his toothbrush from the rack and used the handle in a vain attempt to pulverize the obstinate tablets. With bits of alka-debris churning defiantly in the water, he swirled the glass in his hands, grimaced, drank and chewed the remnants of his medicinal misadventure. Gingerly he replaced the glass on the counter, put a hand towel over his head and pushed the red touch-pad on the autofaucet. Steaming water sloshed into the sink, his head sank between his shoulders and he moaned. It was going to be a long day. Then the bulb in his Mighty Mouse nightlight flickered and died with a single tinkle.

Chapter 9

"I have met the enemy and he is you."

In October the Colorado sky from the plains to the high country is impossible to forget. From the Robin's-egg blue crowning the summit of the front-range peaks, it grades to dense cobalt at its zenith. Beyond, the blackness of space beckons and reminds the observer that the heavens are a mile closer here. At special times along the Continental Divide, it seems possible to leap and grasp the edge of the void.

This was such a morning and even the mist clinging tenaciously to the running paths in Washington Park could not dull its brilliance. After a blender breakfast of orange juice, bananas and strawberries, Forster was feeling somewhat repaired. The temperature was already climbing and as he stretched his legs against a picnic table, he knew he wouldn't need his sweats for long. He snugged the laces, retied his cross-trainers and discarded his jacket, revealing a worn, sweat-stained, gray Army t-shirt. Turning like an NBA point guard, he jumped, arched the wadded garment through the side window of his PTV and proudly shouted, "two," as it settled on the seat. Personal Transport Vehicles replaced multi-passenger gasoline powered transports shortly after the end of the Third Gulf War back in 2034, when OPEC unceremoniously discarded its non-Middle Eastern members, renamed itself the Pan Arabic Oil Consortium and shut off the oil supply to their list of "non-allied" nations. Since then, under duress, the consuming countries of the world were forced to mandate the acceptance of mass transit. PTV's and turbocycles were now the only remaining legal option for solo road travel.

Forster switched the digicom on his wrist from *STDBY* to *ET*. He started the stopwatch and jogged from the parking pad to begin his morning 10K. He started slowly, heeding the warning clicks and pops from his aging joints. After the first mile sweat formed on his cheek, reflecting the low sun into his eyes. His muscles warmed as he fell into his rhythm and he savored the park's sumptuous autumn smells. Leaves in a panoply of colors scurried across his path and crunched underfoot as an early breeze rose. The park's more than abundant waterfowl were not yet with the program. Geese and nearly grown goslings huddled together on the dewy grass and among the waterweeds; only their heads visible above the mist. As he glided past the boathouse pavilion, Forster spied a clutch of canvasbacks and a rare pair of buffle-headed ducks going inverted to feed in the shallow pond. The buffle-heads made him smile, cartoonish things that they were.

For the city, it was a decidedly pastoral scene. But enough sightseeing he thought, it was time to run. Forster accelerated displaying the strength and form of the first class athlete he had been for so many years. Nearing the end of his workout, he powered into a full-out sprint. Face contorted with the concentration of maximum effort, he turned to his right and looked over his shoulder fantasizing that he was in a collegiate meet. Pursuing him in the mock event was the ghost of an old nemesis. The memory was vivid. He was reliving the dual track meet with Navy in his senior year at West Point.

That day his performance became legend - the stuff of officers club bar brags and interservice taunts for a decade to come. Once again, he heard the crowd noise build as he relived the moment of his triumph when he crossed the finish line three one-hundredths of a second ahead of the strongest, fastest, blackest man he had ever seen.

His adversary was so close Forster felt steam from the guy's nostrils curl the hair on the back of his neck. Feeling the need to recreate the victory, the former cadet his comrades called "The Flash," after an old comic book superhero, put his mind to it. The moment he beat the "Monster Midshipman from Americus" in the four-forty was so realistic he could taste the adrenaline oozing from the back of his jaw. He put the pedal to the metal. Almost out of control, Forster lunged forward, grunted with a surge of effort and "felt" the finish line tape break. Grinning like he did when it actually happened, he raised his arms and waved his hands in victory. As imaginary spectators went into a frenzy of worship and adulation, his feet slapped the pavement and he slowed to a walk, hands on hips.

Then someone addressed him, breaking the spell of his reverie. The man spoke with a pronounced burr. There was gravel and depth in the voice, like a used-up radio announcer's. Forster took only a moment to recognize it. With that cognition came ripples of disgust and the recall of a hatred that cut to his core.

"Slowing down," the voice said. "Not the Lucas Patrick Forster, I remember."

The old man attached to the voice wore a faded trench coat two sizes too big. The tattered tweed hat he wore shaded a sallow, scruffy face. He was tall but stooped. An ovaline cigarette hung precariously from his mouth and flopped between his lips as he spoke.

"Up yours, asshole," Forster barked, his eyes squinting with revulsion.

"I should kill you where you stand, MacLaren."

"Easy old man," MacLaren whispered hoarsely. "I don't think you're up to it. You look like you're about to puke. Anyway, how do you say it out here in the wild and woolly West? I've got the drop on you."

The Scot, eyes fixed on the younger man's, drew his right hand from his coat pocket to reveal the silenced muzzle of a .380 magnum.

"Your right hand…and slowly," MacLaren ordered, his tone devoid of emotion. "I'll have that wrist digicom. We don't want interruptions, eh?"

Eliminating Forster's opportunity to alert his headquarters, MacLaren put the device in his coat pocket and commanded, "Walk."

"With my wife's murderer?" Foster asked, incredulous at the request.

"I've no more to say about that," the Scott dismissed the remark.

"She's dead and I'm dying. Now walk", he said icily.

"Fuck you, MacLaren" Forster spit back, "As much as I'd like to hear about the details of your, I hope, imminent death, I'm out of here.

Sure that the Scot's index finger was already inside the trigger guard of the weapon in his pocket, Forster said, "Shoot me in the back if you like, shithead. It's your style."

As Forster turned to walk away, he thought the Scot would act on his suggestion. Killing without hesitation had been his job for forty years and he was the best there was. *Was*, being the operative word. For a moment, given the man's condition, Forster thought of turning on MacLaren. He wanted to kill him. Without reservation, his handlers would support him and bolster his claim that the homicide was self-defense. But he was unarmed, his hand-to-hand combat skills were unpracticed and to his further disadvantage, he was too angry to think clearly.

Why was MacLaren here? To terminate him? For what purpose? Where did he come from and who in hell was he working for? Army Intelligence had cut their ties with the old assassin years ago. But, why hadn't he been warned that the Scot was back in the country? This meeting couldn't have been authorized by INTELCOM.

As Forster began to put some distance between them, MacLaren pursued, but in a few meager strides he was huffing. Forster approached the pedestrian underpass at the north end of the park as MacLaren struggled to keep up. Curious about why he hadn't felt the impact of a bullet, Forster looked back.

They were both in the tunnel now and to Forster's horror, MacLaren was drawing a second pistol, this one with a much longer barrel. Forster began to run in a defensive zigzag. If he could just make it to the far end of the tunnel, he could…

Despite the Scot's wobbly gait, he drew the weapon with the smooth sure motion of a master, assumed the classic Weaver stance, turned his face off-center to the sight and steadied. Holding the breath in his rotting lungs, MacLaren fired. Forster heard the shot but the noise from the weapon's muzzle was oddly muffled.

It was too late to react now. Forster realized he had made a huge mistake in not trying to kill the Scot when he was close enough to have a chance at succeeding. He felt the stinging of the pistol round impact the back of his thigh. Propelled by the impact of the projectile and unbalanced by the reflexive contraction of his thigh muscle, he fell onto the wet leaves covering the tunnel floor. He knew the Scot would fire again, and he bridled at the thought of dying at the hands of his wife's killer, but a strange warmth crept into Forster's chest as he anticipated joining his beloved in the next life.

The *coupe de gras* didn't come. Straining to focus, Forster turned and saw the Scot shuffling toward him returning the pistol to its holster. MacLaren took out a handkerchief and wiped the sweat from his face. Snatching his hat, he swiped the rag along the soaked inner band and tried to catch his breath. He began to cough, chunks of mucous spewing from his mouth, as if he was expectorating a lung. Blood stained the hanky as the Scot's body wracked in spasm. Undeterred he leaned over Forster, grabbed the woozy man's leg and twisted it to get a better view of the tranquilizer dart. The syringe was empty.

"G'night," said the Scot.

As Forster looked into his assailant's rheumy eyes, the sedative hit him like a right hook. His ears rang. His vision irised down and he whispered, "Tricia, Tricia, Tri-"

There was a "whoosh" in his ears and he blacked out.

Chapter 10

"She's come undone."

Forster thought he was dead and that the surreal tableau unfolding before him was a prelude to eternity. He was at The Pentagon. It was a summer day in 2021 and he was above it, floating above the massive edifice. His eyesight seemed supernaturally enhanced; capable of fast action zooms or pullbacks at will and he saw everything in birds-eye view. He zeroed in on a tree across from the building - a tall and graceful Magnolia in full bloom. In the first, low crotch of the trunk a sniper nested in his Ghillie suit. Camouflaged or not, Forster knew it was MacLaren.

It was happening again. The diabolical events of that day were unfolding in heart-breaking detail and once again he was powerless to stop it. As if he was in the tree with the assassin, Forster heard MacLaren release the bolt, lock and load the Cheytac .408, the long-barreled sniper rifle prized for its low trajectory and hitting power.

Preparing to fire, MacLaren leaned into the custom cheek piece that brought his eye into the proper alignment with the scope. Following the sniper's line of sight, Forster zoomed in on the River Entrance as one of the polished brass revolving doors began to spin. He struggled to close his eyes but the vision wouldn't allow it and though he tried to scream through his mounting panic, he was struck mute.

In his perch MacLaren anticipated Sergei Gorkov's appearance, but the figure emerging from the door was not yet the military attaché (and recently outed double agent) from the Georgian Republic, just a tall WAC with overloaded briefcase and handbag trying to negotiate passage through the cramped passage in issue pumps. As she exited and began her descent down the cascade of concrete steps, the revolving door slowed to a stop. Forster knew it would only be a moment, now.

The door began to spin again and Forster saw MacLaren tense. A balding, middle-aged man in a nondescript gray suit emerged from the portal. MacLaren fired. It was then, in the time it took the bullet to close the distance to the man's forehead that the tragedy began to unfold.

As MacLaren squeezed the trigger, Gorkov gave a last little push to render assistance to the attractive female in the compartment behind him. He even looked back to smile at her and see if she acknowledged his chivalry. He had seen her as they approached the door and couldn't keep his eyes off her long, shapely legs and form-fitting skirt. Returning his attention to where he was going just an instant too late, the diplomat/spy caught his heel in his pant cuff and stumbled onto the broad landing outside.

The misstep didn't save him but there were disastrous consequences to his clumsiness. The rifle round hit Gorkov on the top of his head, cutting a deep groove through his cerebral cortex. The impact flattened the bullet but with substantial momentum remaining, it ricocheted, tumbled and crashed through the door glass into the chest of the woman he had leered at just a moment before. The steel and lead wad hit Tricia Forster's sternum like a brick, biting through the bone, tearing away a major portion of her aorta and liquefying the top lobe of her left lung before it fragmented and perforated the muscles in her upper back.

Forster, wracked in pain and with no way to express it, saw Gorkov's lifeless form hit the concrete. The door kept turning however and he now beheld the dreadfulness of his wife's death.

Tricia wore her favorite white suit and blue silk blouse. She always dressed her best to meet her husband and today, while Luke was at the "puzzle palace" for a briefing on his next mission, she wanted to look especially pretty as she dropped off the sealed file he had inadvertently left in the floor safe in their garage.

With dark blood oozing out of the hole in her blouse, she reeled out of the door, her eyes huge and full of fear. Like a sapling felled with the cruel stroke of a woodsman's ax, she slumped to the ground. Demurely she twisted and sat knees together, arms at her side. She teetered in that position, and fell sideways as her life expired.

When the first of the Pentagon's security force gathered around her only seconds later, all but ignoring Grinkov's corpse, all the men in black could think of was the tragic image of Tricia Forster's beautiful face surrounded by scarlet red, cloud white and navy blue.

Chapter 11

"No way out."

Suddenly, Forster heard screeching like rusted train wheels clawing to a stop on cold steel. It was the sound track to the finale of his flashback and it grew louder by the second.

He felt as if he were being propelled downward. His head twisted from side to side as he gasped for air and tried to loosen the grip of his dream. Then, his eyes opened and he heard himself weeping. His pupils were still dilated from the drug in the dart and the pain of the light slashing through them merged with the noise in his ears until he thought the talons of Satan himself were dragging him straight to hell. He wasn't dead but he wanted to be and what he saw next didn't mediate his longing for annihilation.

It was MacLaren. He was so near that Forster could smell the nicotine stains on the old man's mustache. He wanted to spit in his face but he had no saliva and was still out of touch with his faculties.

MacLaren shook Forster violently and hissed a guttural whisper.

"Get up. We've got business."

The Scot released Forster's shirt and Luke fell back, his head bouncing on the turf.

"Jesus," Forster yelled in protest.

While Forster was out, MacLaren had dragged him from the tunnel into the daylight, setting him upright against the earthen burm at its entrance. He had covered Forster's body with the wretched trench coat and turned him on his side, the less to resemble a corpse. To the casual observer, they were just another brace of park bums.

As Forster tried to clear his head, MacLaren sat beside him. Kicking off the erstwhile blanket, Forster mumbled a few more expletives and like a feisty drunk, tried to assume a martial arts attack stance. With hate on his face and the tranquilizer still in control, Forster slurred, "Kill... you-"

The Scot retrieved the .380 from his pocket and gestured with it.

"Sit down before you fall down," the Scot said wearily. I shot you with a tranquilizer, but if you don't shut your trap, I'll put a hole in your head and be on my way. Now, sit!"

Alert enough now to see the wisdom in compliance, Forster gave in.

Keeping his pistol trained on Forster, MacLaren owled his head around to see if they were still unnoticed. Convinced they were as yet a part of the scenery, he started to explain how Luke Forster's life and maybe everyone else's on the planet was about to change.

Chapter 12

"Incredible"

As it will, the day's weather had changed, and a bank of inky clouds ran before a cold wind as MacLaren told his story to the suspicious operative.

"I'm not here for myself, Forster. I know you despise me but I'm just a messenger."

As the Scot spoke, passing runners and dog-walkers cast curious looks at the two men.

"He's all right folks. The klutz tripped."

MacLaren attempted to dismiss the peaked interest of an older couple out for their morning constitutional. Fortunately for all concerned no one stopped to press an inquiry, though most of them couldn't resist an over-the-shoulder double take.

"You're going to get a call from your handler today," the Scot continued.

"There's no way you could know that," Forster said skeptically.

"You've been in the cold for years and clueless forever. I haven't pulled routine duty for three years. I'm 'special projects' now. And, I'm short. Two pieces of official business to wrap up and in three weeks, I'm a civilian."

"Your tour is over, today," MacLaren said. "And, the mission you're about to take on isn't for the Army or the United States. It's bigger than that. You are to disregard any orders other than those from The Ten. All other entities and individuals are to be considered hostile. Is that clear?"

"Bullshit. You don't have that authority. And, what the hell is The Ten?"

"Tell you what, laddie," the Scot continued. "Shut your yap for a few minutes and I'll promise you two things. One, after today, I'm out of your face for good and two, if you do what I tell you, you'll get to stay alive for a while, unless your former associates get to you."

"Former associates? Why would they want to harm me? Screw you!"

"Hey, MacLaren," Forster said, "I'll make *you* a promise. When this shit wears off I'll spin your head around one-eighty so you can watch me kick your ass."

"Feeling frisky, eh?" MacLaren said. "Well, if your vaunted intestinal fortitude is more than just legend, dig deep; you're going to need it. What I'm about to tell you has global implications. You must do exactly as I say. The world social order and the continued existence of every living thing on the planet will hinge on your actions. Do you understand?"

"Drama MacLaren? This is novel."

The old Scot rasped a barrage of deep, hacking coughs. He wiped a trickle of blood from the corner of his mouth with the back of his hand and laughed hatefully.

"You know something, you fart in the wind? I told The Ten that assigning you to his mission was a bone-headed mistake. No matter that you're probably the toughest and street smartest punk to ever play the game. But now," he said with regret in his voice, "I have no time to change that."

"Who or what is The Ten?" Forster asked, again.

"Finally, I have your attention!"

As MacLaren spoke, the wind came easterly, the clouds knit together and it got dark. Bushels of leaves lofted high into the air and sailed west toward the foothills. A flock of geese, as if threatened by the Scot's tale, launched themselves and soared off in formation. The men stood and walked. The old spy, never taking his eyes off Forster, continued. As the Scot spoke, the Captain's expression changed in turn from hate, to incredulity, to angst. The fear would come later. In the distance, a solitary runner braced himself against the newly raw day. Ducking his head to fend off the onslaught of a light drizzle, he saw one of the scroungy men hand the other what looked like a large wristwatch. He watched as the two men parted.

Buffeted by MacLaren's news and the worsening weather, Forster stood, bowed his head and studied the ground. Whatever had passed between the two, the passing runner thought, the younger man looked like he had just learned of a death in the family. He couldn't know that the death Forster was contemplating was the death of the Family of Man.

Gathering himself against the gloom, Forster re-fastened the digi-com to his wrist and with his throbbing thigh hindering his gait, trudged back to the parking pad. He beeped open the PTV's door, settled into the leather seat now stiff with cold, and violently shook the steering wheel, his knuckles blanching. He caught his eyes in the rear-view mirror and uttered the single word that summed up the morning, "Shit."

As Forster reached for the starter his digicom warbled, the clear tones piercing the fog in his mind. After four rings, he picked the device up, read the display announcing the identity of the caller, pushed the *Talk* button and barked his recognition password, "Genoa."

"Venice," came the reply. This week it was Italian cities. The voice on the other end was urgent, "Meet me at the downed house," it said.

"Control, I had a companion on my run this morning," Forster said.

"A canceled number?" Control said, referring to the Scot's status.

"How'd you-"

"Never mind. No more talk on the 'com. Get to the house, on the double."

His handler disconnected. Pulse quickening, Forster clicked off the communicator, fired up the PTV and turned out of the park. An unruly mob of rock maple leaves chased his wheels down the street. He didn't like his handler's tone. The Scot's prediction that Woodless would call was accurate. Was his warning?

Chapter 13

"Reality bites."

Turkey Creek canyon meanders along beside an ancient creek bed. Forster loved this road. In summers past he would reel his motorcycle through the switchbacks at speeds that would terrify his female companions. Impressive as his driving skills were, he occasionally would yell, "Oh, oh," just to thrill the voluptuous, long-tressed play mates he favored in his salad days, only later to soothe their anxieties with a bottle of champagne, a loaf of salty rye and a pungent wedge of Cambazola.

Those days of grass-stained clothes and sticky rides back to Denver were barely memories now. As important as the gentle dalliances were to him then, they seemed a trivial and selfish delusion as he made the ascent to Mt. Falcon Park today. The drizzle of the city park had turned to snow in the chill air of the foothills and the slick road and his foul disposition squelched the old joy.

He pressed on, gliding by the hamlets of Idledale and Kittridge as the scenery whizzed by and painted soft impressionistic scenes on his windows. Forster's mind was so boggled he nearly overshot his turn. But, tugging hard on the wheel and adding some body English, he made the sharp left onto the Parmalee Gulch road and eventually up the serpentine, washboard trail to his destination. Before he knew it he gained the park entrance and braked to a hard stop.

For a while he sat motionless, hands on the wheel, and thought about fleeing to a sun-drenched island in Mexico. It wasn't like him to run scared, but if there was a chance the world was about to become the hell that MacLaren had described, maybe the best thing to do was to buy a sack of limes, a case of tequila and sit on the Playa Cancun until the dread came to get him. On the other hand, maybe things weren't really this dire. Maybe, probably, the old man was paranoid, schizophrenic and delusional.

He had no reason to trust MacLaren and why would he have anything to fear from the Army? He was one of the most decorated officers in the branch and his efficiency ratings were the envy of his peers.

Stiff-legged from his drive and sore from the tranquilizer dart, Forster climbed out of the PTV and began the quarter-mile walk to the ruins of the old house and the rendezvous with his handler. After a few paces, he remembered MacLaren's warning and returned to the vehicle for his 9mm. He clipped the holster to his waistband, secured the PTV and set out again, adjusting his jacket to conceal the weapon. Though he had little doubt that Woodless would clear things up and dispel the doom and gloom MacLaren had preached, he was intuitively ill at ease and his pulse was tripping faster than the physical effort of this short hike demanded. As he walked, the snow changed from the big puffy stuff that proclaimed the arrival of a transient snow shower to the smaller flakes that implied a prolonged siege.

The wind freshened as Forster approached the ruins. From seventy-five meters, the stocky silhouette and ever-present cloud of cigar smoke broadcast like a bullhorn in church that it was Conroy "Connie" Woodless awaiting him. He was sheltering in a corner of the burned out shell that was planned by the entrepreneur and *Cosmopolitan Magazine* publisher, John Brisbane Walker, to be President Woodrow Wilson's Summer White House. Economic setbacks, his wife's untimely death, and the advent of World War I diminished Walker's interest in the project until finally, in the 1930s, a merciful lightning strike demolished the pseudo-palace and he abandoned the project.

Woodless, buttressed against the weathered split-rail fence encircling the ruins was gnawing on his cigar and smiled as Forster approached. Forster grabbed and shook his colleague's hand, but the look in the senior officer's eyes reinforced the hinky feeling Luke had about the meeting. Connie had bad news.

"Luke," Woodless nodded, Forster's hand still clamped in his. "It's great to see you. You look great. Your leave has done wonders."

Then, his expression changed.

"But, as much as I'd like to chat and catch up on things, there's no time for pleasantries. Effective now, your leave has been extended indefinitely. You're going cold."

Highly alert now, Forster took a deep breath and expanded his diaphragm in a search for the secure feeling of the 9mm pressing back against him. The semiautomatic pistol held thirteen rounds that in *his* hand meant instant death to thirteen people if the situation demanded.

Threatened by Woodless' tone and replaying the encounter with MacLaren, Forster instinctively began to scan the tree line for any suspicious shapes or movement that would conceal a back-up man. Coming back to Woodless' comment, he stammered.

"Whaddya mean, Connie?"

"You heard me," Woodless said in his most serious command voice. "Effectively immediately, you are not to have contact with anyone in the unit, at Defense, foreign intel, NSA, no one. We'll find MacLaren and he'll be terminated. Command thinks he's lost it. He's been marked and tailed and now he's made a connection with you. We've got big problems, partner."

"You're serious!"

"You were seen in the park with him this morning."

"I told you that," Forster responded defensively.

"Yeah, Luke. That was righteous. I never expected anything different."

"Then, what's the problem?" Forster balked, his anger rising. "I sure wasn't expecting that sonofabitch. You know I'd as soon kill him as look at him."

"What did he want, Luke?"

As much as these two men had meant to each other over the years, and as much as they had trusted one another, Forster knew the answer to Woodless' question would determine his fate. He would have to phrase his response carefully. As Forster tried to discern the best, safest way to reply, Woodless sensed his anxiety and, for the sake of their relationship, interrupted to clue his friend in before Luke's answer forced his hand and resulted in calamity.

"Luke, we've confirmed the existence of an emerging weapons technology, superior to anything we've got in the field or on the drawing board. It's not ours yet, but we're determined to have it. We think MacLaren has joined a rogue political faction that will try to keep us from obtaining that technology. If his masters beat us to it, confidence is high that there will be disastrous implications. It may be that we're talking about a weapon of mass destruction. That's all I know. I need to know your part of it and I need to know it now."

To underline the gravity of his request, Woodless, with a speed belying his age, drew his Glock 27. At this range, even Woodless' legendary poor marksmanship wouldn't save Forster. Disoriented by the hostile actions of his close friend, Forster wondered what in the hell was going on, that twice in the same day people had pointed loaded weapons at him.

"I want precise details, Luke," Woodless continued. "What did MacLaren tell you? Don't leave a thing out. What were you doing; a: together, b: speaking and, c: how did it happen that neither of you are in the morgue? Your answers make sense and I may be able to turn this thing around before it's out of my hands. You lie to me and your part of this ends right here."

Forster had to make his move.

"Jesus, Connie," Forster yelled, "Back off. I'll tell you. MacLaren, that crazy fuck, shot Tricia through the heart. What do I owe him?"

The venomous intensity of Forster's statement and the vicious look in his eyes broke Woodless' concentration for a split second. Normally, that wouldn't be nearly enough time for Forster to be assured of safely disarming an assailant, and if he botched the attempt, a .40 caliber round didn't have to hit a vital organ to be fatal. But, he didn't know if he'd get another chance, so he had to try. Luckily, there were the magpies.

As Woodless flinched from the fury of Forster's reaction, a playful squirrel accosted a pair of magpies huddling in a lodgepole pine above the men. Startled from their intimate repose, the big black and white birds burst into the open, the sudden relief of their weight on the branches flinging a few pounds of accumulated snow into the air. The cacophony of the birds' cries in the solemnity of the ruins was ear splitting. Woodless ducked instinctively. In a heartbeat, Forster grasped the man's wrist and forced the muzzle of the Glock up and away from his torso. Stepping back to gain sufficient clearance to strike, Forster released his right hand from the man's arm and in a blur, brutally drove a flattened palm into Woodless' nose, exhaling a plosive "Kiai" for maximum force.

Woodless' head snapped back, blood and mucus flowing from his nostrils, defiling the snow at his feet. As if in stop-action the stunned man stumbled backward, lost his footing and crashed his skull into the rubble of John Brisbane Walker's ruined home. There was a grisly "whap" as bone hit stone. Woodless' hand relaxed its grip on the Glock and the pistol fell to the ground. Forster quickly snatched it up and tried to process what just happened.

When MacLaren told Forster his astonishing story, it had all the credibility of a fairy tale. Given the Scot's erratic behavior after he killed Tricia and was court-martialed out of the service, Forster had every reason to distrust him. But now, with Woodless spread-eagled before him, and the man's pistol in his hand, Forster considered that MacLaren had been playing it straight with him. It was time to face the probability that the Scot had spoken the truth.

Forster let loose with a wrenching primal scream, borne of frustration, betrayal and the soulful regurgitation of the memories that MacLaren's visit had rekindled.

When Tricia died the fire went out in Luke Forster. He was sullen and forlorn and his friends, unable to rescue him from the crushing depression of her loss, eventually abandoned him to his misery. He lost faith in the righteousness of the quest and the sacred motivations of "God and country" waxed meaningless. Words like honor, decency, devotion and friendship prompted only cynical retort and his belief in a merciful higher power vanished. His desire for physical love was buried with her remains. It was all blown away in the millisecond it took the Scot's bullet to tear her chest apart.

It took a year of sedulous and skillful therapy before he returned to duty. Even then his mates recognized a greatly reduced version of the supremely capable, complex and happy man they had known. In stark contrast to the affable, gregarious man he was, he only seemed to tolerate the presence of others now and that only under the influence of copious amounts of liquor. When finally he returned, he rededicated himself to his craft and honed his military skills to a fine edge, achieving near perfect scores on every evaluation they could throw at him. But, excellence brought no satisfaction and finally, accepting the spoliation of his soul, he opted to leave the service. Today's events validated the wisdom of that decision.

As Forster's scream echoed from the rampart of trees that formed the park's perimeter, Woodless stirred. Forster, anguished eyes to the sky and his back to the man, was unaware of his surreptitious movement. But, when Woodless bent to retrieve the small caliber Beretta he kept strapped to his ankle, he gasped in pain at the dislocated teeth gnashing in his mouth. Forster reacted to the noise, whirled and fired. The massive round coughed through the silencer.

Before the spent shell casing cleared the receiver, the back of Woodless' head was torn away. Forster was always amazed at how a hollowpoint made such a little hole in the front and such a big one in the back. A few seconds passed and a post-mortem twitch closed Woodless' finger around the Beretta's trigger. The pistol spit its tiny round harmlessly into the air, a last futile act by the now lifeless pile of dung that had once been Forster's compatriot, drinking buddy and often, apologist.

When Tricia died, Woodless spent endless days listening to Forster's heartbreak and consoling him. He called in a boatload of personal markers to wrangle a staff helicopter to ferry the despondent Forster from Lowry AFB in Denver to a private helipad at the pristine Vail mountain resort, where he helped the young man recuperate with long hikes along the Gore Range and long nights at Russell's bar with the locals.

Forster looked at the body; wretched his breakfast on the ground and cried.

Chapter 14

"Good guys, bad guys"

Luke felt his senses were under assault from every direction. The lingering pungency of vomit soured his taste. His balance had not returned following the encounter with MacLaren and the flashback to Tricia's death. He could still see the blood pouring out of the head shot he put in the friend who had betrayed him, and his sixth sense was clouded by his inability to see where this was all headed. His skin prickled because he knew there would be others sent to hunt him down.

He had no choice. He would have to contact MacLaren.

Gathering his wits, Forster unfastened the digicom from his wrist, pitched it to the ground and crushed it beneath his heel. They couldn't track him electronically now, but they'd be curious about the cessation of his ID signal. Or, perhaps, they were expecting him to go off the air and he could buy a little time with the deception, at least until the cleaner team arrived and found the wrong body. Regardless, Connie's digicom had already alerted them that the handler's pulse had stopped. Forster had to beat feet. He jogged to his PTV, pulled his personal digicom from the glove box, strapped it on and drove down the winding road back to Denver. His body felt leaden and his head throbbed as he fought to keep his eyes focused on the road.

He knew there was no chance of retrieving his belongings from his home. His home. That was history. It and every approach to it would be under surveillance. That part of his life was over. His life as Luke Forster, U.S. Army, was over. His friends would likely never hear from him again. Their communications and activities would be closely monitored. He was a huge liability to Woodless' associates and for all he knew, that group could include half the Federal Government.

He had to go somewhere to think. But, where? Using his PTV for much longer would be folly. Maybe the best course of action was to put his pistol to his head and end it now, on his terms. Maybe he would find MacLaren and kill him first. This must be his doing. It had all been his doing since he shot Tricia.

As Forster drove on his mind reeled with wretched, fateful images and he sensed a new smell pervading the now dark morning dank. He'd smelled it the first time he faced combat and every time since. It was coming from him and he knew he must be leaving a trail of it on his descent. The scent of fear.

Then, his digicom lit. The ID screen said *UNK*. Tentatively he pressed the *Talk* button and tried to hear whatever the instrument would tell him about the caller.

"Answer the phone," the voice said in its familiar, cold tone.

"MacLaren, what the fuck have you gotten me into?"

"I know about Woodless."

"You what? That's impossible, unless…you were there."

"I told you this was serious", the Scot said. "Listen carefully; we can't talk on this thing. Meet me at location Bravo in one hour." MacLaren hung up.

"McLar- Hello?" Forster said in full-blown frustration. "Damn," he said as he braked the PTV and twisted the reluctant vehicle into a screeching, one hundred eighty-degree turn.

There was only one "location Bravo" they had in common and it would take sixty minutes to get there, in good weather, with no traffic and no cops.

Location Bravo was the Golden Bee tavern in Colorado Springs. It was tucked away in a Hobbit hole near the main entrance to the Broadmoor Hotel. When Forster was completing his agent training at the reopened Fort Holabird, Maryland, MacLaren, then the headquarters G2, had taken the top five trainees in that class to a briefing on interservice counterintelligence operations at NORAD Headquarters beneath Cheyenne Mountain.

Days spun into nights as Forster and his comrades worked physical security swing shifts - a disorienting watch rotation that had him on duty the first day of the cycle from zero seven hundred to fifteen hundred hours; the second day from fifteen hundred to twenty-three hundred; and the third day from twenty three hundred to zero seven hundred. He had the fourth day off, and then repeated the cycle. By the end of the first cycle the circadian rhythms that subliminally told him when to sleep, when to eat, etc., were out of whack. He wanted breakfast for dinner. He wanted to work out in the middle of the night and he wanted to sleep at noon.

Feeling sorry for the trainee and having remembered that an entry in Forster's dossier reported him to be handy with a tennis racquet, MacLaren challenged him to a match. Though he was physically exhausted, Luke accepted and the two, dressed in the traditional battle whites of the sport, took to the courts in the pines, hard against the slope of the Pikes Peak massive.

The match was grueling. It was summer and the temperature on the court was measured in three digits. There was no wind, the air was thin and the humidity hovered around a sinus-cracking twenty percent. Worse, during play for the first point of the first game, the contest became a battle not between competitors, but between adversaries. MacLaren, in his mid-forties then, was a reluctant convert to the baseline game, his knees and ankles already showing signs of arthritis in rebellion against his years of playing on city hard courts. He played well as a young man, in the main due to his physical prowess. Now, having gained the experience of more than a million serves and service returns and four times that many forehands, backhands, overhead smashes, drop shots, cross-court kills and lobs, he was crafty and nastier than ever.

Forster had the game MacLaren had lost. He was a dyed-in-the-wool serve-and-volley man. Hit, attack, parry and kill. First or second serve - it didn't matter to young Luke when he charged in. If he wasn't at net, he was doing everything he could to get there. This match would pit brute force against savvy. It went on for a long time. Three hours later it was over; 7-5, 7-5, 10-8.

In a gesture that spoke volumes and that MacLaren never forgot, Luke didn't shake hands and offer the traditional and annoying but gentlemanly, "Good game."

Instead, he headed straight for the shade of the player's bench and shouted.

"Tough loss old man. Thanks for the workout," leaving MacLaren, standing at mid net. The Scot glared at him and shook his head.

"Prick," he said.

Luke heard the comment, but let it go. He wasn't a bad sport and he did feel guilty about acting like one. It was just that McLaren was so goddamn good at what he did and the only edge Forster could find on the old pro at this point was annoyance.

Forgiving Luke his boorishness, MacLaren disclosed that there was a place nearby with no sun and glass yards sloshing with copious quantities of English ale. It took almost five minutes for the sweat-soaked combatants to cover the hundred yards from the tennis court to the tavern, though Luke never did slow down enough to walk abreast of his benefactor.

Toweling off as he walked, Forster swore to his friend he saw the shimmering mirage of a nine-story high draft beer floating above the tree line, its frothy head glistening in the sunlight. MacLaren took a salt tablet out of his duffel and made Forster gag it down.

Snapping back from his daydream and disliking the return to the present, Luke could almost taste the salt again as he turned into the Golden Bee's parking lot. He didn't know what MacLaren was driving and he didn't yet see him, but he felt the Scot's presence. He unbuckled his seatbelts, dismounted the PTV and whacked the door closed. The splendor of Pikes Peak's east face rose into the mist behind the stately stonework of the hotel's porte-cochere.

"When would beauty be beautiful again?" He reflected as he touched his pistol through his jacket.

Ducking his head, more against the murky interior of the bar than the low door transom, Luke tensed at the prospect of another encounter with the Scot. It revolted him that, once again, he would have to dance with his own private devil.

MacLaren waited within. Silhouetted by the sunlight pouring through the doorway the athletic form stepped in and hesitated, waiting for his eyes to adapt. He made a good target, the Scot thought.

"Here, MacLaren said," not loudly.

Eyes still adjusting to the blackness, Forster stepped in and walked toward the voice.

"Beer," MacLaren hailed the bartender.

"Coffee," Forster issued his redirect.

"Suit yourself," MacLaren replied. "Sit down. We've got a lot to cover."

"Were you there, MacLaren?"

"Where?"

"Mt. Falcon."

"Not at the ruins, but near. You didn't think I'd let you face him alone, did you? I told you that you've got things to do."

"He could have killed me!"

"He didn't," the Scot said, taking a long pull on his beer. "Now, let's have it. I couldn't hear Woodless. I want the play-by-play."

For the better part of an hour in the damp womb of the subterranean bar, enveloped in the odor of stale beer and smoke, MacLaren continued his interrogation. He was disturbed that Woodless knew the machine to be a weapon of mass destruction or WMD, as the boys in war business called such things. If Woodless knew about the machine, so did every man-jack agent working for any government with even modest intelligence assets. Soon the whole friggin' world would be after this damn thing. The faster Forster got out of Colorado and on his way, the better.

Then it was MacLaren's turn to relate current events. There was no longer a need for him to deploy to the USS Kendall and escort the machine to The Ten for further study, as the plan had been relayed to him this morning. Now, there was no machine. By a twist of fate, the device had been destroyed, accidentally they thought, by the builder herself. But, confidence was high that the computer disk containing the plans for the device had survived the helo crash and was now in the hands of a myrmidon they suspected to be freelancing for someone or some group with a boatload of money and a big ax to grind. Now Forster's mission would be to make a pit stop on the Kendall and then head to Bergen to interview, believe or not, an eyewitness. Forster couldn't help but wonder, "An eyewitness to what?"

MacLaren also told Forster that the thermonuclear explosion in Norway had torn The Ten's veil of secrecy asunder and there were already teams from a handful of Norwegian and outside intelligence agencies sifting through the residue that had been Dr. Luknar's complex. So far, only globs of melted metal, bits of circuitry and a few corrupted file fragments had been found. Most of the data had been scrubbed clean by the electromagnetic pulse from the blast, but microscopic bits of memory chips had been found and were being packaged and shipped to facilities around the world for analysis.

Satellite intel showed no missile launches prior to the explosion. There were however, two helicopters in the area - one just before and one just after the detonation. According to The Ten, four highly classified air operations took place that night under their direction. There were two takeoffs and two landings by a Navy helo, from the USS Kendall to the doctor's lab and from the lab to an unscheduled touchdown a short distance away. The satellites had also recorded the infrared signature of a second, unidentified aircraft that entered the sector from the east-northeast, landed near the blast site just after the detonation and departed four minutes later; heading back in the direction it came from. The satellites lost the mystery helo's signature as it approached the Swedish border, probably due to the activation of some on board stealth technology.

"How do you know all this?" Forster asked.

"Luke, we're all in great jeopardy. I'm going to have to do something I never thought I'd have to do. I'm going to have to trust you."

"Fuck you," Forster burst out, much too loudly for the comfort of a few locals at the bar. But, most of them were working on their third round of drinks by then and were unaware of the gaff.

Leaning back and forcing a smile at the patrons, MacLaren endeavored to make it seem to the onlookers that the profanity was just a friendly chide. Forster continued *sotto voce*, staring his hate into the older man's eyes.

"Don't trust me, asshole. I don't want anything to do with this. I've told you, I don't give a shit what happens to you or the Army, or Norway, or the fucking government that's out to terminate my ass with extreme prejudice. You said the machine is gone. There is no more threat. I'm out of here."

As Forster put his hands on the thick wood to push himself away, the Scot reached his left hand across the table and held the Captain's shooting hand fast.

"Hear me out boy. Or you become an instant legend in this place."

Forster thought momentarily about making a move to break free. Although there was probably a herd of armed and hostile agents closing in on him, any potential hazard seemed less repugnant than being in physical contact with the Scot. He was going to go for it. Then, he saw the position of MacLaren's right forearm under the table and heard the distinctive click of a hammer being cocked.

Forster recalled the excerpt he had read from an old, well-circulated field report, about the time the Scot had taken out an Iraqi double-agent in a public place just like this, by firing one silenced .25 caliber magnum round into the man's genitals. Surprise still on the man's face, MacLaren fired a second round into the man's forehead, at the hairline. The impact of the small caliber round wasn't sufficient to knock the man over, it just set him up against the wall, eyes wide open, dead as a doornail and fit to sing soprano. Afterward, MacLaren calmly stood and left the premises. Patrons saw only a man in a dark corner staring at the headline news on the television.

"Sit," MacLaren said.

Forster sat.

"You know what were talking about here?" MacLaren resumed. "This machine, if it can be rebuilt, could bring about the complete reordering of political and military power on Earth. This isn't about you and me. It's not about capitalism or petrol or religion. It's about freedom and survival of the common man, Forster. Either you sit and listen, or I'll escort you outside and leave your sorry ass under a tree for the squirrels to hide their nuts in. What'll it be?"

The Scot started to cough again. Helpless, he let go of Luke's arm, pulled another bloody rag from his pocket and blotted at his nostrils. Realizing he had to surrender to the indelicacy of the moment,

MacLaren surreptitiously holstered the pistol and used both hands to stifle the bleeding as he hacked. People at the bar began to show interest. Forster slumped back in his chair and watched dispassionately. Finally, pity overtook him.

"Here," Forster handed the Scot a wad of napkins from a dispenser on the next table, scowled at the old man and shook his head in disgust. "What is wrong with you?"

"Wrong? With me? Nothing, short of my lungs rotting away. Something I caught in Cuba, the doc says. He says I've got some time, if the hooligans don't nail me first. I'm coming to a bad end, you'll be glad to know. Not exactly going out in the blaze of glory we drank to when you were a fresh new butter bar, eh?

"Look, MacLaren, I don't care how you die, as long as I get to watch. Maybe I will hang around."

"I don't care why you hang around lad; just let me paint you the rest of the picture. I haven't told you everything. Hear me out. I think you'll do the right thing."

Resigned, Forster pointed to MacLaren's empty glass and wagged two fingers at the seemingly disinterested, but obviously vigilant bartender. After the beers came, they ate crackers and cheddar from the crock on the table and Forster listened.

As the last golden rays of the day backlit the clouds and the sun set behind the big mountain, MacLaren related the panoply of his incredible saga. He talked of a stalwart and resolute band of operatives working at the highest levels of government in the most militarily and monetarily powerful nations on Earth. These magnanimous conspirators called themselves, "The Ten." Their purpose, at once elegantly simple and confoundingly complex, was to keep the psychopaths of the world from activities that threatened democracy. In the last three-quarters of a century that meant, among other things, preventing the development and deployment mega death weapons - devices so powerful that a single use incident had the potential to wipe *Homo sapiens* from the face of the Earth.

He spoke of the real reason the super powers had started to disarm in the mid-1970s. It wasn't, as most had thought, that the U.S., China and the old Soviet Union had come to their senses and agreed not to destroy the planet. It was because The Ten and their friendlies had demonstrated through incontrovertible and brilliant mathematics that the nuclear winter theory was not a theory. They provided the superpowers' top physicists, mathematicians and meteorologists with a holographic demonstration of how the dinosaurs died when a mid-sized meteor crashed into the earth sixty-five million years ago, effectively ending the Cretaceous geophysical period and beginning the proliferation of species that would lead to human domination.

They showed the awe-struck scientists how there would be more energy released in a multiple warhead exchange between two, nuclear-capable antagonists than was released in the dinosaur-killing cataclysm and they showed how the next species to become extinct would be Man. Then they showed the probability, after such an event, for long-term survival of any life form more sophisticated than an insect. It wasn't probable. It got their attention. For a while, The Ten's presentation had returned sanity to the world. Treaties were signed, tests were banned and warheads were destroyed. Now, the threat of global destruction loomed again.

Mega computers had made it possible for any nutcase physicist or crank biologist to invent, refine and build horrible weapons. Usually, by the time The Ten uncovered the threats, theoretical errors or economic unfeasibility had shattered the inventors' plans and sent them back to their megalomaniacal daydreams. In this case however, the threat was tangible and MacLaren and his cronies believed the machine's use would follow its reconstruction in short order.

They knew that Eva Luknar's machine was not built to be a weapon. It was built to heal, but something went wrong. They knew that the doctor was despondent at her inability to correct the problem and they believed that she knew the machine's killing potential. They believed her suicide came when she realized that the deadly effect was replicable and reliable and that she would be powerless to keep it a secret.

MacLaren, who assuredly was not a scientist, didn't understand how it worked, but The Ten explained it in layman's terms. The thing disintegrated living things, including humans. If it were true, the first group or individual to possess a working model would gain a terrible and possibly terminal advantage over whomever they determined to be the opposition. Moreover, if the device could be mass-produced there may be no other way to destroy them than by the use of thermonuclear retaliation.

In fact, that may have already happened in the Norwegian fjord and The Ten had nothing to worry about. Maybe someone else did them a favor. But MacLaren thought it more likely that the detonation at the doctor's compound was simply what The Ten had thought it to be, an over-dramatized suicide. In any circumstance, The Ten were unwilling to call off this operation until they were sure that the device wouldn't be rebuilt. The only way to be certain of that was to seek out the plans and secure or destroy them.

"One last thing," MacLaren explained. "I need to emphasize that we're not working for the United States government. There are people in this country who are completely ignoble and no better than the worst fanatic or terrorist. We work only for The Ten. In my book, most humans aren't worth this effort. But, on the eyes of my sainted mother and your Tricia and everything else worth loving in this vale of tears, we must erase this threat. There may not be intrinsic good in all the actions of mankind, but there is within us the collective struggle to live, love and reach out to salvation and I won't let some sick bastard in a black mask put an end to that."

"Don't you dare speak her name, MacLaren...I-" He stumbled for words through his sudden anger.

"It was an accident, Luke. My God boy, do you think I wanted to hurt her?" MacLaren, who hadn't cried since the doctor slapped his newborn bum, felt tears began to well in his eyes as the poignancy of the memory and the pain of his disease fatigued him to gentility.

"Luke, you're the best commando we've got and our best chance to succeed. At one time, you were considered the brightest and deadliest man in the service. It's time to shit or get off the pot."

The Scot ended his soliloquy and waited for Forster's answer; fully aware that if the man's reply was negative, his next action on behalf of The Ten would be killing Luke Forster and beginning the search for his replacement.

Luke knew his options were limited. He would be able to evade his pursuers for a while, but he didn't know anything about the assets under control of The Ten. His gut told him that running from them would be risky business. He didn't like being trapped, but trapped he was.

"Let's get out of here," Forster said, being civil to MacLaren for the first time since their encounter in the park.

"Answer me, Luke," the Scot said emphatically.

"Outside. We've drawn enough attention to ourselves." Forster gave the bartender the air check sign.

"Eight bucks gentlemen," the tapster gruffed.

MacLaren paid the bill and they opened the door to a blinding sun.

"From snow to summer in the same day," MacLaren griped reaching into his coat for his sunglasses and finding none. As they walked through the parking lot, Forster, still finding it difficult to look the Scot in the eye, spoke first.

"MacLaren, if half of what you told me is true, you do need my help. Today's omens don't bode well. First, you show up and send me to dreamland. While I was out, I flashed back to the day Tricia died. I know it sounds twisted MacLaren, but I was there. As much as I wanted to kill you this morning, I had a vision. I saw how it might have been an accident. Not that you didn't fuck the mission up totally and I don't forgive you and I never will, damn you to hell. But why was I given the vision? Why? Am I *supposed* to give you a break? Listen to you? Trust you again? What for? You know I'm not a religious man. God's given me no reason to have faith in anyone but myself. But there's something dark going on out there and maybe "the force" needs some help in making it right. Whatever the reason, I'm out in the cold and may not live through the day…especially now that we've been seen together, again. So what the hell. What can I do?"

"The force? The force?" MacLaren wheezed a laugh.

"You still getting your moral guidance from old movies? Why not Tolkien? We can just call Bilbo, Frodo and the Strider and set upon the dark forces of Mordor together. Maybe the elves and the dwarves will join up!"

"Look MacLaren, what do you care why I'm going to help. I'm going to help!" He shouted.

"I just don't want you to underestimate the threat here, boy. This isn't fantasy. You fix this, or a lot of people are going to die. You may die trying. Whoever we're up against, they have unlimited assets and are willing to murder millions to get what they want. They may be so far ahead of us this mission is already futile. I want you to be prepared for a confrontation with the most determined evil you can imagine. These brutes will not relent until they get the machine operational. If they do make it work, reach deep into your pockets, Forster. There will be hell to pay."

"I got it! What's next?"

"Leave your vehicle," the Scot instructed, slipping easily from his emotional pleadings into the cold efficiency of his craft. "It's got a target painted on it by now."

They walked past Forster's PTV to an electric hauler MacLaren had stolen that morning. As they opened the doors MacLaren turned and, over the roof of the small truck, said, "Forster. Welcome to the team."

"So what are we now, MacLaren, The Eleven?" Luke asked, unsure of the significance of the return of his sense of humor.

"Ten and a wee dram," the Scot replied, not smiling.

"Fuck you," Luke derided. "I think you just want this killing machine for yourself, so you can chase the Brits out of Scotland once and for all."

"Get in," MacLaren said.

Forster chuckled at putting a burr under the Scot's blanket for a change. Or, maybe it just felt good to let a little of the hate go.

Chapter 15

"The knight errant"

MacLaren turned out of the Bee's parking lot and headed back down the resplendent tree-lined boulevard, away from The Broadmoor and toward an evening appointment at the Jeffco Airport.

Both men were nearing exhaustion and Forster's hip was still sore. He rubbed the numb spot around the wound. The men dropped the hauler's windows and the crisp air whistled in, refreshing them as MacLaren talked Luke through what he knew of the next steps of his mission.

The first clots of the rush hour mired them to a stop in Castle Rock, just south of Denver and as they melded into the rhythmic crawl of the miles-long queue, the men had time to savor the fiery orange and dusky blue twilight. The aluminum and graphite tide pulled them along like flotsam as MacLaren heel-toed past the glass towers and office camps of the Denver Tech Center; the myriad windows reflecting the final golden glimmer of the sun as it dipped behind the jagged silhouettes of the Front Range peaks. As they gained, then passed the downtown skyline, they turned northwest onto the Boulder Turnpike. Half an hour later, they escaped the glutted six-lane near Jefferson County's commuter airfield.

The stars were out and a pale, gibbous moon rose as they wound through the airport entrance and crept onto the tarmac. A minute later, they arrived at what looked outwardly to be a disused hangar. They were expected and as they approached, a small door opened within a much bigger one. Dousing his headlamps, MacLaren pulled into the structure and parked the hauler against the back wall.

An ominous-looking jet dominated the hangar that, even in the dim light, Forster saw was spit-shined top to bottom. An airworthy thoroughbred of obviously exotic bloodlines, the plane seemed to strain at its chocks with the engines off. Its color was unusual and it was clear that the designer intended the jet to be invisible against the sky. It was tinted in various hues, grading across the stealth-angled surfaces to more and less dense grays and pale blues in a mottled, cloud-like scheme. It looked at once ethereal and spooky.

"Nice paint job," Forster commented to MacLaren.

"Highly functional against prying eyes," another voice spoke.

Foster turned around to see a smiling leathered face beneath a carrot-colored flattop.

"She's got the full stealth package, but that won't prevent a keen-eyed pilot from picking us up in flight and wondering why we're not being scoped," the flight-suited, man said. His blue eyes sparkled disarmingly like a cocky jet driver or an enthusiastic kid.

"I'm Red," he said.

"Obviously," Forster agreed, grinning back.

"I assume you're Luke Forster," Red said, offering his hand.

"He told you I'd be here? Forster asked, suspiciously. "Sure of yourself as ever, MacLaren," he said as he cast an incredulous look at the Scot.

"No, Sir. He didn't tell me that," Red countered. "He said he'd either come back alone or with Luke Forster. He said the odds were better he'd be back alone."

"Never mind", MacLaren snapped. "Everything that's happened until now is history." He looked sharply at Forster and repeated himself, "History. Got it?"

"Yeah, yeah," Forster shot back. "What do you do?" He queried.

"I'm just your driver, Luke," Red said, holding his hands up to fend off any ideas that he was in command or a key player, "Okay?"

"Okay," Forster said, "Is this our ride to Norway?"

"Affirmative," Red nodded.

"What are we flying here, Red?" Luke asked.

"Well, as you can see from the 'attack porpoise' lines, the plane is built around the old Raytheon Premier 1 airframe. But, we've kicked up the specs a little bit and fit her with a new radar deflection suit. We call her Hellion III. She's still subsonic, but she'll cruise at better than six hundred knots. Her range is unlimited as you can see by the refueling tap growing out of her beak. Her stealth technology is classified. Works like a charm. We only take off from civilian airfields at night. In daylight flight, she's damn near invisible to the naked eye. The Navy brass is still studying the paint palette for force-wide application. We didn't wait," the pilot said proudly. "We, uh, 'liberated' a few drums of the coating for our trip."

As the flyer was speaking, Forster noticed the only markings on the craft. A small Roman numeral X rode the underside of the port side canard, just visible as a negative space with no cloud pattern behind it.

"Weird. Have you flown in this thing?" Forster turned to MacLaren.

"No, and I won't be flying in it tonight."

"Wait a minute…"

"Listen, Luke. We don't have time for hugs and I'm out of fresh hankies. Red has your orders."

"Orders?" Forster bristled.

"Sorry lad. You're right. You're a civilian now. Let's call them instructions. You can open them after take off. Hey, don't pout Laddie. You can ride in the two seat."

"Oh, goody."

"At least as far as Wright-Patterson. You'll pick up a co-driver there for the hop to the Kendall. Hey, don't sweat the small stuff, Luke," MacLaren got serious. "You know the drill now. All you have to do is retrieve the plans. The Ten will handle the rest."

Forster wanted to dispute MacLaren's oversimplification but husky electric motors began to whine beneath his feet and the false front of the hangar door assembly disappeared below ground, opening the entire front of the structure for the Hellion's exit. A moment later a massive blast deflector on shiny hydraulic pistons rose behind the aircraft to prevent the engine exhaust from blowing the old building onto the turnpike. Running lights strobed as the pilot wound the twin Williams/Rolls Royce FJ75 engines. Then, the engines lit, their initial screams quickly blending into a throaty harmonic.

"Luke, this is your mission now." The Scot strained to be heard. "Get to it. You'll get what you need aboard the Kendall. Goodbye."

The old man turned and saluted the pilot. Red returned the gesture. He had completed the pre-flight checks and was anxious to be under way.

"MacLaren, I can't…" Forster protested, after the happenings of the day and reliving Tricia's death, he felt emotionally drained and a little short on bravado.

"You can," the Scot hissed, grabbing the collar of Forster's jacket in clenched fists and pulling him to within an inch of his nose.

"You will."

MacLaren released him, stepped back and an admonishing look on his face, pointed at the Hellion's open hatch. In Forster's mind the gleaming steps were really a pair of dark, serrated mandibles, thrashing viciously, ready to devour him. He couldn't help feeling this was a one-way trip.

Resigned, Forster summoned his courage and turned to board. He mounted the steps stiff legged and disappeared inside. In the cockpit, Red flipped a toggle and the hatch ate the steps and sealed them in. Red goosed up the RPMs and the needle-nosed plane powered onto the tarmac and rolled toward takeoff.

The Scot doused the strobe lights, secured the hangar and, thumbing a small trickle of blood from the corner of his mouth, remounted his hauler. At Denver International there was a commercial airliner headed to Hawaii and one seat had his name on it. Whatever the outcome of Forster's mission, he would hear about it while reclining on a chaise scuffed into the black sand at Kona Village. If he lived that long.

The Hellion's afterburners lit and twin trails of brilliant white shock diamonds pulsed through the elongated cones of blue flame trailing her engines. MacLaren watched for a moment as the mighty little jet, the cocky pilot and the reluctant warrior jumped into the blackness.

"Farewell, Luke Forster," MacLaren whispered. "Farewell."

Part Two

Deep Threat"

Chapter 16

"Into the breach"

The Hellion gobbled the distance between Denver and Wright-Patterson AFB in under two hours. That gave Forster all the time he needed to read his instructions and reinforce his trepidation.

"Red, what do you know about this?" Forster queried the carrot-topped pilot.

"Not much, Luke," he said. "When we work for The Ten we all know bits and pieces, but never enough to put the puzzle together. Need to know and span of control drive the decision about who knows what and when they get to know it. I think the only people who have the whole picture are the Triton, The Ten's ruling committee. They rely on us individually for loyalty and commitment. I got no problem with that. You?"

"Not now," Forster replied, humbled. "After reading this briefing I understand the problem but Red, I don't know if I can hold up my end. This is '007' stuff and I don't think the bad guys in this operation watch movies much. I hope there are some cavalry and stunt men behind the scenes."

Red laughed. "I don't think you have to worry about that, Luke. When The Ten takes on a mission, the point men have unlimited assets under their control. How do think you got your 'limo' here? The network is full of people who understand the implications of the threats they deal with. I can't tell you anything to make you feel better other than I've been part of this team for five years and we've never failed to complete a mission."

"Now, I've got the hot potato."

"You better finish your reading, Luke," Red said. "We've got landing priority at Wright-Pat and we'll be down in a few minutes. Our turnaround time, including refueling will be twenty-five minutes. You'll have time to inspect your gear, repack it and get your rear back on the jet. We're picking up a crew mate to help me jump the pond and we're outta here."

"What gear?"

"Dunno, Luke. It's not my gig. My job is to drop your ass on the carrier deck and return this baby to NATO in Brussels. Then, it's back to my unit and I never heard of you. To the rest of the world, I'm coming back from simulator training in the F-30. I wish I was, actually. Not that playing chauffeur for you in this little beastie is all that bad, but it would have been cool to grab some single-seat cloud time at Mach 3."

"Yeah, I've never been *that* much fun," Forster smiled.

"Stow your stuff and cinch-up your harness for landing, Mr. Forster," Red smiled in acknowledgment. "We is here."

After a brief chat with traffic control, Red pulled a tight right bank, leveled out smartly and put the Hellion down on the moonlit runway like a butterfly with sore feet. Forster gulped hard during the turn, felt his stomach hit bottom and grabbed his chair, not letting go until he heard the wheels screech. He had never spent much time in jets this small and he was pleased to be on the ground. The run out took a few minutes as the pilot followed a trail of purple lights to a hangar flanked by two F-16 revetments. A gang of ground crew was prepping the now obsolescent war birds, trainers for the Ohio Air National Guard, for mock battle. The weekend warriors stopped their ministrations momentarily to gawk when the Hellion rolled by. They had never seen a craft quite like it and, if they weren't preoccupied with preparation for a major exercise, they would have sneaked in for a closer peek. As it was they looked up, craned their necks for a look-see and swiftly returned to their work.

Red gentled the ship to a stop and began his shutdown procedures as a crewman in a black jumpsuit appeared from the hangar with a pair of wheel chocks.

"Time to stretch your legs and run your checks, Luke," the pilot said. "Our next hop is a long one so make the most of it. The latrine's at the back of the building. If there's food or coffee in there, I'd grab it. We've got mess hall food aboard for the crossing, but I'd rather eat the seats."

"Thanks, Red."

Forster slapped the harness release buckle and began to wriggle out of the cockpit. The hatchway opened and the stairs spidered out and reached for the pad. As he ducked his head to exit the aircraft, he began to survey the area. Immediately his eyes were caught fast by the figure before him. The black jumpsuit he had taken for a ground crewman was definitely not Air Force, or, a man. It was a civilian female; one in fine form he thought, with a ponytail gushing from the back of her ball cap. When she turned to face him, he was engaged by the most captivating green eyes he had ever seen.

"Captain Forster?" She yelled over the whine-down of the turbofans.

"Yes, Ma'am. Who are you?"

He asked as he strutted down the stairs. He had made his query a little brusquer than he had intended, so he quickly manufactured a smile.

"I'm Natalie Katrova, your handler for this mission."

The fans had quieted to a level at which she could be heard in a normal voice and he couldn't help notice the sultry huskiness in her voice. Then, what she said registered.

"My what?" He asked, angrily.

"Your handler, Sir," Katrova repeated as a flight services fuel truck pulled along side the Hellion.

The fuelers jumped to their task like a NASCAR pit crew.

"We just have a few minutes, Sir," Katrova said. "If you'll join me in the hangar, we need to inventory your gear and give you an updated SITREP on our mission."

Still suspicious of her claim to be his handler and curious to know what in hell she was saying about "our" mission, he preceded her into the hangar.

She was nearly as tall as he and easily kept pace. As they entered the hangar's service bay, she hurried past him and with a hand gesture that was more commanding than courteous, motioned to a gray steel door stenciled, "Authorized Personnel Only." Forster reached for the knob… locked. Before he could ask if she had the key, Katrova unzipped the front of her jumpsuit and reached in. There wasn't much room for her hand. She didn't find what she was looking for right away and Forster kind of enjoyed the little fantasy he was having as she groped her own bosom. She cast him a scolding glance as she saw what he was thinking and turned her back.

"Long time no nookie for this one," she thought, his puerile behavior lowering her expectations.

She found the lanyard around her neck. Drawing the cord through her fingers she produced a thin aluminum card on a snap swivel, turned back toward Forster and displayed the reason for her actions. He raised his eyebrows and nodded to acknowledge her success. Then, he blushed.

She inserted the key card into a slot concealed on the side of the doorjamb. A small, mirrored plate slid out from the jamb just above the card slot and announced its presence with a single beep. The plate presented a small keypad and next to it what looked like a laser scanner; its beady red eye sweeping to find something it could recognize. Katrova stepped closer to the device, blinked and opened her eyes wide. The machine beeped and a green LED flashed in slow sequence, apparently in approval of what it saw. She punched four keys on the pad and it beeped one long beep before it retracted back into the jamb. She pulled out a similar card and lanyard from an outside pocket on her suit and handed to it Forster.

"You're next. Look in the mirror, center your eyes between the marks and blink. When the green light comes on, enter a zero, then your mission ID number - six zero niner".

"I know my number Miss; it was in my briefing papers. My "EYES ONLY" briefing papers. How do you know it?"

"I know everything about you Captain, I mean Luke Forster," she said smugly. "I'm your handler."

"I heard you the first time." Her assertiveness pissed him off but he imagined there would be a lot of things happening from now on that would piss him off.

"If you're such a big shot, why can't your card open the door?" He asked in an intentionally snotty tone.

"Because the infrared sensors know there are two of us," she replied, parroting just enough of Forster's attitude to let him know that she wouldn't put up with his crap.

He repeated the procedure. The door unlocked with the slam of metal bolts and swung open noiselessly.

"Please," she motioned him forward again like an MP at a base gate.

In the middle of the brightly lit room were two trestle tables covered with gear, weapons and clothing. Some things were familiar to Forster at first glance, others were strange to him and some others seemed out of place. At the far end of the room was a ratty looking card table with a coffee maker, what looked like a crock of something that smelled like beef stew, plastic bowls and spoons and a red rope file folder three inches in thick.

"Mr. Forster, I've taken the liberty of pulling your kit together based on what I know about your capabilities, where we're going and the objectives of our mission. If there's anything else you…"

"Where *we're* going?" He asked, raising his voice. "*Our* mission?" He was now thoroughly agitated; both at MacLaren's assumption that he would accept this mission and that he would be working on a mission this critical with a complete stranger - a pushy, female, stranger.

"*We're* not going anywhere."

"Yes *we* are," she replied, maintaining serious cool. "Mr. Forster, I know you don't know me and I know how you were recruited for this mission and by whom, but listen up. The Ten have put us together for this job because they think we have the best chance to get it done. My dossier is in your SITREP file and I think you'll find my qualifications acceptable."

As she finished her little speech, Forster sprang at her and pushed her forcefully against the cinder block hangar wall. She was too light to resist his weight and he moved her as if she weren't there.

Grasping her under the jaw, thumb pressing firmly on her carotid, he began to lift her off the ground as her eyes startled and she began to feel light-headed. He pressed his shoulders against her arms pinning them to the wall and put his nose on hers as he made his point. His face was quivering as he tried to contain his fury.

"Lady, my life and apparently the lives of a few billion other humans are on the line here. If I get an assistant, I want a ten-foot high defensive lineman with a grenade launcher under each arm and a thousand pounds of bad intent between his legs. I need *military* help, not someone with big pretty eyes and painted fingernails to get in my way. You're not handling anybody, least of all me. Qualifications or not."

Before he could ask if she understood she crashed a knee into his scrotum. He released her like his hands were spring-loaded and she dropped to the floor. Forster went to his knees and clutched at his groin with both hands, sucking lungs-full of air and never taking his eyes off her. She landed on her feet in a perfect defensive horse stance; knees slightly bent, feet shoulder-width apart, fists clenched and ready to strike again.

"Bitch," Forster hissed through his teeth.

"Bully," she spit back at him, stretching her neck to see if still worked.

"I oughta…"

"You oughta check your gear, Mr. Forster," she said, emphatically. "Red will have the plane ready to turn and burn in…" she said looking at her digicom, "eighteen minutes. By the way, you try anything like that again and I'll kill you myself. You may be our best chance, Captain Jackass, but you're not our last."

Standing uncomfortably, still rubbing his crotch, Forster was unapologetic; "I want you off this mission lady."

"My name is Nat."

"Spelled with a 'G' no doubt," Forster thought to himself.

"And, unless you're prepared to co-fly this thing through two mid-air and one carrier refuelings, you're stuck with me. At least 'til we get your six on the Kendall."

"Of course. You're the copilot," Forster said, disgusted and surprised.

"That's right. Everything else you *don't* know is the SITREP. I suggest again, Sir, in the interest of getting the hell out of here that you inspect your gear, help me stow it aboard and stop being such an asshole.

"Asshole?"

"All right, sorry. This mission has us all a little jumpy and I'm sure you haven't had the time to let any of it sink in. The best thing for us to do is get on our way. We can fight on the plane."

"Looking forward to it, Pat," he added just to bust her chops.

"Nat."

"With a 'G'?" He said, aloud this time.

He turned his back on her slowly, letting his head twist on his neck just a little to watch her reaction. He wanted her to understand that he didn't trust her.

The gag didn't impress her. She didn't trust him either.

Defying the conclusions a casual observer would draw from viewing the pugilistic and childish events of the past few minutes, Natalie Katrova and Luke Forster had much in common. Both their characters had been tempered hard in the cruel forge of life.

The only child of a second generation Russian-American father and an Irish-Catholic mother, little skinny Natalie had been the most gifted child in her classes from pre-school through her post-graduate studies at Cal Tech. It was there that her academic career hit a speed bump that knocked her off course.

Her doctoral dissertation had been rejected by a board of professors who had grown tired of her aggressiveness, quirky viewpoints and disdain for societal convention. In what would, around the campus, come to be known as one of the most brilliantly written and thoroughly logical arguments ever constructed, Natalie penned a treatise that her mates affectionately called the "The Mookie Manifesto."

The basic premise of the tome and what essentially killed her chance for attaining her Ph.D. at Cal Tech, was that "all gods are one," and that every day, science proved God's existence. She held that right was intrinsically right and wrong was objectively wrong and that religion was created to help man rationalize the extremities of the continuum and give feeble-bodied and feeble-minded priests a job with some status in the community.

To Natalie Katrova, Mohammed, Jesus, Buddha, Confucius and Lao-Tse were all great philosophers; probably with good hearts and certainly with good intentions, but they were just humans who "got it."

They understood that eventually, the people who inhabited planet Earth would have to come into harmonious co-existence or face the inevitability of self-destruction. In her mind all the other moral rules and political interpretations could be judged by their tactical political utility in meeting the needs of some transitory war lord or head of state.

"The Mookie Manifesto," she thought the moniker had once belonged to a professional athlete or two, was just a name she gave the perpetual desire of the ruling class, (democratic, despotic, economic, oligarchic or theocratic) to engender elaborate philosophical rationales for what was, according to their rules du jour, acceptable conduct. Hence, Fascism could rationalize genocide against the Jews in the early half of the twentieth century. Communism could excuse theft of personal property and assassination by the state, and the redistribution of wealth could be justified by Socialism, just as avarice and selfishness could be forgiven under the banner of Capitalism. To Natalie, morality was absolute and self-determinism as proselytized by Ayn Rand was the only true, inalienable right.

Of course, her professors were personally and professionally offended. They couldn't understand how a gifted infoscience protégé, a multi-engine rated jet pilot, and a Tae Kwon Do practitioner of renown (though her appearances at organized competitions were infrequent), could forsake the opportunity to contribute to her university, her field of study and her nation and instead be wasted in the effort of writing seventy-five thousand words of "mean-spirited, sociopathic, blasphemous drivel."

Natalie didn't see it that way and she fought back hard. She told anyone who would listen that nature was ruled by mathematics. Things were definitively right or wrong because the physical universe was built on dichotomy. Binary bites were either 1 or 0. Round was an absolute characteristic. The Yin and the Yang didn't have shades of gray between them. Black and white simply interfaced, with neither gaining the upper hand. "He created them male and female," she reminded them. Good and evil co-existed as a matter of balance but neither melded and there was trouble when the weak-minded tried to blur the distinction. Those abominations of thought, those amendments, revisions and compromises were just attempts to excuse mediocrity, absence of character and lax judgment. It was sloppy thinking and it caused indecision and confusion among the masses. It was all that simple and all that complex.

Reviled in academia, "the godless witch from Cal Tech," as the religious right on campus had labeled her, packed up her considerable charm (she could turn it on when it mattered to her), striking good looks and lithe body and struck out on her own, appearing on every broadcast and digital media outlet she could entice to let her speak, in an ill-fated effort to rally supporters to her side. In the end, there weren't many. As with most everything for which the public has a passing fancy, the pejorative headlines made juicy news on vidscreens and in the few remaining printed tabloids around the world, then the public tired of it. Natalie ran out of energy and Cal Tech stood pat. So, up in a puff went seven years of study and just under a quarter-million of her father's tuition money (in turn-of-the-century dollars), and the entire affair vanished from the public conscience like so much swamp gas.

Disenchanted with philosophy and exhausted from attempts at sharing her brilliance, she did what any self-respecting entrepreneur would do in her situation. She went commercial and sold her skills to the highest bidder - Interis Worldwide, the planet's largest and most powerful infotech consortium. For twelve years, Katrova led a multinational legion of infotech nerds who built the servers, switches, fiber optic links and peripherals that gave birth to, sadly, the only "living" entity she ever felt close to...*Librex Hominorum*, to her "Rex," her wunderkind; the largest, fastest and most accessible database ever created. In Rex, she had an offspring, companion and confidante. After Rex was "born" she needed nothing and she thought, no one else.

Then, in less time than anyone thought possible, the project was complete and she was a born-again media darling. But, after the initial round of hype and a fusillade of scientific kudos gave her a year of electronic face time with the world's two and a half billion InterVid viewers (the successor to twentieth-century television and the Internet), the populace once again lost interest. They thought kindly of the accomplishment but were never able to comprehend the "Gestalt" of the project. Most of Rex' users settled into a monotonous, predictable pattern, using Rex to suck up grist for their children's school papers and to settle tavern wagers.

Of course, the scientific community raved about Rex for years afterward. They were voracious and insatiable users and craved interaction with the esoteric, voice rec accessible, "physiomniscient" side of the machine. Eventually, steadily increasing logon fees relegated access to the brain to those with the deepest pockets.

Some good came of it. In 2019, under the direction of an obscure mathematician (now a Nobel Prize winner), Rex wrote a program that demonstrated how to take food and feed crops from the producers of the world and distribute it with a small profit for the growers, to the five dozen or so countries still incapable of growing enough food to sustain their populations. The solution was still, more than a decade later, in its infancy and there were myriad problems the mega-brain didn't include in its problem/solution matrix (warfare, the black market, and meteorological catastrophes), but mass starvation was already a thing of the past. The brain also had a sociological impact. Rex turned most of the people in the "linked" nations into outdoor enthusiasts. With the ability to recall on demand any entertainment product ever produced or to find an answer to a tricky research question in seconds, no one spent time surfing cable television channels or sitting at desk-based terminals anymore.

So, as the world approached the mid-point of the twenty-first century, it was outdoor activity; close to nature in the real sun with clear skies and none of the foul, gritty rain that still visited a demoralizing darkness on Earth's industrial centers that brought participants the exuberance of being alive. People weren't, however becoming more robust; they still managed to over-serve themselves all manner of biologically grown and synthetically-derived comestibles and intoxicants. They we're just a little more sunburned.

The latest problem posed to Rex had been to create a program for identifying and converting the space, and it was massive when considered as a planetary whole, that had for decades been used as indoor entertainment venues and video production facilities, to outdoor eco-parks.

Eco-parks weren't amusement parks like the fantasy tot lots founded by the old film and cartoon studios. Eco-parks had no electricity and as few creature comforts as practical. Camping in the dark, under the stars with the family, was the latest fad. Wyoming had actually become one of the richest states in the union in late 2030, when it started renting open space by the day. Rex projected that by 2050 the state would be booked solid for three years out. North Dakota was licking its chops to get in on the game. Alaska was already being overrun by tenderfeet speaking every imaginable language acting out their Davy Crockett fantasies - electronic predator repellers strapped to their hips instead of pistols and long knives.

Sometimes Katrova thought that this was the course of all of the grand fantasies of her life; visualization, realization, ennui, and evacuation. She never wanted to hang around long enough to watch her creations crumble. Even as a little girl in Crystal Lake, Illinois, when the winter provided abundant raw materials to build snowmen, she wouldn't build them in her yard. She would build them in a secluded clearing in the little woods that surrounded the hockey pond at Veteran's Acres. When she finished, she'd giggle, give the frosty creature a kiss and go home, never looking back. She couldn't handle hearing the gleeful shouts of the mean children when they discovered it and knocked it down. Nor could she bear the pain of watching the sun turn her jolly sculpture to slush. She'd just slink away quietly and keep her creation in her heart, where no harm could come to it.

As a kid Natalie had been popular, even though she would frequently forsake the company of her pals for weeks at a time, enthralled with the content of a particularly salient scientific text.

Her friends called her "Awky," a kiddy insult that nicely melded the pejoratives "awkward" and "gawky." Her giraffe-long legs and frenetic behavior often put her in laughable, if not constitutionally threatening predicaments and although her cumulative overnight time in the local hospital wasn't all that impressive, she did know the emergency room physicians at the nearby trauma center by their first names.

She loved her father deeply. He was a socially ungracious but honest man who adored and doted on her until his premature death by heart attack at the age of fifty-two. He called her "Tuffy."

Her mother was a hard case. Whether she was jealous of the pretty and popular girl, or envious of the precocious child's accomplishments, her mother kept putting her down and pushing her toward her own lofty definition of perfection. Natalie tried hard to please and appease her, but soon learned from her mother's admonitions and occasional emotional cruelty, that she would never be perfect enough. Throughout the girl's childhood and adolescence, her mother endeavored to control and manipulate every situation that involved her daughter; times, venues, outcomes and lessons learned, until she died of stress and abuse of the substances she used to treat it, at age sixty-one.

Her father taught Natalie that everyone would always love, protect and encourage her. *He was wrong.* Her mother taught Natalie that she would never be quite good enough. *She was wrong.*

Regardless of parental shortcomings, Natalie was clever enough to glean a useful legacy. She gave herself the fitness, character and intelligence to *adapt* to new situations and *overcome* obstacles with only fleeting moments of self-doubt. She grew into a remarkable, if stubborn and willful woman. But, regardless of the reinforcement of frequent public adulation, the unabashed envy of her peers, her spectacular feminine form and the seductive quality of her intellect, she was alone.

No matter how coy and demure she tried to be, she intimidated most of the people she met. It wasn't that she was ill mannered or snotty, she was just so *much* - brainpower, looks, confidence, self-discipline and what really put most people off; an uncanny knack for solving puzzles.

Natalie saw solutions before most people could define the problem. It made her impatient to share her opinions and at times, she came off like a braggart and a know-it-all. Of course the media, the bevy of syco-phants clinging to her coattails and her beneficiaries loved this charac-teristic. It made her a controversial and flamboyant celebrity. But, over time her enthusiasm and sincere wish to share her knowledge began to wear thin and was taken for conceit and arrogance. When those attribu-tions persisted, she fell out of favor with the star makers and her fans and she decided to seek shelter in the quietude of her research. Maybe she was better off dealing with machinery after all.

In due time, the afterglow of the Rex project waned. She resigned her position at Interis, sucked up a wad of courage from the deep reposi-tory inside her, camouflaged the psychic and emotional scars from the view of any curious or opportunistic predators, and hid away in the con-trolled environment of her private research facility.

It was shortly after she began her self-imposed exile that The Ten made themselves and the problem of Dr. Eva's machine known to her. She perceived the danger of the situation at once. She also identified and empathized with the doctor's quest to find a cure for breast cancer. She, like many of her time, had lost friends and colleagues to the disease. This time though she didn't have a ready solution to The Ten's dilemma. She wasn't a physicist and paramilitary operations where certainly not her thing. She was in shape and a formidable martial artist, but she wasn't an action hero. Weapons scared her and she was smart to fear them. She was aggressive and capable of defending herself, but she didn't have the killer instinct. More often than not, after a spirited *kumite* at her Karate dojo, she would drop an opponent with a blurry roundhouse kick and just as quickly go to the mat to offer comfort. But The Ten's problem intrigued her. So, after being briefed about the missing death machine and learning about The Ten's suspicions of who may be competing with them to uncover its secrets, she was fired up and ready to do what she could to help.

Whatever they required of her, she would do her best. Even if it meant working with Luke Forster. A man she was warned would be struggling through a rough emotional patch himself. Altruism aside, she needed this challenge to regain her self-confidence and give her life renewed meaning. It was an end game with values important enough to die for and she knew when it was over, if she survived, she could walk away with a renewed sense of pride.

Forster too, had his share of hard knocks early in life. He lost both his parents while he was in basic training at Fort Leonard Wood. He was called back from bivouac in the frozen Ozark Mountains and took his first flight on a commercial airliner to Denver for the funeral. They were killed instantly when a drunk flipped his pickup on a swervy road outside Delta, a small ranching community on Colorado's Western Slope. The wreck was still caroming toward them wheels-up when they rounded the uphill turn. The impact knocked their big old Ford sedan forty feet into an irrigation ditch.

Luke was an only child (a brother, five years his junior had been killed at age eight when he was thrown by a neighbor's horse) and his emotional manhood began that day, when his support system was crushed in the twisted wreckage. Though he was never known as a particularly brave or confident youth, after their passing he did his best to internalize the qualities that marked the lives he admired so; honesty, sincerity, determination and a fearlessness born of knowledge. He didn't have anything like Natalie's technological savvy. His solitude engendered within him a commitment to learn what he needed to know to thrive and compete in the mainstream. He was above all, practical. The way he figured it, if you prepared for everything, you'd be ready for anything. It also meant that he knew right away when he was in over his head. Like, now.

Forster finished inspecting his gear.

"I have no idea what some of this stuff is or what it's for and I hate the toothpaste you picked, but I guess I've got most of what I need. And, Katrova…dental floss? You want me to face the bad guys with good gums?"

"As far as I'm concerned, you can use it to strangle yourself if you fail. They don't give out cyanide capsules anymore. I asked."

"Well. Now you know everything there is to being a handler," he said, his sarcasm approaching insult.

"Get dressed, Forster. There's a jumpsuit in the wall locker. I'm going to help Red with pre-flight."

"Don't you want to watch me change? Afraid to see a really big weapon?"

"Keep your squirt gun to yourself, hot shot," she replied, not smiling.

"I prefer machinery. It's much more reliable and it never talks back in the morning."

She turned and left Forster to wonder if she really meant it.

Ten minutes later, still trying to shake the imagery of Natalie playing with a vibrator, he was dressed, packed and headed for the Hellion; bloated black duffel slung over his shoulder and a wheeled trunk trailing at his heels.

Both agent and handler had in their minds that this would be a very prickly relationship.

CHAPTER 17

"REPRIEVE"

Confused, frightened and just awake, Markus Haukken flailed his arms and yelped his panic into the quiet of the ICU. He tried vainly to sit but found himself restrained by thick belts at his waist, arms and legs. Why was he bound? Captured? Through fuzzy eyes he saw IV tubes dangling above him. He could only guess what was in them and where they went. He had an oxygen canula in his nose and his head was a helmet of bandages. He felt as if he was suffocating.

A voice, female he thought, tried to calm him but he couldn't make out her words over the high-pitched bleeps of the bedside monitors. His throat was dry as dust and though he tried to talk, he could only make a wheezy, rasping noise. Trying desperately to make sense of it all he bore down with all the strength he could muster and strained to find a hold on consciousness. As Markus's mind gradually assembled random bits of reality he saw that he was in a bright white room. Or, maybe he was just buried in snow, lying rigid and hallucinating in the fjord.

There were big people in white clothes standing near, their gleaming face shields and helmets occasionally leaning in and swelling to goofy proportions, then soaring back out of focus.

Was he dead? He didn't think so. The beings attending him looked neither like angels, nor the horned and hoofed preternatural beasts foretold in his religion's version of hell, but like his countrymen; though their biohazard suits and gloves made him feel like an infected animal or an alien from which they needed protection.

Then, a composed female voice spoke to him in Norwegian. He was in hospital. Strong hands held his head down and pulled the breathing tube from his throat. He coughed hard. Another tube approached his lips and he fought to keep it out.

"No, Sir. Still please, Sir," the woman urged gently.

"It is water."

Markus understood.

He sucked down the coolness greedily and stopped coughing long enough to gasp.

"Where am I? How long have I been here?

Overcome by the feeling of safety, he giddy-whimpered like a rescued prisoner.

"Try to keep still or the pain will come," a man pleaded, trying to calm the sled driver.

"I'm Doctor Tellis," a man with glasses behind his mask said. "You are in Prince Haakon Magnus Hospital, in Bergen."

"How did I get here?" Markus begged.

Another man spoke. He appeared not to be a doctor, but a policeman or military officer.

"We picked you up on a glacier face near the Fensfjorden," the man said in official sounding, emotionless English of American dialect.

"Three days ago."

Markus screamed as a flash of pain shot up his back, into his arms and out through his fingertips.

"More! Hurry!" The doctor ordered the anesthesiologist.

The pain doc struggled to catch the IV control valve as the tubes wriggled before her.

Markus screamed again, "God, I can't feel…what are you putting into me?"

He tried to rip the tubes from his arms but the narcotic brew hit him hard and he slumped back into the bed with a moan. Head spinning and mind reeling, he went back to the fjord, with all the discomforting apparitions and illusionary fragments of his ordeal.

"The blood. Where…are…legs? Can't…move…him. There. You won't die. Don't! Die. Dead. Dead."

He screamed. "Tracker! The light. Down! Can't save…Who are… Where are you going? My disk…Klax? Klax. Take me. Take me with you! Going. No. No. Eva. Mr. Tyrone. Eva. Ev-"

Then, his eyelids twitching in the anguish of his dreams, he slept. The man in the military uniform rubbed his eyes in frustration. The interview would have to wait. But, did he say "Klax?"

"Doctor Tellis, will our giant friend survive? I need your best guess," the American officer said.

"Guess? Yes, well," the doctor replied, bristling at the man's request for a shot in the dark. "What we have here, Commander Lang, is a man in grave condition. He's delirious, dehydrated and suffering from hypothermia. A bullet, a big one, has torn away one of his ribs, collapsed a lung and remains lodged near a vertebra. Too, he's been exposed to a potentially lethal dose of radiation. If we can get him through the next forty-eight hours, he has a chance. But, he'll not be talking or let's say not making any sense, until we can stabilize him. His recovery, of course, doesn't just involve treatment of his body. Given his physical constitution the odds are good that, if the radiation doesn't do him in, we will eventually heal his wounds. But, his psychological well-being may not be such an easy thing to repair. Sometimes after such a severe shock, memory is affected. This man has been near a nuclear bomb explosion and, by the condition of his clothing; we know that he's been in contact with someone other than himself who has lost lots of blood; perhaps this Eva or Tyrone he mentions. At any rate, the blood on his clothing is not entirely his. Different types. After all that, he was left to die. The fact that he's here at all is a testimony to his fortitude, his God or his luck. I assure you that I will call you as soon as he shows signs of improvement. Now, Sir, you must leave us to our work."

"Thanks, Doc," Lang said disappointedly as he turned to the intercom on the wall.

Beyond the safety glass was a burly and heavily armed SEAL, one of the Navy's elite sea, air and land commandos. He snapped to attention as he heard the order from inside the treatment room. In the sternest tone possible, Lang impressed upon the SEAL that the sled driver's welfare was his personal responsibility. As the guard acknowledged the order with a crisp, "Aye, Sir," the naval officer checked the exposure badge on his radiation suit and, relieved that it hadn't changed color, turned from the intercom and walked into the adjacent decontamination room.

Half an hour later, scrubbed clean as a bosun's whistle, Commander Wolfgang Lang, USN, left the hospital by a back entrance and, the door held open by his bodyguard/driver, slid into the rear seat of his staff sedan. Selecting the white handset from the communications console he punched in the number for his contact at The Ten. Though the scrambler encrypted the voice until it sounded like a duck quacking English, he recognized at once the characteristic inflections of the voice on the other end.

"Three," he addressed his party, "Wolf Lang here. We have to assume total compromise. There's nothing useful in the wreckage. The aircrew is dead. The machine, whatever it was, is micro-junk. We have one witness in critical condition and in no shape to talk. He's under guard. The nuke blast took a seventy meter-wide crater out of a glacier where our girl's lab was. It looks like a self-destruct. I think she was making sure no one else could duplicate her work. We've got a forensic team in there now and I've asked for more satellite shots from SPACE-COM; a bigger area, at least a five hundred kilometer radius around the place, from today and back a week. Whatever went down here, we need a cover story fast. Every diplomat in Scandinavia and Western Europe is fainting and seeing the sky fall, so we need to make sure it's plausible. I think we should include an environmental impact statement and an estimate of the potential for latent casualties. It was a small device and initial readings don't show much fallout but I'm no expert and we don't want to underestimate the downside and encourage more investigation. I'm sure you have some ideas about how to spin this. Now the bad news, Sir. I'm afraid that someone beat us to the good stuff. We have reason to believe that a freelance terrorist named Dagon Klax may have made off with an important piece of the wreckage at the helo crash site, maybe an info disk. We don't know if Klax is going solo or working for a third party. More when I finish debriefing our survivor. In the meantime, I'll need a download of everything you can find on Mr. Klax. First name; Delta Alpha Golf Oscar-"

The voice on the other broke in, "Yes Commander, we're very aware of Mr. Klax."

"Yes, Sir," Lang said, not surprised. Thanks. Out."

Wolf Lang was a man of action and rarely worried. He was whip smart, tenacious and intolerant of sloppy thinking. He was career military, devoted to his work and his shipmates and for good or bad, had no diversions in his personal life to distract him from his mistress, the United States Navy. The Ten counted him among their most valued operatives. He was single-minded when it came to accomplishing his goals and he was cock-sure that he would eventually ignite the fire that burned down the bad guys' house, whoever they were.

Chapter 18

"Malevolence in motion"

When Dagon Klax was angry nothing and no one was safe. The venting magma of the man's furor enveloped everything in the immediate vicinity. This was a miscreant, a man solely in nomenclature. He respected only destruction, death and the remuneration that supported his sybaritic lifestyle. He wasn't about subtlety or finesse.

The first thing Klax did when he returned from the melted fjord with only a computer disk in hand was typical of how he handled disappointment. He called a meeting of his lieutenants for zero six hundred and made them sweat the reason for the parlay for nearly an hour before he entered the room. Then, calmly and without warning, he drew a large bore pistol from his waistband, casually let it hang at his hip, walked to his place at the apex of the triangle-shaped table, turned toward the unsuspecting gray-haired man to his left and put a bullet through his larynx. A pink cloud gushed from the back of the dead man's neck and air brushed the wall. His chair rocked backward in slow motion until it toppled and both inanimate objects hit the carpeted floor with a dull "whumpf."

The death of his chief of staff was no loss to society. He was as perverted and pustulant an individual as Klax himself. But, when Klax whirled to face the glass étagère behind him and dispassionately emptied the remaining rounds in the clip into his stolen collection of rare Chinese artifacts and vases, it became yet another demonstration of the depravity that was the hallmark of Klax' misbegotten life.

Even as his bullets were dashing the priceless antiquities to powder, and noise and smoke and flying glass harassed the surviving members of his dark minion, Klax knew that he may be the next to be destroyed. His masters didn't suffer mistakes and this one would cost the powerful cartel that pulled his strings their best and perhaps only opportunity for power in the world politic.

MAL had already anted up millions of dollars to generate the necessary intelligence and equip the expedition to liberate Dr. Eva's machine and now, just before the device was to have come into their hands, the fey scientist had outsmarted the Malthusian Advocacy League and their most capable thief.

The thought of all those anus-anchored egos and schizophrenic personalities on MAL's high council being denied their prize was enough to make even the coal-hearted Klax apprehensive about their retribution.

"So," he thought, "This is what it's like to be afraid."

No one had ever seen him wince, even in combat. During the '98 Bosnian War, when tracer bullets ripped past his ears like malevolent mosquitoes and the more robust artillery projectiles caused his Serbian commando unit comrades to shit their pants, Klax had maintained control and coolly pressed the attack on NATO's peacekeepers.

Klax was orphaned by the brutality of yet another in the long chain of Intra-Balkan conflicts that had plagued the "powder keg" of Europe for a millennium. Old men, searching for survivors after a skirmish initiated by Croat militia, found the scrawny boy beneath the bullet-riddled corpse of his mother. His nose was shorn off by a ricocheted shell fragment and his cheek was deeply gashed, the upper row of his teeth visible through the ragged wound. He still wore a chunk of shrapnel the medics pulled from his leg on a chain around his neck to remind him of the occasion. It wasn't just his body that suffered insult in that war. Other souvenirs of that bitter time mutilated his personality; the most poignant of which was the tattered photo his mother took of him while he and so many other children from his neighborhood frolicked in the whimsical costumes they wore in the opening ceremonies of the 1984 Winter Olympic Games in Sarajevo.

The memory of the night he pranced carefree before the world's television cameras had vanished in the same flames that consumed his little, pearl-white costume. His mother, his home and most of his friends were now buried somewhere beneath the foundations of the rebuilt city. But, he knew where the phantoms were. To recall them he only needed to look at the scar; a spear point of gristly tissue that ran diagonally from chin to temple, and the dull, copper-colored prosthesis that badly simulated his severed nose.

The Croats hanged his father two days before the man's twenty-seventh birthday. Klax had no memory of him. They strung up Januscz Klax and four of his cell in a bus barn after they were outed by a whore who for the first time had more to sell than her body. From that point on, Klax personified hate in black boots.

When the smoke cleared in the conference room and the body and the pottery shards settled to the floor, Klax felt better. There was still a chance that MAL would spare him. His deputy had been suitably punished for the failure of his plan to beat the Americans to the objective and Klax had secured the info disk from the wreckage of their helicopter. If the electromagnetic pulse from the blast or the heat from the exploding helo hadn't corrupted or erased the data files, it may still be useful.

There was also the small bit of strangely unencrypted digital mail his men had intercepted from what they presumed to be Eva Luknar's last InterVid transmission. It was a short text message and they only got a small piece of it before all the servers in Scandinavia and Northern Europe jammed with traffic about the explosion. It just said, "cannot generate sufficient power…" That could be significant. MAL's scientists would know.

Coming down from the rush of the impromptu execution and the heady, self-satisfaction of having purloined something useful from the fjord, Klax shook off his euphoria and returned to the moment. His men were staring at him, their eyes wide open and alert. In his perverted mind, he thought the expressions on their faces to be humorous. He smiled. That scared them all the more.

"*Pa□nja*," he yelled. The two men closest to him twitched visibly at the command. They all blinked, then stood and snapped to attention.

"You will get further orders at zero six-thirty tomorrow. Ernst Jost, you are now chief of staff."

A tall, crew cut German with an angular face and sweat on his upper lip bowed and clicked his heels.

"*Danke shoen, Mein General*," Jost replied.

Klax turned to regard the man and, forcing his breath through a sneer said, "Rossovich also thanked me when I made him chief of staff. Now, his brains decorate my briefing room. Surveying the mess on the wall, Klax said, "Nice upgrade, don't you think?" No one answered.

"You are advised, Comrade Jost, to do better."

"*Jawohl, Mein General.*"

"You are all advised to do better," Klax screamed.

"All!"

Klax turned to make his exit, but stopped after a few paces, his back to his lieutenants. For a moment he stood motionless and let the tension build. When he was sure the pregnant pause would have them all ready to push the FREAK button he drew a noisy, deep breath and the men braced for the onslaught. Instead of railing, Klax tossed his pistol back over his shoulder and continued his march down the dimly lit hallway. Arching in a lazy somersault through the doorway to the briefing room, the weapon landed hard and twirled a few times in the center of the table like a macabre, spin-the-bottle-of-death pointer. When it stopped spinning, a wisp of smoke rose from the muzzle.

It was a hump from the briefing room to Klax' quarters at the far, seaward end of the MAL complex. As he strutted down the corridor, Klax momentarily broke stride and laughed, still amused at how his staff looked after he blew Rossovich away. It was tricky managing his lieutenants. To get them to do the awful things he wanted, they must be motivated, well compensated and in abject fear of their commander. These were mostly desperate and all deadly men. Not all were psychotic killers but they shared a desire to avenge various injustices in their past lives. Some were motivated by revenge, others by religion or politics. A couple of them were just garden variety schizophrenics. Klax knew he was juggling some very sharp knives.

Ten minutes later, Klax arrived at his quarters and entered. Discarding his fatigues as he walked, he stripped to his under trousers and grabbed a black karate gi from the front closet. All his clothes were black, even his civvies, in tribute to his parents and his sundered homeland. He pulled the pants on, secured the drawstring, wrapped the jacket around him and cinched the thick black belt around his waste, making the traditional knot.

In the commodious living room there was a bar cart with an intricately ornamented decanter encircled by a dozen filigree-etched tulip stems. Selecting one, he poured himself a glass of Slivovitz and drained it in a single draught. Empty glass still in hand, the weary madman sank into the overstuffed chair before the fireplace his orderly had set ablaze. An ember popped and sparks flew. Parroting an old American western he had seen as a child, he feigned being shot, clasped his chest and recited a line from the film in a sham Spanish accent.

"Hey hombre, you put a hole in me." It was a childish bit of fantasy, but he knew someday that was likely to be the way he…how did the Americans say it? "Bought the farm."

As he lingered, feet toward the hearth, he was satisfied with saving what he could of the mission. He contemplated with zeal the wealth and power that would come to him when MAL triumphed and brought the world to their "Darwinian Destination," the ultimate expression of their mission.

He didn't realize that in his exhaustion, he had verbalized this last thought.

"What did you say, darling?" A soft voice cooed from the bathroom. He heard the slosh of bath water.

"Nothing," Klax said, pleased that his loyal orderly had also arranged companionship for him this evening. "Finish your bath and go to my bedroom. I don't want your tits to shrivel."

"Ah, a romantic," came the reply.

"Come here. I've changed my mind, he said. "I want to see you by the fire."

An exquisite redhead emerged from the doorway. She had thrown a towel around her broad shoulders. It was long enough to conceal her ample breasts but too short to disguise her gender, as if that could ever have been in question. She glided toward him, drawing her fingers back through her wet hair, her hips swaying a salacious rhythm. When she reached his chair she stood behind it, bent over him and massaged the knotted muscles in his shoulders. When she felt the tissue slacken she stepped to the chair arm, sat with the endless yards of her legs draped across his, nudged his head down toward her lap and pressed his cheeks to her warm, silken thighs. Her nipples loomed above him and he could see the full perfection of their undersides. He let himself linger there and inhaled her fresh and feminine essence. He guessed her to be twenty years of age. Her considerable charms were at their peak. The curves of her breathtaking body glowed angelically in the amber waves of flame from the hearth. Her shoulder length tresses framed the insouciant sensuality of her face and a silken tuft of the same hue decorated the mound between her thighs. A few tenacious bubbles perched astride the flawless expanse of her décolleté, accentuating her tender perfection. Klax couldn't take his eyes from her. Raising his head from its alabaster pillow, he scanned her from head to toe and back again, his attention riveted by lust.

She rose in glory to her full height, crossed languorously to the door to Klax' bedroom and teased him with a rear view that she knew would try his restraint. Turning to face him, she crossed her arms and leaned against the wall, canting her hips forward and offering herself fully to his view, as if he needed encouragement. He met her there and they walked into the bedroom. Playfully, she broke from him, giggled and covered herself with carmine-tipped fingers in the appropriate places to lighten the mood. He took the bait and approached. She bounced down on the bed and tossed hair back. She landed on her stomach and, spreading her legs wide, turned to look at him.

"Are you ready to play, Mr. Klax?" She purred with as much sincerity as she could summon.

Klax let the gi drop to the floor, shucked his boxers and, his tumescent penis pointing the way, strode to the bed. He took her that way, as she glanced back at him over her shoulder and bit her lip in mock ecstasy. As he thrust into her, she clutched the pillow and bucked her hips against him, hoping to end it quickly. She could have saved herself the trouble. Klax rarely engaged in prolonged intimacy. The honesty of considerate sharing and mutual surrender made him nauseous. It wasn't fucking a woman that made him queasy; it was when they fucked him back.

Klax never made love with his partners; he just ravaged them and sent them away. So it was tonight. He was rough and without any outward sign of passion, he released himself into the girl. Without taking even a short pause to savor his satisfaction, he pulled out, her buttocks still quivering, stood at the foot of the bed, and donned his gi.

"Leave me," he said.

Sensing the meanness of the moment and suddenly afraid, she rolled off the bed without protest and complied. The party was over. Klax' lover *du jour* stepped into her spiked heels, wrapped herself in a deep-green dress, secured it with a faux-jeweled belt and departed without a word.

She thought it better not to antagonize him with attempts at social pleasantries. She would just leave the bunker, collect her money from the orderly, clean herself as best she could with the tissues in her handbag, and retreat back across the water to the small flat she shared with her young lover and their daughter. Three or four more visits and she could buy her way out of her meaningless life as a "dancer" and fly away to start a new life; she hoped as a singing talk show host on American television.

That didn't happen. Two of Klax' men drove her to a mist-shrouded wald near the base helipad, took turns raping her, shot her and left her nude body for the animals. Her personal effects would become gifts for the men's wives back home. Those who didn't get the presents this time would get them the next. Or, the next.

Whenever MAL's senior military commanders returned from their indoctrination and recruiting trips for some rest and recuperation, a sleek black turbocopter flew the one hundred miles from the MAL base, cut into the sand on the islet of Ahvenanmaa (the largest in the sixty-five hundred island archipelago at the southern entrance to the Gulf of Bothnia), to a covert pad near Stockholm to pick up returning mercenaries and supplies for the base. When Klax was in camp, his personal helicopter usually accompanied the cargo transport. The ships that flew these nighttime "sorties" stayed fully cloaked in electronic stealth to avoid Swedish and Finnish patrol aircraft. While the ground crew loaded supplies Klax' flight crew set out on secret forays to the capital's nightclubs to recruit from the extensive cadre of exotic dancers, prostitutes and club girls in the district. There were so many bribes paid along the way for young flesh, munitions and materiel that nothing that left from their guerrilla airstrip on MAL's aircraft could ever be traced to or from the island.

Whether a girl made it home or not was a matter of who accompanied her on the ride back. If there were civilian scientists or consultants aboard the flight she had a chance to see the sun rise in Stockholm. If she returned solo, she was doomed. Those that did make it back were careful not to talk about their experiences with what they were told was a company of wealthy oil wildcatters. They were plied with alcohol and the recreational drugs of their choice as soon as they boarded and none of them were capable of reckoning their destination in the dark.

Like the organization that employed it, the system was sinister and effective. None of the girls went back for a second visit. Some were paid and went home. Some gave their all and died on the island.

To MAL people were expendable, a whole lot of people.

The cabal was founded by a militant pack of environmental pseudo-scientists who corrupted the ideas of Thomas Malthus and Charles Darwin to form their twisted ideology. The core of MAL's credo was created from Malthus', 1798 *"Essay on the Principle of Population."* In the piece, Malthus offered the premise that, when unchecked, the human population on the planet would rise so rapidly that food supplies could not be produced in sufficient quantity to sustain an orderly society. Unless the proliferation was curbed, there would be famine and ultimately mass starvation. However, Malthus believed that God in his goodness had provided two kinds of checks to save man from self-extinction. These were preventive checks and positive checks.

Preventive checks included moral restraint (abstinence from sex or willfully controlling family size, as in the case of the "higher ranks of humans" who chose to have fewer children so their familial wealth would not be diminished by distribution to a large number of heirs),

vice (assumedly sodomy and masturbation) and mechanical or medicinal birth control.

Positive checks included war, famine, plague, and misery resulting
in murder or suicide, and natural disasters.

Where the group had usurped a basically sound observation and
vivisected it to rationalize their rotten aims was in the war part. MAL
figured that if human nature wasn't reliable in the matter, weapons of
mass destruction were. If the undesirable could be eliminated using dangerous density or environmental pollution as a justification, perhaps the
accidental elite of the world (those who remained alive after such a mass
cleansing) would yield to the inevitability of their circumstances, realize
the need for such draconian actions, and become manageable. Surely,
they would benefit from the beauty, solitude and eco-recovery of the
expunged territory and be appreciative. If they weren't, they could be
the next to be cleansed.

Until now, MAL's plan had serious drawbacks. Chemicals or
microbes capable of homicide on that scale would be difficult if not
impossible to control. Also, the rot of tens of millions of corpses and
the disease attending such decay would render the land around them
useless for decades or more. Thermonuclear explosives left the ground
uninhabitable for centuries and caused tremendous ecological damage,
although such devices did a great job of corpse disposal.

Dr. Eva's machine changed their leaders' way of thinking. With such
a thing in their control it might be possible to build a ray gun that would
dissolve people. It could be aimed. Its effect could be broadcast over
large areas and when its work was done, only a steamy, mineral-rich
residue would remain. The ray could dissolve flesh, not just where it
contacted a body, but throughout it, like a contained chain reaction, and
if more power was all it needed to make the effect bigger, MAL had the
scientific genius at its disposal to make that happen.

Chapter 19

"Up against it"

After ten hours of transoceanic flight the Hellion didn't seem as roomy as it had at takeoff. Red and Nat had stayed busy flying the little jet through some rough weather, two in-flight refuelings and one carrier-based top off, but Forster had memorized every thing there was to read by now and he had nothing left to distract him from the lack of circulation in his own tail section. Their only respite had been when they were allowed to leave the aircraft for fifteen minutes while they gassed up on the flattop in the mid-Atlantic. The flyers got fresh java, Natalie got to powder her nose in private and the unusually good-natured CAG gave Forster a pocket flask of succulent small-batch aged rum. Then it was back into the big blue for the final leg of the journey and a pre-dawn landing in Bergen. They were met by an SUV with blackout windows and ferried to a safe house not far from the airfield. Forster was happy to be on terra firma.

After a shower and a three-hour nap (only Red slept), Forster and Katrova changed into less conspicuous civvies and said goodbye to their flame-haired friend. Red was going to miss them, especially the bickering, but he was happy his part of this was over, or so he thought.

"Thanks, man," Forster said. "You fly good." He was certain that it was Red who had done all the work in the cockpit, even if Katrova had made like she knew what she was doing.

"Good luck Mr. Forster," Red said. "You too, Ma'am. You give good right seat."

"My pleasure, Red," Katrova extended her hand. "Anytime."

"Where next?" Forster queried the pilot.

"Don't know. Couldn't tell you if I did. Back to the States, I guess. But, who knows? The Ten calls and I'm there. Maybe I'll blip you on my screen somewhere down the line. Take care and for Christ's sake, you kids try to get along, will ya?"

They looked at each other, then back to the pilot and mumbled.

"Yeah."

"Sure."

An hour later, Katrova and Forster stood in a pristine sky lit day room at Prince Haakon Magnus Hospital and awaited their turn to debrief Markus Haukken. Shortly, they were introduced to Dr. Edmund Tellis, Haukken's attending physician who filled them in on the sled driver's condition. The prognosis was grim. The barrage of photons from the weapon damaged Haukken's retinas and they weren't sure his eyesight would ever fully return. He had second and third degree flash burns on his face and hands from absorbing nearly six hundred roentgens of gamma, X and who knows what other kinds of rays. His gastrointestinal system was under severe stress and vomiting and diarrhea were dehydrating him. He was able to speak but for only for short periods of time. His voice was hoarse and frail and the gunshot wound to his chest made it difficult to breathe. He was bleeding internally and externally through some hideous skin lesions. His hair was falling out in places but seemed to be growing abnormally fast in others. He looked a weak and ugly mess, but he was for the moment alive and an eyewitness. The interview had to happen today.

The dour doc took his leave and returned to his patient.

"If you know a 'God please help the nice musher survive the atom bomb blast' prayer, you'd better say it, Forster," Katrova said.

They both looked at the floor and hoped for the best.

Then they were distracted by the clack of cleats on the floor. Striding at a quick-march toward them were Wolfgang Lang and a stout, stern-faced SEAL, Steyr AUG at the ready. Instinctively, Forster stood at attention as the senior officer approached.

Nat looked at him openly amused and said, "Forster, you're not a soldier anymore."

"Right," he answered, embarrassed, "Old habits…"

Lang introduced himself as the manager of "Project Repo" as their mission had come to be called. The Commander motioned for the two to be seated. The SEAL remained standing, his back to the small group and his eyes scanning the windows around and above him. Katrova wondered what in the situation had deteriorated to the point that they needed such protection in this quiet setting in broad daylight. Forster knew why the man was there and had a high level of confidence that more of his team were close by. A barely defensible facility, accessible as it was to staff, visitors and vendors, it seemed an open invitation to the enemy to come get the sled driver. Despite the presence of the SEALs, a rapidly deployed force could be effective, especially if the enemy had superior numbers and a disregard for collateral damage. For that reason and the questions engendered among the local population by the ostentatious force needed to control the outer perimeter, Lang wanted to move Haukken to the Kendall as soon as the ICU released him. Unless he went directly to the morgue.

"We don't know much yet people but here's what we have," the Commander began.

Keeping his voice low, with practiced clarity, he succinctly related what he knew. Much of the tale had already been laid out for Forster and Katrova in their briefing materials. What The Ten had learned since gave them no comfort. Dagon Klax had been identified as the first man on the scene after the blast. That was very bad. Not only was Klax dangerous and persistent, he never worked alone. Someone had hired him. Whoever it was, they must be very powerful and in possession of copious amounts of cash to lure Klax into their service.

According to Lang, some of the information the sled driver passed along was thought to be reliable and relevant. Parts of his tale were suspect. A psychiatric consultant thought the man had a hard time distinguishing dreams from reality. If the shock of his experience hadn't addled his mind, he hadn't slept on his own since they brought him in and he was often delirious. The anesthesia was starting lose its effect and Haukken repeatedly screamed in pain. He chanted, "Tyrone," and "arms and legs" over and over. Once in a while he'd mumble something about a "record" but he had no recorder on his person and there was no evidence of a written log found at the scene, although evidence teams were still melting snow and sifting mud for clues.

Just then, Lang's briefing was interrupted by Tellis' return.

"He's conscious again," the doctor said enthusiastically and added with urgency, "You have just a few minutes."

Nat and Forster looked at Lang as if to get permission to proceed.

"Let's get in there," he said, leading the charge to the ICU.

Gathering themselves for what was sure to be an unpleasant sight, Forster and Katrova followed the officer in single file. They wouldn't be allowed to enter Haukken's space. There was no time for scrubbing and suiting up. They would have to conduct the interrogation using the intercom in the anteroom. Arriving in the cramped quarters, Lang encouraged Forster to get things underway.

"Go ahead," Lang prompted. "If I have a question, I'll relay it to you."

"Me too," Nat said.

Forster turned to regard the patient through the thick glass. He was a sorry sight. For the bandages, machines, tubes and wires, they could see little of the man. Forster supposed that was a good thing. What they could see was yards of white sheets and a gallery of framed vignettes of peeling skin; some black, some red, some the color of old callus. Swatches of hair pouffed from the bandages on the patient's head and a splotch of pink oozed from the dressings over his chest wound. A covey of technicians in full-body protective gear and breathers that looked like small scuba tanks, attended him. One was dangling a microphone above his mouth like a child teasing a sibling with a rubber spider on a string. They could hear him moaning softly through the headsets on the hooks beneath the window.

Each donned one of the headsets. Forster pulled the mic to his mouth.

"Mr. Haukken?" Forster spoke softly.

Markus stopped moaning at the query, but he couldn't quite figure out where the sound was coming from.

"Who is this?" He asked, groggy and wary.

"Mr. Haukken?"

"I'm Markus," he said. "Who... Where are you? I can't much see, very well."

"My name is Luke Forster, Markus. I'm trying to find out what happened to you and Dr. Luknar."

"I don't know, Mr. Luke Forster. I just think I'm going to die like Eva and my dogs."

Forster had little practice at bedside manners but over the course of the next ten minutes, he learned much and hearing direct testimony, he was sure that these were not the ravings of a dying man. He believed Haukken's report to be accurate.

Markus confirmed that Klax didn't have the machine. The prototype had been smashed in the crash after Eva set off her bomb. That negated the theory that Klax had beaten the Americans to the punch, stolen the machine and incinerated the physicist's compound.

The only remaining clues about the invention must be imprinted on the disk Klax had pried from the sled driver's hands. If there were schematics on the disk, the bad guys would still have a tough row to hoe. First they would have to decode the most likely encrypted information on the disk. Then, they would have to gather the raw materials and engineering expertise to build a new machine and test it. They all agreed The Ten would have some time to implement countermeasures but no one could speculate about the how long that window would stay open, and Forster and Katrova might need a big chunk of that time just to find Klax. By the time they found him, the disk certainly would have yielded its secrets. Klax was a hired killer, not a scientist. He would already have passed it on to his masters. Still, he was the key to the next door that had to be opened.

"Thank you, Markus. Do your best to get well, will you?"

"Yes, I will do this," Haukken replied, weakened by the questioning. "Please also, Mr. Luke Forster, find who did this and punish them," he said.

"Maybe I will be healed soon and help."

He coughed phlegm as he tried to speak.

"You get these bad…men," he strained and collapsed onto his pillow.

The interview terminated, Forster and the team replaced their headsets and left, just avoiding a run-in with an irritated Dr. Tellis who was already on his way to halt the questioning.

Back in the day room, Katrova turned to Lang.

"What's next, Commander?" She asked.

Forster and Lang answered together.

"Find Klax."

Lang continued, "A helo's to take us out to the Kendall. Your gear's been shuttled ahead."

"Great. More air time," Katrova bitched.

"It's secure out there," Lang said, obviating the primary advantage of working from a carrier.

"We can map our moves and get our shit together under cover of the fleet. If anyone aboard the Kendall asks and nobody should, you two are civilian consultants. But, no one needs to know squat 'bout nuthin'. There are six others on the Kendall's crew who work with The Ten and they'll be your aides and advisors until you depart the ship. They will make themselves known to you when and where appropriate. Clear?"

"Yes, Sir," Katrova replied, aware that responding with military courtesy may keep her out of the Commander's dog house.

Forster simply nodded and they left the hospital staff and Mr. Haukken to their work - they to heal, he to survive.

Seventy nautical miles west of Bergen, in a relatively light chop for this part of the Norwegian Sea, the aircraft carrier USS Kendall, flagship of the Atlantic fleet, sat in its towering, hulking majesty awaiting the arrival of Commander Lang and his charges. It was a relatively short hop to the deck of the "Nighthawk," as the crew called her - a tribute to President Kendall's tribal name and an allusion to the fact that big ship could strike hard and decisively against her foes, even in the black of night.

Ten miles out, Katrova and Forster got their first look at her from a broken cloud deck at six thousand feet. She was huge. Built by the Newport News Shipbuilding Company in Virginia, she was topped out in '36 and completed her sea trials in '38. She was singly the most feared and capable surface ship in the Navy. Since her launch, she had been "the sharp end of the stick" in the Third Gulf War, the Taiwan Intervention and the Indo-Pakistani War. Her crew was already the most decorated in the fleet.

The Nighthawk was powered by two Westinghouse A4W reactors that made screw turns and generated electricity for all on board systems and propelled her over the world's oceans at more than thirty-five knots. With space for her air wing (eighty-five fully loaded combat and support aircraft), accommodations for Marine security and ship's crew (nearly six thousand men and women strong), the ship measured out at one thousand and forty feet in length. Her beam was one hundred and thirty-four feet. The Kendall displaced nearly ninety-six thousand tons, more than two and quarter times the size of the legendary USS Hornet of World War II fame. Had it been possible to lift her there, the old "Grey Ghost" would sit with room to spare on the Kendall's flight deck.

Although Wolf Lang had made hundreds of carrier landings in fixed wing aircraft, both he and the novices in the back of the helo who had just made their first such "controlled crash" for the Hellion's refueling just hours ago, appreciated the relative gentility of a helo landing versus smashing a relatively delicate fixed wing aircraft onto a tossing steel surface at over one hundred knots, the typical landing speed for a jet with wings that didn't twirl. The craft's rotors had no sooner started to wind down than the main hatch slid back and Lang was confronted by a man in a helmet who politely yelled, "Follow me, Sir," above the din.

The salt-spiced wind vectoring across the deck hit the passengers square in the kisser as each in turn stood in the doorway. Lang held his lid on with one had and a brushed aluminum attaché case in the other as he leapt without hesitation and landed squarely on the deck. Forster thought it looked like the Commander had done this before. Natalie misjudged her jump but made a cat-like correction and caught herself upright with the assistance of a helmeted safety officer who was all too ready to lend a hand. Finally, Forster made his leap. He thought he had judged his landing well and he had, but for the downward plunge the deck executed while he was mid-flight. His personal landing gear now in a bad position, he put down on stretched out toes, instead of the balls of his feet. Rather than risk rolling an ankle, Forster used his jump school training to duck, tuck and roll out of the fall. No matter how well executed, the maneuver wasn't quick or agile enough to avoid detection, as the pointing fingers and open laughter of the deck hands and bridge officers who caught his trick proved. Chagrined, but unable to resist seizing the moment for a little self-promotion, he took a single bow and marched the remainder of his dignity toward the hatchway dead ahead.

"Tell me Katrova didn't see that," he prayed.

She had.

A short dash later, the trio was off the tumultuous flight deck and in a cramped electric elevator headed down three decks to their temporary quarters. There was no air moving in the conveyance and the car smelled of jet fuel.

"Miss the wire on that landing, Mr. Forster?" Lang ribbed.

Natalie snarfled, trying to smother a laugh. Shaking off the temptation to let it pass, she turned to Lang and said, "I'm thinking, call sign 'Grace,'" she grinned, about to lose it.

"At least I didn't hafta gwab onto a big, stwong sailor," Forster cooed in his best baby talk.

"You want another clip to the *cajones*?" She shot back.

"Stow it, children," Lang beefed, bored with their bullshit.

Lang gave the antagonists fifteen minutes to stow their personal gear and report to Ward Room 4 on C deck. Their mission gear was already being secured in a bay near the flight deck for final inspection and testing by the ship's armorer, one of The Ten's most committed agents and the world's only plasma weapons specialist. LJG Malachi "Big Mo" Moroder was the best insurance policy the good guys could buy.

To the casual observer Moroder was a bespectacled dweeb. Katrova outweighed him by ten pounds. He was small in stature and could stand invisible behind Luke Forster. But, when it came to skill with hand-held weapons, the man was large and in charge. To him, targets were just images in an arcade game that vanished with funny noises when he destroyed them. He was as close to a killing machine as a human could be. He had the knack of being able to find the right weapon for the right skirmish and bring it to bear with certain and effective brutality. Fast and fearless, his tactical planning never missed and he always provided maximum safety for his team and minimum survivability for the enemy.

These days Moroder was at the height of his powers. That was comforting, because the new tools of his trade no longer depended on the mechanical loading of lead and powder to splinter bone and liquefy flesh. With the new stuff, he could make lots of people die fast and where the Repo team was going, they would need every bit of Big Mo's attitude and expertise.

Even with directions from well-intended crewmen, most of which sounded like gobbledygook, the maze of the ship's companionways got the best of them. Nat and Luke were five minutes late to their meeting and Lang bristled when they jostled each other through the hatchway and into the cramped briefing room.

"You two stop for a smooch?"

"I'd rather kiss a lizard," Nat huffed back at Lang.

Forster winked at her.

"Stow it. You're late," Lang said. "Mr. Forster, Miss Katrova, this is Lieutenant Colonel Jim Comstock, CIA." Hands were offered and shaken.

He's going to give you an updated SITREP and the latest on Dagon Klax. When you're through here," he said, checking the chronometer on his wrist, "report to Bay 88, B deck. If you don't think you can find it, use the nearest black phone. Push 555, read them the number off the first bulkhead you see and ask the person that answers it for an escort. Clear? If you're not on your way by thirteen-thirty, I'll assume you've driven Colonel Comstock mad and I'll come and get you myself. I won't like that and you won't either"

Before Forster could acknowledge the instructions, Jim Comstock started talking and Lang was on his way elsewhere.

Comstock pushed two folders with red and white striped cover sheets across the table. He had serious eyes.

"This is Project Repo."

For the next three hours they learned everything The Ten had developed since their last briefing on Dr. Luknar, her machine and Dagon Klax. It was a demoralizing afternoon. By the end of the session, Forster felt like he needed a change of underwear. Katrova, reading Forster's eyes, tried to lighten the mood and quoted a line from an old movie about naval aviators at Miramar.

"Just a walk in the park, Kazanski," she said.

Forster despised her perky optimism. It was naïve and he found her effort at humor in bad taste given what had already happened and what may come to pass.

They finished in time to make their assignation with Lang and found him and two junior officers hunched over a chart table tiled with aerial reconnaissance images of what looked to be a giant black crater in the center of a massive snowfield. Each of the men wore magnifying loupes and had their noses inches above the photos. No one looked up as Forster rapped his knuckles on the bulkhead and announced their arrival.

"Commander?"

Without turning to face the pair, Lang raised the magnifying glasses from his nose and issued curt instructions to his associates, returning to his analysis work without waiting for acknowledgment or recognizing Forster.

Forster was assigned to Moroder for training on the new weapons he'd be taking on the mission. Katrova was left on her own to ferret out her workstation, a dim, sequestered nook in Air Ops where she had been provided with the tools she needed to establish a secure link to Rex, her *wunderkind* computer. It was time for her to do her thing and begin the hunt for Dagon Klax. That night, after she and Rex had spent all day sniffing after the miscreant mercenary's tracks; she turned in, the very personal smell of the previous occupant of her tiny rack offending her sensibilities. Too exhausted to let it deter her, she nodded off.

Later, Klax, at least Natalie's mental projection of him, visited. The last vision she carried to consciousness was of the dank cavity that had been Klax' nose, just inches from her own as he throttled her with one hand and groped her naked body with the other. Twitching and tossing in fevered fear, she beat her elbows and knees to bruises against the bulkhead. She awoke suddenly in a clammy sweat, just before dawn, bolted upright and mashed her forehead into the wire underpinnings supporting the mattress in the rack above her.

"Ow! Shit," she vented and collapsed back on the sparse bedding. "Nightmare," she exhaled.

Still groggy, she checked and found blood seeping from a small cut above her eye, but she was relieved. Klax wasn't really there and she wasn't naked. Just the same, she unfolded the blanket she had earlier disdained, kicked it open and pulled it to her chin with both hands. He couldn't reach her here. Could he? But of course, he had and she felt his evil like a bruise on her soul.

Chapter 20

"The Vatican violation"

Halberdier Willi Berlith was serenely unaware he was about to die. Everyone in his village thought that the Swiss Guard was a silly pretense accurately outed by the whimsy of their sixteenth-century regalia. But since his boyhood, he always thought that it was the perfect job for him and his family thought it was an ideal army to join for a shy German-Swiss Catholic boy with more courage than vigor.

Established in 1506 by Pope Julius II, the unit had a long and distinguished tradition of service, though they had never actually gone to war. Their primary duties were ceremonial though there were times they had to make a fuss in an effort to sort harmless wandering tourists from actual kooks. Like everyone in his unit, Willi was a qualified expert with small arms, but in his wildest dreams, he never thought he would have to deal with anything more vexing than a dressing down by his commander for a missing button on his uniform or a scuff on his boot.

Today though, he had passed his morning inspection without a gig and he assumed his post outside the Vatican library actually looking forward to a quiet day in a quiet place. Guarding the antiquities of the *Biblioteca Apostolica Vaticana* meant that his only interpersonal communication would be an occasional, subtle nod to a Cardinal here, a black-cassocked librarian there, or a custodian scuffling about the place to repair the fair wear and tear of the day.

He loved his outdoor postings when they came, especially when he was stationed with a view of St. Peter's square and the ever-present throng of pilgrims there, but it was warmish and muggy today in Rome and his head was sweating profusely in the confines of his plumed helmet. Yes, he mused, today it would be better indoors. No, it wouldn't. Today, Willi met Dagon Klax.

He didn't see the terrorist's face. He never knew his name. But he felt the sting of his stiletto as Klax plunged the fine blade upward through the base of Willi's skull and into his cerebellum, ending his life with a quick thrust, rip and twist. As Willi's body toppled, one of Klax' men emerged from behind a grand marble column, clasped the victim against him to prevent a noisy collision with the floor and dragged the corpse; helmet, pike and all, into a dark niche beside an ancient bookcase. Klax entered the library behind them and cautiously closed the door, looking out to assure they remained unseen. Although the Swiss Guard carried swords and pikes for public amusement, modern weapons were always nearby and the Guard wouldn't hesitate to use them in defense of the Church and the Holy Father. Or, in this case, to avenge the murder of a brother-in-arms. Haste was in order.

The assassin's aide was quickly into Willi's uniform and pulled his headgear down to shadow his face. It would be difficult though to remain inconspicuous for long. The garments reeked of Willi's evacuated bowels and bladder.

Klax hissed at the man to hurry back to Willi's post. It would be less than five minutes before the watch commander would come to verify that Willi was on post. The hope was that the supervisor would simply do his usual reconnoiter from twenty meters or so across the dusky marble canyon of the vestibule, wave to Willi in passing and move on to the next post.

As Willi's impostor assumed his position, Klax moved into the library to keep the covert appointment with his agent inside. Everyone there was so jaded by the security the Guard provided that no one took extraordinary notice of Klax as he walked the polished stone floors of the great athenaeum. He had chosen his most realistic-looking nasal prosthesis for this adventure. With that and an unobtrusive suit of clothes, he drew not a glance. Strolling amid the antiquities, Klax chuckled to himself that in spite of the presence of the finest literary and theological works of human kind, it was an obscure notebook of mathematical scribblings by a prominent Jewish physicist of the mid-twentieth century that he would steal away. Maybe he would return one day soon with fast helos, heavy weapons and enough muscle to make a good haul. He had known a few desperadoes who had amassed great fortunes with misappropriated rarities. Or perhaps, after MAL built the death ray, he would come back and merely raze the place to the ground. Most of these writings were based on sloppy thinking and maudlin sentimentality at any rate.

No time for browsing now. MAL's schedule and the threat of discovery kept him on his course and he continued his march toward the rear of the huge room.

"Signore Klax," a gentle voice called to him from behind one of the high book stacks to his left. He could barely make out the figure of the woman motioning to him. He approached her casually, being careful not to look around; making it look as if he was greeting a friend. A clerk who had been mildly curious about his arrival watched him disappear between the shelves where Adelina was working and, thinking him to be nothing more than another scholar in search of answers, returned to his work.

No matter what Adelina Calabrese did to disguise her physical beauty, it radiated. Her convent school bearing, her proper manner of speech, her detached awareness of everything around her, gave her at once the ability to command a room and to put off everyone in it. Her vixen/virgin aire made people uneasy, as did the dichotomy presented by her plain dress and striking form. But, she just wasn't friendly, even to long-time coworkers who occasionally tried in vain to cajole her into cordiality. Some of the males, unable to accept that their charms were insufficient to turn her head, thought she preferred women. Actually, she had sparse appetite for companionship of either sex.

It was the woman's reclusive nature, an intimate knowledge of her family history and her access to certain archived papers that had attracted MAL's attention to Adelina. They needed that information to make Dr. Eva's machine work and she was the surest means to obtain it. Adelina's father, a Sicilian, had been a mercenary in service to the Palestinian Liberation Organization's Arafat Brigade. He was killed by an Israeli gunship attack in the Second Sinai War. The video of her father being shredded by a burst of machine gun fire during a live broadcast of the battle of the Golan Heights had damaged her psyche beyond repair. She was the last surviving member of her clan. Simply, Adelina wanted revenge and she'd gladly sacrifice her freedom or her life to assist any adversary of the West. She would exact retribution for her father's death and if her assumptions about the nature of the information she was handing over were correct, the price would be high. Deep in her tortured heart she hoped the humble act of piracy she would commit today would make development of a super weapon possible and she would live long enough to see her father's murder avenged by the death of millions of his, and now her adversaries.

MAL had proffered another weighty incentive. Adelina was a poor girl, modestly educated and with more ambition than potential. To her delight they had promised that when she delivered on her part of the bargain she would be compensated with money, power and position in the new world MAL would build. She had never imagined great personal success and the dreams of such things coming to pass had for a fortnight kept her sleepless with anticipation.

She was better off in her dreams. Klax took the information from her, a fist-sized box of data disks, smiled his quivering snake-sneer and whispered.

"Arrivederci Signorina."

Before she could ask about her rewards, her new title or her duties with MAL, he whirled behind the maiden, clenched her roughly by her soft hair that smelled of vanilla and broke her neck with a muffled crunch.

Minutes later Klax and his now plainly attired accomplice mounted twin turbobikes and headed for a private hangar at Rome's venerable but discreet Ciampino airport, fifteen kilometers southeast on the Via Appia. In a few hours, they would deliver Adelina's precious diskettes to MAL's scientists at the Ahvenanmaa compound.

The murders at the Vatican were explained creatively to the world press. The story was that Willi and Adelina had given their lives thwarting a terrorist-led raid aimed at misappropriation of ancient and priceless religious treatises. With a single, masterfully orchestrated press conference, the Vatican simultaneously disarmed concerns of more sophisticated intrigue and bored reporters to tears with the details of arcane religious mystery in the writings, effectively dousing their journalistic fervor. The disclosure that the escaped perpetrators were unknown and that technical difficulties had prevented a video record of the incident, left little to tell and provided a convenient explanation for an obvious increase in security.

In fact, Adelina never came into contact with religious manuscripts. Her job was to oversee access to and retrieval of original writings of the greatest scientists of the age; including the sensitive and controversial musings of chemists and physicists whose works the Church thought sacrilegious or too dangerous to mankind to ever again see the light of day. Despite the outwardly low key-dismissal of the incident the Vatican was deeply concerned. The Ten were terrified.

Willi was buried with full military honors beneath a splendid linden tree in his tiny village cemetery. The family wept in silence, bereaved but proud.

No one inquired after Adelina's body. After the autopsy she was interred beneath a rude marker in a potter's field on the outskirts of Rome. Her landlord was told someone would come for her things. That was an understatement as he learned when a small hoard of investigators arrived on his doorstep. Local police inspectors, forensic technicians from Interpol and a detachment of CIA operatives under the guidance of The Ten dismantled her flat and scrutinized every square centimeter. The only thing they found of a suspicious nature was a series of numbers written on a postcard from Warsaw, apparently a digicom number. It was unregistered and inactive, the first of many dead ends.

As a small army of librarians began a tedious inventory to learn what was missing and Europe's best info-techies sought to uncover digital document compromises, the ever-vigilant Ten were left to ponder the probability of a connection to the events in the fjord.

Chapter 21

"Good stuff in bad hands"

It was late afternoon when Klax' plane leapt into the verdigris sky over the Baltic Sea. Traveling at over three hundred knots and clinging to the mist just fifty meters above the wave tops, the plane soon spent the fuel from their stop in Dresden and now had only sufficient reserve to keep to the flight plan, going "feet wet" just West of Kozalin, Poland. The pilot corrected slightly east to reduce the risk of visual sighting by Gotland's inhabitants, and circled out over the channel east of the hamlet of Lapgnas to a landing North of Geta.

MAL's leadership called their northern outpost Alpha Island because this was where the new way of doing things would begin. Everyone else called it the "Black Hole," a less romantic but more truthful description of the place where everything; laboratories, hangars, barracks, mess halls, workshops and infocenter had been built below ground to avoid detection from space-based sensors.

Here it was also most unlikely that the accidental tourist or off course fishing boat would discover them. Most landfalls in this sea of islands were casually charted and the ever-changing sea and cloud patterns altered the look of the landscape by the hour. From the air the islands looked like the Everglades on steroids. The sixty-five hundred tiny emeralds of the Ahvenanmaa archipelago had a storied past and since MAL's infestation, a fetid present.

Less than a percent of the islands (strewn across a five-hundred square mile expanse) were inhabited, which made concealment of men and munitions relatively easy. The only remarkable population center in the sector was the modest provincial capital of Mariehamn.

MAL avoided contact with the natives. Everyone knew everyone there and news and secrets were hard to keep. It was better to do even minor trading business in the large cities of Scandinavia's capitals where bustle and commerce would obscure the comings and goings of the league's drones as they went about their black business. Alpha Island was an ideal base for MAL's operations in this part of the world and there, they were virtually invisible.

It was twilight on the island when the plane from Rome arrived, the smoke from the tires swirling in the jet wash on touchdown. Minutes later the crude strip that had been cleared for the landing would once again be concealed beneath an overhang of dimensional camouflage. The ground crew had the exercise down to a science. Under the direction of a single choreographer wagging luminescent wands from his roll stair perch, a chorus line of electric tugs danced a flotilla of wheeled rafts bearing bogus brush and thin sheets of Mylar "water" into place. Instant bog.

Klax was fatigued but he looked forward to delivering his newly plundered booty to Dr. Llorca. Veral Llorca was high prelate of the Wardens, Klax' immediate supervisor and his most ardent champion on MAL's ruling council. As his plane rolled into its revetment, Klax was already impatient for the arrival of the electric cart that would shuttle him to the council's chambers.

It was a short ride through a garishly lit access tunnel to his rendezvous and soon the cart's tires squeaked to a halt outside the great hall. Without acknowledging the driver's service, Klax dismounted the vehicle and straightened his clothes.

He was not one for silly sentimentality or subject to being moved by symbolism but the sight of the imposing logo atop the council door spoke to him as he anticipated his audience. Red-orange flames encircled the bold "M.A.L.," it in turn superimposed over silhouettes of the earth's continents. Purposely, there were no geopolitical divisions to indicate the borders of Earth's countries. When MAL had achieved its goals no such delineations would be necessary. There would be one language, one economy and one governing body for the surviving world. Klax was energized by thoughts of the imminent conflict that would bring it all to reality. At last in their hands, Eva Luknar's machine would be the instrument of this change. Klax salivated over the possibility that it would be operational soon and that he would be the first to bring its demonic force to bear.

As Klax relished his daydream Llorca's secretary appeared on the threshold of the gargantuan doorway and beckoned him inside.

"Mr. Klax, Warden Llorca will see you," the gaunt old man said.

The Warden was concluding a quiet conversation with two others of his ilk on the raised dais that formed one end of the High Council's chamber. Tolerating the delay with forced patience, Klax stood immobile and awaited recognition. His hands clasped the diskette case at the small of his back and he rocked on his heels like a boy about to present his mother a posy.

Llorca finished the palaver and descended the short steel mesh staircase to the floor. He was clad in the standard Warden uniform; dark green suit and robin's egg t-shirt. He was tall and swarthy with a thicket of mono-brow surmounting deep-set black eyes. At sixty, his hair was still mostly raven.

"Mr. Klax, you were successful?"

"Sir, I give you the answers to your questions." He proudly presented his prize.

Llorca took the box and held it reverently in both hands.

"Oh. You know the questions we pose, Mr. Klax?" Llorca said haughtily, sure that his soldier was incapable of understanding what it was that he had just conveyed.

Irritated but unwilling to venture a display of emotion, Klax said in measured tones, "I know only that these are Einstein's notes on generating great quantities of energy and that we need much to power our machine…Sir."

"The answers may be here, or they may not," Llorca said brusquely, a tremor creeping into his voice. "Even if this is what we seek, I must remind you that we don't know what effect the machine produces or how we may employ its power to-"

Flustered, Klax interrupted, "But Sir, we know it kills and that we can make it kill bigger and better."

"Better killing? Mr. Klax," the man said sternly, "We know no such thing. It has killed yes, but only small animals according to our spies. We are quite some distance from the ecological super weapon we need to prosecute our program on the inept governments of this decaying planet. It is promising though. You know Mr. Klax? Our best minds believe as you do, that it could be a very useful tool but it will be some time before we have a functional prototype. The disk you found in the fjord is only now being restored from the corruptions caused by the thermonuclear blast. Fortunately, the disk is not a magnetic storage unit. It's optical, but the release of so much photonic energy has presented its own set of obstacles. I am told we will have holographic schematics of the machine not before two weeks have passed." Klax looked forlorn.

"Patience my cruel friend, patience," Llorca cajoled. "It would serve you well in the meantime to work with our logistics group on preparing the plans for the transport and testing of the device, so that when it is ready, you will be ready."

He reached out to shake the crestfallen Klax' hand and offer a measure of reward for his accomplishments but in his typically anti-social manner, Klax stiffened ignored the gesture and said, "By your leave, Sir, I have much to do."

Dismissing his leader, he turned on his heels and squeezed through the doorway as soon as the opening permitted his exit. Llorca watched the madman's retreat and shook his head.

"Necessary evil," he thought and shuddered, mildly curious about the origin of Klax' verve for destruction.

MAL's analysis of the data provided by the late Ms. Calabrese revealed that she had done well. Most of the files contained high-resolution images of the handwritten notes of Albert Einstein. During the period in which Einstein was evolving his theory of relativity, he explored for a short while a mathematical equation for a "transformer coil" that could take a source electrical current and convert or multiply the output by the power of ten. Then, through the use of a precisely of an ingeniously designed feedback loop, it would again, take the output and multiply it by the power of ten and so on; again and again. What made Einstein apprehensive about this discovery, an ironically similar problem to Dr. Eva's foil, was that his calculations pointed to the undesirable creation of a self-sustaining phenomenon that would continuously accelerate the flow of electrons, thus producing tremendous heat and vaporizing any mechanical method of control or transmission including the destruction of physical devices like cables, rheostats, switches and those humans unfortunate enough to be in the general vicinity. Einstein quickly abandoned the project and put his notes in a Manila folder marked "*Sackgassen*." German for "dead ends." It was conceivable that someday, someone would be able to accelerate electrons to such a speed and that the very building blocks of matter itself would be made evident, but he thought it would be a long time in the future before such a robust flow could be restrained and made useful.

Many years after the savant's death, Einstein's intimates at Princeton sent those of his writings perceived to be of little scientific or museum value, including the "dead ends" file, to auction. After all, if Professor Einstein thought the studies were useless, who would disagree?

Appreciating the social and moral value of his works and their relevance to the history of man on Earth, a representative from the Vatican secured the minor manuscripts for inclusion in the voluminous repository in Rome. Finally, after a few years of sporadic inspection by die-hard devotees and erstwhile biographers of the German-American physicist, they were scanned into the digital record and the papers were processed for archiving.

The file went unnoticed and unopened for a long time until in 1987, Fr. Michel Denís, a Jesuit scholar and mathematical genius in his own right, ran across the documents while hunting for new areas of theory to explore. The name of the file had intrigued him. He didn't like what he found, especially in light of recent news about the creation of a new class of electrically powered weapons being unveiled at the time. He feared that with the advent of the supercomputer, people with less integrity and moral judgment than the late genius may, with the aid of the old notes, revive Einstein's quest for a mega-generator. Denís was troubled by rumors that there were teams of arms makers around the globe seeking to develop powerful weapons with the emerging Light Amplification by Stimulated Emission of Radiation or LASER technology.

Once it was discovered that an intensified light beam could be projected across great distances with remarkable precision, the natural question from the military-industrial complex was, "can we use it to destroy?"

Of course they could. It wouldn't be much of a leap from punching a tiny hole in a tomato can, to the invention of bar code readers, to the manufacture of heavy discharge laser artillery. But, as of yet, no one knew how to generate the massive amounts of electrical power required to fire a big ray gun. Back in Denís' time, the most powerful laser weapon under study was merely capable of delivering a nasty burn to a single soldier, if one would hold still long enough to be singed and if he wasn't wearing reflective clothing. A bigger limitation was that the time it took to recharge and fire again made it impractical for use in a firefight. So, Fr. Denís, in a vain attempt to alter history and delay the inevitable, turned the file folder inside out, re-labeled it, "Hellenic Archeology" and deliberately misplaced it. He knew this simple intrigue would make it highly unlikely that the paper file would ever be found again.

Sadly for the world, Adelina Calabrese knew precisely where the digital *Sackgassen* file lived and Einstein's notes were now in MAL's hands. If anyone could turn his idle musings into an unspeakable horror, it was them and it was now very likely that the men of America's Manhattan Project would no longer be the only ones to help a bloodthirsty genie escape the bottle.

Chapter 22

"Something's rotten, but it's not in Denmark."

Katrova and Forster had been at it for two weeks and life aboard the Kendall had settled into routine. Mornings for Natalie began at zero five forty-five with breakfast in the Officers Ward Room. The only interaction she had with the crew was the inquisitive and sometimes needy looks of the young men who messed with her. But their superiors had warned the gentlemen off. So unencumbered by the need to deal with their flirtations, Natalie took her usual low-fat yogurt from the modest buffet board, sat a discreet distance away from the men, perused the morning "Eyes Only" reading file through the fog of an oversized cup of hot java and prepared for her next session with Rex.

Lang rarely slept, repairing to his quarters for what the team called a "bat nap" whenever he began to nod off.

Forster and Moroder were the early birds; up at zero four-thirty and joining the ship's SEAL company in a testosterone-venting round of weight lifting, calisthenics and sprints around whatever perimeter they could navigate without testing the patience of a deck safety officer. Then it was a quick shower and a review of yesterday's lessons from the weapons manual. No one knew what occupied Comstock until the zero six-thirty SITREP briefing. But then, he was a spook by trade and no one really felt they would get a straight answer if they had inquired.

By zero seven-thirty, they were at their individual duty stations. Lang spent the day in the Combat Direction Center, maintaining his liaison with The Ten and reviewing downloads from their HUMINT and ELINT assets. Forster and Moroder drilled relentlessly on the rapid and efficient application of both mechanical and physical weapons. Essentially, it was their colleagues' job to find the damn machine. Moroder and Forster just had to kill it.

The team spent the afternoons analyzing raw data to sort legitimate clues from the extraneous and irrelevant and, despite some heated arguments and the suspicion they were all chasing wild geese, things were starting to look up.

In Bergen, Markus Haukken was recovering and remembering details; like the hazy outline of markings on the tail of the helicopter that bore Klax to the fjord and the direction it went when it departed and abandoned him there.

Then a field agent sent security camera video of Klax and an unidentified man boarding the jet in Ciampino. In Lang's mind that confirmed Klax was the perpetrator at the Vatican. The Ten would soon know from were the plane had come and where it had gone.

Investigators determined that Signorina Calabrese had copied the Einstein files to diskettes early the morning of the intrusion and assumed they were now in Klax' possession, although they were still searching

Adelina's flat and interrogating co-workers to determine the extent of the theft.

Satellite intel confirmed that no missiles were sent against Dr. Eva's compound the night she died. Radioactive residue from the site showed the source of the fissionable materials to be the generator that powered her compound. Not much more information would be gleaned from the blast site until the spring thaw.

In a seemingly unrelated but disturbing side bar, Natalie reported that Swedish police may have a mass murderer on their hands evidenced by a growing number of missing strippers, waitresses and club chicks. What perked Natalie's interest was that street people had supposedly witnessed some of the abductions. Through rheumy eyes and alcoholic breath a few of the local derelicts told of seeing scantily-dressed and apparently intoxicated party girls stumbling through a dark alley in the company of two stout men in short haircuts and black clothes. The bums called them "cunt commandos." It seemed like, for a short stretch of time, they would come nightly and disappear into the mist. Then for a long time, they wouldn't come at all.

"Bad guys preying on bad girls," Natalie shook her head, unsympathetically.

"Don't think there's news there Ms. Katrova," Lang said. "And our bad guys aren't into white slaving, they're into terrorism." Lang dismissed the report as irrelevant and asked Natalie to continue her briefing.

Then came a knock at the hatchway.

"Mr. Comstock, we just downloaded this image from your operative in Bergen, the messenger said. "The cover transmission just says, 'Bingo'."

Comstock handed an optical disk to Natalie.

"Let's have a look," he said.

Natalie inserted the shiny object into a CPU behind the conference table and a couple of mouse clicks later an image appeared on the monitor. It was a hand rendering of what looked to be a symbol or logo.

"What do you make of this Commander?" She queried Lang.

"I'm not sure," Lang said, leaning in. "What does the caption say?"

Natalie read aloud, as they all looked over her shoulder. "Reconstruction of helicopter markings, as reported by Markus Haukken, eyewitness to nuclear blast, Fensfjorden, Norway, 100416/21:18Z. Origin/definition UNK.

Superimposed over a ring of what appeared to be flames, were three capital letters – M.A.L.

"MAL?" Natalie looked quizzically at Comstock, then Lang.

"What or who is MAL?"

"Don't know, Nat," Comstock admitted. "Military Air Lift? Commander?"

"Nothing flicks up for me," Lang said, shaking his head. "Do anything for you, Luke? Moroder?"

They shook their heads.

"Negative," Forster said.

"Maybe a paramilitary group or an armed forces insignia from a field unit somewhere. But, I don't like the symbolism of a ring of fire around a globe. 'Kind of looks like someone wants to incinerate the world or something," Forster speculated.

"Katrova," Lang said, "Let's break this session up. I want you to get that image into Rex and see what he, I mean, *it* comes up with." He had picked up the habit of using a personal pronoun from Natalie. It was a slip. He thought it weird she did that.

"Sure thing," she replied. "If it's been used in any publication or electronically transmitted message or been sent somewhere for reproduction, Rex will find it."

"This ring a bell, Comstock?" Lang asked the CIA man.

He didn't reply.

"Comstock!" Lang raised his voice, "You with me, Boy?"

"Huh?" The man snapped out of his fog."

"No sir. The graphic doesn't register, but the acronym…MAL…I think I've seen it before. Something I picked up at Langley, maybe while I was in training back in ought-twenty. I'm going to get on the digicom and see what I can squeeze out of the analysts at HQ."

"You do that." Lang was starting to believe they were actually going to make some headway on this one. Experience had taught him that with the right people vetting the problem, even a tiny puzzle piece could lead to a solution and he had a hunch about this one. There was still the possibility that Haukken was hallucinating or that he had combined parts and pieces to manufacture it in his mind. The letters could be part of a navigation number, aircraft make or model, but he didn't think so. The goose flesh on his arm was Lang's subconscious telling him he was onto something. He went to help Katrova.

Nobody drove Rex like Natalie could. There were good ways to ask questions and there were ways that would spin the computer into a chaos of circular logic. Natalie had built Rex to be user-friendly though, even when the user was naïve about the brain's predilection for sophisticated heuristics. At such times, rather than voicing a rude, "Query invalid," Rex would reassuringly respond, "Abundant information is available on that subject, not all of which may be relevant. Would you like to be more specific about the nature of your inquiry?"

There was no such problem with Natalie at the microphone. After exchanging greetings, Natalie inserted the disk into the drive slot and asked her protégé, "Do you recognize this, Rex?"

He answered almost before she finished, "No, Natalie, I don't."

"How about the initials, M-A-L?"

"I have records of thirty-four million humans with those initials, surnames and given names, alive and deceased, including English transcreations of ideographic, cuneiform and hieroglyphic approximate translation matches. I also have sixteen thousand forty-one commercial enterprises, eighty-four hundred twelve governmental and quasi-governmental entities, four-hundred fifty-seven military para-military, police and political interest groups and seventy-seven musical organizations, mostly build around the letter "M," as in Mahler, Men-delssohn, Mozart…

"Rex?"

"Yes, Natalie."

"Limit your search to current day and show me only non govern-ment-affiliated militant, paramilitary and political action groups."

"Here they are, Natalie. There are sixty-six such organizations with the acronym, MAL. Would you like a printout, download or file trans-fer?"

"Let's look at them on screen first, Ms. Katrova," Lang's voice star-tled her.

"Eavesdropping, Commander?"

"Just thought I'd add another brain," he replied, unaffected by her rebuff. "Computer, scroll down," he ordered.

"He doesn't hear you," Natalie said, chafing at Lang's rudeness and lack of understanding about how Rex worked. He needs to recognize you and your voice before he'll respond.

"Okay, Miss Katrova, how do we get that done?"

"Rex, we have a partner for this session."

"Please identify yourself," Rex spoke to Lang.

In obvious discomfort, Lang addressed Rex, "Commander Wolf-gang Lang, USN."

"Welcome Commander Wolfgang Lang, USN.," Rex acknowledged. "How would you like to be addressed?"

"Sir," will do.

"Fine, Sir Willdo."

"No. Just, Sir-" Lang shot back, annoyed at the machine's lack of respect and its inability to get it right.

"He was making a joke, Commander."

"Shall I just call him Commander, Natalie?"

"Yes!" Lang affirmed.

"Very well, Commander Natalie."

Lang was getting angry and looked at Natalie with a full metal scowl. Natalie's smile vanished and she directed Rex.

"Suppress your humor program for now Rex; we've got some serious work to do."

A now serious Rex replied, "Commander, I need to sample and store your voice patterns for proper interaction. Would you please repeat after me? The quick brown fox jumped over the lazy dogs."

Lang repeated the tried and true phrase from the ancient days of high school touch typing class and Rex responded with a friendly, "Thank you Commander. How may I help you?"

Satisfied that they were now on speaking terms, Lang asked the machine to scroll through the list on the screen.

Macedonian Army Loyalists
Malaysian Legion
Mauritanian Army League
Mexican Army of Liberation
Michigan Aryans for Liberty
Mohammedan Army of Libya

This was going nowhere.

"All of these groups look like fronts for something or other", Lang said.

"Right," Katrova acknowledged. "I think we should look under a different rock."

"Let's take two tacks," Lang said. "First, let's check on the movements of Klax' known associates. He's got a small cadre of unsavory characters he runs with on and off. If we find them all in one corner of the world, we might at least be able to pin down the country they're working from. Secondly, if someone's planning to build this thing, they're going to need some pretty damn good scientists and some pretty exotic materials, maybe even more people to build or secure quarters for them. It might be that they intend to build a base of operations, if they don't already have one up and running."

"I think you've got something there, Commander, this operation has to be big. And Klax, moving around in heavy iron? Not his usual *modus operandi*. Whatever expense account he's using has taken him from eating combat rations in a hole somewhere in Eastern Europe to making trips to Rome in a private jet in broad daylight."

Lang said, "Another thing. I think he's too slick to use a front like a paramilitary group or terrorist cell. I think he's got legitimate cover, deep enough to let him operate in the open."

"Rex," Natalie was into it now, "Give me all known associates of Dagon Klax. Go back," she turned and glanced at Lang for confirmation, "five years."

He nodded. Then just for moment, he got caught in the depth of her eyes as she looked up at him. He could smell her too.

"Jesus," he thought and unknowingly said under his breath. He was unable to look away, even thought he wanted to.

Natalie caught him looking at her for longer than he ever had.

"Commander?" He was making Natalie uncomfortable.

"What?" Lang said, snapping out of it.

"You said, 'Jesus.' Something bugging you?"

"What?" He hadn't recovered. He was unaccustomed to being this close to a truly beautiful woman.

"Yes", he said, trying to reassure them both that he was paying attention to…something.

"Something on the screen?"

She thought she knew what had just happened and for all the grief he'd given her, she really didn't want to let it go. She enjoyed prolonging the awkwardness; another quirkiness in her personality from the days when the world's scientific community, and every man who had ever been close to her, had treated her badly.

"No.…Yes!" Lang stammered, now with a little extra sweat above his lip and a little more color than he wanted in his face.

"Never mind. I was thinking of something else," he said. "You and Rex just keep at it. And, you might want to check satellite intel for unusual flight plans for non-military air traffic. We know MAL's got a private jet and a helo; they may have a whole friggin' fleet of aircraft. I'll be briefing Forster. He's going to Rome tomorrow to follow up on the murders and see what the connection is."

Nat tried to catch his gaze again and said, "Thanks Wolf." She was shameless. "We'll keep digging."

She missed her shot at the befuddled officer. Lang was walking away.

"That's Commander Lang to you, Miss, and you're welcome." He felt sea sick.

For the next two weeks everyone went their own way.

Comstock wrangled Langley's efforts to identify MAL.

Forster got some good stuff in Rome. After waiting almost three days for clearance (not even The Ten could strong-arm The Church), Luke interviewed the pathologist who had performed the autopsies on Willi Berlith and Adelina Calabrese. Both were killed by an expert assassin; quietly, quickly and efficiently, with no noise and little mess. They never had a chance to defend themselves or even to react to the assault. The suspicion was that someone in MAL's hierarchy had gotten to Calabrese. She was one of three people on duty that day authorized to use the library computer system for duplication and release of files and her login to the Einstein archives had been noted at zero seven forty-five the morning of her murder. The disks she had checked out of the supply cabinet to make copies were missing and presumed to be in Klax' hands.

The Swiss Guardsman was probably killed because he got in the way. He could have been an accomplice but his background and psychological profile didn't support that assumption.

Forster took copies of the compromised files, obtained a duplicate of the security videotape from Klax' visit to Ciampino, and returned to the Kendall, impatient to see how his pieces fit into the big puzzle.

In the U.S., Lieutenant Dennis Rackoff, an ace Naval Operations investigator had at Lang's direction, begun his debriefing of Professor Larry Craigh from the University of Illinois. Luknar's machine was headed his way when the bomb went off. When it didn't arrive, he contacted the Navy to inquire about its transit status. He was devastated to learn that the device had been destroyed. The Navy was happy for the lead out of the blue. Craigh wasn't informed about the missing disk.

Since it never made it out of the fjord and he had seen neither plans nor prototype, Craigh wasn't able to tell Rackoff much about the device itself, but he had two pieces of information that were relevant. He confirmed that Luknar had abandoned her project and was sending the machine to him to, if possible, correct a disastrous flaw. Somehow, an unforeseen glitch had turned the thing from a therapeutic treatment device to a death ray so powerful and unpredictable that Luknar couldn't live with the guilt of its invention, especially knowing that others, perhaps military people or terrorists, may be aware of its existence. Craigh showed the agent the InterVid transmission he had received from her and they discussed the power problem. The doctor unknowingly prophesied, "Well, Mr. Rackoff, it may be a good thing that Eva's machine was destroyed. It won't cure anybody without radical modification and operating the thing as it is would be unwise and reckless."

Rackoff raised his eyebrows at Craigh's Pollyannaish point of view, "I think that's inevitable Doctor."

"Why would anyone want to do such a thing? He replied. "If these people can make the necessary modifications, they would own the most important piece of healing technology since the AIDS vaccine. It would be worth millions, billions if they could achieve the ends for which the machine was intended. You said you have evidence that the group who has the machine plans has also obtained information that may help them generate a large volume of electrical power?"

"Yes, apparently at the cost of two more lives," Rackoff confirmed.

"That makes sense. It was a power problem that Dr. Luknar identified as the machine's shortcoming. She needed more power to eliminate the possibility of starting a chain reaction and to localize the effect of the primary particle beam so it could be used for microsurgery. If that power could be generated, controlled and focused, the machine apparently would work the way it was intended. A single such device could save a dozen lives a day. If it was mass-produced, thousands of lives a day. Greed is a terrible sin, Mr. Rackoff, but if the outcome saves so many, the end may justify the means. I tend to think that your villains have an economic motive, if not one based on the needs of someone's inflated ego or quest for acclaim and celebrity. It's not like such a thing is without precedent in science."

"Dr. Craigh…" He paused to think out his words before he spoke. "What if our villains, as you call them, are not looking to generate more power to control the beam? What if they are looking to add more power to generate the beam?"

"Surely not, Mr. Rackoff," the doctor replied, disturbed at the possibility. The machine is, or was, already sufficiently dangerous to cause the emotional breakdown and suicide of one of the most brilliant physicists of our time. Who would want to make it deadlier by adding more power to the beam generator? It's a frightening thought."

"How so?"

"Dr. Luknar was operating in what many of us believed to be a very dangerous area of research. But, but, let me take you back in time, just a little. Please bear with me. The use of particle beams in commerce and industry has not progressed much since the proliferation of laser technology in the 1980's. Today, we can precision-cut some hard industrial materials. We can entertain football fans at half time with some pretty flashy light shows. The military uses lasers for missile guidance and they developed the laser rifle just after the turn of the century. But, these are trivial applications when you look at the overall potential of particle beam physics. Medicine as well has not done much to further particle beam utility. We can do some minor ophthalmic and plastic surgery procedures and permanently remove unwanted body hair. Beyond this, no quantum leaps have been made. The reason is that adding power to such energy streams has not yet resulted in better output, just stronger. Have you ever heard of the work of Barbara Van Anter?"

Recalling who he was talking to, Craigh answered his own question, "No, no of course not. Van Anter was the first to follow-up on the earlier work of McDonald, New and Chang. Late in the twentieth century, they published the results of experiments that confirmed that when dense, powerful light is shot through the air, the air itself can generate more light, even ultra-broad bandwidth light, not just passing along highly stimulated photons, but propagating the very energy that propels the light. Their results excited many people and led to a profusion of new studies back then. People even began to believe that highly intense energy could be broadcast through ambient air in beams that were several meters wide and equally deep. It never came to pass. What happened instead was, the energy dispersed instantly in all directions. The photons in the beam followed the very molecular matrix of the air itself. The force of the beam, regardless of how much power was used to generate it, dissipated, weakened and dispersed, harmlessly.

You could almost hear the collective sigh of disappointment from the dreamers in science and industry. The long-anticipated tunnel boring machines that would cleave great roadways through the world's impassable places and terrible battle field "enemy sweepers" that would kill thousands of infantrymen in one pass were never built because the very vehicle that provided the medium for the transmission of the energy was an amorphous cloud of gas, not a directed flow. Do you understand?"

"I think so," Rackoff said, straining his recollection of college-level physics and his attention span. "What you're saying is that they were never able to produce, focus and aim a beam wide enough to be broadcast with any significant force. A wide beam can't be fired like a rifle. It goes off in all directions like a bomb.

"Yes, precisely. The energy radiated like a bomb but without the force. That's why you soldiers still use explosives to do the heavy killing today."

Rackoff felt the scientist's distress, "Why the glum look, Doc? It sounds like we're all better off without the big beam."

"Yes. I think we are, Mr. Rackoff. But, Eva Luknar wasn't working on a light beam concentrator. Before her death, we had many conversations about her device. I'm afraid she came across something much more dangerous than a high output laser."

For the next two hours Larry Craigh described in layman's terms what he knew of Dr. Luknar's research, her hopes for TVap therapy as a viable cancer treatment modality and the incredibly effective carbon atom rending effect of her machine's beam. He then detailed the problems she encountered and the horrific lab animal fatalities.

Then he told Rackoff the worst of it. Eva Luknar's beam didn't dissipate in the air like a laser. As well as being transferred by physical contact from carcinoma to healthy body tissue, the air passed its effect along, handing it off from carbon molecule to carbon molecule. From tumor, to tissue, to table, to the air itself, and so on to any matter in the immediate proximity. If a molecule contained carbon, it took a hit, disintegrated and passed the energy on - four carbon atoms each loosed to break the bonds of four others, multiplying by a factor of four every time it struck. The denser the air, the faster it worked. It became a self-sustained chain reaction that carried the effect through the air like a shock wave.

Rackoff listened carefully, his mind boggled, and when the scientist was finished with his explanation he knew that The Ten had not exaggerated the peril in which the world had been placed.

"I hate to be rude Dr. Craigh, but you still haven't answered my question. What if the other people we suspect to have an interest in Luknar's machine are successful in rebuilding it and they add massive amounts of power to the beam generator?"

"I don't know. What I've told you is very general information and I haven't seen Eva's plans."

"Guess."

"Catastrophe. Cataclysm. The Apocalypse!"

"C'mon Doc, I need accurate information here, not exaggeration."

"Exaggeration?" The doctor's face reddened and he stood, knocking an avalanche of papers from his desk. He screamed at the agent, "Look Mr. G-man or whatever you are, you don't get it, do you? If they add power to the generation side, the effect could be huge. It might dissolve a city block. Or, they may start a chain reaction that can't be controlled. Period! It won't start and finish. It will start and keep going. Each atom of air firing up each successive atom of air until everything in contact with the effect disintegrates. You see," he said still exorcised, "You are made of carbon. The trees and the grass are made of carbon. It's in the earth, in every plant and flower, in steel and plastic and…"

"Dr. Craigh," Rackoff said, trying vainly to calm the man. "Please."

Two lab-coated women burst through his office door, alarmed at the clamor.

"Larry, are you all right?" The older of the two women asked. She glowered at the agent.

"Get out of here!" The younger woman barked at agent Rackoff.

"No. No. I'm okay. It's my fault," Craigh tried to reassure her. "I'm fine. Really Jessie, Meg. I'm fine. I was just venting some frustration on this young man." He smoothed his course white hair, centered his glasses back on his nose and bent to pick-up the strewn papers.

"Dr. Craigh, are you…"

"Yes, Meghan. I'm fine. Please, let me finish my conversation with Mr. Rackoff."

The women looked at Rackoff as if he were a thug and grudgingly slid from the room.

"We're here if you need us," Jessie spoke coolly, not taking her eyes off Rackoff as she backed through the doorway.

Craigh turned to the agent and said, "I am sorry, Mr. Rackoff. Until you find the plans or Eva's notes and bring them to me, there's nothing I can do. Eva Luknar and I were colleagues and good friends. Good friends. I haven't slept well since her death and my work and my health are suffering. I want to help you and I will help you. I know very well the seriousness of this matter, but you must find something for me to go on. Something. If that information cannot be retrieved, destroy whatever you find. Another machine cannot be built, unless I build it. Do you understand?"

"I understand," Rackoff said, reading the fear in Craigh's reddened eyes. I do."

Rackoff left the building in a funk. It was a rare, warm and cloudless November day in Chicago, but he felt a chill as he keyed open the door to his rented PTV. He slumped into the seat, rested his hands on the steering yoke and hung his head. Looking out through the windscreen but seeing nothing, he took a deep breath and began punching Wolf Lang's number into his digicom.

Aboard the USS Kendall, Lang listened to Rackoff's report with dismay. Forster was on his way back from Rome, but Lang summoned Katrova and Comstock and gave them the update, "Now we know why Klax wanted the notes on the power transformer."

"Yes," Katrova said, "but we also know that he and his associates may be charging headlong into an event that could destroy them and everything around them. They can't be aware of the danger of putting so much power into the device that they might create a self-sustaining chain reaction." She looked at Comstock for concurrence.

Comstock wasn't sure. "We don't know what they know, Natalie," he said. "Maybe our friend Dr. Craigh is right and they really just want to perfect the thing for medical use. You think a few billion dollars is enough motivation to make the bad guys go straight?"

Natalie brightened. "Well, we don't even know we have bad guys on our hands, do we? Maybe MAL stands for Medicine Against Lesions or something, and Klax being part of the group is just a bad personnel decision."

Lang burst her bubble.

"Here's what we do know Miss Katrova. Someone connected to Klax or his people got to Connie Woodless. The guy was Forster's handler, and he operated at the top echelon of this country's intelligence infrastructure. Whatever they offered him or threatened him with, it must have been somethin' to break that man's faith. I knew him. The man was a goddamned patriot. When Woodless wasn't able to turn Forster, he tried to terminate our boy on the spot. That's some freakin' change of attitude for one of his best friends. Then Klax shows up in Norway. He enters a nuclear blast zone, rips off some highly classified U.S. Government property, shoots an already seriously injured man and leaves him to die. Then the bastard jets to Rome and wastes two more individuals within the walls of the Vatican. All this to benefit mankind? Bullshit! We're not dealing with Mouseketeers here Miss. And Comstock, you should know better than to blow sunshine up her skirt."

"Sorry, Sir," the CIA man responded sheepishly, "It's just that an army of mad scientists working to create a weapon that could very well destroy them along with their enemies is sounding pretty far-fetched."

Lang struggled to maintain his demeanor. The distended veins in his neck punctuated his ire.

"Far-fetched or not Mr. Comstock, we'll keep at it! The Ten is concerned. Dr. Craigh is concerned and I'm concerned. This mission will continue until we find Klax and the plans to that device. Clear?"

Two heads nodded, both already contemplating the prospect of living out their days aboard the Kendall.

Weeks went by and the Repo team still had nothing on Klax, MAL or the plans for the machine. But no one in the group was willing to fold. Whether it was the gargantuan dimension of the egos involved or their raw competitive natures, the tensions that evolved from their lack of progress had been converted into a stubborn determination. Lang finally had them all believing that a breakthrough was more likely to come from perspiration than inspiration or waiting for the enemy to make a mistake.

Through the Christmas holidays, except for Comstock and Moroder who had families with whom to share the joy of the season, the team persisted. Lang kept daily liaison with The Ten. Katrova and Rex were alternately creating and exploring ways to scout MAL's tracks. Everyone and everything left traces of their movements, no matter how subtle. They just had to find out how to interpret the signs.

Forster started grueling two-a-day sessions with the Kendall's hand-to-hand combat chief, honing mental, physical and fighting skills to a razor's edge and pushing the instructor to the limit of his abilities and endurance. Forster and Katrova even sparred a few spirited rounds with pads and headgear. Luke declared himself the winner after the bout. She never acknowledged defeat. Deep down, he admired her mastery of the martial arts and he admitted to himself that it was his strength that gave him the edge. She was exceptionally fast and had better technique. But, could she really fight against an opponent who was trying to kill her? He hoped she never had to find out. She had a tendency to lose her temper and even a momentary lapse of concentration could give a more disciplined foe enough of an edge to triumph.

Mostly the time dragged, but they persevered, hardly stopping to acknowledge the birth of the new year. Then, in the bitter darkness of a January morning in the Norwegian Sea, Natalie and Rex broke through.

The intercom woke Lang in his quarters. Trying to make his eyes work with the dim night light above his rack, he groped for the handset. "Lang," he said his throat thick and his voice sleep-fuzzy.

"Commander, it's Natalie. I have something you need to see."

"On my way."

Lang was still buttoning his shirt when he entered Natalie's workstation.

"Whatcha got?"

"Two arrows, Sir, pointing in the same direction."

"A little more clarity, please Miss Katrova."

"Yes, Sir. When we launched Project Repo, I asked Rex to stay alert for any signal intelligence containing the letters M-A-L, with our without punctuation, in any language or letterform. Rex, tell Commander Lang what you found."

"Good morning, Commander Lang," Rex greeted the officer.

"Yeah. 'Morning Rex," Lang responded, uncomfortable with pleasantries, especially at this hour and with a smart-ass computer. "What's up?"

"Commander Lang, I have recovered an NSA recording of a short wave radio transmission, sent four days ago from an unidentified sender, at an unspecified location in the Ahvenanmaa Archipelago, addressed to a registered recipient in northern Germany. Would you like to hear it?"

Lang rolled his eyes. Natalie read his impatience.

"Yes, Rex, she said. We'd like to hear it."

"It's in German."

"Translate to English, please, Rex," Katrova said.

"Do you want a literal or a colloquial translation, Natalie?"

"Just, get on with it!" Lang was burning as he motioned to a passing yeoman to get him coffee.

It says, "Gerd, is that you Gerd?"

"Yes, Helmut, this is Gerd, go ahead please, sun flux is making your signal weak. I'm trying to hold you."

"There is more static, Rex said, "Then, the sender says,"

'Gerd, tell Mutti I won't be home for Christmas. I'm sorry…so sorry. This year I won't be there to light the *Adventskraanz* with you and Hilde. MAL keeps me working. I won't see *Der Weihnachts-mann* and the presents. None of your fine Christmas carp for me. I shall miss it all. Gerd, will you tell her? Tell her please. They won't let me-."

"There is more static," Rex said, "Then, the transmission ends."

"MAL," Lang said, narrowing his eyes. "Is this our MAL, or is this just a name of a lonely Kraut's Scroogey boss? And, what do you think that 'Vy nots man' is all about? Another code name?"

"Perhaps Commander Lang," Rex voiced. "But in German, *Der Weihnachtsmann* is Father Christmas, in some western cultures, Santa Claus. The *Adventskraanz* he speaks of is what Christians would call in English an Advent wreath. You know, pine boughs, candles, that sort of thing. It signifies the imminent birth of -"

"Christ! I know what it signifies, Rex," Lang said, losing the last smidgen of his patience. "I'm a recovering Catholic. What do you think, Katrova? Is this code-speak?"

"Could be, Commander," Natalie said. "But I don't think so. It doesn't sound sinister. I think we just have a homesick boy telling a relative he won't be home for the holidays," Natalie said. "Lucky for us he used a radio with an unencrypted signal to phone home."

"What else do you have?" Lang chaffed.

"Rex, recall the pix from the Stockholm Police file, please."

"Here it is Natalie," the computer complied and displayed what appeared to be a human forearm with a tattoo.

"Zoom in on the tattoo, crop to the full window and rotate counter-clockwise to vertical please Rex."

They watched as the tattoo enlarged, filled the screen and straightened. It was very much the same as the symbol Haukken had described as being on Klax' helicopter at the blast scene.

"That's it! That's MAL's insignia," Lang exclaimed. "Where is this guy? We've got to interrogate him now." Lang was energized by their good fortune.

"Not possible, Sir," Katrova said. "The man attached to this arm was found floating face down off a pier at the *Stockholms Hamn*. According to the police report, a bullet punched a whole in his heart. The local police were stymied for days. Pistol killings are pretty rare in Sweden. Then a club girl, name of Karinna Stenstrom, turned herself in. According to her police statement the dead guy and an accomplice tried to convince her to go with them to a private party. She was pretty high and she said the guys were cute and flashing wads of money, so she was game at the start, but the more the two started talking about a helicopter ride and asking if anyone would mind if she were gone for awhile, the more she sniffed trouble. She knew about the Stockholm kidnappings. She has a friend who's still missing, so she started to resist.

One of the perpetrators, evidently the dead guy, started getting rough. She panicked and started yelling her head off. He roughed her up, popped her a black eye and grabbed at her shirt. She got loose, managed to pull a .25-caliber pistol from her bag and plugged him. She knew having the gun would mean big trouble, so she ran. Evidently the guy's partner panicked, too. I figure he didn't want to carry the corpse around and he didn't want the police to find it, so he dumped his buddy in the channel. A longshoreman found him, head banging against a piling in the wake of some passing boats."

"A cunt commando?" Lang asked, recalling Natalie's earlier report.

"I guess the old sots weren't imagining this stuff. But Commander, could we just call him an asshole? That other thing you said is repulsive."

"You can call him a lead, Katrova. A dead lead, but a lead. So what we've got here is a dead MAL guy who's into bar chicks and a homesick Kraut on an island…where? Where is that Aven Mama place, Rex? Show me."

"Here is Ahvenanmaa, Commander Lang. Sixty degrees, two minutes, north latitude, twenty degrees east longitude."

Rex brought up a graphic showing the island cluster in the Aland Sea separating Sweden from Finland and connecting the Gulf of Bothnia with the Baltic Sea.

"Looks like a great place for a rat's nest," Lang said. "What's there?"

"Fishing villages, small tourist inns and a few miles of bike paths, Commander. The text on their InterVid tourism site says it's very pretty and the natives are congenial," Rex editorialized.

"Show me where this place is in relation to Stockholm, Rex."

"It's proximal, Commander. What you might call, right next door."

Rex zoomed out on the map. Stockholm came into view to the southwest in just a few clicks.

"Estimate the distance between Ahvenanmaa and Stockholm, Rex."

"From Mariehamn, the principle city on Ahvenanmaa to Stockholm is one hundred and forty kilometers or eighty six point nine nine six miles, Commander. As the crow flies."

"Good work, Katrova. Congratulations," he was sincere in his compliments.

"Thank you, Commander," Rex added.

"Yeah, uh…you too, Rex." He instructed Katrova, "Comstock and Moroder are due back at fourteen hundred hours. I want you all in the briefing room at fourteen-thirty. We're going to put that island under the microscope. In the meantime, I want you and Rex the wonder brain to give me everything you've got on that place, including air and sea traffic for the last year, and let's have our intelsats take a look at it under infrared, radiation, photo and thermal sensors, the full array. I want that placed jacked up and looked under if we have to. I'm going to call The

Ten and see if we can get some ground intel in there. And, I'm putting four SEAL teams on standby."

Lang took a step to leave before Katrova caught him. "Sir, I think we should check out that short wave transceiver, too. The sender used a bogus call sign - no registration on file, but the guy that acknowledged the message used a real one and it was in the registry. Gerd Bogaert resides 42A Shifdorfstrasse, Schleswig."

"Right," Lang responded, a little embarrassed that she had to call the oversight to his attention and that his excitement at the new smells on the ground had blunted his usual penchant for thoroughness. "Give that one to Comstock," he ordered. "Let's see if he still remembers his street stuff."

Comstock and Moroder returned from holiday leave just before the afternoon briefing but beyond a quick greeting, there was no time for fellowship and telling family stories. Being the good Midwestern boy he was Comstock brought each of the males on the team a pint of top-shelf booze (mashed bows on the bottles and all) and Natalie a box of Belgian chocolates.

Moroder brought them each a rosary blessed by the bishop of his diocese. He knew that Lang would dismiss the gift as superstitious clap-trap, but that he would keep it anyway. Mo knew the group could use the help.

After some perfunctory grats from the boys and a smooch from Natalie (Moroder went googly and didn't wash his cheek for two days) they got down to business.

Lang and Katrova shared their progress with the team and afterward they all got butterflies. Then Natalie asked Comstock whether he had come up with anything on his recollection of MAL during his training.

"Jeez, I almost spaced it," he admitted. "I'm not sure this is relevant, but at least I know I didn't dream the initials up."

He drew a single-sheet fax from his attaché case and began.

"Back in the '80s and '90s the agency was involved in some sensitive field work infiltrating eco-terrorist groups, as they were called then, to see if they had more sinister activities in mind than hugging trees and harassing fishing boats. Some of our senior people suspected they were being manipulated by people hostile to the U.S. to help them stall development of our natural and petro-resources and keep us at the mercy of an organization called OPEC, a price-fixing cartel with Middle-Eastern and South American membership. As it turned out there was nothing there and the investigation was kyboshed. But, while we were patting them down, we uncovered some stuff about some extremists calling themselves the Malthusian Advocacy League. It was run by Amazon rain forest preservationists who thought there should be more population control so the world wouldn't need to whack down all the trees on the planet to build condos and grow corn to feed beef cattle. They talked a big, mean game, but their assets were limited and no one outside of Brazil gave a damn. But, that was a long time ago and I can't imagine a group that wanted to save the environment for humanity would be trying to build a machine to kill people and save the plants. Sounds kinda convoluted to me."

Wolf Lang looked puzzled.

"Comstock, what's a Malthusian?" He asked in his simple, 'there are no dumb questions' manner.

Katrova took the question.

"Thomas Malthus was a late eighteenth and early nineteenth century political philosopher, Commander. He and Charlie Darwin wrote some papers that outraged a lot of people back then about how, if human breeding couldn't be brought into check, that people, just like animals in a contained eco-system, would eventually over breed and outstrip the environment's ability to provide food. In short, they would eat and breed themselves into extinction. Subsequent true believers took Malthus' theory to more of an extreme and said that disease, war and famine were

God-given means of natural selection and that they provided a control mechanism to keep populations down and prevent over-habitation."

Comstock caught her drift and a light went on in his head. "Natalie, you may have nailed it."

"I thought you said this was a blind alley, Comstock?" Forster countered.

"Well, I thought it was, until Natalie said that Malthus' successors took his theories to an extreme." He tilted forward and everyone at the table leaned in attentively.

"You see it wasn't only Malthus' contemporaries that pushed the limits of logic with the philosophical extension that famine and plague were God's control system for long-term human survival. In the late twentieth century a guy named Paul Ehrlich, a Ph.D. from the University of Kansas, published a book called, 'The Population Bomb' that expounded Malthus' ideas in a new wrapper. He even founded a group called ZPG, short for Zero Population Growth, and sold memberships to raise money to push his agenda. He was pretty harmless and perceived as part of the lunatic fringe, but he was the first to be so globally aggressive in presenting Malthus' theories, or his derivations of those ideas, and he was the first to have the benefit of mass communications and an interconnected world press to spread his gospel. At one point, he claimed the U.S. had achieved zero growth and attributed it to his intervention and wise, widespread use of the just-introduced birth control pill. Although most of the countries in Asia, Africa and India never did buy into the idea and just kept on doin' what comes naturally.

When his predictions that tens of millions would die of starvation in the '70s and '80s didn't come to pass, he kind of faded from sight. But, Erlich brought Malthus back into the intellectual fray on the subject and inspired extreme thought on both sides of the argument. In the '90s there were huge political battles over the 'right to life' and the consequences of uncontrolled population growth. Some still think that the increase in mass murders, mass starvations and disease epidemics in Africa and youth violence at the turn of the century was the natural product of the escalation of competitive economic and societal pressures, and sheer overcrowding.

Eventually, a new crop of madmen picked up Ehrlich's philosophy and all of a sudden, there were a half-dozen tin-horn dictators, armed madmen and bio-weapons terrorists using Ehrlich's and Malthus' writings to justify mass murder and genocide. Remember the *Lettino Silenzioso*, the silent cradle killers in Italy in ought-16?"

The team as one bent and nodded their heads, recalling the slaughter of sixty-two infants that year.

"The killers were never caught and it was only the assignment of armed *Carabineri* and similar security moves in hospitals throughout Europe that brought and end to the carnage. Remember the sound bites of the phone call to the television station saying that there were enough people in Europe?" Again, they nodded.

"Yeah," Comstock continued, "A lot of people, sick of bad air, bad water and rush-hour traffic started to ignore large-scale tragedy, like it wasn't really happening - you know earthquakes, floods, the Bosnian and Hutu ethnic cleansing episodes, the AIDS and Ebola virus epidemics? Some experts thought it was just desensitization or emotional overload. Others took it as evidence that we reached the limit of humanity's ability to tolerate each other."

"That's dumb." Moroder disagreed with what the CIA man was saying.

"People need each other, especially if there's a lot of them around in a cramped space. Remember 9-11-01? Bad things tend to bring us together."

Natalie smiled at Mo's provincial view.

"You're right, Mo. But, that's a uniquely Western view of the sanctity of life. Unfortunately, not everyone shares that philosophy. What if overpopulation is what this is all about? What if this is the twenty-first century version of that same ZPG faction? But, for the sake of argument, let's say our MAL guys aren't just political activists? What if this group is bigger, more vicious and what if it has the resources to gear up and kill a lot of people? Maybe the plan is to kill millions of people and do exactly what you said, Jim Comstock. Get rid of the people to save the plants."

"Natalie," Forster chided. That's rid-"

"No, Forster, hear her out," Lang said, listening hard.

"Look at it their way. With millions, even billions of people dead, the planet, in a few hundred years, would start to heal itself. We know that there have been catastrophic natural disasters much worse than man has caused, things like the meteor impact that killed the dinosaurs and the Tunguska blast in Siberia, and the Krakatau volcano eruption that stressed the planet's geophysical structure to the max. But, whether it took decades or centuries or epochs, Mother Earth repaired it all herself.

From that point of view, MAL could rationalize taking out a few major cities, eliminate the consuming masses that are beating down their precious environment and in just a few moments of relative geological time, all would be well. The whole joint would be green as the felt on a pool table."

She finished, breathing hard. She was internalizing the possibilities and she was scared.

"*Dio Mio*," Moroder said as he made the sign of the cross.

"What happened to Medicine Against Lesions?" Lang asked.

"Not funny, Commander," Natalie said, humorlessly. "I have a creepy feeling about this."

"I think we've all had our heads in the toilet for too long," Forster said, "After a while, everything starts smelling like shit."

"Look," Lang replied. "We don't know what we're dealing with here, but Katrova and Comstock have given us something to go on. We won't know for certain until we get out there and pound some ground."

So, Wolf Lang gave the team their assignments; Comstock to track down the radioman in Schleswig; Moroder and Forster to make for the

Port of Stockholm to see if they could bag one of Natalie's "assholes" and Natalie, following an especially noisy protest, back to Rex to corroborate and cross-correlate the information they would soon get from space intel.

Why should she have to stay cooped up on this can when the boys got to breathe fresh air and stretch their legs?

"Asset allocation, Ms. Katrova," Lang retorted intolerant of her protest. "We put the brain with the brain and the feet on the street."

No one liked the way he put that.

"We'll meet again for debriefing in forty-eight hours," Lang said. We've wasted too much time already.

"Wasted?" You-"

"Ms. Katrova, Rex is waiting for you," Lang interrupted with emphasis. "Gentlemen, you're dismissed."

Chapter 23

"Insectus slaughterus"

MAL's scientists, some working on their own accord under personal contract with the leadership, others conscripted through intimidation and the threat of violence against their families, had been working around the clock for months and progress came with great difficulty. The hastily assembled mob of eggheads, most of whom had only a working knowledge of each other's languages, had to rely on Simultrans sets for communication and depending on each individual's diction and articulation, the voice-activated digital translators either mediated the problems or exacerbated them. Occasionally, comical fisticuffs resulted from the combination of problems caused by the idiosyncrasies of the translator's programming and the idioms of a particular language. One very surprised Hungarian man got his nose broken by a Spanish female colleague when he thought he was commenting about the warmth of the building that morning but his Simultrans had erred and called her a "little hottie." These were though among the least of their problems.

The biggest challenge was the myriad disagreements about the physical design and assembly of the machine - joining the components into parts, turning parts into sub-assemblies and finally shaping the finished device. Eva's disk had provided them with the electrical and mechanical schematics, but without an assembled prototype they were left to their own visions of the product's ultimate appearance. Eventually, it was decided, with Klax' input, that the thing should look threatening, like a mythical monster, perhaps a Cyclops or maybe an ugly bug. Yes, a scorpion. Klax had offered that from a public relations standpoint, the more terrifying the thing looked, the faster MAL would be able to dictate the terms of surrender. They took his advice.

That decision made, there was still the problem of locating supplies of the rare earth metals and sophisticated alloys for the beam generator and the hyper-dense, matte-black ceramic shell that would shield the carbon-based components within from the effects of the beam. Without the shell, the machine would certainly dissolve itself. The thing was coming together though, and today there was great excitement on Alpha Island. It was to be the first test firing of the beam generator.

All morning the tension in the cavernous main laboratory had been palpable. Dozens of technicians in white jumpsuits and anti-static booties, some in hazmat helmets, some with headsets and some with hand-held computers, buzzed around the ugly structure that would eventually become the business end of the venomous arthropod's doppelganger.

The beam generator was designed to simulate the bug's hideous telson - the poison gland and its aculeus (the venom needle itself). That was mounted atop a re-curved aperture that faired down in thickness from base to tip and pointed ominously forward from a height of five meters above the floor. A series of decreasing-radius concentrator mirrors wrapped the aperture in ovoid, telescoping scales from the point of the needle back three meters or so. The mirrors were made of enhanced liquid mercury to maximize reflectance and ensure beam containment. That particular feature was one of Eva's proudest technological triumphs. Exposed, as it was in MAL's iteration of the device, the weird random rippling motion of the substance gave the impression that the thing had life, but out in the open as it was, it made a few of the workers queasy during assembly and no-one could look at the undulating content of the mirrors for long without being overcome by nausea.

The stinger-like aperture had been MAL's innovation. Eva Luknar had built the device to heal and had incorporated the beam generator into a benign-looking hospital white hood to avoid disquieting her patients while they were being treated. To suit its reincarnation as a weapon, MAL's designers concurred that the need to aim the device at ground targets and elevate it for anti-aircraft use dictated a more practical configuration. A user-friendly cosmetic was now superfluous.

As Klax prowled his room, watching the assembly on one of a small bank of video monitors, a tone from his digicom announced an incoming call. Warden Llorca's voice scratched from the small speaker.

"Mr. Klax, we are ready for the static and live target test. Please, you will meet me in the control room."

"On my way, Sir." Klax exited his quarters and boarded the electromotive cart outside. As he headed down the dim tunnel toward the main lab, he was not nearly as excited as he had been the day before, when he thought the first firing would be on a human target. Today's test would only involve a dry firing at a fraction of the machine's power capacity then a test on an animal subject.

When he arrived at the thick blast doors to the main lab, the two guards had already begun to open them. Because of their heft, it would take some time before he could clear the portal. Klax waited impatiently as the two-foot thick concrete and steel slabs pulled back under the whiny strain of electric motors. As the crack between the doors widened, Klax' heart leapt at the evil revealed before him.

Overhead, sodium vapor lamps were switching off all around the machine and photofloods were being pushed into place to permit thorough video documentation of the event. As he entered and circumnavigated the assembly pit and turntable that facilitated access to the machine's innards, he could see sparks and molten metal shards falling and bursting like mini-fireworks on the lab floor as fabricators made the most of the final minutes before the test. A spotlight snapped on and focused on the first test target, a cross of wooden rails. Each axis was four meters long. The rails were a third of a meter square, mounted like a giant "X", ten meters in front of the tip of the Scorpion's elongated, crystal blue beam needle. Behind it a cove of white ceramic tiles spanned the wall to the ceiling to assure containment of the beam and its effect on the target.

Klax revolved where he stood, slowly, to drink in the scene. Behind and above him a small observation gallery was beginning to fill with MAL's senior scientists. A few of the Wardens also had taken their seats and were adjusting the protective eyewear and Kevlar vests provided them. At regular intervals, Klax could hear nervous laughter above their anxious whispers.

Beyond the machine was a second pit twenty meters in diameter, covered in a low glass dome. It resembled the primary lens of a compound eye, for beneath it were rank on rank of control and sensor monitors; the glowering blue data screens like so many sub-lenses, and a technician studying each, reciting checklist items into their headsets in monotone, multi-accented English.

There was good reason for anxiety. No one in the room knew precisely what was about to happen. During the development of standard laser weaponry there had been hundreds of failed tests resulting in the death or maiming of dozens of technicians and observers.

MAL's scientists still anticipated that the machine's beam would affect only the designated target. Yet, among the re-builders of Dr. Luknar's machine, there was great controversy about potential outcomes.

Could the effects be localized? Some said the target would absorb the beam and its energy would only be transmitted within the target itself by intercellular or intermolecular contact, much the same way that the process of osmosis transported liquid from cell to cell.

Others said the beam would hit the target and wrap it in a cloud of charged particles that could only be contained by an instant reduction of electrical power to the beam generator. They worried that too much power or too long a burst would create a ball of searing-hot plasma that would envelop everything in the room in a sphere of death.

A third group had a more dire prediction. These and they were very much in the minority, surmised that once the beam was generated it would become self-sustaining and feed off the energy released by the destruction of organic material around it. This theory implied that the effect, once begun, would be transmitted through the disintegration of the organic molecules of ambient air; the carbon monoxide, methane, suspended dust particles, spores and bacteria, and would continue until the organic matter around it was no longer dense enough to support continuation of the reaction. If the beam were to be employed in a desert environment, these men believed, there wouldn't be sufficient organic material density and destruction to sustain the effect. But, if it were fired in a rain forest, it could continue unabated until the entire expanse was destroyed.

They were all partially right and wrong and they would know to what extent shortly. They all agreed precise control of the power input would be critical. Eventually MAL would have a complete understanding of how to create just the right results, but prudence dictated that they proceed slowly.

The Einstein coil was still under construction and would not be used for this test. For now, a comparatively anemic input would be used, with no more power than it would take to light and heat a small home. Cautiously, they would increase the power and measure the results.

Unlike Eva Luknar's version this machine, MAL reasoned that the Scorpion had no need for a secondary power supply to constrain the beam's effects, or for the tertiary patient comfort circuitry. They wanted maximum devastation from the thing. Frills were unnecessary.

A loudspeaker punched through the spit of the arc welders and the technicians' chatter. The words clanged off the walls.

"Counting down ten minutes to initial test. Ten minutes to test. Start primary generator," the voice from the control room said. "Observers, to your places. This bay will lock down in one minute. One minute to lock down."

Klax ascended the staircase to the observation gallery and took his seat in the row behind the Wardens, feeling the slight of not being able to sit in the front row next to Llorca. As the final clutch of Wardens arrived and took their places, they and the scientists among them made an attempt at upbeat banter, even as the sweat from their palms warped the papers on their clipboards.

On the main floor, the fabricators were clearing the last of their equipment from the area and fastening the access panels over the machine's innards. A serious-looking, twitchy little man sat behind the Scorpion at a mock-up of the machine's firing station and manipulated the joystick at the center of his console. As he did so, a fine sighting laser projected cross hairs on the timber target. When he was certain that the cross hairs rested at the crux, he spoke into his headset.

"We are sighted and standing by," he said, his voice thick with apprehension.

"Power to the primary generator...now," the test director commanded. "Set for one one-hundredth of capacity," another man said.

A low hum vibrated through the floor as the rpm's from the turbine that drove the machine's generator began to build. That stopped the casual conversation in the gallery. As one, the people seated there stiffened and faced front. The moment at hand had their complete attention. As titanium panels irised in and isolated the gallery from the potential dangers on the test bed below, a trio of video monitors motored down from the ceiling and bloomed on before them, the split screens giving the VIPs the option of close-up views and long shots of laboratory, machine and target. A countdown clock superimposed on the screens read 00:02:16:04.

The voice on the loudspeaker spoke with noticeably more emotion now.

"Primary generator at desired power, fluctuation is nominal. Aiming is complete and locked. We are now at test minus two minutes, ten seconds and counting. At two minutes, command will switch to Mr. Maximovich at Scorpion fire control. Acknowledge."

Mr. Maximovich acknowledged, "Fire control standing by."

The man at the trigger felt his heart pound. His pulse surged into his ears. The final checklists were reviewed and at two minutes, Mr. Maximovich took control.

At one minute, headsets fell silent and all conversation stopped. At thirty seconds, Goran Maximovich, stammered into his mic, "Char, charging beam generator...now."

A disturbing noise arose in the room; static, electric crackling at first, then sub notes of fingernails on a blackboard, finally a counterpoint of rending metal and a low growl just at the threshold of human hearing. The sound level climbed - 80, 95, 120 decibels. Everyone had their hands to their ears.

":20 Seconds, :19, :18, :17," the air in the lab thickened. It was getting hard to breath. ":11, :10, :09, :08, :07," A ball of plasma started to grow about the needle, the energy and noise built to a frenzied crescendo and suddenly, the tip of the needle disappeared in blinding white light, ":02, :01-"

"FIRE!" Maximovich screamed, drowned out by the din and squeezed the red trigger on the joystick.

Out of the plasma ball an intense, brilliant blue beam of light an inch in diameter sprang straight at the target.

There was a loud WHOOSH followed by a visible shock wave that rippled the dense air like a videotaped mirage on fast forward. The whole room looked as if it was trapped inside a mold of clear Jell-O and someone had bumped the plate. All eyes were glued to the target awaiting an explosion or…something. Then it all stopped. Light, sound, shock wave, everything. The target was still there, intact. Klax was incredulous.

As Llorca was about to bombard him with hysterical invective a man pointed at the *Close Up* monitor.

"*Alors,*" the Frenchman yelled, his eyes wombat-wide with wonder.

At the center of the target the effect of the beam was taking hold. Spreading outward at increasing speed and size was a clear view to the ceramic plating behind the target, surrounded by what appeared to be erupting bubbles spewing thick, black smoke as they burst.

Accompanied by a sound like the effervescence in a giant glass of seltzer, the timbers were disintegrating into sulfurous ooze that dripped in fist-sized globs into a swelling, putrid puddle on the floor. In fifteen seconds, the entire target was reduced to a steaming pile of yellow-green sludge.

A huge cheer went up in the room and the scientists' collective angst evaporated with the timbers. Klax' eyes narrowed in delight. He stood trance-like and contemplated the future. No one clapped him on the back or shook his hand. Unless one was well paid to do so, one never had intentional physical contact with Klax, but the scientists exchanged awkward attempts at high-fives all around. As MAL's minions jigged to celebrate their triumph, Klax took a deep breath, his lips squeezed into his customary sickly smile, and softly hummed the famous four-note bar of Beethoven's Fifth Symphony through his nasal appliance; "Da da da dum."

He was already impatient for the next test, firing on a live animal with significantly more power input.

The loudspeaker interrupted the party.

"Test two in twenty minutes and counting," it blared.

The test director added his orders.

"Target team two, reset target stand. All power on safe. Mr. Maximovich, prepare to re-aim. This test will be at one-tenth power."

The shield protecting the VIP gallery was open now and technicians renewed their fussing around the machine. Two men rushed the remains of the wooden target and began to scrape at the droppings from the floor with broad shovels. They took turns pitching the acrid-smelling residue into a wheeled bin. There wasn't much left to gather and the remains were soon hurried away for analysis.

As quickly as they moved away another team replaced them and began to assemble a bright metallic platform a meter and a half high and a meter square. Atop it, at each corner, four round dowels protruded ten centimeters above the base. The cage that would be mounted on them was wheeled into the room on a flatbed dolly, a man each at front and back. In the cage atop the dolly, the doomed target glowered and hissed at the men and ostensibly, its fate.

The fifty-pound *Gulo gulo*, from the Latin word for glutton, was a vicious vortex of flying fur and slathering spittle. It had been snared in a steel net near Alpha Island's trash incinerator where it had just devoured a giant Norway rat in two snaps of its razor-lined jaws. Even for the men that loved animals, it was difficult to feel pity for the Wolverine; endangered species or not. A homely, squashed-face bear with beady eyes and yellow-white stripes, the thing was a repulsive, nasty creature that knew no retreat and gave no quarter. They had been known to face down grizzlies and drive them away.

Cautiously and with difficulty as the stout creature scurried about, the two men wrestled the cage into position and secured it on the pedestal. One cursed at the animal in his native tongue, smiled and made a throat slashing gesture. The other faced the control booth and gave a thumbs up.

"Target in position," the voice boomed over the loudspeaker.

The next few minutes was a repeat of the steps and checks employed to ready the machine for the first firing. With now practiced precision, the machine was aimed, the generator was charged and the observers once more took their seats.

"Mr. Maximovich, prepare to fire," came the test director's command.

Goran replied, "At one tenth power, standing by to fire."

As the power was again applied, the mind-rending noise of the machine proclaimed its presence. In the target cage, the curious Wolverine turned to face its antagonist. When the beam generator needle began to glow, the animal's eyes grew huge, its ears began to twitch, and it bared its teeth.

"FIRE!" Maximovich yelled.

This time, at ten times the power of the previous shot, there was no delay between the release of the beam and its effect on the target. Instantly the Wolverine's body became a mass of sizzling steam. For a second, it screamed. Then the animal's flesh was rent from its body and fell to the cage floor; pooling into goo. For a moment the skeleton was visible. Since its bones were primarily comprised of calcium, the beam appeared to be having no effect on them. Then the connective tissues that held the animal's inner structure together let loose and the bones detached like Tinker Toys poured from a box. They quivered there for a few seconds on the floor of the cage before the heat and pressure from the disintegrating marrow burst them from the within in a series of crackles and pops that broadcast shards of bone and teeth through the bars of the cage and into the air. The observers were spellbound.

Then, before anyone could react to the eye-popping scene, the test itself came apart. The ball of energy that had dispatched the Wolverine so thoroughly began to grow. In a blink, it engulfed the entire laboratory bay. Ceiling fixtures began to spark as their carbon-based wiring and reflectors disintegrated and left banks of hot quartz halogen bulbs to free fall onto the equipment below. Test equipment and assembly tools, pushed back to the lab's outer walls for safety, melted.

Reacting as quickly as he could, but not soon enough, the test director shouted into his mic, "Maximovich, take cov-"

The men in the bubble and the observers in the gallery turned their attention from the target cage to the man at the firing controls and a sight they would never forget.

Maximovich was dissolving before their eyes. In a trice, his flesh was gone, his skeleton twitched and his bones exploded. Then as suddenly as it had appeared, the beam's energy dispersed and the bay went dark. No one cheered this time, but Klax and the Wardens knew at once they had achieved their goal. With a few modifications, not the least of which would be an enclosed firing station to prevent the operator's suicide, Scorpion was ready to come off the drawing board and into the nightmares of those responsible for maintaining Earth's *status quo*.

No one had anticipated that the effect would expand through the air in all directions, sustained by its own chain reaction. No one thought Maximovich's misfortune to be anything more than feedback from mistaken firing of the weapon in an enclosed area. A lack of an understanding of that phenomenon would soon prove disastrous.

Klax rejoiced. A particle beam weapon capable of killing multiple proximal targets in a single firing was a reality. Before long hew would have his finger on the trigger of the ultimate ray gun.

CHAPTER 24

"NOBODY HOME"

The Project Repo team was chafing at the bit to share what they had learned over the past two days. When Wolf Lang walked into the briefing room, he saw in their eyes the look of kids fresh back to school from summer vacation, squirming in their seats to be the first to step to the front of the room, stand and deliver.

"All right people, let's get down to it," he said amused by their enthusiasm.

"Comstock, what did you find out about our boy in Schleswig?"

"Well, at first the guy denied he had a radio," Comstock read from the notes on his PDA. "After I suggested that we could arrange for the German *BfV* to search his home, his memory improved. I guess the joys of a visit from the state security police escaped him. The conversation we intercepted was with an old school chum named Hansel Brueckner, an electrician specializing in high-energy control systems. Not exactly the kind of skill you'd think would be in big demand on an isolated island in the Gulf of Bothnia. He told me his *freund* had been out of the country for about a year and that Hansi was excited that in the last few weeks he been able to work at his specialty. Before that, he had been assigned to a team of construction electricians, building underground structures. He was not a happy camper then, but lately he was getting into some stuff that challenged him. Interestingly, he told Bogaert that he thought he would be home soon, in a few weeks. It looks like whatever project he's working on up there is about done."

"That jives with what we found out about the missing girls in Stockholm," Moroder added.

"Right," Forster said. "All that action has come to a sudden halt. Police interviews and accounts from bar and club workers confirm there have been no reports of missing females in the last month. That's unusual they say, given the one or two a month they've averaged over the past year. Not that anyone's complaining. It's been bad for business. We talked to a bunch of locals and street people and they haven't seen any black-suits either. Looks like our 'wildcatters' have pulled out and gone back to wherever they came from Commander."

"How 'bout you Katrova? Rex, have anything new for us?"

"Not much from Rex directly Sir," Natalie said, opening a folio and spreading out a half dozen glossy photographs on the table. "But we got some great stuff from the satellites. Take a look," she said with some pride.

"What're we looking at?" Lang said as he cranked his head around to orient himself and make some sense of the photos. The rest of the team stood to do the same.

"These are thermal and infrared shots of Ahvenanmaa Island. If I didn't know better, I'd say we were looking at the Port of Stockholm for all the activity."

"No, shit," Jim Comstock said, used to interpreting such images.

Natalie began her presentation.

"I asked the bird-boys to make me a series of time-lapse images so we could see not only the thermal and IR radiation from the fixed facilities, and as you can see we've got some small surface structures and one big mother underground facility, but showing the combined movements of all surface, sea and air craft in the vicinity. These heat trails show hundreds of trips by all kinds of vessels to the island from northern Germany, Denmark, Finland, Sweden, specifically Stockholm, Latvia and Russia. It looks like enough traffic to support and supply a small city. Way too much activity to conclude that it's routine logistics for an oil or mineral exploration outfit. And, look at this." She moved a single photo to the center of the table atop the pile of images.

"These trails from northern Germany show the telltale hotspots of ultra-dense materials, probably lead; the kind of stuff our STRATCOM guys use as shielding to transport weapons grade radioactive materials. There have been at least three shipments like that in the last month."

Katrova handed Comstock a magnifying loupe for a closer look and he bent over the image.

"Casing that thick could only be used for one thing guys," Comstock said, his concern apparent. "Plutonium."

"You think they're using plutonium to drive Dr. Eva's beam?" Forster asked.

"Maybe," Comstock replied thoughtfully. "There were traces of plutonium found in the debris in the fjord and we know she used plutonium to power her laboratory. But, I'm thinking our bad guys are more likely building Einstein's coil with the stuff."

The team looked at him, hoping he was wrong, knowing he probably wasn't.

"Maybe they'll blow themselves up in the process of testing the damned thing," Moroder added optimistically.

"Mr. Moroder, if I'm right," Comstock continued, "and they test that thing at full power, they'll not only take themselves out, they could take Scandinavia and northern Europe with them."

"I've seen enough," Lang said. He put the loupe down, planted both hands on the table and said in as serious a tone as anyone had heard him use, "We're going to dig these bastards out of their hole and spoil their party."

He grabbed the intercom from the bulkhead and spoke as he winked at Forster.

"Get the SEAL team leader, TACCOM and the Air Boss down here, on the double."

The earpiece crackled back, "Aye, aye, Sir."

Over the next few hours, a small herd of people cycled through the frenzied briefing room, each in turn carrying the mission parameters down the chain of command to those that needed to know.

Within hours, the SEAL recon team Lang had ordered to MAL's island reported no detectable operations on the island's surface or in the surrounding sea. Either the people on the island knew something was up and had and had hunkered down or the activity underground had reached a crescendo and required all hands to be at their subterranean stations. Lang had no time to deliberate the alternatives. It was time to move in.

They were too late. MAL's own commandos had locked onto the radio signals from the recon team, found and eliminated them. Three Zodiacs of six men each were ripped to shreds by fast moving, heavily armed patrol craft and sent to the bottom. Four men survived to report. In SEAL tradition, they vehemently refused extraction until the dead men could be retrieved.

Alerted to the presence of and discovery by the Americans, the Wardens directed a hasty retreat of the key people and machine components they would need for the next phase of their plan.

When Lang's assault team hit the beach at dawn the next day they found only remnants of the hive and a few demolition technicians left behind attempting to destroy anything significant that wasn't evacuated. None of the stragglers had witnessed the test of the machine and they knew nothing of its purpose, but under extreme duress and with some psycho-chemical prompting, they gave Mr. Comstock plenty of scuttle-butt about a cannon with "awesome destructive power" and some disturbing information about the multinational scale of MAL's operations. Even this small group was diverse, with men from Sri Lanka, Egypt and Korea.

If this information was factual, even without the threat of the machine, it became clear that The Ten was facing a formidable foe in MAL, perhaps equal in intellectual and economic assets to its own organization and determined to become so powerful it could dictate the course of global events if not the terms of total planetary surrender.

Pursuit was now the order of the day.

Chapter 25

"Cry havoc."

There was acrimonious dissension among the Wardens about the next steps to take in accomplishing their fiendish ends. The cramped quarters of the hovercraft in which they made their escape from Alpha Island reverberated with their shouting. Some, supported by Klax, wanted immediately to attach the beam generator to the nearly complete Einstein coil and go into battle. They knew that there wasn't a bomb, missile, laser weapon, aircraft or warship in the world that could withstand the withering onslaught of Scorpion's beam, and in a short time, there would be more, newer and highly mobile versions of the device coming off the assembly line. The proliferation and distribution of the machine's clones would make resistance folly. The order of battle they favored would wreak instant destruction on the forces responding to Scorpion's first deployment, probably against NATO forces in Poland or the Czech Republic, then onward to face the industrial and social infrastructure of each territory they conquered until, country by country, the world could be made clean again. When the world stood witness to MAL's victories and the dear price of resistance, the attempts to stop them would surely end and the Wardens could dictate the terms of surrender.

Others in the group were frightened by the possibility that, given the extent of the destruction they had seen during the low-power test, there was a great risk of inadvertently demolishing excess territory while mounting their defense against what would certainly be massive retaliation by every technologically capable country on Earth. After all, they would have to live in the aftermath and the potential of catastrophic and uncontrollable collateral damage left them as vulnerable as their targets.

A third faction, convinced that there had not been sufficient testing of the device, wanted to follow a less aggressive plan; perhaps by demonstrating Scorpion's power with the destruction of a small, especially dirty factory. Afterward they could dictate terms and demand the forfeiture of say, Australia. There, MAL could fashion a private Utopia and show the world how things could and should be done. Scorpion would make a marvelous shield against intervention.

In the end, it was Warden Llorca who ended the debate and dictated the events to follow. There would be a demonstration of Scorpion's might, but on a massive scale. He would send a communication in the clear to the Secretary General of the United Nations. Then with precisely twenty minutes warning, enough time to assure that governments capable of linking up with MAL's satellite video feed could do so, but not providing sufficient time for a preemptive attack, he would order the weapon fired at full power, Einstein coil engaged, against a large, disgustingly polluted city. Over the period of an hour, multiple targets would be selected and vaporized, until there would be no doubt of MAL's power or invulnerability. Scorpion and a small task force of technicians and security troops under Mr. Klax' command would be inserted into the target area by helicopter and removed immediately after the demonstration.

For two days following the demonstration there would be no communication with the U.N. or anyone else. This would allow the world to assess the devastation and give them time to fully "appreciate," their plight. Afterward, MAL would relay its demands. Punishment for failing to accede would be the systematic destruction of Europe's then Asia's industrial centers. Governments would either comply or the Wardens would turn a nest of Scorpions loose on the world to destroy its smog bound cities one at a time. Then, starvation, civil war, anarchy and finally pestilence, would take the lives of enough humans to give Mother Earth a chance to build herself anew. Llorca knew in his heart that even the most selfish and greedy among the world's Kings, Presidents, Prime Ministers and Generals would quickly relent and bow to MAL's enlightened despotism.

"At this time we will begin our retreat and deliberate our choice of target," Llorca's flat tone and half-smile emphasized the finality of his decision. "Warden Biletnikov, your fine people have three days to assemble Scorpion in its final configuration. Remember we are not doing this to, but for the world. Small sacrifices must be made for the greater good."

With that final pronouncement, Llorca and the four senior members of the cabal stood and moved forward into the hovercraft's wardroom. The last man through the hatch threw an iron latch and closed the water-tight door behind him.

Three hours later, as the hovercraft prepared to dock at a private mooring in the Port of Gdansk, Warden Llorca sent for Dagon Klax. His instructions were brief.

"Shkodra, Albania," he said. "Three days from now."

Even before the last of Scorpion's scaly sub-assemblies had been unloaded, technicians began its final assembly in a dingy warehouse on a disused alley abutting the Vistula River. A day later, they began mating the monster to the Einstein coil.

Within forty-eight hours, a huge custom-crafted cargo helicopter would ferry Klax and the Scorpion deep into Albania, where they would inject mayhem into the suspended murk of a winter afternoon in Shkodra, one of that country's most densely populated and eminently polluted cities.

Aboard the Kendall, Wolf Lang selected a secure line on his digicom, contacted The Ten and brought his liaison up to speed. In typical "Langese," his briefing didn't take long.

"Three? Lang here. We found 'em. Went there. Missed 'em. Took some casualties. None of the primary team. We are in pursuit. The enemy is considerably stronger than indicated by prior intel. We have reason to suspect the machine is operational. More, soon."

"Proceed," the man known to Lang only by his numeric moniker said.

"Out," Lang said.

Lang logged off the digicom and lurched down the passageway to meet with John Patrick, Captain of the Kendall. Lang commandeered Patrick's ship and two escort frigates under auspices of The Ten and asked perfunctorily for permission to commence the air, sea and intelsat search for the fleeing MALs. It took no time to determine that the fugitives had scattered in every direction and that the Repo team was in for a protracted search. If the detection of the SEAL recon team had rousted the MALs before they were able to finish their dirty work so much the better, but Lang's intuition told him that MAL was still acting; not reacting. If they had a working machine, there would be evil afoot straight away. Klax' odor filled Lang's nostrils. If he could just get wind of the direction it came from.

Forster was taking the air on the deck and thinking hard about where the bad guys could be headed, when Natalie touched his shoulder.

"Luke, do you-"

"Jesus, Natalie," he started. "I damn near jumped off the deck."

"Sorry, Forster."

"Forget it. What do you want?" Once again, she had aggravated him.

"Nothing, it's just that I'm feeling like the odds are against us and I guess I'm a little frightened."

"What do want me to say? That we're gonna hunt down these Morlocks and save the world? I don't know that. Hell, I don't even know what these guys are up to. You know, we've got bits and pieces and guys like Lang and MacLaren are all full of doom and gloom, but we really got nuthin,' bupkus, zip point shit! It's too bad you're scared. I'm tired, pissed off, half seasick and, if I have to listen to Moroder tell me one more time to hold my weapons tighter when I fire, I'm going to pull off his clipped little jar head and shit down his neck! That's what I'm feeling, if you want to *share*. These bastards have me combat ready, I want to kill something, and all you fuckers are starting to look as good a target as the MALs. Christ, how did I get sucked into this?"

Nat took the full force of Luke's frustration and without comment, turned on her heels and walked back down the flight deck. She wouldn't show him the mist in her eyes. Sometimes, she hated being a woman.

Later that night they chanced upon each other in the passageway as she returned from her shower, damp-haired and fresh-faced. She looked hurt and vulnerable but Forster didn't apologize.

"Hey, uh, Katrova," he said, gently, as if he were about to ask forgiveness, "You know, you're not bad looking...for a geek." He smiled at his little joke. She didn't.

"Up yours, Forster," she said, forcing a smile. She'd never again make the mistake of revealing her feelings to him.

By morning, things hadn't changed much. Intel hadn't a clue about which of the multiple fleeing targets was Klax. Rex suspected the machine was destined for one of five ports, each of which had the equipment to off-load heavy machinery and radioactive materials. RECON teams were sent to all; Gdansk, Helsinki, Riga, Leningrad, and Copenhagen.

Forster, Moroder, Comstock and Katrova were assigned an elite SEAL team escort and told to make ready and stand by for immediate deployment. Mo spent the better part of the day familiarizing everyone but Forster with the special weaponry they would carry into action. Forster had qualified as an expert with them all and Moroder noted he was smiling during target practice. His edge was plenty fine.

Mo was pleasantly surprised by how fast Katrova learned and at her deftness in field striping, cleaning and reassembling the grenade launchers and light machine guns. The SEALs had never seen the M-90 laser rifle and were like kids at a new video game during qualification. The men that had to carry the twin twenty-five kilo power cells for each of the weapons weren't as impressed.

In the early evening, the team assembled full aft on the Kendall to practice arming and throwing the compact but deadly vibration grenades. When the gritty-skinned black balls exploded, there was no flash or bang, just an irresistible thump of air pressure expanding outward at the speed of sound. Enemy troops within eight meters of the detonation had their guts turned to jelly while their eyeballs exploded in their sockets and their brains liquefied. It was an unpleasant close-quarter, antipersonnel weapon with no tolerance for user error.

So, with bravery shielding their taught, tattooed skins and supreme confidence in their weaponry and leadership, the young SEALs were convinced of their ability to thwart MAL and retrieve Dr. Eva's machine. At the end of the day there they were; Forster, Katrova, Moroder and the SEALs, all dressed up with no place to go.

They didn't wait long. One of Comstock's deep cover men spotted Klax disembarking from a harbor shuttle in Gdansk. He was now under surveillance and the operative on his tail awaited orders.

The intercom in Lang's quarters warbled. He looked up from the low-altitude aerial printouts he was studying.

"Lang," he said, perturbed at the interruption.

"We've got Klax," Comstock said on the other end.

"The briefing room, now! Get the whole team, Jim." Lang used his most sincere command voice and hung up the phone. His face turned deep red and he got a far away look in his eyes. He squinted, as if he were staring directly into the villain's eyes.

"Stay put you sucker. Stay put!" He said, he thought, to himself.

A sailor stopped and stood at attention outside the door to Lang's quarters. "Aye, Sir," he replied, surprised.

Lang came back to the moment and looked curiously at the sailor.

"Can I help you, Seaman?"

"No, sir. You just said, stay put."

Lang looked at him sheepishly, realizing the cause of the man's confusion.

"Never mind son. As you were."

"Aye, Sir," the man said as politely as he could, trying to avoid looking at the officer like he was nuts, and moved on thinking, "SOB" (standard officer behavior).

Moments later, the Repo team stood in the briefing room dressed in their dark battle fatigues.

"It looks like we have a break here people," Lang said. "One of Comstock's spooks eyeballed Klax this morning in Gdansk. He was coming off a hovercraft in the harbor. "Let's have the details, Jim."

"I have an update, Sir," Comstock said. "At zero seven eighteen local time, Dagon Klax and twenty or so others disembarked from a large cargo-capable hovercraft and piled into a deuce and a half. About a mile from the dock they unloaded themselves and the shrouded contents of three larger haulers in their convoy into a jumbo-sized warehouse. The dock and the warehouse are unusually secure; not just the usual chain link fence and video camera thing. Our guy counted two perimeter guard squads with automatic weapons and four canine teams. The fences around the place are electrified and topped with razor wire. For the next half hour he watched a crew of about thirty men from the inside unload the haulers with forklifts and power dollies. His last report, the one I snatched on the way down here, says that more haulers have been showing up, one about every ten minutes. They all have the same symbol stenciled on their doors."

"Let me guess," Katrova, said, "A globe in flames?"

Comstock nodded in response.

Lang said, "Mr. Moroder, get your gear to the flight deck. It's time to bag some game. Comstock, I want the same reports you get, on the fly. Mr. Forster, the resources of the Kendall's battle group are behind you. Use your discretion. You are at the point and in command. You know what's at stake here. Good luck." He shook Forster's hand, then the others in turn. "Good bye," he said, looking each of them in squarely in the eye.

Natalie wondered if they would see him again.

Thirty minutes later, Forster's team, in a Super Sea Stallion, accompanied by a Marine Aircobra III attack helo, jumped off the deck of the Kendall and vectored toward Gdansk. There would be one refueling stop in Goteborg, then straight on to the objective. Everyone on the mission was thinking the same good thought, "Be there." Forster wondered why helicopters were so "bleeping" slow.

With the delay for refueling, the team would arrive in Gdansk at fourteen hundred hours, local time. They would put down far enough away from MAL's warehouse to avoid detection, but close enough to bring force to bear quickly. While they were in transit, Comstock used his PDA to download a satellite close-up of the warehouse in question and Moroder and Forster busied themselves making attack plans with the SEAL team leader, Captain Stan "Stosh" Juracka, a rough Polish kid from Chicago.

"You speak the lingo?" Forster asked, recognizing Juracka's ethnic origins.

"Enough to order dinner at a restaurant in the 'hood, Sir!" He replied, a little ashamed that he hadn't spent more time at his grandfather's knee practicing his "Vs" and "Ws."

"No sweat Captain," Forster reassured him. "I don't think these boys will be in the mood for lengthy conversation."

The satellite close-up showed an LZ big enough for both the transport and attack helos to put down simultaneously and they passed the image up to the pilot. Forster's helo would land first. The Aircobra would stay aloft briefly to provide high cover.

Forster decided to split his assault team into three groups. Natalie would stay in the helo with the aircrew, maintaining voice and data links to the Kendall. Comstock and two SEALs would establish a defensive perimeter around the LZ. Forster, Moroder and the remaining SEALs would reconnoiter and assess the threat at the warehouse. Depending on the situation, they could then surround the building and wait for reinforcements, attack and hope surprise gave them the edge, or clear the area and let the Aircobra blast the building to rubble. Of course all those options assumed Luke and his team were in control. They would have been, but an intel analyst on the Kendall had made a mistake.

On the satellite shot the analyst interpreted the big white buttons on the roof of MAL's warehouse to be nothing more than translucent skylight covers. They were, except for the fourth one from the front of the building. That particular dome masked a low power radar unit. It didn't pulse with enough wattage to be detected by local civilian or military authorities; it was just powerful enough to alert the operator of the approach of any aircraft within a quarter mile that was not squawking an authorized frequency.

To avoid arousing curiosity, and not knowing whether The Ten's people in Poland had had time to clear their presence in the area, the Aircobra's pilot was operating in full electronic stealth mode. The Sea Stallion however, was not and the bulky old workhorse made an elephantine blip on MAL's tiny radar screen. As the helo began its descent, a squad of heavily armed men led by Klax himself was already on the way to greet it.

Enshrouded by a cloud of dust, the noise of its engines greatly amplified in the confines of the small LZ, the Sea Stallion set down on a concrete quadrangle amid the derelict warehouses near MAL's. Before its skids had settled, Forster's men threw the hatch open and exited the aircraft, machine guns at the ready and laser rifles fully charged. Forster,

Moroder and the SEALs gained the nearest building and, completely exposed, crept low along its siding.

Comstock and his SEALs found cover behind stacks of old chemical drums and wooden palettes and settled into the correct positions to create a triangular field of fire around the helo.

Advancing in short sprints between the long buildings, covering each other's backsides as they snaked forward, Forster and his men approached their target. But, as they stopped to gather themselves before entering the building, they heard the unmistakable sound of automatic weapons fire. Amidst the echoing reports and ricocheting whines of the fusillade, Forster heard Natalie scream in his headset.

"Luke, help! We're taking heavy fire!"

Ignoring the warehouse, Forster and the SEALs scrambled back to the LZ. When they arrived, it was chaos. The helo and its defenders were totally defensive. Comstock and the SEALs were outnumbered three to one. They were only alive because of their angled field of fire and the fact that Klax and his men had entered the LZ in a cluster. For the moment, the three men and the helo crew were holding the MALs down with their autopistols and side arms. Three of Klax' men already lay dying in pools of glossy crimson.

The Aircobra's crew had also heard Natalie's cry on the radio and the ship was already rounding to attack Klax' position. Its miniguns and grenade launcher would make short work of the gunmen. Then, another squad of Klax' men entered the LZ from the alley nearest Comstock. One of them held a Stinger antiaircraft missile on his shoulder. He was aiming directly at the Aircobra even as the gunship began to rain fire on Klax' position. Four more MALs fell in the first burst from the helo. The rest dove for cover. Now, Moroder and the SEALs loosed their laser rifles and cut through a few of the new arrivals.

Katrova heard Comstock over her headset, "Hang on Nat!"

"Jim, they've got a Stinger."

"Shit!" Forster yelled as he heard Katrova's warning and saw the man with the missile. But, Forster was pinned down by a fusillade of suppressing fire. Grasping the rapid deterioration of their situation Katrova gathered herself and pulled a vibration grenade from her ammo belt. She grasped the indention in the top of the grenade between her thumb and forefinger and twisted the arming cap, breaking the safety tab. It started to whistle. She twisted the cap to the second position and it beeped. It would now detonate on contact. She stuck her head out of the cargo door to sight the missile man only to be met by the whine of a full metal jacket whizzing by centimeters from her ear. She threw herself back inside and crashed onto the helo deck. The grenade was still armed and she nearly blew the helo and herself to kingdom come but she held it fast.

Gasping at the near miss, she scrambled back to the cover of the doorway. Once again she sucked up her courage, stuck her head through the hatch and saw her target taking aim at the Aircobra. The Repo team was reloading or behind cover and the MALs were about to go on the offensive. She had no time to think. Bullets or no bullets, she had to drop the guy with the Stinger. With bullet fragments ricocheting all around her and in total disregard for her safety, she stood, drew back her arm and, relying on body memory from her days as an intramural league softball pitcher at Cal Tech, fired a perfect underhanded strike at the missile man. The vibration grenade exploded on impact with his belt buckle. Whvvvvrrrr!

He and four of his mates slumped to the ground - bags of blood and bile and mushed-up organs. It was an Olympian hurl, but it came a split second too late. The missile man had already fired.

As the Aircobra's gunner prepared to launch a rocket salvo, the smoke trail of the Stinger rose to meet it. Like a dragon slain with a fiery dart, the helo plummeted to earth. On impact the airframe shattered with a deafening roar and filled the LZ with an expanding ball of flame. Rotor shards, burning fuel, shrapnel from detonating munitions and disintegrating turbine parts tore through bodies and buildings alike. The Sea Stallion's cockpit took a direct hit from a massive piece of flaming debris. The aviators there were immolated in their seats. If Natalie's door had been facing the fireball, she would have been toasted herself. As it was, the searing heat from the flight deck chased her back against the fuselage and the concussion from the explosion clanged in her ears like a church bell. A ragged chunk of metal the size of a golf ball pinged through the Sea Stallion's fuselage and lodged in her right calf catapulting her to the deck. Natalie could smell her hair burning and she panicked at the thought of being cooked alive in a deluge of aviation fuel. As tongues of flame rose and spread around her, she jumped out of the doorway and loped on one foot across the LZ, every inch of forward progress commanding all her strength. After a few steps, she realized she didn't know where she was running to.

She didn't hear Jim Comstock calling her, screaming at the top of his lungs. She was running directly at Klax and, as he raised his head from the cover of his arms, he saw her and raised his pistol. Comstock and Moroder both responded and sprayed his position with hot steel. Uncannily, Klax pitched himself back into a cranny between the buildings and cheated death once again. His henchmen were not as fortunate. Bullets and beams cut the rest of them to ribbons.

The LZ was still being zipped by exploding ammunition when, in the smoke and fury of the firefight, Klax weaseled down a narrow alleyway and fled back to MAL's warehouse.

Forster was angry and ready to press the attack but first he had to account for his people. Katrova had made it cover, but was bleeding badly and needed medical attention fast. The SEAL he had left to guard the helo was dead, cut in half by a rotor blade as it spun through the air – a turbocharged guillotine. Moroder was unharmed and already scanning the area for new threats.

Comstock leaned against a wall opposite the gristly scatter of Klax' dead. His face was white, and as Forster and the SEAL team medic approached, he slumped to the ground, a gaping wound in his abdomen oozing blood. He was going into shock, but managed to ask for a cigarette while the team medic attended him. No one smoked though and nobody knew he had the habit. They were sorry they couldn't give their comrade this one last comfort.

"You give 'em hell, Luke," he said softly as Forster pressed his ear close. "And, look after Nat, will ya? I think she...she's sweet on...you."

He coughed, his breath burbling through the blood in his mouth. Then he was still, his vacant eyes still engaging Luke's.

Forster felt like he had taken a round through the heart. He liked Comstock and knew the guy gave it up to cover Natalie's pitch. Before he could say goodbye to his fallen friend, he heard the wail of sirens in the distance. This operation was about to be blown all over the front pages. Forster had to make a fast decision. He had two options left. Put Nat and the retrievable bodies in a safe place and press the assault on the warehouse, or deal with the local authorities and wait for extraction. The choice was made for him.

Klax sent a MAL gunship to finish them off. Before Forster's people could regroup, its grenade launcher opened up. The flash of each grenade brought a new hail of shrapnel and glass shards. The concussions nearly dropped them to the ground and made it impossible to aim their guns. The dense shock waves diffused Moroder's laser rifle beam rendering it useless. Still they tried to return fire as they scattered, but before they could mount a defense, the gunship rose out of small arms range and hovered ominously above the LZ. Forster didn't understand why it just hung there, watching. It must be preparing to launch a missile. A moment later he had his answer. The air once again thickened with a steady thumping noise but, this time it wasn't from weaponry.

It was the sound of rotors - big rotors. As the remnants of Team Repo watched helplessly, two huge cargo helos rose from the direction of MAL's warehouse and headed southeast. A last burst of fire from the gunship reminded them that intervention would not be permitted. As the aircraft banked away and shrank in the distance, Forster keyed his digicom to brief Lang on the failed mission.

Chapter 26

"The Albanian tragedy"

Lang squinted and hung his head as he listened to Forster's report, but there was no time for sadness or anger and the details would come soon enough. He hung up on Forster without comment, grabbed the command phone and directed the Air Boss to dispatch an E2F Hawkeye from the Kendall's battle group to hunt down MAL's aerial convoy. Five years ago, the Navy had compromised the Chinese-developed stealth technology MAL was using and though Klax thought his helos were invisible, the Hawkeye's thermal target sensor would display them like lightening bugs at midnight. The Ten was locked on now and neither Klax nor the machine would escape.

There was still the snafu in Gdansk to deal with though, so Lang made his emergency calls. The Ten responded quickly with assurances that Forster's team could count on the full support and cooperation of the Polish government. They would handle the wet clean up.

Natalie's wound was not life threatening so she was sent to a nearby private hospital. It seemed she was a whole lot more pissed off about her singed tresses and the subsequent emergency room nurse haircut than she was about the sizable hole in her leg. What really upset her though, to the point were she earned herself a hypodermic full of sedative, was that Comstock was dead and Forster was going forward without her. Her wound was treated and as she slept she was transferred to a safe house near the U.S. Consulate in Gdansk. A day later, she was back aboard the Kendall.

Lang arranged an overnight rest and rearm for Forster, Moroder and the SEALs at a long-abandoned Soviet Army barracks outside the city. They were to hole up there until Lang's scouts could determine Klax' destination, then the chase would resume. If Lang could only be sure that the machine was in the helos with Klax, he could call off Forster and order a single sortie by an F-22 to finish the job once and for all. Talk about a duck on a June bug. With two super cruising thrust-vectored engines the F-22 Raptor was, at speeds exceeding Mach 2, capable of acquiring a target over the horizon and destroying it before the enemy knew they had been fired on. But no one was sure if there was yet a machine, where it was, or who had copies of the plans. Lang's best bet was to stay the course and assume that Klax = machine.

The SEALs, re-supplied and refreshed somehow by the foil wrapped "doggy snacks" in their rucksacks, sat amid their gear quietly contemplating the day's events. These were not men who placed blame, cried over battle losses or complained. Each of them in their own mind was reliving the battle and critiquing their own performance. According to their protocol, after every training session or combat mission, each stood before the group and gave an objective-as-possible overview of everything he or she did right and wrong. The team leader went last and had the final say. He debunked the *mea culpa*'s when they were not the individual's fault and just as quickly rebuffed any self-criticism offered up to deflect responsibility from another team member. He offered praise when deserved. After the session it was his job to absolve the offenders, educate the mistaken and encourage improved performance in the next action.

Forster and Moroder were not as disciplined. They sulked together in a dim corner. They blamed themselves for what happened to Comstock and Katrova, and they were angry at having underestimated the enemy. The bastards had their own radar?

But, things were starting to add up. The evidence techs The Ten sent to scour MAL's warehouse had found latent radioactivity in the facility along with some cast off scraps of a material unlike anything they had seen before. It was matte black, light and flexible, but it had the look and texture of a ceramic. Some kind of new armor plate? When Forster got a look at the sample, he swore that the helos that attacked his team were covered in the same stuff. He conducted his own field tests by standing the stuff against the wall and shooting at it, first with a 9mm pistol, then a sniper rifle and finally the M-90. The bullets from the small arms smacked it good but only scuffed its surface before falling to the floor harmless, stubby wads. No ricochets either. The stuff seemed to absorb all of the round's energy on impact. The laser rifle made it glow and scorched it but was unable to penetrate. Moroder scratched his head. Maybe a shaped charge would do it.

While Mo explored a solution to the problem with the armorers on the Kendall, Forster discussed the evidence from the warehouse with Lang. Lang reported back that the technicians thought the latent radiation emissions were definitely from a plutonium source, maybe the power supply for the machine. Traces of it had been found at Luknar's lab, there was evidence of it in shipments to Ahvenanmaa and now it was here. Forster took some courage from the information and felt they were finally closing in.

As the first ray of sunlight peaked through the barracks window and hit Forster between the eyes, his digicom warbled.

"Forster, Lang. We have Klax' helos down in Shkodra, Albania. We don't believe this is a fuel stop. They've been on the ground for an hour, on a plot of ground adjacent to the Rozafa fortress. It's kind of a landmark. They picked up two more gunships along the way and they're using them to fly continuous cover over the area. Satellite shows they've built a twenty-foot square tarpaulin between two heavy cargo helos and we think they're off-loading equipment. They could be assembling the damn thing. You need to blow it to hell, whatever it is. We're sending you new transportation and the Kendall is making flank speed to a better support position just north of the Frisian Islands. We can have the whole air wing behind you in two hours if you call us in. Be ready at zero eight twenty-five. Let's stop this thing right here, Luke."

"Right, Sir. Time for some payback."

At the appointed time the V-26C Osprey Lang dispatched touched down at the old barracks. The Osprey was bigger and faster than a helo and time was of the essence.

"Move out," Forster yelled as he chased the SEAL team and Moroder into the craft.

Morning in Shkodra city was never pretty. Albania's ancient capital was, in the early twenty first century, one of the most polluted cities in Europe.

In an effort to mediate the ecological impact of their own industrial effluvia, Russia and the Ukraine had convinced the Albanians to accept construction of all manner of smoke-belching, toxin-spewing enterprises. The Albanians, still in dire economic straits from the deformation of the Soviet Union, and in desperate need of work for their burgeoning population, had mortgaged their environmental future for a chance to eat regular meals and clothe their beloved children. The *quid pro quo* for the impending rape of the Albanian environment was the guarantee that the capitalist investors would purchase the output from the foul factories and rebuild the telephone system that had been dismantled by the peasants in the 1990's when they ripped down telephone wires and re-purposed them as cattle fences.

This day, a typical early-Winter temperature inversion coddled the sun in a sky as milky-yellow as the water from the spring that issued from the walls of the Rozafa, the old fortification that commanded the highest point in the city.

Local lore held that three brothers were retained in ancient times to build the Rozafa, but the place was somehow enchanted and everything they built during the day collapsed each night. An old seer explained to the puzzled masons that the ground was cursed and would have to be purified by a human sacrifice. The brothers were horrified but determined to succeed. They agreed an equitable solution would be to sacrifice whichever of their wives climbed the hill the next day to bring them their midday meal. The elder brothers selfishly warned their wives of the plot, so it fell to Rozafa, the wife of the youngest to give up her life that the others might prosper. The noble Rozafa also learned about the pact the brothers had made but agreed to be buried within the walls, demanding only that a small hole be left so that she could feed her infant child. Milky water still seeps through that small breach. In sum, Shkodra was a dismal place with a sad history that would end this awful morning.

At zero nine hundred, Dagon Klax received his final orders from the Wardens. He was to establish a defensive perimeter around the Scorpion and wait for the order to fire the weapon. Then they were to destroy every industrial target of opportunity they could hit within a twenty-minute time frame. The factories would be razed one-by-one with Scorpion at full power to make the destruction as spectacular as possible. First to go would be the venerable electric cable works, then the aluminum mill, the malodorous chemical plant and finally the plastics foundry with its halo of acrid fumes crowning the towering smokestacks. All of the plants had yawning culverts and broad open sluices that poured hundreds of thousand of gallons of acids, contaminated resins, petro-chemical waste and heavy metals into the Kiri river. The toxic soup had already found its way into the *Skadarsko Jezero*, the twenty-five mile lake on Albania's northwestern border with Montenegro, and the efflu-ent could be seen from space befouling sea water and river deltas all the way to the Adriatic.

Llorca and his cohorts believed that Shkodra was the poster child of eco-spoilage; an overcrowded, used up and defiled place that needed to be cleansed and reborn. Surely, the demonstration would bring the world to its knees. They believed retaliation, if any, would be slow in coming. No one ever helped the Albanians.

Minutes after Klax got his orders, the Wardens, looking dour with their faces puckered and their eyebrows furrowed, appeared on the vid-screen before Jayne Whitehurst, secretary general of the United Nations. When the alert tone commanded her attention, the diplomat, a tall and graceful Jamaican of indeterminate age, looked up from the substantial sheaf of docs on her desktop and was dumbfounded at the image before her.

"Ms. Whitehurst?" Llorca queried, fully aware that it was she.

"Yes?" She replied, quizzically, "Who are you and how did you get this call past my staff?"

"That is irrelevant," he replied dispassionately. "But I suppose an introduction is in order. My name is Veral Llorca, high prelate of the Wardens, the group you see with me here."

"And, what are Wardens, then?"

"Please Ms. Whitehurst, explanations are forthcoming. First, I want you to know what will be happening today and its meaning."

"Happening? What is it that's happening?" She said, with sarcasm, beginning to lose patience with the arrogant talking head before her. She pushed a red button on her com console and two aides, a dark-skinned man in black suit and turban and an alert young woman in a U.N. guard's uniform, rushed into the room. The guard had her sidearm at the ready.

"Ah, I see we have witnesses," Llorca said. "Good. It is better that way, yes? So, what I say to you will not be misunderstood. You will all pay close attention, if you please. We are the Wardens, members of the leadership council of the Malthusian Advocacy League. We are a worldwide organization dedicated to bringing social order and environmental sanity back to the Earth. In about fifteen minutes…sorry, but I couldn't have your defense forces interfering, so this is…¿*Como se dice?* Ah yes, '*short notice.*' In now, fourteen minutes, we will demonstrate our power by reducing the major factories in the Albanian city of Shkodra to rubble.

We will employ a new weapon of magnificent power. We are invulnerable and any attempt to prevent this demonstration will result in the total loss of your forces. Believe me; I do not overstate our capabilities."

His voice was getting louder.

A shock of hair fell across his forehead, dislodged by his animation.

"As you will see," he fought to gain control of his emotions, "We are prepared to go to great lengths to scrub clean our Mother Earth and restore her glory. We will do this or we will all perish, Madame," he said. "Your members refuse to unite and take the necessary action to save this planet from the filth caused by the unchecked infestation of humanity. Is this not so? Let me illustrate my point by refreshing your memory about what the governments of the world have inflicted upon their people.

Every sixty-seconds we are adding three new mouths, net, to the world's population. Similarly, every minute, three people starve to death. Two acres of wetlands are lost. Seven hundred tons of CO^2 are injected into our atmosphere and seven hundred fifty tons of topsoil is eroded. ¿*Comprende?* Your member nations provide a poor stewardship in the care of this precious vessel, our Earth. So, we are going to take that responsibility from you. Forever!"

The people in the office looked at each other skeptically but with fear in their eyes, completely taken aback by the ramblings of the obviously insane man on the screen.

"The video you are about to see is live," he continued. "Momentarily, we will begin satellite transmission on a frequency that your news bureaus can intercept and broadcast around the world. Don't miss it," Llorca intoned like a network programming pitchman. "We will communicate again just before our presentation. Now, as the famous American journalist used to say…'Stand by for news!'"

The Warden's image faded from the vidscreen but the audio level stayed up and the observers could hear him chuckling off camera.

Whitehurst furiously accessed the speed dial list on her digicom and shortly her office was full of emissaries and their aides. None knew why they had been summoned so rudely. The only available representative from Albania was the ambassador's personal secretary and he was praying to himself that whatever was going on here had nothing to do with his tiny country.

While Whitehurst made her best attempt to explain to the puzzled crowd the events of the last few minutes, her vidscreen brightened once again. This time a cityscape appeared before them.

"Madame Secretary," Llorca said, composed now. "This is an aerial view of Shkodra from one of our helicopters."

The Albanian in New York wobbled on weak knees.

"Here, for centuries, humans have willfully contaminated the air they breathe and the water they drink. Pitiful, isn't it? The haze you see is from an aggregation of chemical and particulate air pollution. It is making the people here sick with all manner of respiratory diseases and cancers. This poor city is a veritable canker on the face of Mother Earth. A contingent of our scientists will now remove this blemish!

We are using a weapon of our own creation so devastating and impervious to attack that you will recognize your helplessness against it with the first volley of its dreadful ray. After we have razed Shkodra's factories to the ground we will begin to talk, you and I, about our terms for world surrender. Most certainly, you will not want us to loose our Scorpion on the major cities of the industrialized West. Make no mistake, Ms. Whitehurst, if you hesitate or attempt to negotiate in bad faith, the next targets may be in England or perhaps in your own back yard... America. Watch closely now."

Their fear mounted as the camera zoomed slowly in from a wide view of the city to a location on a hill overlooking the city. The shot zoomed in tighter and they could now make out a large tarpaulin. When the tarpaulin filled the screen, on cue, Klax' men furled it back to reveal a sight that sent a chill up their spines.

It was Scorpion, complete and terrible.

The main body of the weapon, looking dreadfully like the insect itself, was mounted not on legs but on eight bloated wheels, each twice the height of a man. Over the wheels were bulbous fenders that made it look as if a giant, armored beetle was riding atop each one. Fire control was now a gimbaled black leather and titanium throne, mounted beneath a dome of pure, clear silicon. The entire carriage was ten meters long; comprised of two articulated segments, the trailing part of which contained the Einstein coil, and a cabochon-shaped, black-scaled ops cabin cum troop carrier of sufficient size to transport three technicians and a squad of light infantry. Here, Klax and his men would be safe as Scorpion advanced. Each segment of the rig was the width of a main battle tank.

Scorpion's business end, the crystalline blue beam needle and liquid mercury concentrator mirrors, was poised menacingly at the very tip of the tail aperture. Its front grille flared out and faired down in a plow-like concave arc toward the ground. Two 100mm laser cannons were recessed into the front fenders, one at either side, and a pair of xenon searchlights perched like glowering eyes on bifurcated pan-swivel mounts that sat astride the rounded hump that ran from just in front of the fire control station, along the machine's length, to form the machine's head shield. It resembled the real bug's carapace.

The sight left everyone in the room slack-jawed. Who were these people and what was this abomination?

"Impressive, yes?"

Llorca's voice startled Whitehurst's audience and made them flinch.

"Oh, you won't have to wait long to see what it can do," he said, forcing a smile. His face went quickly serious.

"Firing in ten seconds."

The video continued to zoom in to extreme close up. They could clearly see Fritz Jager, Scorpion's gunner maneuver the control yoke between his knees. They couldn't see Scorpion's laser sights locking on to the entryway to Shkodra's huge electric cable plant. They didn't have Jager's close-up view of the workers coming and going through their daily routines oblivious of the threat atop the hill.

Then, the video began a pullback and a countdown clock was superimposed on the vidscreen.

"Ten, nine, eight," the numerals read.

"Goodbye, Ms. Whitehurst," Llorca said, coolly.

"Seven, six, five," the clock read.

"We'll talk, soon."

"Four, three, two," the clock read.

Then a sickening noise came from the vidscreen speakers and the witnesses pressed their palms to their ears.

"One," the clock read.

There was a dreadful pause. Whitehurst would later say that she felt "every living thing on Earth hold its breath."

"At full power, Fire!" Llorca yelled.

A ball of bright white light shown from the beam needle and bloomed for a moment at its base. A heartbeat later, Scorpion fired.

At this power level, the width of the beam increased to the diameter of a trash can lid. It ripped through the air and covered the quarter mile between the beam needle and the factory in a fraction of a second. Instantly, the two hundred thousand square foot, three-story structure and everyone and everything in it were enveloped in brilliant blue light and began to disintegrate. Men and materials began to fizz, bones began to explode and everything on the screen was reduced to muck.

In fire control, the man kept the beam coming and the effect continued. Stuff that moments ago had been solid matter, was now burbling and venting heat from the chemical oxidation. The macabre ooze flowed in foot-deep rivulets onto the city streets and down into the sewers to mingle with the polluted effluents the workers themselves had been pouring there just a little while ago.

A minute passed and, as the building slumped, the man at Scorpion's controls heard Klax' command to cease fire in his headset. As he began to release the trigger, Llorca broke in.

"No," he said. "We must demonstrate that the machine can completely cleanse the Earth of this blight. Select the next target."

But as he began to pan the sights to acquire the next target, Jager could see something was wrong. The effect of the first firing of the beam continued. Already the newly built machinist's union hall behind the factory started to glow. Panicking at the thought of killing hundreds in an office building, Jager killed the power to the beam. It didn't help. At first everyone watching thought that Scorpion's operator had failed to adjust his sights as the first factory went down and now he was accidentally overshooting his target.

"Re-aim fire control," Llorca screamed. Select another target. "You have hit an office building, correct your aim!"

"I've stopped firing and initiated emergency shutdown, Sir. I'm not, repeat not, firing!"

The beam surely had stopped issuing from the needle, but the destruction continued.

Two adjacent buildings flanking the primary target now began to glow. Then it was the people on the sidewalks and the vehicles on the road that began to waste away. The beam's effect was spreading like wildfire in all directions. Now, the air itself was aglow and the ball of blue light grew, seeming to feed on itself. Scorpion's beam had started a chain reaction, sustained by the energy from disintegrating organic matter on the ground and in the air. It was spreading, ever faster.

Soon it overwhelmed Scorpion's position and began to overtake MAL's helos on the ground and in the air. Scorpion's armor kept the men inside safe. The escort and camera aircraft and crews were not as fortunate. One helo attempted take off to rise above the effect, but was enveloped in the blue glow. Instantly the rubber and hydrocarbon composite parts on the aircraft began to dissolve. The light followed the helo's exhaust gases into the engine, turning the oil to a super-viscous varnish. The engine seized within a few revolutions and exploded. As the crew's bodies fell from the sky, they had already been partially vaporized and their bones were exploding like Roman candles. The helo providing the airborne video coverage turned abruptly to flee only to meet the same fate. The camera aboard the aircraft whirled and, their stomachs already churning, two of the people in the Secretary General's office swooned to the floor at the vertiginous images. Unable to cope with the sensory overload the people around them just let their colleagues fall. Then, Whitehurst's vidscreen went black and a pall settled over the room.

"What is happening?" Llorca screamed in his command center. "Stop! Cease fire!"

The man at Scorpion's controls screamed back, "I told you, I'm not firing! I shut down," he looked at his event chronometer, "sixty-seven seconds ago." The effect is self-sustaining. I can't stop it!"

"Tell me what you see, Fritz!" Klax said in frustration, blinded to outside events by the static on the internal video monitors. He knew the man at the firing controls well and found it strange that the man had lost control of his emotions.

Forgetting protocol, the gunner answered him. "Dagon! It's like an atom bomb. Blue light is everywhere! As far as I can see, things are melting into slop. People, a dog, buildings…like the sky is falling.

There is a fizzing sound…I saw a woman's bones explode! What have we done?"

No one knew. To the horizon nothing withstood the death ray. From Fritz' vantage point atop the hill he could see the concentric rings of smoking bubbles and the blue haze still expanding.

"*Mein Gott*, I have ended the world," he thought. Then, eyes fixed on the mayhem before him; he pulled his pistol from its holster, ate the barrel and pulled the trigger. The contents of his skull spattered the dome.

Everyone heard the shot in their headsets. Klax knew Fritz was over.

Now who would be their eyes? The cameras were still out. Fritz was gone and as far as anyone knew, the beam was continuing outward, spreading death beyond the city to…where? Would this continue? Had they gone too far with this machine? What the hell was happening?

"Klax, are you there?" Llorca asked, sounding exhausted. "Klax, you must tell me. What is going on, please?"

"Fuck!" Klax exclaimed. "I can see nothing in this tin can."

Then, as the destructive beam advanced far away from the machine, the interference moderated and Scorpion's video vision cleared.

"We have regained our signal, Warden Llorca," Klax said, leaning over the monitoring station.

"Transmitting external visuals now, Sir," the video technician said.

The flattened plain of what had moments ago been a boisterous city of eighty thousand souls appeared before him. No matter how he panned or zoomed the cameras the view was the same; a putrid yellow-green sea. Here and there tiny islands of stone or piles of glass rose above grade, but basically, it was a featureless lagoon of dreck. As they continued to watch, they saw the mess was still dynamic and before their eyes, it shrank back and began to solidify into the crusty substance they had only days ago scraped off the floor of the laboratory on Alpha Island.

Analysis had shown that the leftover stuff was comprised of everything that humans and plant material were made of, less the carbon. It

was calcium, phosphorous, potassium, sulfur, sodium, chlorine, mag-
nesium and traces of iron, copper and other metals, all suspended in
gas-infused water. Shkodra had been reduced to hectare upon hectare of
steaming inorganic stew.

Pushing the cameras to the limit of their resolution, Klax reported
that all was not as bleak as it seemed. There on the fringes of the city,
about five kilometers from Scorpion's position, Klax thought he saw
trees; unless it was a mirage caused by the heat ripples dancing in the
still air. No, they were definitely there. The fizzing noise stopped.

Shkodra had been annihilated, but it was over. There was something
else. As the heat began to dissipate, the air cleared. The atmosphere
had been wiped clean of hydrocarbons and was transparent as the trade
winds that rode the seven seas. The damned thing worked.

With the sludge on the surface shrinking away, desiccated solids
blew away in multihued dust devils and the sun shone brightly above. It
was as if someone had opened the door to an electrically cleaned oven
and it was just a matter of wiping away the ash. But the residue was
people. Tens of thousands of people; their hopes, dreams, possessions
and potential all gone up in a single zap from the Scorpion.

Un-phased by the tragedy, Klax said gleefully into his mic, "Look,
Mr. Llorca, its over. It has worked beyond our greatest hopes! You there,
crack the hatch," he said to the trooper nearest the door, "I want to stand
on this new ground." The man threw a toggle switch and the vehicle's
rear wall dropped to become an exit ramp.

Klax hopped out of the machine and sank an inch into the barren,
loose earth. Convinced the effect had truly ceased, he yelled to the
uneasy troops queued up behind him.

"Move out, move, move. Stay alert!"

The men formed a perimeter around the machine and looked about
in disbelief as Klax crowed into his mic.

"Gentlemen, we have achieved a wonderful victory here today.
We…"

"Mr. Klax, please," Llorca interrupted, weeping softly as he spoke.

"The murder of eighty-thousand people is not what we wanted and it is certainly not a victory. Something went wrong. Please, please tell me the destruction has stopped. Tell me, the destruction…"

Llorca couldn't continue. He put his head in his hands and wept.

"Llorca? Llorca!?" Klax called. There was no response.

What could be wrong with him? This was the high prelate's moment of supreme triumph and he was sniveling like a whipped child. Yes, they had only meant to destroy a half dozen factories and had anticipated only a few hundred casualties, but this was so much better. Today's victory would mean immediate capitulation of the world's leaders without so much as a passing consideration of opposition. This was as grand a day as Klax had in his life and the tears of all the Wardens combined would not mediate his joy.

Klax decided he would take the machine for himself. The Wardens be hanged. MAL be hanged. The machine had exceeded his grandest expectations and he would decide from now on when, where and how to wield its magnificent power. First though, he had to get Scorpion out of there. His air cover was gone. The gunship had been vaporized, but the armor clad cargo helos were intact. For now, he would need MAL.

A short time later a replacement gunship appeared to assure Scorpion's safe recovery and Klax directed the retreat from the hilltop. They would go to ground at what was to be MAL's New World Capital on the island of Corfu at the southern tip of Albania where the Adriatic became the Ionian Sea. There, in the sub-marine womb of MAL's impregnable fortifications, Klax would execute his internal coup and make preparations to lay siege to the world.

Chapter 27

"Licking the wounds"

Forster's face was a tortured mix of disappointment and anger when the Osprey's pilot told him they had just received orders to return to the Kendall. What in hell could have happened to halt their pursuit just as it began? Before he could form the question the aircraft pulled a hard right bank and headed northwest, back toward the carrier, now bobbing like a bathtub toy in enormous swells off the windward side of the Netherlands Frisians.

Moroder, feeling he same frustration, pointed to Forster's digicom. Forster was too preoccupied to hear it ring. Stifling his furor (he was so ready to avenge Comstock's death and Katrova's injuries) he pushed the button that put Wolf Lang on the other end.

"Commander-"

Lang cut him short and explained about Shkodra. Forster was incredulous. Lang assured him it was true. They had seen real-time streaming video of the city's demise. It was no camera trick.

"We're reevaluating, Luke. The Ten are meeting now. We need you back here ASAP. Sending you in now would be like going to war with a cap gun, son. We've seriously underestimated the problem. Again."

Forster thought back to the look he had seen in MacLaren's eyes, back in Colorado. Now, he was hearing that same dread in Lang's voice. He didn't argue. He looked at Moroder and said, "Fast as we can, Sir."

Moroder caught the fear.

With a fuel stop and a weather delay it was half a day before the Osprey lit on the Kendall's deck. Natalie stood in the Air Boss' perch and watched as Forster, Moroder and the SEALs, eyes downcast and shoulders slumped to a man, dragged their gear to the aircraft elevator and slinked below decks. She refused the crutches offered her by the doc in Gdansk, preferring the less complicated task of maneuvering on a walking cast through the big ship's narrow passageways. Encumbered by her bandages, with her glorious hair shorn and her complexion wan from her ordeal, she looked like they felt. The pain medication was making her dizzy and for the first time since she accepted the challenge of this assignment, she wanted to go home.

A robust CPO helped her down the passageway to Lang's briefing room. There, she thanked the chief for his chivalry and awaited the reunion with Forster and Moroder. Fifteen minutes later, they still hadn't shown up, so she put her arms on the table, lay her head down and, weary from the effort of her recovery, dozed off. Lang arrived solo some time later. He slowed his entry when he saw the sleeping woman and briefly stood and looked her, guilt overtaking him. He tried, but couldn't resist gently stroking her hair with his fingertips. He felt like a complete asshole for putting her in harm's way without knowing the enemy's strength. He shucked his sweater and draped it over her shoulders, adjusting it with care to cover as much of her as possible.

He didn't see Luke and Mo standing in the doorway. He turned, saw the mocking grins on their faces and gave them a sharp gesture to move back into the passageway. He pressed an upright index finger against his lips, squinted his eyes to show he meant it, and closed the hatch behind him. He would brief the two men in the CDC. Katrova needed her rest.

They were joined in the Combat Direction Center by Captain Patrick, his XO, the Air Boss, and a brilliant battle tactician named Brian Christopher. This was one of the most capable and accomplished group of line officers in the Navy and although The Ten had put Forster at the point on this mission, he couldn't help feeling like the weak link.

Following curt introductions and perfunctory handshakes, Lang began.

"Gentlemen, the cat's out of the bag."

He nodded to a seaman stationed at a nearby console and the monitors above them flashed on with the Shkodra video.

"In a few hours, every vidscreen in the world will broadcast what happened and you can bet your sister's cherry that every news organization on the planet is flocking there for more."

Forster looked at Moroder for assurance that he wasn't hallucinating.

"The video ends when the helo carrying the camera is apparently consumed," Lang said.

To our knowledge there were no defensive sorties launched by the Albanians. It happened too fast."

Another nod from Lang and the seaman selected a second video source. The scene switched to a low earth orbit satellite view of the area.

"This is digitally enhanced imagery from twenty-eight thousand miles up. Watch the center of the screen."

Zooming in to a view so clear they could make out vehicles on the streets, the camera gave a bird's eye view of Scorpion as it fired. They watched the destruction of the factory and the building beyond, then, as if it were a nuclear detonation, they saw a fast moving ring of bright blue light swell and envelope the entire city. As the time coding on the screen ticked off the seconds, they watched the city evaporate. One hundred and eight seconds had elapsed since the Scorpion fired and only a tiny dark spot remained, centered in a yellow-green sea.

"Sailor, mark the center of that image and magnify," Lang ordered.

"Aye, Sir," the technician complied.

"Fill the screen with the freakin' thing," Lang instructed, impatiently.

The image on the screen continued to grow until they had the best view of the monstrous machine they were going after. Astonishingly, they could see the man under Scorpion's fire control dome. He had fair hair.

"What is that thing?" The Kendall's Captain asked.

"That is what MAL has done with Dr. Luknar's machine, Sir."

"Damn thing looks like a beetle…maybe a Scorpion or something like that," Brian Christopher added.

"Right, Sir. But this Scorpion is over twenty meters long and its sting just wiped out a city…and the eighty-thousand human beings who lived there."

"Why in the name of God, would someone want to destroy, Shkodra, Albania?" The XO asked. "It has no strategic or political importance. Hell, they're just coming out of the stone age there."

"It's not that," Lang said. "Shkodra wasn't a military target. Before they did this, MAL sent a video transmission to the Secretary General of the U.N. This was apparently a demonstration to prove their power and their intent to hold the world hostage until their demands are met. They picked Shkodra because it was polluted. They wanted to show how they could clean up the earth and put it back in what they called 'order'."

"All they're going to get is retaliation." John Patrick was angry.

"I'm not so sure, Sir," Lang said. "I think everyone's kind of frozen in place, at least until we hear from them again. It's the first time civilians have heard of MAL and they know less about them than we do. Governments won't know who or where to strike, and I wouldn't underestimate the impact this 'demonstration' has had on people. They're probably sweating who's next. Anyone living in a city with a pollution problem is probably making for the nearest national park, on the double."

"Do we still have them under surveillance?" Forster asked.

"Affirmative," Lang replied. "The last images we have showed the machine being loaded in sections into two very large helos. They went e-stealthy but we're tracking three airborne heat trails heading due west, out over the Adriatic. The third ship is an escort craft; also rotary-wing, probably the same type as the gunship that shot you guys up in Poland," he addressed Forster.

"They could be making a rendezvous with a ship in those waters or they could be making tracks for Italy. We've scrambled four F-22's from the 31st Fighter Wing out of Aviano and they should intercept the bastards within the hour."

"Is my team out of this, Commander?" Forster was kind of hoping the answer would be, yes.

"No, Mr. Forster. You are not," Lang replied firmly, emphasizing the "not."

"Seven aircraft, including two commercial airliners, MAL's helos and a pair of Albanian MIGs on a training exercise, went down over Shkodra when they were hit by whatever the hell was fired down there…that… Scorpion. We don't know that this thing can be successfully attacked from the air or by any machine. The Ten's forensic evidence guys have analyzed the samples from MAL's lab on Ahvenanmaa and they say the thing works by busting carbon molecules out of organic matter. That means people, buildings, machinery and the like. It also means that pet-rochemicals will break up under the effect. So, aircraft fuel, engine seals, even polycarbonate plastics will be eaten up. If we can't take it out with tactical weapons, we have to hope we can isolate the device somewhere where there aren't a lot of people and nuke it. Of course the success of a missile strike depends on the sophistication of MAL's target acquisi-tion technology and the beam's range. We're thinking we can send an air-launched cruise missile with a tactical warhead over the horizon at treetop level and whack it before it sees the thing coming. Admiral Christopher's people in the Mediterranean are working on an ALCM solution now. If they see us first though, they can probably toast our bird as it's inbound. Our guys at Weapons Command are having a devil of a time analyzing the ceramic compound you guys retrieved and even if we can duplicate the stuff, we don't have much time to re-engineer the aeronautics on an ALCM to account for the added weight of a ceramic skin. Regardless of the probability of success of attacking it from the air, you and your team are still our best hopes for destroying the Scorpion.

"What about a satellite-guided Joint Direct Attack Munition?" Moroder asked. "With a JDAM, the jet can drop the thing and boogie. The satellite guides it home."

"Good thought, son," Lang said. "But we've got to get a bomber within fifteen miles to launch one of those critters and like I said, we don't know the Scorpion's range. Mr. Forster, Mr. Moroder, get some sleep. In about four hours, we're putting your team back in the Osprey to make for Aviano. If MAL is concealing that machine anywhere in the area, that will be a good place to start from. Thank you gentlemen, you're dismissed."

"What about Katrova?" Forster asked, looking for confirmation that she would be staying behind to heal up.

"Yeah…Katrova," Lang looked at his shoes. "I suppose it'd be best if she stays here with Rex. Maybe it…he can help us figure out a way to bust that thing."

"You want to tell her, Forster? She won't be happy."

"Yes, Sir," Forster said, knowing how she'd probably react and that he had already weathered a couple of her storms.

"I'll tell her."

She was already angry. She had just awakened alone in Lang's darkened briefing room and knew that the men had begun their meeting without her. When she got hold of Lang, she would…

Just then, Forster appeared in the hatchway.

She was in his face in a single step and she shouted at him.

"Forster, what the hell?"

"Easy, Katrova, easy," he scrunched up his face to look mean and deflect some of the steam from her nostrils

"You needed the down time and actually, no one wanted to be the one to rouse you."

Knowing he was in for a hard time, he pressed into the room cautiously, backing her up until he could close the door behind him.

"I'll fill you in."

He did, as gently as he could and taking his time, trying to stall the part where he would tell her she wouldn't be going on with the team. The tone in his voice was different than he usually used with her and she quickly figured out there was something up.

"A fighter sortie and cruise missiles won't work, Luke," she said.

"I saw the video, too. It's going to take a small team, our team, to take this thing out face-to-face. It has to be a surprise. Their technology is too good. I've been thinking about a way-"

"Natalie," he interrupted. There was no more avoiding it and he steeled himself against what was sure to be a fierce response.

"We need you here, on the Kendall."

She didn't jump at him, claws bared. She didn't hang her head. Or cry. Or bash him with the water pitcher on Lang's file cabinet, although he would never know how close he came to wearing the vessel as permanent headgear. She didn't yell either. She just looked through his eyes and straight into his defenseless core.

"Why, Luke?" She asked.

He saw her hands shaking. She was trying her best to be professional but she had worked hard and taken her lumps and she didn't understand why he wanted to cut her from the team. Over the past few months, she had grown to enjoy being part of a team. Going back to her days of playing it solo now scared her.

"Nat," Forster said, steeling himself to tell her the hard truth.

"This is going to get awfully tough from here on. We're probably going to take more casualties before this over. You need some time to heal up and I can't be there to protect you. I've already let you down once and almost got you killed! You're better off here. Hell, if they turn that thing loose again, we may all be goners. The team needs you here where you can work with Rex and come up with some kind of defense against that thing. You're the brains of this outfit and it just doesn't make sense to have you at the point!"

He made his best argument and he thought he impressed her with his sincerity and concern. At least she was still listening.

The silence hung thick in the room. Still, she didn't speak.

"Natalie, stop staring at me. Say, something. You agree with me don't you?"

She stood and pulled Lang's sweater from her shoulders. Still not taking her eyes off Forster, she folded the sweater a little too deliberately and laid it across the chair back.

"No, Luke, I don't," she said.

Luke felt the temperature in the room drop.

"I've been a loner and a social outcast for most of my life. I taught myself to read, play and write music; I'm a qualified master of three martial arts and I've taken my share of honors in international competitions in both. I've built the single most powerful computer ever built by…woman…a triumph by the way, that our most respected minds have called brilliant and the most significant technological achievement of the modern age. I'm a damn fine scientist and a fast thinker, mister team leader and because I'm a damn fine scientist and a fast thinker, The Ten has enough faith in me to believe that I can be a part of the solution to this problem. I'm not a quirky overconfident tomboy looking for an adventure. My motivation is simple and straightforward. I can't stand by and watch a few million or billion people die. Besides," she said, giving her primary, self-assessed weakness its due, "this is so damn black and white and easy for me to get behind. There's no finesse here. Not much chance of making an emotional screw-up with this one. We're up against pure evil, Luke Forster. Whipping these bastards will take everything we've got. Maybe it's latent mothering instincts, I don't know. But, I don't want anything to happen to you or Mo or Wolf Lang or anyone else on our side. MAL just wasted some of our best SEALs and Jim Comstock, and tens of thousands of innocents in Shkodra without a blink, and if we don't take them down, I don't think they're going to stop until everyone and everything on Earth is turned to slime. I can do thi-"

Tears fell down her cheeks and she started to shiver. Her leg wound, the deep sorrow in her heart for those lost, and the feelings for Luke welling up in her were just too much to handle. She started to weave and felt the blood rush from her head.

Luke caught her as she toppled and held her uneasily, like he was a kid in school and a girl had just tossed him a rag doll. Her beautiful face, the tears glistening on her cheeks and her soft kid-cropped hair made him look at her closely, probably for the first time. Suddenly, he felt like a voyeur. He shouldn't be holding her like this. Not this gently. Not knowing his ambivalence toward her. Not knowing that, as Comstock had disclosed in his last moments, that she was falling for him.

Yes, he knew it. He saw the way she looked at him out of the corner of his eye when they worked together. When she was wounded, he had to fight to keep control of his feelings and his command, though he wanted to run to her and blow away the people who hurt her. She was brave and kind and tough and God, she felt warm and lax and good in his arms.

It seemed like an hour that he held her there, close to him. He cradled her head in one of his big mitts and tenderly brushed a wayward lock of hair from her face. He wanted to kiss her. He wanted to surround her. She wasn't all that bad. She was just so blasted stubborn and…he did care. Damn it to hell, he did. That's why she had to stay aboard ship.

He couldn't go on with her on the assault team because it was too late to take back his love. He did love her and his heart couldn't withstand another loss like Tricia.

With her near, he could never bring himself to take the risks he'd have to take. He couldn't make the clear-headed tactical calls and cold-blooded kills to beat the bad guys if she were in peril.

Natalie came to while he was lost in thought.

"I feel like dog shit," she said as she steadied, found her feet and backed out of his arms. He helped her into the desk chair, wrapped Lang's sweater around her again and turned into the passageway.

"Sit tight, Katrova," he said gently, relieved to be leaving.

"I'll get the doc."

Natalie hung her head, put her elbows on her knees and cupped her chin in her hands, trying to keep from doing a face plant on the deck. She couldn't know that Luke's head was spinning too. As the doc escorted Natalie to sickbay, Forster moped up to the flight deck for air. Whatever he was feeling he had to sort it out and get himself squared away, fast. There was no time for romance. He saw Moroder leaning on a safety rail watching the whitecaps seesaw atop the deep green of the sea.

"How's she taking it, Luke?" He asked.

"Still fuzzy from the painkillers, I think. She didn't shoot me but she's not happy."

"What did you expect? Luke, you haven't done this team combat thing very much have you?"

"No, Mo, I've worked pretty much alone 'til now. What's your point?"

"Well, now that you've asked. Ya know, the team we put together, it's like every other gang of jamokes you throw into a platoon for the first time. Ya know, just a bunch of folks. See, at first, it's like it was in basic. There's a herd of guys from all over the map. Different ages, races, classes, schooling and like that. First, everybody digs at each other about bein' hicks from the country, or fast Eddies from the city or gooks or wops or spics or camel jockey's or whatever. Then, after a few too many beers at the PX, sharing a mud meal on the night assault range and a few screw-ups in front of everybody on the obstacle course, you start to laugh at things. Maybe even start to like each other a little bit. Then, you find yourself giving a shit and helping the weaker guys do better, so you all look good. The next thing you know, you're mates and you start to work together better than you did alone. *Capice?*"

Forster nodded his head and smiled to himself about how Mo could make a complex social interaction sound like just so much playground common sense.

"*Capice*, Forster replied."

"Yeah, well, that's the way it is with Natalie and us all now. It's not she wants to grandstand, Luke. She only wants to be on the field with her teammates when it's the bottom of the ninth. Myself, I think we're makin' a big mistake leavin' her here."

"How so?" Forster asked, giving the man his due respect.

"You didn't see her stuff at the LZ, did ya?

"No, we were trying to shoot bad guys."

"She did us proud, Luke. The LZ went up in a puff. It was nuts. She saw the Stinger threat, Klax and a few MALs all in a tight little knot, bad tactics if I say so myself, and she made an instant decision to give up her cover and take 'em on. They had us pinned to the wall and she hummed a vibe grenade fastball. Underhand, ya know?"

Moroder demonstrated the move.

"The viber hit the scum bag in the bellybutton, man. You shoulda seen it. I've had guys on assault teams ten years that didn't have that kinda moxie. Or, that kinda arm. She got a bunch of 'em, Luke. Except, Klax. The clean up guys didn't find his body…not even a slime trail. He just disappeared. But, she really gave 'em Hades, Luke. She probably saved our bacon. I'm tellin' ya…I guess, I mean, I'm suggestin', Sir. We need her."

"I appreciate your loyalty, Mo, but-"

Forster contemplated his boots.

"But, what?"

"All right, all right, Mo. Here it is. I'm just worried about her, especially after what happened at the LZ. I can't do my job and protect her."

Mo saw the look in Forster's eyes and finally understood the problem.

"Cool," he thought, "He's not as thick as he looks."

"Luke, see, the thing is (you deluded head case, he thought), what I'm tellin' ya is, *she* can protect *us*. She's smart and tough and she likes me. Why wouldn't I want her at my back?" Moroder forced his big Guinea grin on the man.

"All due respect, Luke, if I was you, I'd get to Lang on the double. Make up your speech on the way. OPS found the MALs. We've got 'em on satellite, maybe headed to Corfu. We're to make ready for a final assault. If we miss 'em this time Luke, The Ten's ordered a nuclear solution.

"They can't do that, Mo," Forster protested. There are a lot of civilians on that island."

"The way they figure it, Luke, if we don't get MAL, that's a small number compared to the casualties we'll take if they fire that damn thing again at like, Athens or Rome."

"Thanks, Mo," Forster said. "You know, you're really not as bad as people say. Or, as ugly."

Forster bolted the deck at a full sprint, leaving Moroder to wonder whether Forster was kidding.

After two minutes of red-faced, tumultuous argument, both men screaming at full-bull volume, Lang said, "All right, dammit. Get your assess and your gear to the flight deck, now! Yours and hers. But, so help me God Forster, if anything happens to that woman, I'll stick that Scorpion up your six and pull the trigger myself!"

"Yes, Sir," Forster replied in his best and most militarily courteous tone. He smiled at Lang.

"Shit fire, mister!" Lang ordered him. "The clock is ticking."

Thirty minutes later, an Osprey with two full SEAL teams, Natalie Katrova, Mo Moroder and Luke Forster aboard, sprang off the Kendall's deck and set course for Corfu and their destinies. When they reached cruising altitude, the smooth droning of the tilt rotors was punctuated by the clicks and clacks of weapons being re-checked, re-cleaned and reloaded. Natalie asked Moroder for an extra viber and the co-pilot for a marker pen and wrote Comstock's name on it.

"This one's going down Dagon Klax' throat," she said aloud, a furrow in her brow, and clipped it to her belt.

Lang in the CDC and Forster in the Osprey were making the assault plan literally on the fly. There was some discussion about weather they would attack by sea. The SEALs were certainly well trained on that tactic, and they were outfitted with the necessary gear, but Forster, Moroder and Katrova were by no means expert swimmers, especially loaded down with so much firepower. As they were debating the logistics and coming to the conclusion that a water attack would be too risky, Katrova found a better solution.

The latest satellite imagery had uncovered heat trail patterns showing that hundreds of tons of materiel had been delivered by surface transport to an area just east of the last known position of MAL's helos. The printouts showed a fan of heavy truck trails leading to a single portal - a dead end that must mean a tunnel door and another subterranean facility.

Immediately, Forster and Lang agreed the tunnel door would be the focus of the raid.

The key to success would be presenting a significant enough threat to entice the Scorpion out of the fortress. The M-90s ought to insure that, especially when they began to sear a hole through the main portal. If the bug went for it and Forster's team could get a hit on a vulnerable spot, they had a chance. Of course, if the tunnel doors opened and a heavily armed battalion of MAL's own troops responded instead, they'd have to fight their way in or wait for reinforcements. That would give the enemy a chance to spring their own trap and set the Scorpion against a much larger opposing force. The casualties would be staggering in that event and as they had seen when the MIG fighters melted over Shkodra, air power would be rendered useless. No. The only way to do this would be to lure the Scorpion out alone and attack it up close and personal, like aphids on an ant.

As Forster and Lang discussed the merits of the plan, the Osprey's intercom scratched open.

"Mr. Forster," the co-pilot spoke, "the pilot would like a word with you. Would you join us up front, Sir?"

"On my way," Luke replied. "Thanks, Commander," Forster signed off with Lang, "I'll draw this up for the team and get back to you."

Unbuckling his harness, Luke cast an inquisitive glance at Katrova and, getting raised eyebrows in response, made his way to the Osprey's flight deck.

As Forster stuck his head into the cockpit, the pilot pulled off his helmet, revealing a familiar shock of red hair and a grin that made Forster smile back.

"Red!" He said, in the relief of recognition.

"Mr. Luke, it's good to see ya'. Take over, will ya' Jackson?"

"Aye, Sir," the copilot replied.

"How the hell'd you draw this duty?"

"To be honest Luke, this whole death ray thing looked pretty much like a run 'n hide to me. If I went with my natural instincts, I should probably be home under the covers about now. Truth is, scuttlebutt says some jackass took a chunk out of Ms. Katrova's trim little leg and there's somethin' about that just pisses me off. Besides, there's an old Scotsman I used to know asked me to," and he slipped into MacLaren's brogue, "Kaep a shaerp eye ferr anyone trrayin' to taern your lights oout."

Forster had to fight off his initial revulsion at hearing the name. Still a reflex. After a moment, he appreciated his old nemesis' concern and thought how he had come to appreciate the accuracy of the Scot's assessment of the enemy.

"MacLaren, is he-?"

"Gone," the pilot confirmed.

"How'd he die?" Forster asked, sounding more interested than he intended.

"Oh. He's not dead, Luke. Sorry…I didn't mean…. I mean. He's alive and all that. He's just, gone. Nobody knows where. He's just disappeared, I guess. No, Sir. Far as I know he's still kickin'."

"Forget it, Red," Forster got the point. "I'm glad you're here."

"All the way, Luke," the pilot replied. "My co-driver's an Army Ranger, such as your own dangerous self and he'll be joining your team. Best rifle grenadier in the service and a passable flyer…for a grunt," he chided the mustached, Errol Flynnesque aviator in the right seat.

"Mr. Forster, Captain Lance Jackson," Red said, as the two exchanged a gloved handshake. "Call sign Stony."

"My pleasure, Mr. Forster."

"Glad to have you, Stony," Forster smiled at the man. "The more the merrier."

"Eh, you want to share the plan, here Luke? We'll be feet dry over Corfu in twenty three minutes and we're already being painted by MAL's radar."

Forster related the dicey details of the raid. In the next hour they would either be victorious or a footnote in MAL's version of history. Everyone knew their odds of survival were slim, but the thing had to die.

Chapter 28

"Under new management"

As MAL's helicopters made their way out over the Adriatic, none of the mercenaries spoke. They understood what they had done. In their minds and indeed in the eyes of the world, they were no longer noble eco-soldiers seeking a better world for mankind. They were mass murderers on the run.

The men who accompanied Klax on this mission were his personal guard; hand selected for their loyalty, courage and expertise. They knew after what happened at Shkodra they were being hunted by every technologically capable military force on Earth. And now, in the air, they were most vulnerable, with no way to activate the Scorpion, It would only be a matter of time before someone got a visual on them. There was a high probability that if they were found they wouldn't even have a chance to defend themselves. A single F-22 fighter could launch multiple eMags from over the horizon and splash them without warning.

No defense had yet been devised for the electromagnetic video-controlled air-to-air missile. They couldn't be fooled by chaff or flares, like the old heat seekers and radar homers. These weapons "memorized" the energy signatures of the mechanical and electrical systems of every airborne, sea and land based weapons transport platform in the world's arsenals. EMags could be launched with digitally encrypted instructions to seek an individual plane, boat, truck or train engine. With the tenacity of a terrier, it would hunt the target down for as long as it had fuel. It was supersonic, delivered a one hundred and fifty pound, high explosive, micro-fragmenting warhead and it rarely missed.

For MAL, it was scant comfort that the eMags could be detected on their sophisticated radars. If the intercept officer aboard MAL's escort gunship was competent and paying close attention there would be time for a short prayer before they were blown from the sky and cast into the sea as pre-macerated fish food. Their best hope was to reach the missile defense zone around MAL's stronghold before their foes could initiate the attack.

"Mr. Klax," the pilot spoke into his intercom, his calm voice belying his fear, "The gunship's RIO says we're being followed. At least two American F-22s are vectoring to our position from Aviano. He's also tracking two Greek Hydra Class attack frigates heading east from Othonoi Island toward intercept. They know we're here."

"Get me Llorca, now," Klax ordered.

"Sir, we've been trying to raise the stronghold since liftoff from Shkodra. There is yet no reply."

"Do you think they've been attacked on Corfu?"

"No, Sir. We are receiving their carrier frequency and there is nothing wrong with our transceiver. They are not responding."

"Keep trying."

"Yes, Mr. Klax, but the fighters will soon be upon us."

If they made it back alive, Klax vowed he would kill Llorca with his bare hands for this treachery.

The Vigileer's of the USAF's 32nd Fighter Squadron at Aviano were among the most lethal fighter jockeys in the air and the men assigned to kill the monster that melted Shkodra were intent on administering punishment.

One hundred and eighty miles behind MAL's helos but well ahead of Forster's Osprey in the time it would take to close on the target, the fighters got their first blips of the MALs on the eMag target acquisition displays just after going feet wet. There were two big blips, likely the cargo helos carrying the weapon components and escort troops, and one smaller blip. Had to be a gunship. The electronic signatures from the aircraft were not stored in the eMag memory chips before the mission, but they were now and they told the system plenty. The target acquisition head-up display read, UR2C1A, signifying - unidentified aircraft/rotary, two cargo, one attack. It was the MALs, all right.

The man behind the black-out visor with call sign "Mako" painted in graffiti red above it announced, "Base, this is Bug Leader, I've got three bogies - helos headed one-four-zero at two hundred knots. I think these are our maniacs. Over."

"Affirmative, Bug Leader," the base controller responded.

"Designate your bogeys Mike one, two and three. The Greek Navy has them on screen too. The helos are headed toward Corfu."

"Roger base, designating bogeys Mike, one two and three. What are our orders?" Mako asked, already knowing the answer.

There was a brief pause while the squadron leader confirmed his response with the wing commander and relayed the message.

"Splash 'em."

"Roger, base," the pilot smiled inside his helmet and snapped a thumbs-up to his wingman. "Bug Two, arm your eMags."

"Arming eMags," came the acknowledgment from the second jet. "How do want to split 'em up, Mako?"

"I'll put two on the gunship; you point one each at the two cargo choppers."

"Bug Leader to base, we are at sixty miles and closing. EMags armed." A high-pitched continuous tone in his headset told him the missiles had acquired their target and locked on.

"Firing on my count Bug Two…in three, two, one. Bug Leader, fox one, fox two!"

Then his wingman loosed his missiles, "Bug Two, fox one, fox two."

Four missiles ignited and sprang from the main weapons bay into the severe clear air over the Adriatic, drawing thin white lines in the sky. In seconds, the weapons stabilized and four, arrow-straight, contrails headed in parallel formation south-southeast toward the horizon. They would impact their targets just as MAL's helos began their descent to the stronghold. With a little luck, there would be no homecoming for Klax and his men, just flaming debris and body parts plummeting into the azure water.

Aboard the MAL gunship, the commander knew that within seconds his life would be forfeit. His only chance for survival was to use his radar-aimed miniguns to acquire the inbound missiles and shoot them down before they could reach the helos carrying Scorpion and the Einstein coil. He would need all his skills as a combat pilot and some masterful gunnery from his weapons officer to survive. No helo driver had ever shot down a supersonic missile with a bullet, but his miniguns would each be spitting projectiles at a rate of more than four thousand per minute. If he could put up a wall of lead in a tight enough group fronting the inbound missiles, he might hit a vital spot and survive to tell his children about the adventure.

"Arm Gatling guns, Yuri," he ordered the man sitting in tandem behind him; "We will make our fight, here." He brought the ship about one hundred and eighty degrees to face the incoming weapons and hovered to await his fate.

"Guns armed, Sir," came the immediate reply from the weapons officer. I have four inbound eMags on radar. Two are locked on us. Estimate impact in forty-three seconds."

"Alert the cargo ships, Yuri. Tell them to go to maximum speed and maintain course and altitude. The Americans will have to go through us to get them."

"Acknowledged, Sir."

At once, Klax knew what the gunship commander was attempting to do. He also knew the man would fail. Unless Klax did something immediately, they were all dead.

He hailed his pilot on the intercom, "Listen carefully, we have only seconds. Do what I say or we die. Clear?"

"Yes Mr. Klax.," the pilot responded. Inside his flight suit sweat ran between the cheeks of his buttocks. What he heard next was either insanity born in the panic of the moment or complete genius.

"Turn off all power. All power," Klax yelled. "Tell ship two to comply as well. NOW!"

It was a desperate move, but it made sense. The eMags used electrical impulses to track their targets. No output meant there was no signal for the missile to home in on. There was however, the problem of flying without power.

Auto gyration was a last resort, emergency option to reduce the rate of fall in rotary wing aircraft that had lost power and in the giant cargo helos, with two counter-rotating horizontal and one vertical rotor to manage the tremendous torque from the engine, they would have some control over their rate of descent and heading. But all that didn't do much to mediate the ultimate consequence of free fall. Hitting the water at over fifty knots would crush them and when the rotors impacted the water there would be shredded metal flying everywhere. But, any chance was better than none and that's what a missile hit would give them.

The cargo pilots complied with Klax' orders. Moments later the helos' rotors went to maximum drag. The noise of engines and radios were replaced with the whoosh of rushing air and the prayers and panicked cries of troops and flight crew. Klax cursed Llorca for sending them on this run without fighter escort. Where the hell was he? Why didn't he answer?

"Incoming missiles at twelve miles and closing fast, Sir!" Yuri was breathing so hard, he had to catch his breath to shout.

"Hold your fire, Yuri, just a few more seconds, now," the commander attempted to sound in control. The weapons officer heard the tremble in his voice. Seconds turned to an eternity as the adrenaline surging through their blood mercilessly stretched time. Yuri saw the four incoming blips on his threat display meld into one. They were so close now his radar couldn't separate them.

"Fire! Continuous burst!" The commander ordered. Yuri squeezed the trigger on his control stick and held the stick tightly for minimum dispersion of the slugs. The miniguns barked in response, the tracer rounds flaring out before them in a choked, elliptical barrage. Spent shell casings rained from the ejectors and a cloud of gun smoke swirled around the craft. They could both see the exhaust contrails as the deadly darts drew near. Then, four hundred meters ahead, the minigun rounds found home. The nearest eMag exploded in a ball of white and orange flame. They got one!

It was a hollow victory. A heartbeat later, the second eMag closed on the cockpit of the gunship. The commander even saw the nosecone before it impacted his windscreen. For a few fractions of a second, Mako could make out the two men in the front seats on his cockpit monitor as the eMag's nosecone camera broadcast the kill.

The flaming carcass of the spent missile continued for a quarter mile after impact without even a small deviation from its course. In the helo, metal and flesh vaporized. The high explosive and micro-shrapnel from the warhead and the atomized helo fuel incinerated the flyers' remains to ash even before gravity could pull them toward the sea. The gunship's main rotor snapped from its drive shaft and continued on, now free of the engine that propelled it. It was the only large piece of the craft left and it sailed through the air like a giant black pinwheel, off on a ghostly flight of its own.

"Splash the gunship, base," Bug Leader reported in. "Two birds still homing." But, as he looked to his display, he realized they weren't. The blips from the cargo choppers on his eMag acquisitor screen had disappeared and the head-up display just flashed, "*Hunt.*"

He switched the target acquisitor from *eMag* to *Radar* and the blips reappeared. Two aircraft were still there, and both were losing altitude. To confirm his target, he switched the acquisitor again to the IR setting. The heat the infrared sensors were made to detect was rapidly dissipating and the blips again faded, "No power?" He thought.

"They've gone dark, Bug Two," Mako said. "Have you got 'em?"

"Negative, Sir. It looks like they're auto gyrating, heading straight for the drink. Without electrical to seek, the eMags'll never find 'em. Ballsy move."

Then the wingman's acquisitor warned, and the computer intoned, "eMagAD."

"Bug Leader, I just got eMag splashdown on my shots, Sir," the wingman spoke dejectedly.

"Repeat, both birds going autodead. We have auto destruct."

Without a target, the missiles had done what they were programmed to do; maintain course for eight seconds, then go ballistic, straight up, until they ran out of fuel, flame out and self-destruct. The missile builders had known the problems with misidentification. The acquisition system was proven in battle but it was not perfect. There had been errors; especially when the eMags were fired during a period of sunspot flux, when the Earth's magnetic field went temporarily wacky. So, they had built in this fail-safe. Better to lose a million-dollar missile than have it mistakenly lock on to a civilian aircraft or a passenger train.

For the F-22s, the failure of the eMags was problematic. They still had their guns to attack the choppers, but they had no infrared or radar-seeking air-to-air missiles aboard. Their best hope now was to overtake the enemy and bring their guns to bear before the MALs could set down on the island.

"Bug Leader to base," Mako called in. "eMags useless now. We've lost lock and have missile suicide. We are in pursuit."

"Roger, Bug Leader," the base replied.

"Get 'em, shark boy."

The Raptors' afterburners lit and a booming shock wave buffeted the fighters' airframes as the jets tore through Mach 1.

"Good thinking, Mr. Klax," his pilot said, grinning at his reprieve. "We have lost the eMags or we would have been cooked by now. We will restart engines and continue to Corfu." There were cheers as the co-pilot relayed the word to the escort troops and the noise of the restart shuddered through the huge helo.

"Pilot, ask the gunship the status of the fighters," Klax ordered, anxious to know how long it would be before they would be overtaken.

"There is no more gunship, Mr. Klax," the pilot reported. "Captain Feduska and Flight Officer Chandrakai gave their lives to save us."

Klax cared nothing that the courageous men were lost. He was angry that they had been deprived of the cover of the gunship's weaponry. The Raptors were out there somewhere and it could yet be Klax' day to die.

"Mr. Klax, I have Warden Llorca for you," the pilot said. "On channel two. Please be brief. There may soon be new eMags looking for us."

Klax switched his headset to broadcast and began to berate the man on the other end.

"Llorca, you bastard. We've been trying to reach you for hours. We are under attack. The gunship is gone. We need air cover now! You cowering dog. Answer me!"

Llorca's reply was as maddeningly curt as his tone was cool.

"Mr. Klax, you are now under cover of the stronghold's defense shield. No need to worry, Dagon. Bring your aircraft into the main hangar bay and report to me when you land. Out."

Before Klax could resume his tirade, the signal went dead. If Llorca said they were safe, he believed him. But the casual way the Wardens had let Klax run the gauntlet to bring them their precious machine, without concern for the physical integrity of his posterior, convinced him that his decision to terminate his relationship with MAL and appropriate the Scorpion for his personal use was correct.

"Bug Leader, this is base. Acknowledge."

"Roger base, Bug Leader," Mako replied.

"Bug Leader, are you still tracking your bogeys? Over?"

"Roger, base. We have two bogeys at low altitude twenty miles out. We de not, repeat, do not have visual, but we are closing and expect contact any second."

Suddenly, a blinding flash of light burst in the sky before them. Had the flyers not had their visors down, they would have been instantly blinded. As it was, all they could "see" was spots before their eyes.

"What the fuck was that?" Mako said, trying to keep his plane on course. His head hurt from the pulse of light.

"Shit, they lit a nuke, Mako," his wingman screamed, trying to steady his bucking fighter.

"Negative, Bug Two," the pilot tried to reassure his comrade. His eyes were watering now and his throat was closing up. "No shock wave. It must have been a britelight weapon of some kind launched from Corfu. My radar never picked it up. Engage autopilot and pray they haven't toasted our eyeballs. Bug Leader to base, Bug Leader to base, we are flying blind. A giant flashgun just went off. The whole sky's gone white. We are using autopilot until we can see again. Breaking off attack. Repeat, we are disengaging. Over."

"Roger, Bug Leader. Advise of your condition as it changes."

The Ten had heard of such light burst weapons but had never encountered them and they were caught completely off guard when the rocket, if that's what it was, penetrated the Raptor's threat warning sensors undetected. MAL continued to show they were a formidable foe. The Ten's opinion their adversary would have grown again, had they been witness to what was about to happen.

On the control panel before him, Klax' pilot saw an indicator light that gave him his first hope he would survive the day. The icon meant his craft was perfectly positioned above the gigantic sea door that allowed them entry to the sub-marine complex that was MAL's principal stronghold.

"Prepare for landing, Mr. Klax," he spoke into his helmet mic. "We are home."

In his headset, he heard the technicians as they exchanged landing control sequence orders and confirmations. He had only to hold the helo at a dead hover for a minute and they would be safe.

"Standby," the landing control officer instructed. "Initiating sea vault entry program...now."

"Roger control," the pilot replied.

As Klax' helo hovered and the second stood off awaiting its turn, the sea parted beneath them.

Making hardly a ripple as it rose toward them from the deep blue water was a two hundred foot long black wedge, its apex pointed skyward. As pilot and passengers watched in rapt amazement, it climbed toward them, the shape's base growing more massive at it rose. Soon it became apparent that the wedge was in fact a steeply vaulted roof-like structure sitting atop a rectangular box nearly as wide as it was long. Then it stopped. It looked like a gargantuan black hotel game piece resting on the royal blue field of the Boardwalk property on a Monopoly board.

The structure stood motionless for a moment before the roof began to open from its peak, like a mechanical Venus flytrap about to devour a passing insect. The scene was surreal. As the doors pealed back, it revealed a colossal caisson excavated into the floor of the Ionian Sea. Beneath the waters, the pilot could now view the high intensity landing lights pulsing and rotating to guide him safely to the sub-marine helipad.

"Release controls to landing guidance computer on my signal, please.

Now," the landing control officer called out.

Though he had practiced the next step dozens of times, the pilot never became accustomed to it. With some reluctance, he released the cyclic, then the collective, and felt the reassuring little jump as the computer took over the flight controls. Capricious local wind gusts and the visual disorientation flyers encountered attempting their first landings here had long ago proven too dangerous to allow pilots manual control.

The pilot looked out the windscreen and watched uneasily as the view around him changed from sky and sea blue, to the black of the peak's steel-latticed interior walls, to the brash glare of the hangar and landing lights. Then…touchdown.

"Power down, Sir, quickly please," came the orders from the controller.

The craft's rotors were still turning when a low-slung and stout tractor latched on and began to drag the helo off the pad. They wanted to recover the second one fast, before more enemy aircraft arrived.

A minute later the second helo landed and the command was given to close the vault and it slithered back beneath the sea. Again the surface was calm and any trace of the structure gone.

Below, the turmoil had just begun. At the same moment the tractor gripped the forward wheel carriage, Klax stood in the helo's cargo bay and spoke to his guard.

"To me," he bellowed and his men gathered 'round. He keyed his command radio mic open and locked it so the pilot in the other helo could hear what he was saying and relay his message to those men as well.

"Listen carefully my soldiers. We have little time and we must act without hesitation or we are lost. Do you understand?"

"Yes, Sir," the reply came from the men as one.

"We no longer serve MAL."

The men, although they would never outwardly demonstrate their emotions to the point where Klax could perceive even the faintest disloyalty or reticence, were confused.

"The weapon they have created," Klax continued, "has been proven to be far more powerful than our timid leaders can comprehend or manage. What happened in Shkodra has made them cowards. Rather than press this advantage to the fullest, I believe they will now destroy the Scorpion and surrender to our enemies or flee like scared rabbits. Should that happen, the world's governments will hunt us all the days of our lives. There will be no safe place."

Helmeted heads bobbed in agreement.

"We, however, will not become scapegoats for these idealistic fools. You see, they have put in our hands the means to secure our future. With the power of this machine, we can dictate terms. We can triumph, now and forever!"

As Klax spoke his body twitched with uncontrollable passion. Spittle formed in the corner of his mouth and trickled onto his chin. His nasal appliance began to resonate adding a metallic hum to the rising vibrato of his voice.

"Today, we take command of the machine and our fate. We will tell the world how it will run. We will liquefy the inferior and the defiant. We-" He heard himself begin to rant and took a choppy breath.

"We together, will put order back into the capitalist-driven frenzy feeding on the labor of the world's workers. We together will build wealth and power for all and force our enlightened will on the shrinking minority of those who would destroy us."

None of the men dared look away, but they all knew that the only "enlightenment" Klax had in his life was the sublime joy he experienced watching Shkodra melt. He was right about one thing. After what they had done, they would all be pursued to the far corners of the Earth, but that would happen some time hence. Refusing to join Klax would mean certain death, today. They listened without comment.

"You who come with me will be the governors and chieftains of my new regime. Do this and the rewards will exceed your most fantastic dreams. Today, we take this complex. Tomorrow we make our attack on the Americans and their allies. In the coming days, we will demonstrate our power against all who would resist us. Arm your weapons men and follow me. Keep a tight formation. Today, the Wardens draw their last breath."

Over Klax' shoulder, the pilot and the co-pilots in their seats looked at each other in disbelief. They too feared him, but they were not a part of Klax' inner circle and after what they had just heard, they were sure the man was mad. They had to act.

The pilot keyed his mic and began to speak softly, "Control, control, do you read me?"

Klax saw the two men with their backs to him, surmised the nature of the whispers and shot them through the backs of their helmets. He gave the order to his platoon leader aboard the second helo to do like-wise. The man complied without question.

"Say again, please?" The control officer requested of the pilot, but there was no answer.

Klax said to his men, "Go!"

The troops in both helos vaulted from the cargo doors weapons drawn and forming a perimeter around Klax and made for the broad passageway that led to the Wardens' meeting room and main control.

Nearby technicians, unaware of what was about to happen, stood and regarded the mercenaries' close combat tactics with minor curios-ity, then went about their business. Moments later, the helos' mechanics found the flyers' bodies and reported the murders.

As Klax and his men reached main control and entered the spa-cious bay to face Llorca and the other members of MAL's high council, the automatic doors closed behind them. Then, from the balcony trace above them, a dozen gun barrels appeared. A rash of laser sights measled Klax' face. A few flared in his pupils blinding him. Instinctively, he raised his hand to shield his eyes. Klax' men turned to face Llorca's troops, creating an instant standoff. Although Klax' forces outnumbered Llorca's two to one, the men on the high ground held the advantage. Some of Llorca's men upped the ante, pulling fragmentation grenades from their belts and thumbed the arming bolts. All it would take now was a wink from Klax or the twitch of a trigger finger from one of Llorca's men and the bodies would start falling. To their advantage, Klax' bodyguards were still wearing their combat body armor. Llorca's were clad in the cloth jumpsuits of the stronghold's security force.

Still dodging the lasers in his eyes Klax spoke, stalling for time, "Is this the welcome you give the heroes of Shkodra, Warden Llorca?"

"There were no heroes at Shkodra, Mr. Klax," Llorca admonished him. "Please ask your guard to stand down and drop their weapons."

"As long as we are in danger, Mr. Llorca, we will remain at the ready. Can you tell me what is happening here?"

"Your services are no longer required, Mr. Klax. We have made a terrible mistake firing the Scorpion. The result will certainly be that MAL will be seen as nothing more than a bloodthirsty pack of psychopaths. We will be driven to ground by the combined military forces of the world and executed. In your absence we have decided we must destroy the weapon and scatter like dust in the wind if we are to survive."

"Why would you destroy the only weapon that assures our victory," Klax asked, casting a momentary glance at the captain of his guard from behind the cover of the hand he raised to shield his eyes. In that brief connection, both men understood that this dialog wouldn't last much longer.

"We will not debate our decision, Mr. Klax. You will instruct your men to stand down or we will force you to do so."

To Klax' mind, the events of the next thirty seconds took an hour to unfold. He had been in pitched battles like this before and he had trained himself to push his reaction time and alertness into hyper speed. At such times one had to see and be aware of the dangers from all quarters.

In the blink of an eye Klax dove to the floor and rolled beneath one of the crescent-shaped tables facing the Warden's dais. As he corkscrewed for cover he drew his pistol, sprang to a sitting position, steadied for a heartbeat and fired a single shot into Llorca's torso, slamming the Warden against the wall, a startled look on his face.

The din in the confined chamber was deafening as small arms fire and grenades filled the air with smoke, flame and flesh-rending metal. Combatants from both sides were dying under the withering hail of bullets, shrieking the pain of their wounds into the turmoil. There was a mist of blood in the air and butchered limbs lay twitching on the floor. It was a firefight in a phone booth and for a moment, even Klax thought no one would escape. Then it was over.

None of Llorca's troops stood. Eight of Klax' had men were unharmed, or had minor injuries. Three were mortally wounded, the rest dead. A rifle round had creased Klax' skull and he was bleeding profusely from the left side of his head. Otherwise he was sound. He stood to assess the situation, took a deep breath and screamed at the top of his lungs.

"Victory, my soldiers! Today we begin a new world order."

The survivors were stunned and had no capacity to share his elation. The stench of death grew in their nostrils as they stared at the carnage around them. All these men had been comrades just days ago.

"Gusarov, my friend," Klax said to the captain of his guard, "Clean up the wounded."

"But, Dagon," he began to protest; knowing that "clean up" meant euthanizing the fallen who still clung to life.

"Yevgeny, remember yourself," Klax ordered.

If he had been assured that one of his comrades wouldn't have put a bullet in him for doing so, Gusarov would have killed Klax on the spot for giving him this order. Surely it was to test his resolve and demonstrate Klax' power over them, even as they were overwhelmed by the loss of their brothers in arms.

"Yes, Mr. Klax," he responded in military manner.

One by one, the man shot the remaining casualties in the head, the survivors flinching in their gore stained uniforms at each report.

Inspecting the balcony level, Gusarov came upon Llorca's bloody form among the fallen. The high prelate of the Wardens was still breathing, his face glistening in sweat and fish-belly white.

"Mr. Klax, Llorca lives," he called down.

"Save him for me, Yevgeny," Klax said. As he ascended the stairs, he slid a fresh ammo clip into his pistol.

Continuing his grim patrol, Gusarov dispatched another pair of Llorca's men. Then the room was silent. No more moans or screams or pleadings for mercy, just the gurgling sound of blood in Llorca's throat as he gasped for breath.

Llorca was slumped against the wall beneath MAL's insignia and Klax stood over him, unmoved by the man's agony. The Warden was clutching his abdomen and dark blood gushed from between his fingers. He looked up at Klax and spoke with a rasp.

"It is right I should die for what I have done…but I must…implore you… Mr. Klax…with my final breath. Please…in the name of humanity…destroy that machine. It's a wicked thing…and we who used it… are damned."

"You are damned, Veral Llorca, and your organization dies with you today. It was childish and optimistic to think that clean air and water are something the world wants. They don't want a pretty environment, you fool. They want to make money at any cost and to hell with this planet and the poor, dumb people who live on it.

But, Warden Llorca," he said with disdain, "I want to thank you for bringing my Scorpion to life. With this instrument, I will give the world what it deserves. I will give it the death, torture and pain it has given me and my family and my country. I will make a terror the world will never forget and if the world will not bend to my demands, I will fire the Scorpion until I burst the bones of every last man, woman and child on this planet. That is what you have accomplished, my sad Mr. Llorca. You have given me the means to cleanse the Earth of the disgusting vermin who crawl on its surface.

Llorca's head bowed under the weight of his wounds and Klax' words and, realizing he was a moment away from oblivion, he cursed the man. Or, was he speaking directly to *his* eternal keeper?

"*Diablo*," he said.

"BLAM!" Klax' pistol replied. The empty shell cashing pinged on the floor.

Part Three

"Fear in the Mirror"

Chapter 29

"Cornered"

The F-22 pilots, their eyes still smarting from the effects of the brite-light weapon, were making lazy circles over the sea when Red hailed them.

"Bug Leader, this is Arrow One, do you read over?"

"Redman is that you?"

The pilot replied, checking his target acquisition radar and seeing the Osprey designated.

"That can't be you flying that twirly-bomb, can it?"

"Mako?"

"Major Zack McDonald, USAF, at your service, you old bird. I thought the Navy grounded your sorry ass back in the twentieth century."

"Affirmative. They just bring me out for the big stuff, you know, like when they need a real pilot, instead of you fly-by-wire jocks."

"Yeah, I suppose it takes a real man…a real stupid man, to fly that coffin."

Mako chided the naval aviator, recalling the Osprey's developmental difficulties. The early models had the lowest takeoff/landing ratio of any military aircraft since the F-105 Thunder Chief or "Thud" as the ground crews called it back in the days of the Viet Nam war.

"Well enough jaw flappin', Mako." Red turned serious.

"Turn to tactical channel two; you have a change of orders."

Curious about how a Navy pilot would know this before he did, Mako flipped to the new frequency.

"What's up Red?" He asked.

"Are you packin' your 20 millimeters?"

"Yep and we got real bullets, too," he said, twanging a little to jab at Red's small town, Midwest dialect.

"I know you'll want to verify these orders with Aviano but let me give you the skinny. We're carrying an assault team to take out those bastards on Corfu. We're going to need air escort and close ground support to put this thing down and off load. You up for it?"

"Affirmative, big Red. We took a slap in the kisser back there and I'd like to return the favor."

"Consider this your official invite to the party."

"Done deal. We'll coordinate with our refueling tanker and standby, over."

"Thanks, Mako. Arrow One, out."

Aboard the Osprey, Natalie was busy downloading new satellite intel and she and Rex were busy interpreting the data. The most curious image was of a surface disturbance in the sea just east of the MAL tunnel. At first it looked like a possible crash site, maybe where MAL's helos went down when they disappear from the radar, but there was no visible wreckage, floating or submerged.

"Luke," you need to see this," Natalie said into her headset.

Forster took the jump seat next to her and they both studied the small video screen on her digicom.

As they replayed the satellite transmission in slow, stop action sequence, the sea door appeared and they beheld the astonishing sight of MAL's helos descending into the immense hangar bay below.

"Holy shit," he whispered under his breath.

"That's some feat of engineering," Natalie remarked, momentarily appreciating the science of the accomplishment.

"We're in way over our heads here, Katrova," he looked her in the eyes as he spoke. His pupils were enlarged and his face had lost its color.

"There must be a squadron of gunships down there and dozens of people."

"If not hundreds," Natalie mused, thinking of the technical, maintenance and security forces it would take just to keep a landing bay that massive, operational.

There was no time left to consult with Lang and Christopher aboard the Kendall. Within moments they would certainly be facing an anti-aircraft missile threat. They needed a new plan and had no time our outside help to make one.

Forster pinched his brows to focus. Natalie replayed the video of the sea door. After two passes she looked forward and stared blankly at the SEALs seated in the jump seats across from her. In a quantum leap of random, serendipitous logic she thought, "SEALs...seals...water... door... screen door in a submarine."

Suddenly she turned to Forster, a wry, nasty grin emphasized by a "bad girl" look in her eyes and said calmly, "I wonder if they can all swim?"

"Natalie," Forster said, fascinated by what was apparently going on in that devious mind of hers.

"Spit it out."

She explained. It was an ingenious plan Forster thought, if one disregarded the number of unknown variables, but there was no time left to consider them anyway. They had cornered the bad guys in an underwater box and he doubted the odds would ever be more in their favor.

Forster leaped into the cockpit and grabbed Red's arm. Unfortunately, he forgot Red was preoccupied with flying the Osprey and for a brief moment, pilot, crew and troops got an unanticipated thrill as the craft plunged through fifty feet of altitude change.

"What the-," Red yelled as he regained control.

"Luke, do you see what I'm doin' here?" Red was more than annoyed.

"Sorry, Red. Nat just got a brainstorm that could turn things our way. Here's how it's goin' down."

The pilot listened and grew more enthusiastic by the word until he heard the part about using the Osprey and everyone aboard as bait.

"Red, call our Raptor drivers and tell them Natalie's bringin' in the Greeks," Forster said. "And, hail those frigates. Who are they?"

"The *Salamis* and the *Spetsai*," she said, checking the readout on her digicom.

"We need to coordinate tactics to the split second," Forster directed Red. "We'll do a conference call in four minutes," he said, sounding more like a business executive than a field commander about to put the future of the planet on the line.

"Cool," Natalie said to Forster sarcastically.

"Then, we'll all *do* lunch."

Moroder smiled at her and raised a pretend wine glass to his lips, tastefully holding out his pinkie.

"I'll make the contacts, Luke," Red said. "You better get Natalie and your SEALs strapped in tight. I expect we'll be doing some real exciting flying here shortly."

"Bug Leader," Red hailed the F-22 flight leader, "Arrow One. Be advised we're bringin' in our friends on the Greek frigates '*Salami* and *Spitzy*'" Natalie grimaced at the botched pronunciations.

"You should see them on your scope to the southwest. We're going to ask them to fire Harpoons from their current position. We'll give you the tactical, shortly."

"Roger, Arrow One, but who's handling strategy on this one?"

"It was CDC on the Kendall, Commander Wolf Lang. But we're doin' it from here now. We've got some new intel that required a change o' plans, Mako. No time for Q&A from the brass."

"Hey, you're at the pointy end, big Red," Mako replied.

"We are refueling and standing by for your orders. Bug Leader, out."

Forster and Katrova jammed themselves back into the hatch to the flight deck and worked out the new order of battle with the pilot. The intricacies of pulling off this gambit were readily apparent. One mistake in timing or one weapons glitch and it would be harp and halo time for the lot of them.

The plan was simple in concept but the execution would require flawless functionality of the most esoteric military technology of the twenty-first century, in concert with raw personal fortitude. It demanded precise timing and accurate delivery of heavy munitions by warriors who had never before worked together. It would rely heavily on the hand of God.

The idea was to create a diversion by popping the Osprey up to radar range from low altitude and vectoring the Osprey toward MAL's sea door - a slow, fat fly enticing a hungry submerged frog. Natalie would direct Rex to broadcast a weapons signature to the highly sensitive electronic ears in the stronghold, making it appear that the Osprey was arming a pair of Mark 50 nuclear torpedoes. Since it was well known that the Osprey carried no defensive weaponry, it was Forster's guess that MAL would open the sea door before the Osprey reached a feasible drop position for the spurious torpedoes and scramble a gunship or two. In the meantime, the F-22s would feign a retreat to escape the anticipated secondary explosions after the torpedo impact, further encouraging the helos to attack.

As the sea doors opened, the Greek frigates would unleash the real threat, two AGM 90A Harpoon missiles. The missile men on the boats would guide the super-smart Harpoons to the target at wave-top level and arc the trajectory severely just before impact, high enough to slam-dunk the five hundred pound high-explosive warheads into the open hole.

The hope was that would do it. MAL, the evil machine and the army of nasties that manned the place would be drowned like tunnel rats beneath a few million gallons of seawater.

To intercept potential escapees, Forster's ground forces and the returning F-22s would set up a reception committee at the tunnel's front door. It was a risky, all or nothing scheme. But, as Katrova and Rex were timing out the components of the assault, the tripping points became obvious. What if they didn't open the sea door? What if the door opened and MAL didn't deploy helos but SAMs, or the Scorpion itself, atop some kind of tower or platform? What if the landing pad was separated from the rest of the complex by watertight doors and the Harpoon detonations didn't flood the entire stronghold? In the end, it was Moroder who provided encouragement.

"Look you guys, this could all go south in a blink but truth is, we're outta time, outta options and we're standing here in the ring facing the bruiser. We've been smacked around about the head and shoulders and our beak is broken and we've got blood on our shorts. It's time to throw a punch."

Moroder's bravado was catchy and they all had had enough of coming up short. Natalie looked at Forster. He was ready. She was ready. She saw him swing around and engage the SEAL team leader's eyes.

The man threw Forster a thumbs up and the rest of the men picked up the sign. They all wanted some bad guy butt.

"Red," he said to the pilot. "Get our guys on the horn."

Natalie was already back on the digicom with Rex.

Forster caught his reflection in one of the vidscreens. For a moment he didn't recognize himself. Focusing, he saw there was fear in the mirror.

Chapter 30

"The battle of Corfu"

Aboard the Kendall the CDC was a confused beehive. Though everyone taken into confidence by The Ten knew Wolf Lang was in charge and why, there were plenty of doubts from the old hands not in the know about why such a mighty battle group was supporting a miniscule commando force making for Corfu. But they were, so every officer in the control center stowed the doubts and got into the game. Suggestions poured forth.

"Negotiate," some said.

"Stall for advantage."

"Attack with everything. And I mean everything."

"You mean, light a nuke."

"If that's what it takes!"

"Hit 'em from the air with standoff weapons, Sir."

Lang's head was spinning.

He knew that reasoning with MAL's leadership at this point was out. If they had been cruel enough to waste an entire city, they would have no hesitation to use the beam again to defend themselves - regardless of the probability and scale of collateral damage to the island's docile inhabitants.

So what could the battle group do from so far away? The consensus was that air-launched attack munitions would meet the same fate the aircraft did in Shkodra, after all, cruise missiles and the Harpoons themselves were in reality small jet or rocket-powered aircraft.

There were no ground forces in the vicinity, so arguing about whether a nuclear artillery projectile would be effective was a waste of time.

Multiple ballistic nuclear weapons delivered from different directions was an option, but if even a single weapon of sufficient yield to take out the undersea bunker survived the beam and struck the target, it would mean instant death for tens of thousands of Corfu's populace and the island would be uninhabitable for centuries.

Then reality confronted the practical officer. Team Repo didn't need help from the Kendall. What they needed was positive thought and prayer. They were at the point, on station, and there was no more time. Forster and Katrova had to find the answer and their small force had to apply the solution. It was too late for group think.

Then, Forster called in.

A communications yeoman attempted to hand Lang a headset.

"On the squawk box, sailor," he directed the man. "Let's all hear this."

"Aye, Sir," the man said and switched the incoming signal to PA.

"Go ahead," Lang spoke at the omni-directional mic above the chart table.

"Commander, it's Forster."

"Luke, what's your status?" Lang wiped the sweat from his upper lip as he grabbed a grease pencil to mark the team's position on the plot table before him. Lang struggled to hear his voice over the Osprey's engine noise.

"We are twenty minutes, two zero minutes, from feet dry over the north coast of Corfu. ETA MAL's stronghold in about thirty, three zero, minutes. We have two Greek frigates in sight, about six miles west of our position and we're bringing them in. They're packing Harpoons. Commander, we don't have much time, so I'll let Natalie brief you. We've struck a plan.

"Let's hear it," he said.

It didn't take long for Lang's head to start nodding. He wasn't convinced the scheme would work but he really liked the thinking behind the tactical sequence - diversion, concentration and surprise presentation of overwhelming force, and establishment of multidirectional zones of fire to thwart an attempted retreat. It sounded like Natalie at her purely logical best and it was obvious she had done her homework.

"What's your contingency plan Katrova?" He asked.

Silence on the other end.

"Nat, what's your backup plan?" Lang repeated.

"We all die," she said.

Lang winced. If MAL responded to the first sign of the attack with a blast of Scorpion's ray, they *would* all die and Lang would be the one drawing up contingency plans. For the retreat of his forces.

Lang regarded the men and women in the CDC. Combat-hardened senior fleet officer and first tour sailor alike had heard Natalie's matter of fact recital of the team's personal price of failure and all returned the same, vacant stare. They understood the situation. They were, the whole battle group was, helpless now.

Forster's assault team, a pair of F-22s and two Greek warships were all that stood between civilization and Armageddon. Lang sealed the world's fate with a single word.

"Proceed," he said.

Exhausted, he braced himself against the plot table with both hands. He leaned on them heavily, hung his head and prayed aloud.

"God save us."

Aboard the Osprey, Forster acknowledged him with respect in the long tradition of the Navy.

"Aye, aye, Sir."

Luke switched his mic to *Intercom* and spoke to the pilot.

"Give me a secure channel to our partners, Red."

"Roger, Luke," he answered. In a few seconds he had the F-22s and the Greek frigates on the frequency.

It took ten minutes to communicate the order of battle and answer questions. When everyone was clear on their responsibilities, Natalie called out a rehearsal by numbers.

"T-minus zero," she said.

"From the IP, commence Osprey run on stronghold sea doors," Red said. "Rex stands by to transmit bogus nuclear torpedo profile," he continued. "Hope they take the bait, Miss Natalie."

"They will Red. They have to. T-plus four minutes, Rex will make it look like we're arming the Mark 50s. The Raptors feign a run for Aviano. T-plus four-thirty, sea doors break surface. T-plus seven minutes Osprey breaks off and turns for landing at the stronghold exit tunnel."

"We put the pedal to the metal," Red said.

"Affirmative, you run like hell, Red," Forster said, "If that thing opens faster than we think, or if the helos jump start to the doors, they'll bring guns to bear on us lickety split. Anyway, when those Harpoons impact the doors, we can't predict the force of the secondary explosions. We need to be well away."

"We'll make for you on a dead run too, Red," Mako called from his Raptor, "But it will take half a minute or so, even with afterburners. Let's not cut this too close."

"Roger, Mako," Red said, "I'll be lookin' over my shoulder for that sweet mug of yours."

"Continuing at T-plus seven minutes," Natalie carried on.

"Launch Harpoons," Stavros Andropos, and Nikolo Savalas, the Greek destroyer captains answered as one.

"Affirmative," Natalie said. "Then, Sirs, we'll need your ships to close in fast. We'll need your five-inch guns ready in case they launch patrol boats."

"T-plus nine minutes. Harpoons impact," Natalie said.

"We are on the ground at the surface entrance," Red said.

"Repo aggressor team in position, locked and loaded," Moroder said.

"M-90s flanking the tunnel door. Rifle teams Alpha and Bravo in position at forty-five degrees to the door center to lay down cover fire."

"I want those laser rifles on wide beam, Mo," Forster added.

"We don't know how many men they have in there. If any live through the Harpoons, they'll come out firing."

"We'll mow 'em down before their eyes can adjust to the daylight, Luke," Moroder replied, grinning.

The SEALs on the laser rifles were already adjusting the settings on their weapons.

"We're in close air support and watching for bogeys," Mako said. "And, Mr. Forster, we've scrambled a full squadron of Raptors with anti-tank stuff in case you engage armor at the tunnel."

"Good thinking, Mako," Forster responded.

"Then it's clean up and round up," Natalie said, sure that it was easier to speak those words than believe that would be the end of it.

"That's it gentlemen. Any questions?"

There was a short pause as they all listened. After a three count of listening to static, the talk was over. It was sweaty palm time.

"On my count," Forster said. T minus ten, nine," his heart was racing and a drop of sweat fell from his brow.

"Eight, seven, six," he glanced at Natalie. She flinched at hearing the SEALs lock and load their weapons.

"Five, four," Forster continued. Moroder smiled.

"Three, two," Red thought and said, "Mary, Mother of God, save my ass."

"One, zero," Luke said.

As Red pulled the Osprey into a steep, diving, right bank, Natalie spoke into her digicom, "Rex, you know the drill. Let's do it on time."

At the optimal moment, as Red put the Osprey into an attack pattern, the supercomputer began its "torpedo lock" broadcast. In a moment, they'd know if MAL would take the bait.

They did. The phony signal worked.

Dagon Klax was standing in Llorca's command center, addressing his lieutenants on the new order of things, when a flustered voice came over the PA speaker.

"Mr. Klax, we are under attack!"

"How?" He yelled into the air. At that volume, his nasal appliance added a tinny resonance to his speech.

"It's strange Sir," the voice said. We've identified two nuclear torpedoes locking on to our sea doors but radar shows only single, small plane approaching, an American Osprey we think."

"An Osprey, with nuclear torpedoes? Americans," he said in disgust. Only a people that arrogant and deluded by their action hero movies could think that a surprise attack by an unescorted flea could take down an enraged tiger.

"Rambo bullshit," he said.

"Launch our gunships."

"But Sir, they will be over the sea doors just as we launch," the voice warned.

"Then, hot launch the ships," he barked. "When the outer doors open, the gunships will be in the air just beneath the doors. They will spring forth and take them as soon as they clear.

Klax knew something was fishy. The Osprey had no hard launch points on the wings or fuselage and would have required some complex jury rigging to give it the capability to arm and launch two nuclear fish. Not even the clever Americans had time to fabricate such a mechanism.

But what were they up to? He decided not to wait to find out.

"Korman," he called to his aide. "Prepare the Scorpion and alert my bodyguard. We're going topside."

The piercing wail of a siren rattled off the tunnel walls in the complex as battle stations were manned. Klax' gunships lifted off the hangar floor in tandem and the sea doors began to open.

"It seems we must again demonstrate the Scorpion's power," Klax hissed. He was salivating at the chance. As he strode through the fumy vehicle bay and mounted the ladder to the machine's ops cabin, he laughed a reedy laugh that backed up phlegm into his nasal appliance. In a moment, he was coughing and spitting on himself hysterically. It didn't slow him down.

The dome over the Scorpion's fire control station was open and the access stairs were already unfolding from their cache in the machine's side when he arrived.

Suddenly, the floor beneath him lurched sideways, pitching everyone in the room to the deck. There was a thunderous roar. The Harpoons from the Greek destroyers had found their mark.

The sight from the air was stupefying. As the outer sea doors opened, Klax' gunships were lurking just below, ready to jump the Osprey when they had sufficient clearance. When the doors opened enough to allow them egress they broke for the open sky, just in time to see the Osprey making a one hundred eighty degree turn. The pilots may have had time to chuckle at the feeble enemy in full retreat. Probably not. For just as the helos turned to pursue the tilt rotor, the Harpoons, mere seconds from impact, arced sharply into the sky from wave top level and, tracing a roller-coaster track with their engine exhaust, dove again, perfectly splitting the distance between the helos, down into the open sea doors, and slammed into the hangar floor.

The men in the front seats of the windward helo had a brief moment to look at each other, then at the men in the leeward ship, before a shock wave spewed a mammoth ball of fire and debris out of the hole and blew them into wads of flaming scrap.

A mushroom cloud of crimson and jet erupted into the blue sky as the waning growl of the first explosion was accompanied by the fresh bang of secondaries almost as large. Flaming aviation fuel and the white hot metal of the melting sea doors met cold seawater. The result was an astounding cataclysm of destruction. The hundred or so men in the hangar and adjacent service bays were killed instantly. Those that escaped the fury of the Harpoon explosions were summarily drowned, cooked alive in scalding steam or electrocuted.

In seconds, the rapidly expanding sphere of super-heated air from the blast overtook the Osprey itself and Red struggled to keep it airborne. Inside, Forster's team was slammed around the fuselage like dice in a shaker. Red saw stars when his head smacked the cockpit ceiling. A crate of vibration grenades broke open and a SEAL lost his front teeth when one of them caromed off the bulkhead and kissed him full on the lips. Natalie's safety harness yanked her hard, compressed her solar plexus and knocked the wind out of her. Gasping, she strained to keep her shoulders back and suck oxygen into her deflated lungs.

Four or five seconds passed before the wings leveled and the horizon assumed its normal position on the windscreen.

"Sorry, 'bout that folks," Red said as he righted the craft. "Remind me to thank the taxpayers of America for these swell seat belts."

"What happened, Red?" Forster had no view to the outside.

"I'd guess it was pretty much a direct hit, Luke. There'll be some soggy rats in that hole. Their gunships were fricasseed."

Aboard the Kendall the CDC exploded with raucous cheers, but even as his compatriots were slapping him on the back, Lang was still tense. There was no telling if the Scorpion had survived the missile attack and without a confirmed kill, nothing had really changed.

"Secondaries?" Forster asked Red.

He was hoping for lot of them and big ones at that. The more and bigger the detonations, the better the chance the Scorpion had been destroyed.

"It's still whompin' and blowin' smoke down there," Red said.

"Good," Forster said. "Real good."

He was starting to feel like they were going to win. He looked at Natalie. She was clasping both hands over her diaphragm, trying to make her breathing regular when their eyes met. It was premature to celebrate victory but he was relieved that she may come out of this in one piece. That thinking was premature.

She wasn't sure what she saw in his eyes. She though he was trying to tell her something but he didn't speak. Neither of them knew how to break the awkward silence.

Red focused their attention. "We're on final, lady and gentlemen. Down in two minutes."

Switching to the tactical frequency, he hailed the Raptors.

"Mako, cover my six, son. Here we go."

"Your fine freckled fanny is safe with me, Redhead," the fighter pilot replied.

"Bug Leader to Bug Base, we're in," he called back, lighting the afterburner and heading for the stronghold at full throttle.

As Red flared the Osprey for touchdown, he centered the stronghold's land entrance in his windscreen.

There was a small force in place near the opening - a platoon of security guards with light weapons and two small armored cars with swivel-mounted medium machine guns. They would have to hover at least a quarter mile off amid a cluster of small rolling sand dunes and await the Raptors' arrival before moving in for touchdown. The Osprey was unarmed, only lightly armored and deploying Forster's team before their close air support arrived would be stupid.

"Mako, this is Red," he said into his headset. "We're all prettied up for the dance but the big bad bouncers won't let us in. We'd appreciate some gate crashing."

As the mighty jets ripped through Mach I, Mako replied, "We are making haste, Mr. Red. ETA your position in thirty seconds."

"We'll be Swiss cheese in twenty."

Red un-keyed his mic as puffs of sand began to chase a path toward the Osprey. Red and Stony Jackson went white knuckled on the controls as tracer rounds from MAL's guns burned bright trails in the air around them. Red eased the craft backward in a flat hover without raising his profile. Skillful flying, but it wouldn't help for long. They'd be zeroed in on him in no time.

Then Mako said, "May we have this dance?"

Now, the dirt puffs were chasing toward the MALs. These were from the Raptors' guns and Red's heart buoyed as he watched the big bullets from the 20mm guns chew up the sand in four parallel lines that ran right at the tunnel door and the men and machines guarding it.

During the ten seconds of the Raptors' first strafing run on the guards' position, their combined canons spewed forty-four hundred rounds at the enemy. Each bullet was five inches long, three-quarters of an inch thick and made of depleted Uranium to penetrate even the densest armor. To the targets, it must have seemed as if a wall of steel hit them. Humans, vehicles and munitions were shredded with equal ease and except for the crackle of flames around the armored cars and occasional screams from the wounded, the position fell silent.

Then the ammunition magazines in the armored cars exploded. Superheated bullet fragments, shell casings, bodies and armor plate flew through the air in all directions. Some of the debris clanked against the Osprey. A large chunk of human torso struck the starboard tilt rotor and deformed one of the blades as it was bisected. The eccentric motion of the bent prop shook the plane violently like a wet rug out of balance in a clothes washer spin cycle. Forster thought they had been hit by MAL artillery. As Red struggled mightily to correct their attitude and level the craft, Jackson feathered the starboard prop. The Osprey began to spin on its vertical axis. Fortunately, they were close enough to the ground that the only result of the mishap was a very hard, ungainly landing. Once again, the passengers were jerked against their harnesses.

"Shit!" Red exclaimed. His hands were a blur as they worked to power down the wounded bird.

"That was exciting! Nice shootin' shark boy," he said.

"Our pleasure, Red" Mako replied. Need another pass?"

"Negative, Bug One," Red said. "But, standby. We're gonna take a look down that tunnel. Stay close; we're deploying the assault team."

As the dust settled around the crippled Osprey, Forster burst out of his harness, approached the exit door portal and saw they were within one hundred meters of their objective. Except for the SEAL with the bloody Chiclets in his mouth, no one had been harmed in the smash landing and Forster was impressed that each of them already had their personal gear secured and their weapons at the ready. Moments later, the pilot and co-pilot were similarly prepared and cued up at the exit hatch behind Forster, Moroder, Katrova and the SEALs.

"Move out!" Forster yelled as they sprang one-by-one out of the Osprey and scrambled for cover.

Most found a dune to hide behind, but some were forced to low crawl behind the shore scrub. Once they got their bearings, Forster flashed hand signals directing the SEALs to establish their fields of fire. The two laser rifle teams assumed close-in positions flanking the main doorway and set the ungainly weapons on their tripods, attaching the power packs with sure, practiced movements. Within seconds, Forster heard the firing circuits charging; the high-pitched tones of the weapons' electronics in stark contrast to the otherwise soothing sounds of the wind and surf.

The remaining SEALs split into teams and dug in as best they could in echelons; each man staggered inward from the man in front of him, assuring clear and safe aim at the door and precise up-angled cross fire along the crude roadway that led to it.

MAL's stronghold was all deluge and inferno. To those in the higher levels of the complex, the increased air pressure created by the rush of the seawater into the main tunnel was a sure sign that something had gone wrong. Then came the steam and rancid smoke. Most of the men between the hangar deck and the first branch of the main tunnel were incinerated when the Harpoons hit. Those that survived the primary blast were drowned. Fortunately for Klax, the Scorpion was located in a bay off the highest tunnel, just thirty feet below grade. But, emergency power was failing section by section as the water rose and the entire labyrinth was in imminent danger of collapse.

A quick assessment of the situation told Klax that he and the remnants of his guard needed to make haste.

"Korman," Klax screamed over his digicom to his aide.

"Get a gunner into the Scorpion, now. Command my guard to the troop carrier. Only my guard, do you understand?"

"Yes, Mr. Klax," he said, "But what of our wounded and the men below?"

"We have no use for them now. We have the machine."

"Yes, Sir," he said, knowing further protestations were dangerous. Klax hated to say things twice.

After Fritz Jager destroyed Shkodra and then himself, his brother Johann was promoted to First Gunner. He had none of Fritz' sensitivities when it came to mass murder and he sorely wanted to be the next to sit at the firing controls. As Klax bolted into the bay followed by a handful of his men, the Scorpion's driver slid the access hatch open and they entered the lower fuselage to assume their battle stations. As they started the drive engines, Johann was already warming up the beam generator and calibrating its laser sights for what was sure to be a close-quarter surface and air battle with the Americans.

"Three minutes to full charge, Mr. Klax," he said as the men buckled in.

Klax turned to the driver, "Are my men aboard?"

The driver switched his headset to *Intercom* and verified that the men were all aboard the troop carrier and sealed in.

"We are ready, Mr. Klax," he said, nodding once.

Ready or not they were leaving. Seawater was already lapping at the machine's wheels.

Outside the tunnel, from the cover of his personal dune, Moroder focused his field glasses and was the first to see the water emerge.

"Mr. Forster, the water's reached the tunnel door," he said into his headset.

"This is it," Natalie thought to herself, pulling a vibration grenade from her ammo belt. In the next few seconds, either the machine would emerge from the hole ready to fight or it would trapped behind the door and this would all end with a whimper, or more appropriately, a gurgle.

Moroder pressed his headset to his ear to better hear the message. The SEALs had just confirmed that the laser rifles were online and ready. Then, to their dismay, the door moved. The fight was on.

They all tensed and each in their own way set their minds to the battle. Some spoke silently and some aloud, their prayers for success and survival. Then there was a moment of reprieve as the rising metal maw stopped dead, six inches above the ground. They watched with renewed optimism as the gap filled and overflowed with rushing water. Surely the power had now failed and everyone and everything in the tunnel would be caught in the cold, suffocating flood. No one took their eyes from the door.

Relief had just begun when again the door began to rise and the grotesque front end of the Scorpion started to emerge, the machine's twin laser guns firing at random. One of the SEALs manning the M-90 took a hit just above the chinstrap and his head turned to char with a sickening crackle.

The Repo team returned fire. Light and heavy machine guns, rifle grenades and M-90s were hurled against the monster in a fury of red beams, orange bursts and blue-white muzzle flash, but to no avail. Natalie stood like a pop-up target from behind her cover and fearlessly pitched a vibration grenade at the Scorpion. It was a long throw and she knew she'd be lucky to hit the target, but the bomblet hit home. The detonation laced a delicate fan of cracks in Johan's dome and made his heart skip a beat, but it was not a serious breach and the thing with the red laser gun eyes just kept emerging from the hole.

As fast as he could load and launch, Stony Jackson put three rifle grenades dead on the Scorpion's nose. Amid the deafening blasts, through the smoke, Forster could see them tearing off chips of the ceramic armor here and there, but superficial pockmarks and surface scorch from the M-90 wouldn't get it done. Not a single round, laser strike or grenade missed its target, but nothing slowed the weapon. It crept forward and cleared the doorway.

Now the Scorpion's terrible stinger, the machine's beam generator needle, began to glow and Forster knew there were just seconds before they would all be pools of goo. Through his headset, Forster heard the Raptor pilots who had rounded back from their strafing run preparing to attack the machine with another pass of their cannons.

"Hold on Luke! We're on it," Mako said as he and his wingman witnessed the Scorpion's withering laser fire.

"Turning to attack vector, break on my mark," Mako shouted, the heat from his face fogging the edges of his visor. "Three, two, BREAK! Let's give 'em hell!"

The Raptors pulled a sharp right bank to bring their guns to bear. As the Repo team concentrated their fire, the Raptors dove like falcons on rabbits, engines screaming their wrath. The 20mm canons poured their lethal rain on the Scorpion. Sand burst around the machine, whipped into the air and for a moment, Forster thought he heard rending armor. But the sound he heard was something much more dreadful. It was the Scorpion's beam generator reaching full power. He watched helplessly as the long blue needle panned away from the ground force and inclined to track the attacking warplanes. From inside the sand cloud raised by the Raptor's cannon rounds, the light intensified, now too bright to watch. Forster's team covered their eyes to stop the pain.

The red bead of light from the Scorpion's laser sight blooming on his canopy was the last thing Mako saw before Johann fired and the deadly blue beam from the machine engulfed his fighter. The wings and control surfaces around him began to glow and turn a sickly green, the jet's engine components lost their integrity and the Raptor exploded. The tight attack formation they were flying in required Mako's wingman to veer violently at the last second to avoid being brought down by the flaming, slimy green carcass of his flight leader's disintegrating plane. Bug Two was next in the Scorpion's sights. As the pilot turned to press his attack and avenge Mako's death, he too saw the red beam and met the same fate as his leader.

"Well done, Johann!" Klax exclaimed gleefully. "Now to the weaklings before us," he said.

"Retreat!" Forster yelled as he watched the beam needle track downward toward their position."

"Where?" Moroder screamed. "There's nowhere to hide, Luke." Then he heard Natalie. She was excited, but strangely composed.

"Luke, we've got to surrender!" Natalie yelled into her mic.

"Surrender?" Forster laughed, almost in panic.

"Yes. Now!" Natalie ordered him. We need to buy some time, or we're dead."

At this point argument was out of the question. The machine's laser guns were laying down fire on both flanks and were scissoring toward the center for the kill. Four of the SEALs had been sliced through on the last laser pass and the Scorpion's beam needle was already beginning to glow for a final shot. That would end it. Forster didn't know what Natalie hand in mind but he was out of ideas and they were out of time.

"Everybody stand! Hands up!" She yelled. "Mo, stay down and reload. When…if they come out of that thing, take 'em and rush the firing station. It's our only chance."

Everyone heard her. None believed it would work. They had just wiped out MAL's forces, except for the troops in Scorpion's carrier. Why would the enemy show the Repo team mercy?

But, Natalie had a hunch. She had spent hundreds of hours with Rex pouring over Klax' dossier, including his psych profiles. Intuition told her he was in that machine and the lure of real prisoners that could be tortured and killed at close range, perhaps by Klax' own hand, would be a strong temptation - especially with one of the enemy being of the feminine persuasion. She was convinced their only chance was to lure Klax out of his shell with fresh meat.

"Cease fire, she yelled again into her mic. Drop 'em and get your hands up!"

Forster, knowing they were all going to die if they continued to fight, added his authority.

"Give it up!" He growled into his mic.

"But, for Christ sake, keep your side arms Moroder, stay down and stay put. You're our ace in the hole."

The team stopped firing, dropped their rifles and stood. Moroder took a deep breath laced with the acrid odor of gunpowder and smoldering glove leather, snatched opened the receiver of his weapon and slapped another ammo belt into his mini-gun. If he could get their troops out in the clear, he could slay them all with one sustained burst. The problem was whether he could take enough of them out fast enough to enable his guys to rush the machine and attack it from the only vulnerable spot they could see - the flank. Maybe, they could slip a couple of grenades under the damn thing from there. Maybe, the armor wasn't as dense on its underside. He hunkered down and waited as ordered. He thought the men inside the Scorpion could hear his heartbeat.

Klax saw Natalie on the video monitor at once. Even as the others stood to reveal themselves he never took his eyes off her.

"What have we here?"

He sneered and leaned forward as the video technician zoomed in. In spite of her attire, her goggles, the dirt on her face and the sand in her hair, he could see she was most assuredly female.

"Stop. Don't shoot, Johann," he commanded. The triggerman was preparing to fire the battle's final shot.

"Maybe we take captives," he said.

"After all, I think my guard would enjoy a taste of revenge. Don't you think so, Mr. Korman?"

"Yes, Mr. Klax," Korman said, aware of the delicacy of his mood when Klax was locked on to female prey.

"Sensors show no further threat from the air, Sir," he said. "Infrared shows only the shapes before you. Nine are standing, bearing sidearms. Five are dead. One by their laser, four on our left and one behind that dune at ten o'clock."

The heat radiating from Moroder's ultra-hot weapon flared on the sensor screen, obscuring his own thermal signature.

"I advise sending your guard only. Keep the Scorpion sealed until these pigs can be disarmed and restrained."

"Yes, yes," Klax said as the camera zoomed in closer on Natalie's face. When she pulled her goggles down around her neck her eyes mesmerized him.

"Disarming," he said, his nasal appliance reverberating. "Bring the woman warrior to me."

Johann kept the beam needle focused on the hapless band before him. Trusting nothing and eager to fire the Scorpion again, he held the beam generator at half power just in case. Forster stood amidst his men and it was his body Johann used to sight on. At this range, the red dot from the weapon's sight made a baseball-sized dot on his chest. Luke knew that if Natalie's scam went bust, he would be the first to die. He was feeling light headed, much like he had been nearly every day since the Scot shot him with the tranquilizer gun in the Denver park.

Then, as imminent capture, certain torture, death and failure loomed over them like the Scorpion's tail, their luck changed. Rather, Natalie's luck changed. From the back of the troop carrier, a ramp dropped and Klax' men emerged. Tentatively at first, then with more authority as their number increased, they began to close the hundred-meter distance to their foes.

"When I say drop, everybody do it," Natalie said into her mic, trying not to move her lips. "Then it's up to you Mo. As we drop, rush the machine. Everyone else, when he rushes, you grab guns and let 'em have it. Clear?"

"Aye," she heard them all say under their breaths.

"Then we kill it," she said, her eyes narrowing to a look of mean glee.

"Put every grenade you've got under the chassis."

Klax' guard was close enough now that she dare not say more. Each of the approaching black-suited men leveled an autopistol at a member of Forster's team. They were past the point of no return. As the guardsmen advanced to within fifty meters of were they stood, Natalie saw that no more people were emerging from the troop carrier. This must be all of them. Then, she heard one of the bad guys yell, "Don't move," to which she replied, as loudly as she could scream, "Down!"

Before they could all hit the ground, some of Klax' men sniffed the rouse and opened fire. A dozen muzzles flamed and three of the SEALs were cut down, their bullet-riddled bodies jerking like crazed marionettes. Then it was Moroder's turn. As the rest of the team dove for cover amid the whizzing bullets and popping sand, he rose to his knees. Leaning forward as if making a saber thrust, he braced his weapon against his tree trunk torso and squeezed the minigun's trigger. His body shuddered with the recoil and the bodies dropped before him as if mown by a giant scythe. Limbs were severed, torsos twitched, and daylight came through bodies frozen in place by the equalized forces of ballistic impact and forward momentum. The pink of rent tissue hung in the air. The targets screamed silently, their cries unheard for the barking of Moroder's weapon as he viciously spewed death into them.

Forster's team had the advantage for the moment and sprang to action. They drew their pistols, thumbed off the safeties and rushed the Scorpion. Inside the machine, Klax ordered the gunner to fire. Johann decided he didn't need the primary beam to exact a toll for the American's arrogance. Instead, he set the laser rifles on *Autofire* and squeezed the red trigger on his joystick. On this setting, the lasers would acquire their targets by infrared heat sensors and rapid fire at everything they saw. Within seconds, both the front lasers were blazing away. Four more SEALs were incinerated before they gained a yard.

Moroder, with no human targets left to kill, saw the carnage and concentrated his fire on the Scorpion's lasers. Defying death and screaming *"Semper Fi,"* he marched toward the machine, his minigun blazing as it disgorged spent shell casings by the pound. Before his luck ran out and he was cut in two above the belt, he managed to destroy one of the laser guns. It was on the side Natalie and Forster were approaching. On the other side, three more SEALs were seared to ash.

"Fire the primary beam!" Klax screamed, fuming. He couldn't believe the persistence of the Americans or the loss of his guard.

"They are too close, Mr. Klax," Johann said as he watched the decimated force, now with only a few aggressors remaining, approach the side of the machine.

"Nonsense," came the retort.

"Fire. *Fire* I say!

It would only take thirty seconds to bring the beam to full power. There wasn't much organic material around the machine, but there was probably enough to broadcast the chain reaction and the carbon atoms and carbon-based compounds in the air would help transmit the effect. None of the Scorpion's remaining crew was worried. They should have been.

Angry at their losses and Mo's death, Natalie, Forster, the remaining SEALs, Red the pilot and Lance Jackson the co-pilot/rifle grenadier put their remorse aside and went into frenzy. As fast they could, they began pulling HE and vibration grenades from their ammo belts.

"Eight second fuses! Chuck 'em and run boys!" Forster ordered as the blue light from the beam generator began to overwhelm the daylight and cast an eerie glow around them.

Seven, eight, nine grenades were armed and rolled beneath the machine before the timing fuses began to run down and threaten their escape.

"Go! Go!" Forster yelled at the top of his lungs.

As he turned to run, he caught one of Klax' men in his peripheral vision. The guard leveled an autopistol at his nearest target, Natalie. Alert to the threat, Forster' drew his .45 lightning-quick, and using his supercharged senses to aim without the sight, put a round between the man's eyes. The impact of the bullet lifted the man's already lifeless body a foot in the air before the corpse planted itself in the sand.

Again, he turned to run. He was only a few meters away when the first grenade, a high explosive fragmentation grenade, went off prematurely. Whumph, it went. Jackson, his short legs failing him, was the closest to the explosion. He took a handful of white-hot steel shards between the shoulder blades. The impact sent him flying forward through the air in a Superman pose, though unlike the Man of Steel, he was vulnerable and hit the ground, dead.

Then the vibration grenades lit. Over the deep bass thump of the HEs came the bizarre twang of resonating metal as the "jiggle bombs," as Mo called them, shredded the frame and cross members of the Scorpion's undercarriage. The machine rumbled on its big tires as burning hydraulic fluid poured from the eviscerated weapon's underbelly. Scorpion's remaining laser gun fell silent as tongues of flame licked out from the gun ports.

Red was the first to stop and look back. Then others joined him. Still backing up as they watched the Scorpion's carcass being enveloped in flames, they were in awe of what they had done. The once crystal-clear dome atop the monster was now filling with curling tendrils of dense black smoke and the terrifying blue-green glow from the beam generator was fading.

Before they could catch their breath, something happened.

A strange, but familiar sound came from inside the Scorpion. At first, it just looked like more smoke, pale this time, emerging from the underside of the dying machine. Then, the same milky-white vapor appeared to fill the control dome until it fogged over like a steam bath door. Then came the realization that what they were hearing was not burning machinery and boiling hydraulic fluid, but the discharge of the contents of a fire-suppression system. Halon gas was being forced into every cubic inch of the machine and onto the smoldering frame beneath it. Either someone was still alive in there or an automatic system had taken over.

But, Natalie wouldn't let it live. Not after Klax killed Jim Comstock, and Mo Moroder and the courageous men in the Raptors and all the innocents in Shkodra and all the brave young SEALs. No, she thought, it must die here and it must die now.

To Forster's dismay, Katrova began to sprint toward the machine. She was attacking. Looking like an avenging angel with righteousness raging through her, she closed to within ten meters of the machine, stopped, planted her feet, wrenched the last vibration grenade from her belt and twisted the thumb catch to *Contact*.

Foster screamed, and began to chase her down. "No Nat. Get back. No!"

Then they both froze. Slowly, the malevolent pinnacle of the beam needle moved jerkily and stopped – the aiming laser glowing again, like Satan's eye on Natalie's chest.

As Forster and Katrova stared and contemplated their imminent deaths, Red and the remaining SEALs spread out behind them in an attempt to gain a clear field of fire and provide them some cover. It was futile. They were down to their side arms. Even so, the brave men sank to a kneeling position and began to empty their clips into the Scorpion. Every bullet they fired ricocheted off it with a dainty ping, like a BB hitting a battle tank.

Natalie braced to toss her last grenade under the Scorpion in hopes of dealing the machine a final deathblow when she saw a sight that would haunt her for the rest of her life.

Ventilation fans whirred in the machine and from the top of the firing control dome the Halon began to clear. She could make out the top of a man's head. Or was it a man? The apparition being revealed before her really didn't resemble a human being. It was what was left of Dagon Klax. He had been horribly burned before the fire was extinguished.

He now looked as much a monster as the machine he rode. Like the Scorpion, his skin was flayed and hemorrhaging patches appeared where his skin had been torn from his body. His tattered uniform smoldered. His hair was gone. Worse, so was his nasal appliance. From where she stood she could clearly make out the profoundly disturbing sight of his nasal cavity, gaping dark and raw. His sardonic grin and the bone protruding from the charred skin of his cheeks overwhelmed her.

Natalie faltered and began to sway. The needle began to glow brighter. Klax was going to fire. They had lost after all. The Scot was right. Forster wasn't up to the challenge and once again it would be his curse to witness the death of the woman he loved. Yes, loved, he thought. At least, this time, he wouldn't be left alive to relive the catastrophe and be tortured by the memory.

Natalie had different thoughts. This would not be her end. It would be Klax' end.

The blue-green light increased in intensity. She saw Klax reach for the trigger.

"Natalie," Forster wailed.

She turned to look at him, perhaps for the last time. "Luke," she said, softly, trying to make him feel her love.

"Natalie," he screamed as she turned to face the monsters - man and machine.

A second later, Klax squeezed the trigger. But before the weapon could loose its terrible bolt of death, Natalie grasped the vibration grenade firmly in a fury-powered fastball grip. Shuffling her feet into the sand, she thrust her left hip forward, wound her hand in a tremendous arc over her head and delivered an all-universe, anti-evil hall-of-fame, underhand fastball.

Amused at the female's feeble attempt to destroy him he followed the flight of the puny ball and waited for it to impact the silica shield surrounding him. Knowing the dome's strength he assumed it would explode harmlessly. He was dismayed though that the warping air wouldn't clear in time for him to see the Scorpion spew its venom on the arrogant bitch.

Then his expression changed. She wasn't aiming at him. Her target was the beam needle and she didn't miss. With a tinny clink, the grenade impaled itself on the needle.

"Strike!" Red yelled, clenching his fist like a major league umpire.

The grenade exploded and the Scorpion fired.

Natalie and Luke braced, but the beam diffused. Instead, they and Klax watched with different reactions as the vibe field from her grenade shivered the air around the needle.

A dissonant, grating sound began to emanate from the beam generator as the effect of the grenade walked back along the machine's high-arched tail, exploding the mercury beam concentrators, each in turn. When it hit the base of the aperture, everything changed. A high-pitched, keening shriek numbed the eardrums of the combatants.

"Run," Forster bellowed.

They did.

Klax had nowhere to go. He could only stand alone in his crystal tomb and await his fate. He didn't have to wait long.

The entire machine, weapon and troop carrier was engulfed in the glow. Brilliant light branched out around the device and issued from every fissure in the chassis. The Scorpion sizzled and trembled in its death throes. Klax grabbed the firing console and hung on. Then the machine's ceramic armor began to come loose, large pieces of it whirring and spinning into the air with each convulsion. Without its protective outer skin, the beam was now free do what it was built to do – dissolve stuff. With its guts exposed, the Scorpion began to devour itself and Klax in the bargain.

Foster, Katrova and the remnants of the team dove behind the only dune large enough to shelter them. They wanted to watch, but they didn't dare. They were still in mortal danger from the beam if the effect spread. But it didn't. The grenade had somehow interrupted the airborne chain reaction and the danger appeared to be contained to an area just around the machine. Instead of hearing burning bubbles rippling outward from the needle, they heard only the fizzing sound of the machine reducing itself to the slime it was meant to be. The dissipating sickly light shot over them as it began to react with the air and the vegetation around them, just missing their heads as they cowered behind the bunker.

Natalie, convinced they'd seen the worst of it and overcome with the need to savor their victory, stood to view the aftermath. She beheld a fantastic scene. The machine was a pool of goo. But Klax, or his core, stood in the middle of the morass, just a skeleton now. As she watched, his bones, like those of the tens of thousands he had so carelessly slaughtered, were exploding like popcorn in sequence from the head down. First his skull, then the shoulder assemblies, ribs, pelvis and finally, his leg bones and feet.

It was over.

The weary warriors heard a few more bones crackle and all fell silent. Then a scream split the air. It was Luke.

Epilogue

The sun shone warm on the infant's sweet face, his already thick hair skirling across his forehead in the gentle zephyr that whooshed wavelets of dusky pine pollen across the redwood deck. The tiny motors in the cyboprosthesis that replaced Luke's dissolved left hand and forearm gave him back the ability to hold little Nate securely in two arms, even if the miraculous limb had not restored his ability to feel the boy child's flawless, olive-tinted skin. He used his good hand for that.

Luke felt blessed. If Natalie's grenade hadn't impacted the Scorpion when it did, the beam's chain reaction might have continued a second or two longer and they all would have soaked into the sand on the Corfu beach. He and Natalie would never have known the bliss they wallowed in today.

She never left his side during recuperation. Through the pain of acclimating to his new limb and the frustrating "trial and error" calibrations of the medullar implant, she was there to comfort and encourage him. They healed each other, mind and body, and today, basking in his son's smile and the glow of Natalie's devotion; he thought his hand a small price to pay for their victory.

His trance was interrupted by Natalie's once-again svelte form walking toward him, her lovely long hair swaying in seductive time with each step. She moved gracefully though she still favored her right leg when the weather turned cold, carrying a tray of fruit and cheese, apple juice for the baby and a sweaty pitcher of cold Sangria to celebrate her beautiful family.

The deep blue Colorado sky and the green of the pine forest renewed them, though the memories of the battle against the Scorpion just three years ago would live in their day and night dreams for a long time to come.

The future would bring peace to their household. Natalie would soon bear Luke twin girls. Little Therese became a renowned concert pianist. She wed a Viennese maestro and lived a long and happy life traveling the world and sharing her gift for music.

Kathleen grew to marry a military man. It turned out well though, he was strong and brave and Luke thought the world of him. In 2048, she became the First Lady as her husband became the fifty-third President of the United States of North America.

Nathan became a Pediatrician, settled in Delta, Colorado and passed the gentle ways of his mother on to generations of farm and ranch families on the Western Slope. He never married, but when he died at age seventy, the town erected a marble monument to him in the square.

Mo Moroder, Zack "Mako" McDonald, Mako's wingman, the SEALs who lost their lives in Gdansk and at the Battle of Corfu, and Jim Comstock were all awarded posthumous Medals of Honor and buried with great pomp and circumstance in a magnificent magnolia grove at Arlington National Cemetery.

Dr. Larry Craigh built his own machine from the recovered Scorpion plans. Breast and many other varieties of cancer would never again threaten humanity and he won the Nobel Prize for Medicine. At the award ceremony, Craigh reminded the audience that it was Eva Luknar, who actually pioneered the TVap technology, but her name never appeared in the medical literature and she was soon forgotten. Industrial variants of the device followed and Man finally solved the problem of what to do with old automobile tires.

The Scott died on the black sand beach at Kona Village watching the sunset, a double Mai-Tai in one hand and a Cohiba cigar in the other, just a week after learning about Repo's triumph.

Wolf Lang retired after the final confrontation, moved to Hermosa Beach, California, married a girl that could have been Natalie's twin and fathered four girls – all dead-ringers for their mother. In later years, they and the girls' significant others all crewed on *Antares*, Lang's red-hulled, 12-meter racing yacht and won more than their fair share of beer can regattas.

Lang was twice called out of retirement to serve The Ten - once in 2051 to handle the mission known as the "Talon Tasking" and the second time some years later, when he was captured and imprisoned by the mysterious Runic Triad, the most serious threat ever to The Ten's existence.

Stuart "Red" Minnick, having flown and fought bravely in twenty more missions for The Ten, retired a highly decorated Brigadier General, lived to be eighty-four and passed away from a massive myocardial infarction on a chair lift while skiing single at Okemo, Vermont. It was a light traffic day on the hill and he went around twice before the lift operator caught on to his demise. Red would have appreciated the extra hang time.

Markus Haukken survived his wounds but lost his hair forever. The Ten bought him a baker's dozen of stout puppies and a new sled.

About the Author

Michael D. Kurz was born in Janesville, Wisconsin. He is the eldest of eight children

For many years, he worked in the advertising field, first in Chicago then in Denver. He is an award-winning copywriter and broadcast advertising producer and still maintains a small roster of clients with whom he consults on advertising and brand development.

Michael draws inspiration from the classics as well as the works of modern authors, James Michener, Stephen King, Tom Clancy, J.R.R Tolkien, Ayn Rand, John Irving and Joseph Heller. Today, Michael and his wife reside in the Colorado high country.